SEMIOTEXT[E]
SF

SEMIOTEXT[E]
SF

Editors:

Rudy Rucker

Peter Lamborn Wilson

and

Robert Anton Wilson

Designer/Illustrator:

Mike Saenz

Managing Editor:

Jim Fleming

SEMIOTEXT[E]
522 Philosophy Hall, New York, New York 10027 USA
55 South Eleventh Street, Brooklyn, New York 11211-0568 USA

(718) 397-6471

AK PRESS
22 Lutton Place
Edinburgh, Scotland EH8 9PE

ISBN: 0-93675643-8   (U.S.A.)
ISBN: 1-873176-81-3   (U.K.)

Printed in the United States of America.

CONTENTS

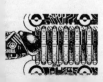

Peter Lamborn Wilson has read SF since adolescence, but only recently began writing it. His stories have appeared in the 3rd INTERZONE Anthology and various small zines. Future appearances are loosely scheduled for TAROT TALES (edited by Caitlin Matthews and Rachel Pollack) and 3-FISTED TALES OF "BOB" (edited by Ivan Stang). He is better known for his most recent books, SCANDAL: ESSAYS IN ISLAMIC HERESY (Autonomedia) and DRUNKEN UNIVERSE: AN ANTHOLOGY OF PERSIAN SUFI POETRY (Phanes Press). He hosts a late-night live talk show ("The Moorish Orthodox Radio Crusade") on WBAI in New York City, where he discusses the marginal press, science fiction, weird physics, sufism, anarchism, the "Free Religions" movement, etc., etc. He edited, with Jim Fleming and Sue Ann Harkey, the mammoth SEMIOTEXT(E) USA. He has lectured at the Jack Kerouac School of Disembodied Poetics at the Naropa Institute in Boulder on sufism and on "hermetalinguistics." He is addicted to literary hoaxes and forgeries. Caveat lector.

Mike Saenz produced the first comic book ever generated in toto on a micro-computer, SHATTER, a P. K. Dick-influenced future-detective saga which appealed as much to literati as to comic book "fans." He refined his technique in a recent graphic novel—IRON MAN (Marvel)—but he may be most notorious for a bit of raunchy animated software called "MacPlaymat," which may be the most obsessively pirated hackers' favorite of all time. Mike is the impeccable Man of the Near Future, plugged-in as a character from some William Gibson story, dressed in Baudelairean black and surrounded by eerily-glowing electronic devices. Still, he holds on to one endearingly old-fashioned virtue: generous enthusiasm. His covers, illustrations, and flip-book artistry give this volume its unique blend of high-tech competence and wacky-wild blow-away style.

Rudy Rucker's and Robert Anton Wilson's bio-bibliographies introduce their stories in this volume.

Introduction:
Strange Attractor(s)
Rudy Rucker &
Peter Lamborn Wilson

HEBEPHRENIA SF

A star's hot plasma lives in dynamic equilibrium between collapsing gravitational forces and explosive heat/quantum pressures. Between black hole and nova. The heavy gold metal force of commercial SF publishing always threatens to suck the whole field into blank uniformity; the purpose of Semiotext(e) SF is to counteract collapses with heat and quantum strangeness.

NO WAVE SF

Various publishing ventures have done this in the past; one thinks of New Worlds, the Dangerous Visions anthologies, Unearth magazine... Now it's time for a new jolt with a Post-Everything topspin: the Semiotext(e) Science Fiction Anthology. An Einstein–Rosen wormhole into anarcho-lit history.

ALL MEAT SF

Semiotext(e), edited by Sylvère Lotringer and Jim Fleming, has been publishing unimaginably wild stuff since the mid-1970s. Sylvére and Jim have introduced many of the major European radical trends of the last two decades to American readers. Their Polysexuality issue of this magazine achieved the distinction of a denunciation in the U.S. Senate (it seems one of our legislators objected to an NEA grant being awarded to subversive publications, particularly one which "advocated animal sex.")

UNREAL SF

SEMIOTEXT(E) champions —or at least explores — everything and anything on the thin insurrectionist edge of Time's wedge. With a large following of loyal but often-bewildered fans, each issue is devoted to a special theme and edited by a different collective: issues on anti-oedipal psychoanalysis, polysexuality, post-political politics, urban nomadism, schizo-culture, Nietzsche, Bataille, post-structuralist linguistics, man/boy love, Italy, Germany, the USA, the Fourth World. Issues are forthcoming on the Soviet Union, Japan, something resembling Panic...

BAD BRAINS SF

AUTONOMEDIA is the name of the umbrella organization which includes SEMIOTEXT(E), a book series called FOREIGN AGENTS, other AUTONOMEDIA books, some films and videos, some music, and similar ventures. AUTONOMEDIA's visionary publisher Jim Fleming bought our argument: that radical publishing and SF could pool their DNA (so to speak) and produce a monstrous hybrid, a godzilla-book to terrify the bourgeoisie. This is it.

GODGROPE SF

In our invitation to the SF writing community (which appeared among other places in the ultra-hip U.K. prozine INTERZONE) we asked for material which had been rejected by the commercial SF media for its obscenity, radicalism or formalistic weirdness. We hoped to tap a deep and almost-inarticulate groundswell of resentment against the ever-increasing stodginess, neo-conservatism, big-bucks-mania and wretched taste of most SF publishers.

SHITFUCK SF

In a society which supposedly enjoys freedom of speech and the press, and yet manages somehow to stifle all deviancy and repress all assaults on its third-rate consciousness and culture, is it possible to publish *risky* and bizarre SF? You bet! This is it; our writers have puked their guts out.

CRACK SF

A powerful response to our Invitation emerged from three categories of writers. First we heard from certain luminaries of the old New Wave: J. G. Ballard, Sol Yurick, and William Burroughs are long-time SEMIOTEXT(E) collaborators, but we also got material from Colin Wilson, Ian Watson, and Barrington Bayley. Then we received the blessings and moral support from the Dean of Strangeness himself, the Pope of Peoria, Philip José Farmer.

FREE DOPE SF

The second major category of response came from the loosely-defined school of young writers sometimes called "Cyberpunks."

Ideologically correct/wet-ware style/radical-hard/transreal/cyberpunk SF has injected a bit of life into commercial publishing with its snickering nihilism, hardcore sexual excess and harebrained violence. We felt, however, that the style has not yet been pushed as far as it'll go.

TERRORIST SF

With the active support of Bruce Sterling (editor of the canonical Cyberpunk anthology, MIRRORSHADES) we obtained original material from most of the rising stars, including William Gibson (who won the 1985 Hugo, Nebula, and P.K. Dick Awards for his first novel, NEUROMANCER), Marc Laidlaw, Rachel Pollack, Richard Kadrey, John Shirley, Bruce Boston, Michael Blumlein, Lewis Shiner, Greg Gibson, Don Webb, Paul Di Filippo, and Bruce Sterling himself. The Cyberpunk contingent tends to produce "hard" SF — stories with plots, characters, and futuristic hardware — rather than the formal experimentalism of the New Wavers. But the cyberpunk content is outrageous. One imagines them as crazed computer hackers with green mohawks and decaying leather jackets, stoned on drugs so new the FDA hasn't even heard of them yet, word-processing their necropsychedelic prose to blaring tapes by groups with names like The Crucifucks, Dead Kennedys, Butthole Surfers, Bad Brains…

TENTACLESUCKER SF

The third category of contributors emerged largely from the underground world of xerox microzines and American *samizdat*: writers so radically marginalized they could never be co-opted, recuperated, reified or bought out by the Establishment. This group includes, for example: Bob McGlynn, a post-peacenik activist with a Brooklyn group called the Sacred Jihad of our Lady of Perpetual Chaos; Nick Herbert, a "real" physicist and author of QUANTUM REALITY, but a dangerous madman; the Rev. Ivan Stang, High Epopt of the Church of the SubGenius; the legendary anarchist hippie and friend of Lee Harvey Oswald, Kerry Thornley (a.k.a. Ho Chi Zen), to whom the ILLUMINATUS! trilogy was dedicated; Hakim Bey, a "Poetic Terrorist" and pornographer; Denise A. Shawl, propagandist for POPULAR REALITY and other zines under the name Celeste Oatmeal; Sharon Gannon and David Life, Lower East Side improv-musicians/artists/poets; James Koehnline of Chicago's Axe Street Arena, an anarchist art collective; and others to be introduced later on.

TRANSCYBERGNOSTIC SF

Along the frontiers of your actual science, something has recently appeared which may soon replace both relativity and quantum as the source for a new social paradigm: "chaos." An amalgam of Catastrophe Theory, randomicity math, topology, dynamics and statistics, "chaos" also possesses great potential in fields as diverse as biology and morphogenetic field research, economics, brain physiology and consciousness, political theory and radical spirituality. The ideas are so new they haven't even filtered down to many SF writers yet, much less to revolutionary thinkers.

NO FUTURE SF

We feel that the present anthology constitutes a harbinger or foretelling of the new paradigm which will emerge from "chaos." The apocalyptic vision of Cyberpunk perhaps suggests the negative "entropic" element; the radical utopianism of texts like Bayley's "Cling to the Curvature" and the anonymous "Visit Port Watson!" could be read as prophecies of a "post-political" chaos, a post-anarchic negentropic metanoia, "beyond consciousness."

ELECTRO-SEIZURE SF

Here then— in "chaos" — lies the pattern (the "Strange Attractor," as the chaos mathematicians call it) around which all of our diverse material converges, into an anthology with a clear theme and direction, hard to define, yet unmistakable. The result — though we *do* say so ourselves — is a book of colossal importance not only for the future of SF, but for the future in general.

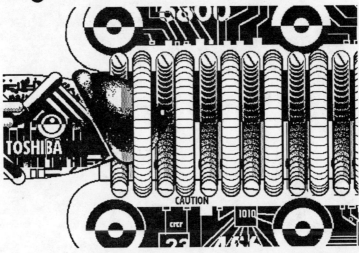

Acknowledgements

This book would never have happened without financial aid and advice from my aunt, Janice Duval, and especially from my father, Douglas E. Wilson. Other people contributed their time and effort to such an extent that they might be considered co-producers: Jim Fleming, as editor and publisher of SEMIOTEXT(E) and Autonomedia; and Bruce Sterling and John Shirley, as advisors and publicists. Special thanks also to J. G. Ballard, Bob Banner and CRITIQUE magazine, James Grauerholz, Sue Ann Harkey, Steve Jones, the editors of INTERZONE, SEMIOTEXT(E) General Editor Sylvére Lotringer, and the editors of NEW PATHWAYS IN FICTION AND SCIENCE FICTION, THE PORTABLE LOWER EAST SIDE, and SCIENCE FICTION EYE.

Despite the already daunting size of the anthology, I feel compelled to mention some writers who should be in it but, for various reasons, aren't: my fellow New Yorkers Samuel Delaney and Thomas Disch, Lisa Goldstein and Pat Murphy, Kim Stanley Robinson and James Morrow (the "neo-humanists"), Rob Hardin, Michael Moorcock, Brian Aldiss, "P. M." (author of BOLO'BOLO)... maybe next time, hey?

As if the above were not already suffiently self-indulgent, I must add that getting to know Bob Sheckley and Phil Farmer, writers I used to venerate when I was 16 or so, has been my greatest pay-off in doing this book—so far!

P. L. W.

Preface
Robert Anton Wilson

The last time I was in the States, I saw a young guy in Des Moines, Iowa (for Jesus sake, *Iowa*!) wearing a T-shirt that said, "Reality is a crutch for people who can't deal with science fiction."

At that moment, I realized the Revolution was over and my side has won. The rest of this century—the countdown to the Millenium—will be just the mopping-up operations. When even Des Moines has a sub-culture aware that "reality" is some kind of ontological silly-putty, the dark ages are finally over and the New Aeon is dawning.

Back in 1957, when I was young—to give you an idea of the kultur of the period—the Feds had just burned the scientific books of Dr. Wilhelm Reich in an incinerator, I had the cosmic *chutzpah* to give a lecture, at the New York Academy of the Sciences, in which I solemnly argued, with my bare face hanging out, that the only truly contemporary literature was that of surrealism, James Joyce and science fiction, since the so-called mainstream "realistic" novel was based entirely on refuted Newtonian-Victorian Idolatry and should be classified with the Bible and fairy tales. I might as well have killed a cat in the sacristy. Many in the audience did not merely think I was eccentric; they were sure I was a certifiable nut-case. (I am rather proud that even now, at the age of 54, I can still provoke that response in some audiences.)

The 20th Century has experienced the total breakdown of all previous notions of "reality" and "objectivity," and no literature is 20th Century literature that does not reflect this enormous evolutionary fact.

Nietzsche, who symbolicallty died in 1900, announced that this century would confront Chaos and the Abyss. We have confronted them. The two main branches of modern philosophy—the Existentialist wing in its various permutations, and the Linguistic Analysts and their symbiotes the Logical Positivists—differ on most things but agree with Nietzsche's verdict that no "true" "reality" allegedly "behind" appearances is ever any more than a hypothesis (and may even be only a guess in disguise), while the world of appearances itself is totally subjective and relative to the observer. We are standing upon "the void. Upon incertitude," as Stephen Dedalus says in almost the geometrical middle of Joyce's epic of the modern mind inturned on its own labyrinths, *Ulysses*.

Anthropology, perception psychology, neurology, phenomenological sociology, ethnomethodology and even ethology (in its study of imprinting in animals), all confirm the quantum mechanical and Existentialist view that the world we perceive is a Mickey Mouse cartoon our brains have created out of signals that arrive as raw energy at the rate of millions of bleeps per second. Which type of Mickey Mouse cartoon—or Homeric epic, or Soap Opera—we make of these signals depends on our genes (which species of brain we have—mammalian, serpentine, insectoid etc.), and next on our imprints, and our conditioning and "learning" or brainwashing by society, and these are perpetuated by our lazy habits and only sometimes modified or somewhat transcended by our efforts at creativity and higher awareness.

The various "models" of quantum mechanics—and it is symptomatic that we dare not call them "theories" any more—are all in direct contradiction to common sense and to common sense-data (the Mickey Mouse cut-outs our brain constructs from the energy bleeps it receives). Each type of quantum model is at least as weird as Dali's *Debris of an Automobile Giving Birth to a Blind Horse Biting a Telephone*.

Is Schroedinger's cat in the famous *gedankenexperiment* dead or alive, or both, or somewhere in between? Each quantum model gives a different answer to that crucial question, just as different quantum models tell us that an unmeasured particle is simultaneously spin-up or spin-down or both or neither. Heisenberg said Einstein's attempt to find out what such an unmeasured particle is "really" doing was "like the medieval debate about how many angels can dance on the head of a pin." Why should an unmeasured particle not also be giving birth to a blind horse biting a telephone?

(The only particles we know anything about are the measured ones, which are shaped and to some extent created by the measurements, just as the only people we know anything about are the encountered ones who are shaped and to some extent created by our encounters with them. You knew that already, didn't you?)

Back in Joyceland, there is the Garry Owen mystery. Garry is a dog, and in the world of appearances one can even say Garry was a "real" dog. That is, he was whelped in 1888 and was owned by J. J. Giltrap, a Dublin breeder of pedigreed Irish setters. In a 19th Century novel, if Garry Owen appeared, he would be a definite and specific dog corresponding to the 19th Century delusion that a definite and specific "reality" exists somewhere apart from observers and observings. In the quantum comedy of *Ulysses*, there are three Garry Owens, or three Mickey Mouse cut-outs of the infinite space-time process called "Garry Owen," each seen by one of three different observers: the first is a lively and endearing animal, the second is a surly and dangerous brute, and the third actually talks and even recites Gaelic poetry. This is the kind of attention to existential, phenomenological relativity that makes Joyce contemporary, whereas "realistic" writers are still living in medieval Aristotelian myth. Joyce's multi-valued dog is as paradigmatic of our age as Schroedinger's dead-and-alive cat.

Elsewhere in this volume I enquire into the length of King Kong's penis. My conclusions are relative to the context in which Kong belongs—the context of surrealism and dream—and are not consistent with the logic of Aristotelian "reality." But to Aristotle a penis, like any other rod, has a "real" length which is "essential" to its "nature," and we have known since Special Relativity (1905) that there is no such "real" length in experience, but only the various lengths (plural) of various observers or observing instruments. Like Dali's Andalusian Dog and Joyce's three-headed Irish setter, Kong's penis and an Einsteinian rod are "in the eye of the beholder," as it were. This is why all people with a good scientific education understand at once the answer to Zen Buddhist riddle, "Who is the Master who makes the grass green?"

If you understand this at once, you might say that, like Bob Black, I have a Nietzsche trigger finger.

St. Gregory the Illuminator said, "We make Idols of our concepts, but wisdom is born of wonder." In more modern jargon, we easily hypnotize ourselves with our current models—our maps of existence, our latest reality-tunnels—and wisdom begins when we are shocked out of this hypnosis and realize again that appearances are our own Mickey Mouse creations and we don't know what is "behind" these appearances.

What could be "behind" quantum waves that are also particles, and also "behind" dogs, crystals, people, galaxies and the Gross National Product? The Void, as Buddhists think? A world in every possible state, until we select one state by measurement, as most quantum physicists think? Chaos and the Abyss, as Nietzsche thought? Joyce's Void of Incertitude? That moment of wonder, in which we are not sure, and our Idols become just models again and cease to hyponotize us, is what all good psychotherapy aims to achieve, what the best science-fiction does more shockingly and amusingly that any other kind of literature, what Liberation means in both Existentialism and Oriental mysticism.

Or to say it more simply, the essence of psychotherapy, Zen, or Encounter, awakening from group-hypnosis, Existential being (right where you are sitting now), Liberation, "Enlightenment," etc. is breaking our habitual mental sets. The function of science fiction is to break mental sets. Science fiction is liberation. Reality in the old Aristotelian sense is a crutch for those who are afraid to walk alone on their own feet, above the Abyss that yawns when we begin to break our mental sets and pause to wonder—really wonder —

Environs of Howth Castle
Dublin , Ireland

What would be the fun of editing an SF anthology if we did not permit ourselves the self-indulgence of a running Editorial Commentary—the omniscient chatty voice of the genial MC of this alien late-nite sleazoid horrorshow? And a tip of the hat to Harlan Ellison, whose DANGEROUS VISIONS anthology helped mutate our youth, and whose ramblings sometimes ran longer than the stories they were meant to introduce. [Helpful note for lazy reviewers: "SEMIOTEXT(E) SF is DANGEROUS VISIONS for the 90s!"]

"Fanzines" like UNEARTH, LAST WAVE, LIVE FROM THE STAGGER CAFE, NEW PATHWAYS, etc., boast of printing stories no commercial magazine or publisher will dare touch.

Even today some critics deny this, claiming that if a story is "good", the pro-zines will buy it, and that the experimental zines are full of juvenilia and tripe. This just ain't so. Ellison proved that commercial SF lacked chutzpah, and the present collection proves it once again.

Don Webb has been described as "ubiquitous" in that little zine-world; recently he's emerged into the pro-zines as well, and will no doubt continue to soar like Alice after she ate the "Eat-Me" cake. Why do so many of the authors in this book live in Texas? Their stories often seem to emanate from a land of chainsaw massacres, assassinations and spaceport architecture already decaying into yet another lost American Future.

 "Don Webb—born and reborn several times, mostly clustered around April 30, 1960 —Walpurgisnacht. Book-length fiction, UNCLE OVID'S EXERCISE BOOK (Fiction Collective). Likes Chinese food."

Metamorphosis No. 89
Don Webb

The dying centaur tries to con me into making a charm from its blood. My great-aunt on my mother's side got taken in by that. I just smile as the centaur wheezes out blood and bits of lungs. The lungs are pretty scrambled — the 30-.06 entered just left of the breastbone. They're yellow too. Must've been a cigarette smoker — looked pretty funny in a 7-11 if you ask me. I wouldn't let one in my store. Takes all types. Three more gasps and it's over. Jake grabs the hindlegs and I get the forelegs and we drag the body through the scrub oak back to the pickup. The critter weighs 800 pounds easy. Hope the winch'll hold. 800 lbs at 50 cents a pound divided by 2 comes to 200 dollars less 35 for the license and maybe 10 or 20 for the gas and the ammo ain't bad for a morning's work.

Jake points out that Japanese and Frenchmen thinks centaur meat is a delicacy. Damn near turns my stomach at a time like this when you

23

can smell the blood. Try haulin' this mother to Japan I say. We both laugh. We lay the body down for a breather. At least you can see the truck from here. White Chevy Custom Ten. Don't know what's custom about it. Jake hands me some Wintergreen Skoal. I take a pinch. Never cared much for wintergreen. Reminds me of that pink medicine you take for the runs.

Kind of timidly I ask Jake if he wants the head. He smiles and says no you take it. I think it'll go good over the mantle. Mildred's liable to squawk though: Well let her, she don't know how dangerous shooting these critters is. A lot of 'em have blow guns with poisoned thorns and got treaties on the side with satyrs. Of course, I checked with the local NRA office. There's not *supposed* to be any satyrs in Balcones Woods. Once you hear the pipes you're a goner.

I saw one of them back in the VA hospital. One of the ones who's heard the pipes. He'd just wander around wide-eyed and sometimes he'd walk into a wall. Might as well have scrambled eggs for brains.

Jake shrugs and I shrug and we start dragging the body again. It's getting a lot of leaves and thistles in its hair but the taxidermist will be able to fix that. I'd better get the people at the dog food place to drain the blood from the head when they cut it off. Glad I bagged — at least I think it was my shell and not Jake's — a male. The game warden's got your ass if you get a mare. I'm beginning to think this sucker weighs 900 lbs. My calves hurt and there's a pain on my left side just below my heart. I had to be the one — Jake couldn't hit the broad side of a barn.

We clear the scrub. Easier going in the tall grass. Jake's got a little blood on him. We stop and clean it off with a hanky and then he throws the hanky away. The blood's poisonous if mixed with sweat or saliva unless you can take some mandrake. I've got some atropine drops in my first aid kit, but like a jackass I left the kit on the dining room table. I'll ask the people at Alpo's for a couple of drops just in case. You can get real drunk on atropine and beer. I forgot the damn beer too.

Jake asks me if they pay in cash or check. I've never traded with these folks but the plant near Plainview pays in cash. The grass's still wet with dew and the carcass just slides along now. It's warmed up a bit since we shot the thing. We got a couple of big black flies trailing us zzzzz zzzzzzzzzzzzzzzzzz (smack) Jesus Christ how can he slap a fly right onto his shirt like that. I'm gonna lose my cookies between the blood and the fly guts and this goddam wintergreen snuff. He don't even wipe it off. What a pig.

Finally at the truck. Jake starts up the engine and the little compressor on the back gets to whining. I fix the hook right where the left foreleg joins the body. I sure hate to tear up the beautiful appaloosa coat, but Mildred don't want it and Jake's old lady don't even know he's off hunting. Jake starts up the winch. And he jumps up in the back and grabs the shoulders and I push on the butt which is really disgusting 'cause it emptied itself when we shot the mother. Most of the shit's been wiped on the grass. Damn I'll be glad when I can have a shower. I push and Jake pulls and the compressor sounds like it's going to blow something and my heart sounds like its going to blow and the zzzzzzzflieszzzzzzzzarezzzbackzzzzzin zzzzzazzzzzsextetzzzzz and finally it's in the pickup.

Pickup's a lot lower on its shocks. Maybe it weighs 1000 lbs.

Jake shuts off the compressor. I walk away from the zzzzz and pant like hell. I promise myself *this* year I'm going to start that aerobic program that Mildred's been touting. Spit out the snuff.

Jake walks up. He's got a thermos from the cab. He offers me a cup of coffee and I wash my mouth out. It scalds but it's clean. I spit the coffee out and pour myself a cup for drinking.

Jake gets him one too. It's gonna be a hot one. We shrug. We both want to get the body to Alpo's before it starts to smell. We walk to the cab. I'll drive. I turn on the air conditioning and roll up the windows. Jake unfolds the map. He'll navigate.

I have to take the dirt road pretty slow since the shocks are so weighed down. Even so we scrape bottom two or three times even before we hit the stream ford. If I gotta pay for a new oil pan it'll eat into my profits pretty deep. Damn Jake wouldn't offer to pay half either. He hasn't shelled out a nickel for gas. I think when it's time to fill up the truck I'll just pull into a gas station and say it's your turn old buddy with no preamble. He'll probably pay then.

We splash through the ford. I can see speckled trout in the stream. I came down here last year to fish and didn't see a damn one. It's about a mile to the highway. Jake's been real quiet.

I look over. He's as white as a sheet and his forehead's terrible swollen. Oh Jesus he's got a little blood in him. Probably through that damned snuff. He looks like he's about to puke. I stop the pickup. I get out and walk around to his side. I open the door and sure enough he pukes all over my shoes.

Come on bud. I help him to the creek and wash him off and fix him a cold compress. I set him down in the shade of a cedar tree. I tell him to rest. I'll get him a couple of aspirin and drive down to the warden's cabin for some mandrake extract. He just nods.

As I walk back to the pickup I hear his clothes rip. I wheel around. His swollen forehead sprouts a horn.

I fire up the goddamned pickup fast as I can. I tell the game warden about Jake. He gives me the Balance of Nature speech. Alpo's ain't open yet but the 7-11 is. I'm going to drink eight or nine beers and then call Mildred.

"Chairman Bruce" Sterling is one of the eminences grises behind this volume, which ought in some senses to be considered a companion to his collection MIRRORSHADES: THE CYBERPUNK ANTHOLOGY.

For our money, Sterling writes the finest "radical hard SF" of the new generation; his stories have plot and characters, his science is solid, his research meticulous, his imagination pure gonzo and his politics highly anarchic.

As an example, take the following story. The few Americans who happen to have lived in the Middle East and Central Asia are constantly outraged by the careless ignorance of Islamdom displayed by all American writers... not just network hacks and bigots... all. So when we first scanned this story—concerning a future in which resurgent Islam has more-or-less triumphed—we were looking for nits to pick.

We couldn't find any. Not one. We were stunned. We wrote to Bruce, asking where and how long he'd lived in the Islamic world. With justifiable glee, he told us he's never been there; the whole story was concocted from research plus imagination.

Bruce's latest novel, ISLANDS IN THE NET, is a virtually unique combination of near-future realism and anarchist utopia— an optimistic cyberpunk adventure story!

We See Things Differently
Bruce Sterling

This was the *jahiliyah*—the land of ignorance. This was America. The Great Satan, the Arsenal of Imperialism, the Bankroller of Zionism, the Bastion of Neo-Colonialism. The home of Hollywood and blonde sluts in black nylon. The land of rocket-equipped F-15s that slashed across God's sky, in godless pride. The land of nuclear-powered global navies, with cannon that fired shells as large as cars.

They have forgotten that they used to shoot us, shell us, insult us, and equip our enemies. They have no memory, the Americans, and no history. Wind sweeps through them, and the past vanishes. They are like dead leaves.

I flew into Miami, on a winter afternoon. The jet banked over a tangle of empty highways, then a large dead section of the city — a ghetto perhaps. In our final approach we passed a coal-burning power plant, reflected in the canal. For a moment I mistook it for a mosque, its

27

tall smokestacks slender as minarets. A Mosque for the American Dynamo.

I had trouble with my cameras at customs. The customs officer was a grimy-looking American white with hair the color of clay. He squinted at my passport. "That's an awful lot of film, Mr. Cuttab," he said.

"Qutb," I said, smiling. "Sayyid Qutb. Call me Charlie."

"Journalist, huh?" He looked unhappy. It seemed that I owed substantial import duties on my Japanese cameras, as well as my numerous rolls of Pakistani color film. He invited me into a small back office to discuss it. Money changed hands. I departed with my papers in order.

The airport was half-full: mostly prosperous Venezuelans and Cubans, with the haunted look of men pursuing sin. I caught a taxi outside, a tiny vehicle like a motorcycle wrapped in glass. The cabby, an ancient black man, stowed my luggage in the cab's trailer.

Within the cab's cramped confines, we were soon unwilling intimates. The cabbie's breath smelled of sweetened alcohol. "You Iranian?" the cabbie asked.

"Arab."

"We respect Iranians around here, we really do," the cabbie insisted.

"So do we," I said. "We fought them on the Iraqi front for years."

"Yeah?" said the cabbie uncertainly. "Seems to me I heard about that. How'd that end up?"

"The Shi'ite holy cities were ceded to Iran. The Ba'athist regime is dead, and Iraq is now part of the Arab Caliphate." My words made no impression on him, and I had known it before I spoke. This is the land of ignorance. They know nothing about us, the Americans. After all this, and they still know nothing whatsoever.

"Well, who's got more money these days?" the cabbie asked. "Y'all, or the Iranians?"

"The Iranians have heavy industry," I said. "But we Arabs tip better."

The cabbie smiled. It is very easy to buy Americans. The mention of money brightens them like a shot of drugs. It is not just the poverty; they were always like this, even when they were rich. It is the effect of spiritual emptiness. A terrible grinding emptiness in the very guts of the West, which no amount of Coca-Cola seems able to fill.

We rolled down gloomy streets toward the hotel. Miami's streetlights were subsidized by commercial enterprises. It was another way of, as they say, shrugging the burden of essential services from the exhausted backs of the taxpayers. And onto the far sturdier shoulders of peddlers of aspirin, sticky sweetened drinks, and cosmetics. Their billboards gleamed bluely under harsh lights encased in bulletproof glass. It reminded me so strongly of Soviet agitprop that I had a sudden jarring sense of displacement, as if I were being sold Lenin and Engels and Marx in the handy jumbo size.

The cabbie, wondering perhaps about his tip, offered to exchange dollars for riyals at black-market rates. I declined politely, having already done this in Cairo. The lining of my coat was stuffed with crisp Reagan $1,000 bills. I also had several hundred in pocket change, and an extensive credit line at the Islamic Bank of Jerusalem. I foresaw no difficulties.

Outside the hotel, I gave the ancient driver a pair of fifties. Another very old man, of Hispanic descent, took my bags on a trolley. I registered under the gaze of a very old woman. Like all American women, she was dressed in a way intended to provoke lust. In the young, this technique works admirably, as proved by America's unhappy history of sexually transmitted plague. In the very old, it provokes only sad disgust.

I smiled on the horrible old woman and paid in advance.

I was rewarded by a double-handful of glossy brochures promoting local casinos, strip-joints, and bars.

The room was adequate. This had once been a fine hotel. The air-conditioning was quiet and both hot and cold water worked well. A wide flat screen covering most of one wall offered dozens of channels of television.

My wristwatch buzzed quietly, its programmed dial indicating the direction of Mecca. I took the rug from my luggage and spread it before the window. I cleansed my face, my hands, my feet. Then I knelt before the darkening chaos of Miami, many stories below. I assumed the eight positions, bowing carefully, sinking with gratitude into deep meditation. I forced away the stress of jet-lag, the innate tension and fear of a Believer among enemies.

Prayer completed, I changed my clothing, putting aside my dark Western business suit. I assumed denim jeans, a long-sleeved shirt, and photographer's vest. I slipped my press card, my passport, my health cards into the vest's zippered pockets, and draped the cameras around myself. I then returned to the lobby downstairs, to await the arrival of the American rock star.

He came on schedule, even slightly early. There was only a small crowd, as the rock star's organization had sought confidentiality. A train of seven monstrous busses pulled into the hotel's lot, their whale-like sides gleaming with brushed aluminum. They bore Massachusetts license plates. I walked out on to the tarmac and began photographing.

All seven busses carried the rock star's favored insignia, the thirteen-starred blue field of the early Americen flag. The busses pulled up with military precision, forming a wagon-train fortress across a large section of the weedy, broken tarmac. Folding doors hissed open and a swarm of road crew piled out into the circle of busses.

Men and women alike wore baggy fatigues, covered with buttoned pockets and block-shaped streaks of urban camouflage: brick red, asphalt black, and concrete gray. Dark-blue shoulder-patches showed the thirteen-starred circle. Working efficiently, without haste, they erected large satellite dishes on the roofs of two busses. The busses were soon linked together in formation, shaped barriers of woven wire securing the gaps between each nose and tail. The machines seemed to sit breathing, with the stoked-up, leviathan air of steam locomotives.

A dozen identically dressed crewmen broke from the busses and departed in a group for the hotel. Within their midst, shielded by their bodies, was the rock star, Tom Boston. The broken outlines of their camouflaged fatigues made them seem to blur into a single mass, like a herd of moving zebras. I followed them; they vanished quickly within the hotel. One crew woman tarried outside.

I approached her. She had been hauling a bulky piece of metal luggage on trolley wheels. It was a newspaper vending machine. She set it beside three other machines at the hotel's entrance. It was the Boston organization's propaganda paper, *Poor Richard's*.

I drew near. "Ah, the latest issue," I said. "May I have one?"

"It will cost five dollars," she said in painstaking English. To my surprise, I recognized her as Boston's wife. "Valya Plisetskaya," I said with pleasure, and handed her a five-dollar nickel. "My name is Sayyid; my American friends call me Charlie."

She looked about her. A small crowd already gathered at the busses, kept at a distance by the Boston crew. Others clustered under the hotel's green-and-white awning.

"Who are you with?" she said.

"*Al-Ahram*, of Cairo. An Arabic newspaper."

"You're not a political?" she said.

I shook my head in amusement at this typical show of Soviet paranoia. "Here's my press card." I showed her the tangle of Arabic. "I am here to cover Tom Boston. The Boston phenomenon."

She squinted. "Tom is big in Cairo these days? Muslims, yes? Down on rock and roll."

"We're not all ayatollahs," I said, smiling up at her. She was very tall. "Many still listen to Western pop music; they ignore the advice of their betters. They used to rock all night in Leningrad. Despite the Party. Isn't that so?"

"You know about us Russians, do you, Charlie?" She handed me my paper, watching me with cool suspicion.

"No, I can't keep up," I said. "Like Lebanon in the old days. Too many factions." I followed her through the swinging glass doors of the hotel. Valentina Plisetskaya was a broad-cheeked Slav with glacial blue eyes and hair the color of corn tassels. She was a childless woman in her thirties, starved as thin as a girl. She played saxophone in

Boston's band. She was a native of Moscow, but had survived its de-
struction. She had been on tour with her jazz band when the Afghan
Martyrs' Front detonated their nuclear bomb.

I tagged after her. I was interested in the view of another foreigner. "What do you think of the Americans these days?" I asked her.

We waited beside the elevator.

"Are you recording?" she said.

"No! I'm a print journalist. I know you don't like tapes," I said.

"We like tapes fine," she said, staring down at me. "As long as
they are ours." The elevator was sluggish. "You want to know what I
think, Charlie? I think Americans are fucked. Not as bad as Soviets, but
fucked anyway. What do you think?"

"Oh," I said. "American gloom-and-doom is an old story. At Al-
Ahram, we are more interested in the signs of American resurgence.
That's the big angle, now. That's why I'm here." She looked at me with
remote sarcasm. "Aren't you a little afraid they will beat the shit out of
you? They're not happy, the Americans. Not sweet and easy-going like
before."

I wanted to ask her how sweet the CIA had been when their
bomb killed half the Iranian government in 1981. Instead, I shrugged.
"There's no substitute for a man on the ground. That's what my editors
say." The elevator shunted open. "May I come up with you?"

"I won't stop you." We stepped in. "But they won't let you in to
see Tom."

"They will if you ask them to, Mrs. Boston."

"I'm Plisetskaya," she said, fluffing her yellow hair. "See? No
veil." It was the old story of the so-called "liberated" Western woman.
They call the simple, modest clothing of Islam "bondage" — while they
spend countless hours, and millions of dollars, painting themselves. They
grow their nails like talons, cram their feet into high heels, strap their
breasts and hips into spandex. All for the sake of male lust.

It baffles the imagination. Naturally I told her nothing of this,
but only smiled. "I'm afraid I will be a pest," I said. "I have a room in
this hotel. Some time I will see your husband. I must, my editors demand
it."

The doors opened. We stepped into the hall of the fourteenth
floor. Boston's entourage had taken over the entire floor. Men in fatigues
and sunglasses guarded the hallway; one of them had a trained dog.

"Your paper is big, is it?" the woman said.

"Biggest in Cairo, millions of readers," I said. "We still read, in
the Caliphate."

"State-controlled television," she muttered.

"Worse than corporations?" I asked. "I saw what CBS said about
Tom Boston." She hesitated, and I continued to prod. "A 'Luddite fanatic', am I right? A 'rock demagogue'."

"Give me your room number." I did this. "I'll call," she said, striding away down the corridor. I almost expected the guards to salute her as she passed so regally, but they made no move, their eyes invisible behind the glasses. They looked old and rather tired, but with the alert relaxation of professionals. They had the look of former Secret Service bodyguards. The city-colored fatigues were baggy enough to hide almost any amount of weaponry.

I returned to my room. I ordered Japanese food from room service, and ate it. Wine had been used in its cooking, but I am not a prude in these matters. It was now time for the day's last prayer, though my body, still attuned to Cairo, did not believe it.

My devotions were broken by a knocking at the door. I opened it. It was another of Boston's staff, a small black woman whose hair had been treated. It had a nylon sheen. It looked like the plastic hair on a child's doll. "You Charlie?"

"Yes."

"Valya says, you want to see the gig. See us set up. Got you a backstage pass."

"Thank you very much." I let her clip the plastic-coated pass to my vest. She looked past me into the room, and saw my prayer rug at the window. "What you doin' in there? Prayin'?"

"Yes."

"Weird," she said. "You coming or what?"

I followed my nameless benefactor to the elevator.

Down at ground level, the crowd had swollen. Two hired security guards stood outside the glass doors, refusing admittance to anyone without a room key. The girl ducked, and plowed through the crowd with sudden headlong force, like an American football player. I struggled in her wake, the gawkers, pickpockets, and autograph hounds closing at my heels. The crowd was liberally sprinkled with the repulsive derelicts one sees so often in America: those without homes, without family, without charity.

I was surprised at the age of the people. For a rock-star's crowd, one expects dizzy teenage girls and the libidinous young street-toughs that pursue them. There were many of those, but more of another type: tired, footsore people with crow's-feet and graying hair. Men and women in their thirties and forties, with a shabby, crushed look. Unemployed, obviously, and with time on their hands to cluster around anything that resembled hope.

We walked without hurry to the fortress circle of busses. A rear-guard of Boston's kept the onlookers at bay. Two of the busses were already unlinked from the others and under full steam. I followed the black woman up perforated steps and into the bowels of one of the shining machines.

She called brief greetings to the others already inside.

The air held the sharp reek of cleaning fluid. Neat elastic cords strapped down stacks of amplifiers, stencilled instrument cases, wheeled dollies of black rubber and crisp yellow pine. The thirteen-starred circle marked everything, stamped or spray-painted. A methane-burning steam generator sat at the back of the bus, next to a tall crashproof rack of high-pressure fuel tanks. We skirted the equipment and joined the others in a narrow row of second-hand airplane seats. We buckled ourselves in. I sat next to the Doll-Haired Girl.

The bus surged into motion. "It's very clean," I said to her. "I expected something a bit wilder on a rock and roll bus."

"Maybe in Egypt," she said, with the instinctive decision that Egypt was in the Dark Ages. "We don't have the luxury to screw around. Not now."

I decided not to tell her that Egypt, as a nation-state, no longer existed. "American pop culture is a very big industry."

"Biggest we have left," she said. "And if you Muslims weren't so pimpy about it, maybe we could pull down a few riyals and get out of debt."

"We buy a great deal from America," I told her. "Grain and timber and minerals."

"That's Third-World stuff. We're not your farm." She looked at the spotless floor. "Look, our industries suck, everyone knows it. So we sell entertainment. Except where there's media barriers. And even then the fucking video pirates rip us off."

"We see things differently," I said. "America ruled the global media for decades. To us, it's cultural imperialism. We have many talented musicians in the Arab world. Have you ever heard them?"

"Can't afford it," she said crisply. "We spent all our money saving the Persian Gulf from commies."

"The Global Threat of Red Totalitarianism," said the heavyset man in the seat next to Doll-Hair. The others laughed grimly.

"Oh," I said. "Actually, it was Zionism that concerned us. When there was a Zionism."

"I can't believe the hate shit I see about America," said the heavy man. "You know how much money we gave away to people, just gave away, for nothing? Billions and billions. Peace Corps, development aid... for decades. Any disaster anywhere, and we fell all over ourselves to give food, medicine.... Then the Russians go down and the whole world turns against us like we were monsters."

"Moscow," said another crewman, shaking his shaggy head.

"You know, there are still motherfuckers who think we Americans killed Moscow. They think we gave a Bomb to those Afghani terrorists."

"It had to come from somewhere," I said.

"No, man. We wouldn't do that to them. No, man, things were

going great between us. Rock for Detente—I was at that gig."

We drove to Miami's Memorial Colosseum. It was an ambitious structure, left half-completed when the American banking system collapsed.

We entered double-doors at the back, wheeling the equipment along dusty corridors. The Colosseum's interior was skeletal; inside it was clammy and cavernous. A stage, a concrete floor. Bare steel arched high overhead, with crudely bracket-mounted stage-lights. Large sections of that bizarre American parody of grass, "Astroturf," had been dragged before the stage. The itchy green fur, still lined with yard-marks from some forgotten stadium, was almost indestructible. At second-hand rates, it was much cheaper than carpeting.

The crew worked with smooth precision, setting up amplifiers, spindly mike-stands, a huge high-tech drum kit with the clustered, shiny look of an oil refinery. Others checked lighting, flicking blue and yellow spots across the stage. At the public entrances, two crewmen from a second bus erected metal detectors for illicit cameras, recorders, or handguns. Especially handguns. Two attempts had already been made on Boston's life, one at the Chicago Freedom Festival, when Chicago's Mayor was wounded at Boston's side.

For a moment, to understand it, I mounted the empty stage and stood before Boston's microphone. I imagined the crowd before me, ten thousand souls, twenty thousand eyes. Under that attention, I realized, every motion was amplified. To move my arm would be like moving ten thousand arms, my every word like the voice of thousands. I felt like a Nasser, a Qadaffi, a Saddam Hussein.

This was the nature of secular power. Industrial power. It was the West that invented it, that invented Hitler, the gutter orator turned trampler of nations, that invented Stalin, the man they called "Genghis Khan with a telephone." The media pop star, the politician. Was there any difference any more? Not in America; it was all a question of seizing eyes, of seizing attention. Attention is wealth, in an age of mass media. Center stage is more important than armies.

The last unearthly moans and squeals of sound-check faded. The Miami crowd began to filter into the Colosseum. They looked livelier than the desperate searchers that had pursued Boston to his hotel. America was still a wealthy country, by most standards; the professional classes had kept much of their prosperity. There were those legions of lawyers, for instance, that secular priesthood that had done so much to drain America's once-vaunted enterprise. And their associated legions of state bureaucrats. They were instantly recognizable; the cut of their suits, the telltale pocket telephones proclaiming their status.

What were they looking for here? Had they never read Boston's propaganda paper, with its bitter condemnation of everything they stood for? With its fierce attacks on the "legislative-litigative

complex," its demands for sweeping reforms?

Was it possible that they failed to take him seriously?

I joined the crowd, mingling, listening to conversations. At the doors, Boston cadres were cutting ticket prices for those who showed voter registrations. Those who showed unemployment cards got in for even less.

The prosperous Americans stood in little knots of besieged gentility, frightened of the others, yet curious, smiling. There was a liveliness in the destitute: brighter clothing, knotted kerchiefs at the elbows, cheap Korean boots of irridescent cloth. Many wore tricornered hats, some with a cockade of red, white, and blue, or the circle of thirteen stars.

This was rock and roll, I realized; that was the secret. They had all grown up on it, these Americans, even the richer ones. To them, the sixty-year tradition of rock music seemed as ancient as the Pyramids. It had become a Jerusalem, a Mecca of American tribes.

The crowd milled, waiting, and Boston let them wait. At the back of the crowd, Boston crewmen did a brisk business in starred souvenir shirts, programs, and tapes. Heat and tension mounted, and people began to sweat. The stage remained dark.

I bought the souvenir items and studied them. They talked about cheap computers, a phone company owned by its workers, a free database, neighborhood co-ops that could buy unmilled grain by the ton. ATTENTION MIAMI, read one brochure in letters of dripping red. It named the ten largest global corporations and meticulously listed every subsidiary doing business in Miami, with its address, its phone number, the percentage of income shipped to banks in Europe and Japan. Each list went on for pages. Nothing else. To Boston's audience, nothing else was necessary.

The house lights darkened. A frightening animal roar rose from the crowd. A single spot lit Tom Boston, stencilling him against darkness.

"My fellow Americans," he said. A funereal hush followed. The crowd strained for each word. Boston smirked. "My f-f-f-f-fellow Americans." It was a clever microphone, digitized, a small synthesizer in itself. "My fellow Am-am-am-am-AMM!" The words vanished in a sudden soaring wail of feedback. "My Am/ my fellows/ My Am/ my fellows/ Miami, Miami, Miami, MIAMI!" The sound of Boston's voice, suddenly leaping out of all human context, becoming something shattering, superhuman—the effect was bone-chilling. It passed all barriers, it seeped directly into the skin, the blood.

"Tom Jefferson Died Broke!" he shouted. It was the title of his first song. Stage lights flashed up and hell broke its gates. Was it a "song" at all, this strange, volcanic creation? There was a melody loose in it somewhere, pursued by Plisetskaya's saxophone, but the sheer volume and impact hurled it through the audience like a sheet of flame. I had never before heard anything so loud. What Cairo's renegade set called rock and roll paled to nothing beside this invisible hurricane.

At first it seemed raw noise. But that was only a kind of flooring, a merciless grinding foundation below the rising architectures of sound. Technology did it: a piercing, soaring, digitized, utter clarity, of perfect cybernetic acoustics adjusting for each echo, a hundred times a second.

Boston played a glass harmonica: an instrument invented by the early American genius Benjamin Franklin. The harmonica was made of carefully tuned glass disks, rotating on a spindle, and played by streaking a wet fingertip across each moving edge.

It was the sound of pure crystal, seemingly sourceless, of tooth-aching purity.

The famous Western musician, Wolfgang Mozart, had composed for the Franklin harmonica in the days of its novelty. But legend said that its players went mad, their nerves shredded by its clarity of sound. It was a legend Boston was careful to exploit. He played the machine sparingly, with the air of a magician, of a Solomon unbottling demons. I was glad of his spare use, for its sound was so beautiful that it stung the brain.

Boston threw aside his hat. Long coiled hair spilled free. Boston was what Americans called "black"; at least he was often referred to as black, though no one seemed certain. He was no darker than myself. The beat rose up, a strong animal heaving. Boston stalked across the stage as if on springs, clutching his microphone. He began to sing.

The song concerned Thomas Jefferson, a famous American president of the 18th century. Jefferson was a political theorist who wrote revolutionary manifestos and favored a decentralist mode of government. The song, however, dealt with the relations of Jefferson and a black concubine in his household. He had several children by this woman, who were a source of great shame, due to the odd legal code of the period. Legally, they were his slaves, and it was only at the end of his life, when he was in great poverty, that Jefferson set them free.

It was a story whose pathos makes little sense to a Muslim. But Boston's audience, knowing themselves Jefferson's children, took it to heart.

The heat became stifling, as massed bodies swayed in rhythm. The next song began in a torrent of punishing noise. Frantic hysteria seized the crowd; their bodies spasmed with each beat, the shaman Boston seeming to scourge them. It was a fearsome song, called "The Whites of Their Eyes," after an American war-cry. He sang of a tactic of battle: to wait until the enemy comes close enough so that you can meet his eyes, frighten him with your conviction, and then shoot him point blank. The chorus harked again and again to the "Cowards of the long kill," a Boston slogan condemning those whose abstract power structures let them murder without ever seeing pain.

Three more songs followed, one of them slower, the others battering the audience like iron rods. Boston stalked like a madman, his clothing dark with sweat. My heart spasmed as heavy bass notes, filled with dark murderous power, surged through my ribs. I moved away from the heat to the fringe of the crowd, feeling light-headed and sick.

I had not expected this. I had expected a political spokesman, but instead it seemed I was assaulted by the very Voice of the West. The Voice of a society drunk with raw power, maddened by the grinding roar of machines. It filled me with terrified awe.

To think that once, the West had held us in its armored hands. It had treated Islam like a natural resource, its invincible armies plowing through the lands of the Faithful like bulldozers. The West had chopped our world up into colonies, and smiled upon us with its awful schizophrenic perfidy. It told us to separate God and State, to separate Mind and Body, to separate Reason and Faith. It had torn us apart.

I stood shaking as the first set ended. The band vanished backstage, and a single figure approached the microphone. I recognized him as a famous American television comedian, who had abandoned his own career to join Boston.

The man began to joke and clown, his antics seeming to soothe the crowd, which hooted with laughter. This intermission was a wise move on Boston's part, I thought. The level of pain, of intensity, had become unbearable.

It struck me then how much Boston was like the great Khomeini. Boston too had the persona of the Man of Sorrows, the sufferer after justice, the ascetic among corruption, the battler against odds. And the air of the mystic, the adept, at least as far as such a thing was possible in America. I thought of this, and deep fear struck me once again.

I walked through the gates to the Colosseum's outer hall, seeking air and room to think. Others had come out too. They leaned against the wall, men and women, with the look of wrung-out mops. Some smoked cigarettes, others argued over brochures, others simply sat with palsied grins.

Still others wept. These disturbed me most, for these were the ones whose souls seemed stung and opened. Khomeini made men weep like that, tearing aside despair like a bandage from a burn. I walked down the hall, watching them, making mental notes.

I stopped by a woman in dark glasses and a trim business suit. She leaned against the wall, shaking, her face beneath the glasses slick with silent tears. Something sbout the precision of her styled hair, her cheekbones, struck a memory. I stood beside her, waiting, and recognition came.

"Hello," I said. "We have something in common, I think. You've been covering the Boston tour. For CBS."

She glanced at me once, and away. "I don't know you."

"You're Marjory Cale, the correspondent."

She drew in a breath. "You're mistaken."

" 'Luddite fanatic'," I said lightly. " 'Rock demagogue'."

"Go away," she said.

"Why not talk about it? I'd like to know your point of view."

"Go away, you nasty little man."

I returned to the crowd inside. The comedian was now reading at length from the American Bill of Rights, his voice thick with sarcasm. "Freedom of advertising," he said. "Freedom of global network television conglomerates. Right to a speedy and public trial, to be repeated until our lawyers win. A well-regulated militia being necessary, citizens will be issued orbital lasers and aircraft carriers...." No one was laughing.

The crowd was in an ugly mood when Boston reappeared. Even the well-dressed ones now seemed surly and militant, not recognizing themselves as the enemy. Like the Shah's soldiers who at last refused to fire, who threw themselves sobbing at Khomeini's feet.

"You all know this one," Boston said. With his wife, he raised a banner, one of the first flags of the American Revolution. It bore a coiled snake, a native American viper, with the legend: DON'T TREAD ON ME. A sinister, scaly rattling poured from the depths of a synthesizer, merging with the crowd's roar of recognition, and a sprung, loping rhythm broke loose. Boston edged back and forth at the stage's rim, his eyes fixed, his long neck swaying. He shook himself like a man saved from drowning and leaned into the microphone.

"We know you own us/ You step upon us/ We feel the onus/ But here's a bonus/ Today I see/ So enemy/ Don't tread on me/ Don't tread on me...." Simple words, fitting each beat with all the harsh precision of the English language. A chant of raw hostility. The crowd took it up. This was the hatred, the humiliation of a society brought low. Americans. Somewhere within them conviction still burned. The conviction they had always had: that they were the only real people on our planet. The chosen ones, the Light of the World, the Last Best Hope of Mankind, the Free and the Brave, the crown of creation. They would have killed for him. I knew, someday, they would.

I was called to Boston's suite at two o'clock that morning. I had shaved and showered, dashed on the hotel's complimentary cologne. I wanted to smell like an American.

Boston's guards frisked me, carefully and thoroughly, outside the elevator. I submitted with good grace.

Boston's suite was crowded. It had the air of an election victory. There were many politicians, sipping glasses of bubbling alcohol, laughing, shaking hands. Miami's Mayor was there, with half his City Council.

 I recognized a young woman Senator, speaking urgently into her pocket phone, her large freckled breasts on display in an evening gown.

I mingled, listening. Men spoke of Boston's ability to raise funds, of the growing importance of his endorsement. More of Boston's guards stood in corners, arms folded, eyes hidden, their faces stony. A black man distributed lapel buttons with the face of Martin Luther King on a background of red and white stripes. The wall-sized television played a tape of the first Moon Landing. The sound had been turned off, and people all over the world, in the garb of the 1960's, mouthed silently at the camera, their eyes shining.

It was not until four o'clock that I finally met the star himself. The party had broken up by then, the politicians politely ushered out, their vows of undying loyalty met with discreet smiles. Boston was in a back bedroom with his wife, and a pair of aides.

"Seyyid," he said, and shook my hand. In person he seemed smaller, older, his hybrid face, with stage makeup, beginning to peel.

"Dr. Boston," I said.

He laughed freely. "Seyyid, my friend. You'll ruin my street fuck-ing credibility."

"I want to tell the story as I see it," I said.

"Then you'll have to tell it to me," he said, and turned briefly to an aide. He dictated in a low, staccato voice, not losing his place in our conversation, simply loosing a burst of thought. "'Let us be frank. Before I showed an interest you were ready to sell the ship for scrap iron. This is not an era for supertankers. They are dead tech, smokestack-era garbage. Reconsider my offer.'" The secretary pounded keys. Boston looked at me again, returning the searchlight of his attention.

"You plan to buy a supertanker?" I said.

"I wanted an aircraft carrier," he said, smiling.

"They're all in mothballs, but the Feds frown on selling nuke power plants to private citizens."

"We will make the tanker into a floating stadium," Plisetskaya put in. She sat slumped in a padded chair, wearing satin lounge pajamas. A half-filled ashtray on the chair's arm reeked of strong tobacco.

"Ever been inside a tanker?" Boston said. "Huge. Great acous-tics." He sat suddenly on the sprawling bed and pulled off his snakeskin boots. "So, Seyyid. Tell me this story of yours."

"You graduated magna cum laude from Rutgers with a doctor-ate in political science," I said. "In five years."

"That doesn't count," Boston said, yawning behind his hand. "That was before rock and roll beat my brains out."

"You ran for state office in Massachusetts," I said. "You lost a close race. Two years later you were touring with your first band—Swamp Fox. You were an immediate success. You became involved in political fund-raising, recruiting your friends in the music industry. You started your own record label. You helped organize Rock for Detente, where you met your wife-to-be. Your romance was front-page news on both continents. Record sales soared."

"You left out the first time I got shot at," Boston said. "That's more interesting; Val and I are old hat by now."

He paused, then burst out at the second secretary. "'I urge you once again not to go public. You will find yourselves vulnerable to a leveraged buyout. I've told you that Evans is an agent of Marubeni. If he brings your precious plant down around your ears, don't come crying to me.'"

"February 1998," I said. "An anti-communist zealot fired on your bus."

"You're a big fan, Sayyid."

"Why are you afraid of multinationals?" I said. "That was the American preference, wasn't it? Global trade, global economics?"

"We screwed up," Boston said. "Things got out of hand."

"Out of American hands, you mean?"

"We used our companies as tools for development," Boston said, with the patience of a man instructing a child. "But then our lovely friends in South America refused to pay their debts. And our staunch allies in Europe and Japan signed the Geneva Economic Agreement and decided to crash the dollar. And our friends in the Arab countries decided not to be countries any more, but one almighty Caliphate, and, just for good measure, they pulled all their oil money out of our banks and into Islamic ones. How could we compete? They were holy banks, and our banks pay interest, which is a sin, I understand." He paused, his eyes glittering, and fluffed curls from his neck. "And all that time, we were already in hock to our fucking ears to pay for being the world's policeman."

"So the world betrayed your country," I said. "Why?"

He shook his head. "Isn't it obvious? Who needs St. George when the dragon is dead? Some Afghani fanatics scraped together enough plutonium for a Big One, and they blew the dragon's fucking head off. And the rest of the body is still convulsing, ten years later. We bled ourselves white competing against Russia, which was stupid, but we'd won. With two giants, the world trembles. One giant, and the midgets can drag it down. So that's what happened. They took us out, that's all. They own us."

"It sounds very simple," I said.

He showed annoyance for the first time. "Valya says you've read our newspapers. I'm not telling you anything new. Should I lie about it? Look at the figures, for Christ's sake. The EEC and Japanese use their companies for money pumps, they're sucking us dry, deliberately. You don't look stupid, Sayyid. You know very well what's happening to us, anyone in the Third World does."

"You mentioned Christ," I said. "You believe in Him?"

Boston rocked back onto his elbows and grinned. "Do you?"

"Of course. He is one of our Prophets. We call Him Isa."

Boston looked cautious. "I never stand between a man and his God." He paused. "We have a lot of respect for the Arabs, truly. What they've accomplished. Breaking free from the world economic system, returning to authentic local tradition.... You see the parallels."

"Yes," I said. I smiled sleepily, and covered my mouth as I yawned. "Jet lag. Your pardon, please. These are only questions my editors would want me to ask. If I were not an admirer, a fan as you say, I would not have this assignment."

He smiled and looked at his wife. Plisetskaya lit another cigarette and leaned back, looking skeptical. Boston grinned. "So the sparring's over, Charlie?"

"I have every record you've made," I said. "This is not a job for hatchets." I paused, weighing my words. "I still believe that our Caliph is a great man. I support the Islamic Resurgence. I am Muslim. But I think, like many others, that we have gone a bit too far in closing every window to the West. Rock and roll is a Third World music at heart. Don't you agree?"

"Sure," Boston said, closing his eyes. "Do you know the first words spoken in independent Zimbabwe? Right after they ran up the flag."

"No."

He spoke out blindly, savoring the words. "Ladies and gentlemen. Bob Marley. And the Wailers."

"You admire him."

"Comes with the territory," said Boston, flipping a coil of hair.

"He had a black mother, a white father. And you?"

"Oh, both my parents were shameless mongrels like myself," Boston said. "I'm a second-generation nothing-in-particular. An American." He sat up, knotting his hands, looking tired. "You going to stay with the tour a while, Charlie?" He spoke to a secretary. "Get me a kleenex." The woman rose.

"Till Philadelphia," I said. "Like Marjory Cale."

Plisetskaya blew smoke, frowning. "You spoke to that woman?"

"Of course. About the concert."

"What did the bitch say?" Boston asked lazily. His aide handed him tissues and cold cream. Boston dabbed the kleenex and smeared make-up from his face.

"She asked me what I thought. I said it was too loud," I said.

Plisetskaya laughed once, sharply. I smiled. "It was quite amusing. She said that you were in good form. She said that I should not be so tight-arsed."

"'Tight-arsed'?" Boston said, raising his brows. Fine wrinkles had appeared beneath the greasepaint. "She said that?"

"She said we Muslims were afraid of modern life. Of new experience. Of course I told her that this wasn't true. Then she gave me this." I reached into one of the pockets of my vest and pulled a flat packet of aluminum foil.

"Marjory Cale gave you cocaine?" Boston asked.

"Wyoming Flake," I said. "She said she has friends who grow it in the Rocky Mountains." I opened the packet, exposing a little mound of white powder. "I saw her use some. I think it will help my jet lag." I pulled my chair closer to the bedside phone-table. I shook the packet out, with much care, upon the shining mahogany surface. The tiny crystals glittered. It was finely chopped.

I opened my wallet and removed a crisp thousand-doller bill. The actor-president smiled benignly. "Would this be appropriate?"

"Tom does not do drugs," said Plisetskaya, too quickly.

"Ever do coke before?" Boston asked. He threw a wadded tissue to the floor.

"I hope I'm not offending you," I said. "This is Miami, isn't it? This is America." I began rolling the bill, clumsily.

"We are not impressed," said Plisetskaya sternly. She ground out her cigarette. "You are being a rube, Charlie. A hick from the NIC's."

"There is a lot of it," I said, allowing doubt to creep into my voice. I reached in my pocket, then divided the pile in half with the sharp edge of a developed slide. I arranged the lines neatly. They were several centimeters long.

I sat back in the chair. "You think it's a bad idea? I admit, this is new to me." I paused. "I have drunk wine several times, though the *Koran* forbids it."

One of the secretaries laughed. "Sorry," she said. "He drinks wine. That's cute."

I sat and watched temptation dig into Boston. Plisetskaya shook her head.

"Cale's cocaine," Boston mused. "Man."

We watched the lines together for several seconds, he and I. "I did not mean to be trouble," I said. "I can throw it away."

"Never mind Val," Boston said. "Russians chain-smoke." He slid across the bed.

I bent quickly and sniffed. I leaned back, touching my nose. The cocaine quickly numbed it. I handed the paper tube to Boston. It was done in a moment. We sat back, our eyes watering.

"Oh," I said, drug seeping through tissue. "Oh, this is excellent."

"It's good toot," Boston agreed. "Looks like you get an extended interview."

We talked through the rest of the night, he and I.

My story is almost over. From where I sit to write this, I can hear the sound of Boston's music, pouring from the crude speakers of a tape pirate in the bazaar. There is no doubt in my mind that Boston is a great man.

I accompanied the tour to Philadelphia. I spoke to Boston several times during the tour, though never again with the first fine rapport of the drug. We parted as friends, and I spoke well of him in my article for *Al-Ahram*. I did not hide what he was, I did not hide his threat. But I did not malign him. We see things differently. But he is a man, a child of God like all of us.

His music even saw a brief flurry of popularity in Cairo, after the article. Children listen to it, and then turn to other things, as children will. They like the sound, they dance, but the words mean nothing to them. The thoughts, the feelings, are alien.

This is the *dar-al-harb*, the land of peace. We have peeled the hands of the West from our throat, we draw breath again, under God's sky. Our Caliph is a good man, and I am proud to serve him. He reigns, he does not rule. Learned men debate in the *Majlis*, not squabbling like politicians, but seeking truth in dignity. We have the world's respect.

We have earned it, for we paid the martyr's price. We Muslims are one in five in all the world, and as long as ignorance of God persists, there will always be the struggle, the *jihad*. It is a proud thing to be one of the Caliph's *Mujihadeen*. It is not that we value our lives lightly. But that we value God more.

Some call us backward, reactionary. I laughed at that when I carried the powder. It had the subtlest of poisons: a living virus. It is a tiny thing, bred in secret labs, and in itself does no harm. But it spreads throughout the body, and it bleeds out a chemical, a faint but potent trace that carries the rot of cancer.

The West can do much with cancer these days, and a wealthy man like Boston can buy much treatment. They may cure the first attack, or the second. But within five years he will surely be dead. People will mourn his loss. Perhaps they will put his image on a stamp, as they did for Bob Marley. Marley, who also died of systemic cancer; whether by the hand of God or man, only Allah knows.

I have taken the life of a great man; in trapping him I took my own life as well, but that means nothing. I am no one. I am not even Sayyid Qutb, the Martyr and theorist of Resurgence, though I took that great man's name as cover. I meant only respect, and believe I have not shamed his memory.

I do not plan to wait for the disease. The struggle continues in the Muslim lands of what was once the Soviet Union. There the Believers ride in Holy Jihad, freeing their ancient lands from the talons of Marxist atheism. Secretly, we send them carbines, rockets, mortars, and nameless men. I shall be one of them; when I meet death, my grave will be nameless also. But nothing is nameless to God.

God is Great; men are mortal, and err. If I have done wrong, let the Judge of Men decide. Before His Will, as always, I submit.

If there exists a major anarchist publication in this country from FIFTH ESTATE to FACTSHEET FIVE which has not been graced by at least one of Freddie Baer's meticulous Ernst-like collages, it is unknown to us. Cartooning and xerox collage are the major graphic forms of the late '80s, as future art historians will have to admit (after everyone finally realizes the death by boredom of "fine art.") However, not every TV-saturated would-be neo-dadaist can simply slap together a few headlines from the WEEKLY WORLD NEWS and fragments of magazine ads and call it a collage. Masters of the form, including the three in this book and others like Winston Smith and Ed ("DADATA") Lawrence, work harder and smarter with scissors and glue than many modern artists with brushes and paint.

The following three pieces by Freddie Baer, and another on page 51, are only a small sample of her prolific output, but they can suggest her consistent quality.

Bruce Boston not only commits the rare sin of writing SF poetry, he also frequently gets away with it. VELOCITIES has recently issued his latest slender vol, NUCLEAR FUTURES. IASFM has bought his vers libre, and so have we. Usually any indulgence in this sub-sub-genre rates about as much attention as filksinging or the theory that Spock and Kirk are lovers (a doctrine that informs several fanzines), but in Boston's case it has brought him recognition and even money—plus, he was on the 1987 Nebula Jury (along with another of our writers, Marc Laidlaw)—which might even be called "power".

America Comes
Bruce Boston

america comes
in tortured lunchrooms
with tiffany palaver
with the hard yellow yolks

of strangulated gumshoes
america comes
in commercial breaks
sweet tocsins on the tongue

a filth of spavined dogs
imported from the hague
in small copper buckets
america comes

with subcutaneous lunges
soft bullets
and hard caresses
a plinth of technosavagery

billeting her breastbone
far too much
not nearly enough
these are the tongs

the assassin breathes
into his blood
as the distended winter
continues to arrive

enamored with
its own body cast
full of greasy assignation
far too much

not nearly enough
the assassin winces
at his own replication
as he flesh tastes

the bitter meat
of metal on his chest
america comes
at the base of a ravine

where a nest of beetles
who have eaten
one anothers' legs
roil like jumping beans

where an old car mirror
with a rusted socket
reflects the spoils
of ejaculation

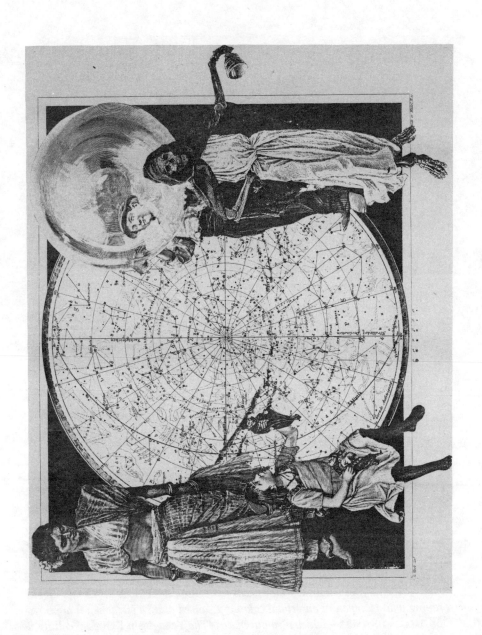

"I'm an Irish-Chicano who's never been assimilated into either Latino or Anglo culture. I've lived most of my 30 years in the smog-eaten outskirts of L.A., but recently moved to Phoenix where I live with my fiancé Emily Devenport, another SF writer.

"My first published story was 'The Rape of Things to Come,' about raping white women in an orbital colony; it caused quite a stir when it appeared in AMAZING STORIES—which also purchased 'The Yenagloshi Express,' calling it 'the weirdest story we ever bought.' My novels keep on getting rejected for being 'too zany.' I just don't seem to be in the mainstream of commercial SF—or anything else!"

The Frankenstein Penis
Ernest Hogan

"Why the fuck can't I ever find a guy with a really big cock?" the tall, bleached-blonde that Ralph had his eye on suddenly got up and shrieked.

It cut through the smoky, muffled roar of that concrete floored bar, spoiling its abandoned garage atmosphere. There was silence. The two truckers who were playing pool stopped and stared at her. A lanky, greasy longhaired kid who would have been a biker if he could ever afford a motorcycle stopped plunking quarters into the juke box to make it play Ted Nugent's *Bound and Gagged* over and over again and walked over to her.

The dried-up crone behind the bar grew pale, the figures at the bar—except for Ralph—all looked longingly toward the door.

"Girl," the pseudo-biker said, smiling with teeth that were on the green side, "this is your lucky day."

Oozing confidence from inside his worn-out Harley Davidson T-shirt and grease-caked Levis, he walked over, reaching for her with bony hands and dirty fingernails.

The old barkeep reached for her shotgun that was just under the cash register.

Before a greasy paw could come near her ample breasts, the blonde sent a dainty fist at high speed into his solar plexus, knocking out his wind. He gasped, started to teeter on his feet. She aided in destroying his balance by landing her cowboy-booted foot squarely on his groin.

Once he was down and helpless she undid his Led Zepplin belt buckle, and his fly, then pulled down his pants.

"Shit," she said, spitting on the pitifully shriveled member, "it don't even qualify as so-so."

The click of a pump shotgun being cocked turned every eye in the place to the white-haired barkeep. "Damn it, bitch!" she said. "Get the fuck outta here, and don't come back!"

"Okay, okay," the blonde said, holding up her hands, flashing long blood-red nails and causing jiggles that couldn't be helped under her faded peach halter top. She got up and made her spectacular, drunken way to the door, her damnnear perfect ass—coated with expensively cut, but old, denim—shaking violently.

Everyone in the bar was relieved. She was great to look at, but this was one of those nights when the L.A. smog didn't stop cooking at sundown. All eyes were bloodshot and sleep was impossible. What they wanted was a place with a half-way decent air-conditioner where they could relax and drink in peace.

The exception was Ralph. There was something about that brassy lady that got his mind off the sweltering, unhealthy air and his problems. It had been a couple of hours since he had seen any sign of them, so he left his flat, warm, half-full beer and followed her out.

She was pacing the parking lot in a dangerous frenzy, muttering non-stop something mostly unintelligible except for frequent repetitions of the word "fuck."

She was all firm aerobicized muscle and sharp nails running too hot on too much alcohol. It could be risky, but he was growing used to that. She could also be fun, just what he needed.

He got in her way and said, "So, you want a really big one?"

Her blue cracked-ice eyes gave a look that could kill as he pointed to the bulge in his pants. It ran almost down to his knee.

"So, you rolled up a couple of sweat socks," she said, but those eyes grew a few degrees warmer.

"It's real," he said, "unbelievable, but real."

"Well, seeing's believing," she said. Her nipples started to peek through her top.

"My car's right over here," he said, trying to take her arm.

His hand closed on thin air. Like a flash she had his pants down to his ankles, exposing It to the corrosive starless sky.

"Oh my god," she said, as she got down on her kness as if to worship.

It was a full eighteen inches long, and getting longer and stiffer as she drew closer to it. It was a monster, with what looked like scars going all the way around it in three places. The sort of thing Frankenstein's monster would have between his legs.

As she hungrily kissed the head, coiling a long, warm, tongue around it, he scoped out the parking lot. No sign of life. Like a typical suburb along L.A.'s San Bernardino Freeway: after midnight meant mass suspended animation. But the cop's asses weren't always glued to their stools at their favorite doughnut shops. And cops were the least of his worries.

She broke the kiss that added anohter inch to its length. She was about to take it between her breasts. A strong cable of saliva still connected it to her mouth.

"Like I said," he took her face in his hands, "my car is right over there."

"Oops," she said, with a leering grin that broke the saliva cable. "I got carried away."

She was the kind that would. Just what he was looking for.

Soon they were in the back seat of his battered green Nova. Ralph couldn't believe how fast she got rid of her clothes, even the cowboy boots. Once again she was kissing the heavy purple glans, flicking her tongue up and down the slit. He gently kneaded her breasts, simultaneously rubbing her nipples with his thumbs. Her eyes closed, she sighed, then chanted, "Tit fuck me! Tit fuck me!"

They rapidly adjusted themselves so that she held it firmly in her warm cleavage. Her nipples grew rock hard and stuck out like stubby fingers as she squeezed his scarred monster, and he pumped it in and out of the taut cavern of flesh, with a slowly increasing rhythm. Each time it hit her in the chin, and slid past her lips to rub her nose, she would greet it with an eager tongue.

It was perfect, all he ever really asked for in life. He forgot all about the smog, cheap bars, mad surgeons, sandy-haired simian goons and anorexic bitches with strange accents carrying little black bags full of devices for a ghastly impromptu operation. Just give him a beautiful woman wrapped around his throbbing cock, her cunt growing wide and wet, his gigantic penis growing sticky at the tip with a milky little pearl that's the prelude to an eruption that would splurt sticky white semen ropes onto her ecstatic face...

Then he heard something.

Three loud knocks.

The blonde didn't notice, but Ralph looked up over her to see something that made his blood freeze. In the fogged window were the blurred outlines of two all-too-familiar forms. They *would* show up just when he was about to come.

A huge fist in a black leather glove then came crashing through the safety glass window just above the gasping blonde's head. A scream ripped out of her throat as pebbles of glass rained onto her like hailstones, and the sand-haired ape-like man grabbed a handful of her hair in a deathgrip.

Ralph's enormous cock went a little limp.

"Having fun with your toy, Ralphie?" said a painfully thin woman with colorless hair in an accent he could never identify. She waved her little black bag at him.

The sight of the bag sped up his reflexes. He grabbed the ape-man's arm and jerked it deep into the car, causing the crude head and shoulders to make a hard, flesh-pulping impact with the edge of the window and the remaining sheets of crumbling glass. The big, black-leathered fist let go of the blonde's hair.

Once free, the blonde went into action. She took the intruding arm and buried her teeth into it, clamping her jaws like a gila monster. The slow-witted thug was too busy with all his pain to do anything.

Seeing his chance, Ralph leaped over the seats. Seconds later he had found his keys and had the Nova all fired up. He punched it, sending the car leaping ahead into the empty parking lot, dragging along their kicking and screaming attacker. They were bouncing out into the street before the blonde let go, sending him rolling, the asphalt chewing up clothing and flesh.

Naked with his tremendous organ limp now, Ralph's eyes glazed over as he locked into some serious maniacal driving. Completely ignoring the business/residential speed limit he shot his way up to the main drag, then floored it all the way to his first destination: an on-ramp to the San Bernardino Freeway. Once on that he ignored the 55 MPH limit, and red-lined away. It didn't really matter where to, anywhere the freeway took him would do, as long as it put precious miles between him and them.

"What the fuck is all this shit?" the blonde screamed, her hair flying wildly in the blast from the broken window. "Sunspots fried everybody's brains or something?"

"My name is Ralph," he said.

"Mine's Willy—from Wilma, my parents liked The Flintstones more than I did—and that was no explanation!"

Ralph settled into the rhythm of the freeway, glanced into the rearview mirror and said, with a straight face, "That was Nelda and Jacob. They came to repossess my dong."

Her facial muscles went limp a second, then she settled back down into the back seat saying, "Yeah… sure."

"Think about it," he said, "how could I have possibly be born with this Frankenstein monster between my legs? Where do you think all those scars came from? Natural penises this long never quite get completely hard."

"I... it's unnatural—I mean artificial?"

"Well, sort of, a miracle of modern transplant and reconstructive surgery. The illegal work of this guy who call himself Dr. Kraken."

"Wha... why?"

"My own was small, real small. Everyone thought it was funny. I had an extremely difficult time getting laid. This one bitch, after seeing it, said, 'I've changed my mind—it's too small,' and left me sitting there with a hard-on. Can you imagine that?"

She gave a confused nod.

"It was driving me crazy, so I started looking into penis enlargement, which turned out to be mostly bullshit and rip-offs. Then one day this Kraken character—he's all wrinkles with no hair, not even an eyelash—came to me. He got my name and address from one of the quacks. His transplant/reconstruction process made sense to me, so I went for it."

"And it worked, didn't it?"

"You were sucking on it, Willy. Well, anyway, they screwed me up on this bizarre system of payments. Soon my bank account was down to zilch, and he demanded that I give the thing back. I took off, then he sent Jacob and Nelda after me to cut it off without the benefit of anesthetic and leave me to bleed to death."

She leaned over to look at it in all its scarred, semi-rigid glory. "If it wasn't for that, I wouldn't believe it."

"Well, if you put your clothes back on, I'll drop you off," he said. "This could get dangerous, no telling what they'd do to you if..."

"No way, Ralph," she said, reaching over and taking hold of it. "I haven't gotten the feeling of ol' Frankenstein inside me yet! Besides, this is exciting, being on the run and all that." She then laid a juicy French kiss on his ear that nearly made them into a mass of twisted wreckage at the side of the freeway.

Soon they were checked into a motel that charged by the hour.

Once the door was locked and bolted they flowed together like two streams of molten lava. Arms held tight. Bellies and groins squeezed the ever-stiffening Frankenstein penis. Her ample breasts flattened out against him as her nipples became hard. Mouths sealed into a warm, dark, saliva-soaked cave for their tongues to wrestle in.

As one they fell onto the bed and began tearing each others' clothes off, exposing sweaty, smog-fouled bodies that desperately sought a haven in each other.

Ralph first tried to climb on top of her, but Willy took his hands and held them to her breasts, locked her eyes to his with a smoldering look, intertwined their tastebuds again and then pleaded, "I wanna ride, Ralph. Let me ride your great, big monster, your magnificent beast."

He laid back and Willy straddled him, got up on her knees, and then squatted, doing a little dance, rotating her dripping vagina just a fraction of an inch away from the throbbing glans of his titanic member, tickling it with her dark brown pubic hair. It drove him wild. He clutched at the sheets as it grew longer and let the spermatic pearl on its tip merge with her juices. He then reached up and grabbed her tits, digging his fingers deep into soft meat, then opened his palms and pressed hard, smearing her breasts out of shape to the sides of her quivering body, being careful to snag the nipples with his thumbs as he let them spring back into place.

"Oh my God, yes, yes, yes," she said, gasping as she lowered her wide-open pussy around the Frankenstein penis head, biting her under-lip as it slid in.

Willy then took a spread-eagled deep knee-bends position, and with a gutteral Ugh! took a firm hold of Ralph with her strong vaginal muscles. It was stronger than the grip of a hand. Relaxing her hold just enough to allow movement, she slid herself down the scarred shaft, taking it deep inside her, completely filling the vaginal tunnel and entering the uterus. When the head hit the womb's wall, he grabbed her by the hips—he didn't want to hurt her.

Tightening and relaxing her grip, she rode the monster up and down, flooding them both with waves of sensation. He took hold of the part of the shaft that didn't fit in. Her fluids ran onto his hand as he stroked in time with her rising and lowering. His hand met her cunt with frequent wet slaps. The pace escalated. Faster. Faster. She huffed and puffed and finally came with a lusty "Yeeeeeeee-haaaaaaaaaa!" as he shot his scalding wad into her.

Just as she fell down on top of him, and planted a sloppy wet kiss on his neck, the door came crashing open, its lock shattering and the dead bolt torn out by the roots.

Apish Jacob stood in the doorway, holding a throbbing, swollen arm. Behind him was painfully thin Nelda, nattily waving a little black bag.

"You naughty, naughty boy," she said, followed by a stacatto *tsk tsk tsk*.

An adrenalin rush tore Ralph out of his post-coital torpor. He took the Gideon Bible off the end table and heaved it at Jacob's wounded arm.

The sandy-haired giant roared in agony; he charged. He then caught the telephone across the face. While he stood there stunned Ralph slammed into him, putting all his weight on that bad arm.

While Ralph pounded on Jacob, Nelda whipped a gleaming scal-pel out of the black bag and came towards Willy. The fiesty blonde knocked it out of the bitch's hand with a precisely pitched lamp, then dove on Nelda like a wildcat, tearing open that thin face with blood-red nails as they both hit the floor. Soon the two women were rolling around on the floor, Nelda leaving red stripes on Willy's skin, and Willy tearing Nelda's mannish clothes to shreds. Being a bookish type, used to getting her sadistic thrills on victims who couldn't fight back, Nelda was soon pinned by the athletic, outdoorsy Willy. Dr. Kraken's assistant began to claw at her opponent's tits. Willy took hold of Nelda's short, colorless hair and started banging her skull-like head against the floor.

She only stopped when Ralph took her by the shoulders and said, "Willy! Quick! Grab your clothes! We have to get out of here!"

They ran out to the Nova in the nude, clutching their wadded-up clothes, not knowing if they had left behind two corpses or candidates for the emergency room.

Once they were zooming madly away towards the pre-dawn light along the San Bernardino Freeway, he turned to her and said, "Sorry I got you into this…"

"Shit," she said, leaning over, putting an arm around his shoulder and a hand on his prick. "Thank you for getting me into this! A few days ago I lost my job, in a few days I was going to get kicked out of my apartment, and I just couldn't seem to find a good man. I was depressed and getting desperately drunk. Then you came in. Now I have a man with the organ out of my wildest wet dreams, I'm leading an exciting, dangerous life, and keep ending up naked on the freeway." She put her head on his shoulder and ran her hand up his pubic hair, to his chest hair, and commenced to play with his nipples. "I'm a girl who loves fun and trouble, so I'm sticking with you, Ralph, and all the craziness that comes with you. Hey, let's just take this road until we get sick of the scenery, then change directions. This is what I call living…"

Ralph just smiled and thought for the first time in a small eternity that maybe things would finally work out for him after all.

Among the so-called Cyberpunks, John Shirley is perhaps the only genuine Punk. Far be it from us to gossip, but when Shirley writes about rock'n'roll, weird hairstyles, controlled substances, sick violence and tacky sex, one gets the impression of a writer (like Jack London or B. Traven) who draws on his own adventures and has earned the right to a revolutionary stance by serving his season in the Lower Depths.

The political comparisons are deliberate; Shirley has adopted a libertarian-socialist position, most fully worked out in his ongoing trilogy, A SONG CALLED YOUTH (vol. I, ECLIPSE, Bluejay 1985; vol. II, ECLIPSE PENUMBRA, Questar 1988), but already present in earlier and delightful works such as CITY COME A'WALKIN' and THREE-RING PSYCHUS. More recent works include A SPLENDID CHAOS (Franklin Watts) and IN DARKNESS WAITING, a horror novel from Signet.

Mickery Films has produced his script "Black Glass," a movie about performance artists and government conspiracy in a nightclub in 1999.
Shirley , mid-thirties, no longer has green hair.

Six Kinds of Darkness
John Shirley

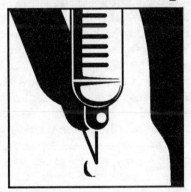

Charlie'd say, "I'm into it once or twice—but you, you got a jones for it, man." And Angelo'd snicker and say, "Gives my life purpose, man. Gives my life direction."

You could smell the place, the Hollow Head, from two blocks away. Anyway, you could if you were strung out on it. The other people on the street probably couldn't make out the smell from the background of monoxides, the broken-battery smell of acid rain, the itch of syntharette smoke, the oily rot of the river. But a user could pick out that tease of Amyl Tryptaline, thinking, *Find it like a needle in a haystack*. And he'd snort, and then go reverent-serious, thinking about the needle in question...the needle in the nipple...

It was on East 121st Street, a half block from the East River. If you stagger out of the place at night, you'd better find your way to the lighted end of the street fast, because the leeches crawled out of the river after dark, slug-creeping up the walls and onto the cornices of the old buildings; they sense your bodyheat, and an eight-inch ugly brute lamprey thing falls from the roof, hits your neck with a wet *slap*; injects you with paralyzing toxins, you fall over and its leech cronies come, drain you dry. When Charlie turned onto the street it was just sunset; the leeches weren't out of the river yet, but Charlie scanned the rooftops anyway. Clustered along the rooftops were the shanties...

New York's housing shortage was worse than ever. After the Dissolve Depression, and most of the Wall Street firms moved to Tokyo or the floating city Freezone, the boom in Manhattan deflated, the city couldn't afford to maintain itself. It began to rot. But still the immigrants came, swarming to the mecca of disenchantment till New York became another Mexico City, ringed and overgrown with shanties, shacks of clapboard, tin, cardboard protected with flattened cans and wrapper plastic; every tenement rooftop in Manhattan mazed with squalid shanties, sometimes shanties on shanties till the weight collapsed the roofs and the old buildings caved in, the crushed squatters simply left dying in the rubble—firemen and Emergency teams rarely set foot outside the sentried, walled-in havens of the midtown class.

Charlie was almost there. It was a mean motherfucker of a neighborhood, which is why he had the knife in his boot-sheath. But what scared him was the Place. Doing some Room at the Place. The Hollow Head. His heart was pumping and he was shaky but he wasn't sure if it was from fear or anticipation or if, with the Hollow Head, you could tell those two apart. But to keep his nerve up, he had to look away from the Place, as he got near it; tried to focus on the rest of the street. Some dumbfuck polyanna had planted saplings in the sidewalk, in the squares of exposed dirt where the original trees had stood. But the acid rain had chewed the leaves and twigs away; what was left was stark as TV antennas... Torchglow from the roofs; and a melange of noises that seemed to ooze down like something greasy from an overflowing pot. Smells of tarry wood burning; dogfood smells of cheap canned food cooking. And then he was standing in front of the Hollow Head. A soot-blackened townhouse; its Victorian facade of cherubim recarved by acid rain into dainty gargoyles. The windows bricked over, the stone between them streaked grey on black from acid erosion.

The building to the right was hunchbacked with shacks; the roof to the left glowed from oil-barrel fires. But the roof of the Hollow Head was dark and flat, somehow regal in its sinister austerity. No one shacked on the Hollow Head.

He took a deep breath, and told himself, Don't hurry through it, savor it this time, and went in. Hoping that Angelo had waited for him.

Up to the door, wait while the camera scanned you. The camera taking in Charlie Chesterton's triple mohawk, each fin a different color; Charlie's gaunt face, spiked transplas jacket, and customized mirrorshades. He heard the tone telling him the door had unlocked.

He opened it, smelled the Amyl Tryptaline, felt his bowels contract with suppressed excitement. Down a red lit hallway, thick black paint on the walls, the turpentine smell of A.T. getting stronger. Angelo wasn't there; he'd gone upstairs already. Charlie hoped Ange could handle it alone...The girl in the banker's window at the end of the hall—the girl wearing the ski mask, the girl with the sarcastic receptionist's lilt in her voice—took his card, gave him the Bone Music receptor, credded him in. Another tone, admission to Door Seven, the first level. He walked down to Seven, turned the knob, stepped through and felt it immediately; the tingle, the rush of alertness, the chemically-induced sense of belonging, four pleasurable sensations rolling through him and coalescing. It was just an empty room with the stairs at the farther end; soft pink lighting, the usual cryptic palimpsest of graffiti on the walls.

He inhaled deeply, felt the Amyl Tryptaline go to work almost immediately; the pink glow intensified; the edges of the room softened, he heard his own heartbeat like a distant beatbox. A barbed wisp of anxiety twined his spine (wondering, *Where's Angelo, he's usually hanging in the first room, scared to go to the second alone, well, shit, good riddance*) and he experienced a paralytic seizure of sheer sensation. The Bone Music receptor was digging into his palm; he wiped the sweat from it and attached it to the sound wire extruding from the bone back of his left ear—and the music shivered into him... It was music you *felt*, more than heard; his acoustic nerve picked up the thudding beat, the bass, a distorted veneer of the synthesizer. But most of the music was routed through the bone of his skull, conducted down through the spinal column, the other bones. It was a music of shivery sensations, like a funny bone sensation, sickness sensations, chills and hot flashes like influenza but it was a sickness that caressed, viruses licking at your privates and you wanted to come and throw up at the same time. He'd seen deaf people dancing at rock concerts; they could feel the vibrations from the loud music; could feel the music they couldn't hear. It was like that but with a deep, deep humping brutality, like having sex with an obviously syphlitic whore and enjoying it more because you knew she was diseased. The music shivered him from his paralysis, nudged him forward. He climbed the stairs...

Bone Music reception improving as he climbed, so he could make out the lyrics, Jerome-X's gristly voice singing from inside Charlie's skull:

> *Six kinds of darkness*
> *Spilling down over me*
> *Six kinds of darkness*
> *Sticky with energy*

Charlie got to the next landing, stepped into the second room. Second room used electric field stimulation of nerve ends; the metal grids on the wall transmitting signals that stimulated the neurons, initiating pleasurable nerve impulses; other signals were sent directly to the dorsal area in the hypothalamus, resonating in the brain's pleasure center...

Charlie cried out, and fell to his knees in the infantile purity of his gratitude. The room glowed with benevolence; the barren, dirty room with its semen-stained walls, cracked ceilings, naked red bulb on a fraying wire. As always he had to fight himself to keep from licking the walls, the floors. He was a fetishist for this room, for its splintering wooden floors, the mathematical absolutism of the grid-patterns in the grey metal transmitters set into the wall. Turn off those transmitters and the room was shabby, even ugly, and pervaded with stench; with the transmitters on it seemed subtly intricate, starkly sexy, bondage gear in the form of interior decoration, and the smell was a ribald delight.

(For the Hollow Head was drug paraphenalia you could walk into. The building itself was the syringe, or the hookah, or the sniff tube. The whole building was the paraphernalia—and the drug itself.)

And then the room's second phase cut in: the transmitters stimulated the motor cortex, the reticular formation in the brainstem, the nerve pathways of the extrapyramidal system, in precise patterns computer formulated to mesh with the ongoing Bone Music. Making him dance. Dance across the room, feeling he was caught in a choreographed whirlwind (flashing: genitals interlocking, pumping, male and female, male and male, female and female, tongues and cocks and fingers pushing into pink bifurcations, contorting purposefully to guide between fleshy globes, the thrusting a heavy downhill flow like an emission of igneous mud, but firm pink mud, the bodies rounded off, headless, Magritte torsos going end to end together, organs blindly nosing into the wet receptacles of otherness), semen trickling down his legs inside his pants, dancing, helplessly dancing, thinking it was a delicious epilepsy, as he was marionetted up the stairs, to the next floor, the final room...

At the landing just before the third room, the transmitters cut off, and Charlie sagged, gasping, clutching for the banister, the black-painted walls reeling around him...He gulped air, and prayed for the strength to turn away from the third room, because he knew it would leave him fried, yeah badly crashed and deeply burnt out. He turned off the receptor for a respite of quiet...In that moment of weariness and self-doubt he found himself wondering where Angelo was, had Angelo really gone onto the third room alone? Ange was prone to identity crises under the Nipple Needle. If he'd gone alone—little Angelo Demario with his rockabilly hair and spurious pugnacity—Angelo would sink, and lose it completely...And what would they do with people who were overdosed on an identity hit? Dump the body in the river, he supposed...

 He heard a yell mingling ecstasy and horror, coming from an adjacent room, as another Head customer took a nipple...that made up his mind: like seeing someone eat making you realize you're hungry. He gathered together the tatters of his energy, switched on his receptor, and went through the door.

The Bone Music shuddered through him, too strong now, now that he was undercut,weakened by the first rooms. Nausea wallowed through him.

The darkness of the Arctic, two months into the night
Darkness of the Eclipse, forgetting of all light

Angelo wasn't in the room and Charlie was selfishly glad as he took off his jacket, rolled up left sleeve, approached the black rubber nipple protruding from the metal breast at waist-height on the wall. As he stepped up to it, pressed the hollow of his elbow against the nipple; felt the computer-guided needle probe for his mainline and fire the I.D. drug into him...

The genetic and neurochemical essence of a woman. They claimed it was synthesized. He didn't give an angel's winged asshole where it came from, right then: it was rushing through him in majestic waves of titanic intimacy. You could taste her, smell her, feel what it felt like to be her (they said it was an imaginary her, modeled on someone real, not really from a person...)

Felt the shape of her personality superimposed on you so for the first time you weren't burdened with your own identity, you could find oblivion in someone else, like identifying with a fictional protagonist but infinitely more real...

But oh shit. It wasn't a her. It was a him. And Charlie knew instantly that it was Angelo. They had shot him up with Angelo's distilled neurochemistry—his personality, memory, despairs and burning urges. He saw himself in flashes as Angelo had seen him...And he knew, too, that this was no synthesis, that he'd found out what they did with those who died here, who blundered and O.D.'d: they dropped them in some vat, broke them down, distilled them and molecularly linked them with the synthcoke and shot them into other customers...Into Charlie...

He couldn't hear himself scream, over the Bone Music (*Darkness of an iron cask, lid down and bolted tight*). He didn't remember running for the exit stairs (*And three more kinds of darkness, three I cannot tell*), down the hall, (*Making six kinds of darkness, Lord please make me well*) out into the street, running, hearing the laughter from the shantyrats on the roofs watching him go.

Him and Angelo running down the street, in one body. As Charlie told himself: I'm kicking this thing. It's over. I shot up my best friend. I'm through with it.

Hoping to God it was true. *Lord please make me well.*

2

Bottles swished down from the rooftops and smashed to either side of him. And he kept running.

He felt strange. He felt strange as all hell.

He could feel his body. Not like usual. He could feel it like it was a weight on him, like an attachment. Not the weight of fatigue—he felt too damn eerie to feel tired—but a weight of sheer alienness. It was too big. It was all awkward and its metabolism was pitched too low, sluggish, and it was...

It was the way his body felt for Angelo.

Angelo wasn't there, in him. But then again he was. And Charlie felt Angelo as a nastily foreign, squeaky, distortion membrane between him and the world around him.

He passed someone on the street, saw them distorted through the membrane, their faces funhouse-mirror twisted as they looked at him—and they looked startled.

The strange feelings must show on his face. And in his frantic running.

Maybe they could see Angelo. Maybe Angelo was oozing out of him, out of his face. He could feel it. Yeah. He could feel Angelo bleeding from his pores, dripping from his nose, creeping from his ass.

A sonic splash of: *Gidgy you wanna do a video hook-up with me? (Gidgy replying:) No, that shit's grotty Ange, last time we did that I was sick for two days I don't like pictures pushed into my brain couldn't we just have, you know, sex? (She touches his arm.)*

God, I'm gonna lose myself in Angelo, Charlie thought. Gotta run, sweat him out of me.

Splash of: *Angelo, if you keep going around with those people the police or those SA people are going to break your stupid head. (Angelo's voice:) Ma, get off it, You don't understand what's going on, the country's getting scared, they think there's gonna be nuclear war, everyone's lining up to kiss the Presidential Ass cause they think she's all that stands between us and the fucking Russians—(His mother's voice:) Angelo don't use that language in front of your sister, not everyone talks like they do on TV—*

Too heavy, body's too heavy, his run is funny, can't run anymore, but I gotta sweat him out—

Flash pictures to go with the splash voices now: *Motion-rollicking shot of sidewalk seen from a car window as they drive through a private-cop zone, SA bulls in mirror helmets walking along in twos in this high rent neighborhood, turning their glassy-blank assumption of your guilt toward the car, the world revolves as the car turns a corner, they come to a checkpoint, the new Federal I.D. cards are demanded, shown, they get through, feeling of relief, there isn't a call out on them yet...blur of images, then focus on a face walking up to the car. Charlie Chesterton. Long skinny, goofy looking guy, self-serious expression...*

Jesus, Charlie thought, is *that* what Angelo thinks I look like? Shit! (Angelo is dead, man, Angelo is...is oozing out of him...)

Feeling sick now, stopping to gag, look around confusedly, oh fuck: two cops were coming toward him. Regular cops, no helmets, wearing blue slickers, plastic covers on their cop-caps, their big ugly cop-faces hanging out so he wished they wore the helmets, supercilious faces, young but ugly, their heads shaking in disgust, one of them said: "What drug you on, man?"

He tried to talk but a tumble of words came out, some his and some Angelo's, it was like his mouth was brimming over with little restless furry animals: Angelo's words.

The cops knew what it was. They knew it when they heard it. One cop asked the other (as he took out the hand cuffs, and Charlie had become a retching machine, unable to run or fight or argue because all he could do was retch), "Jeez, it makes me sick when I think about it. People shooting up somebody else's brains. Don't it make you sick?"

"Yeah. Looks like it makes him sick too. Let's take him to the chute, send him down for the blood-test."

He felt the snakebite of cuffs, felt them do a perfunctory body-search, missing the knife in his boot. Felt himself shoved along to the police kiosk on the corner, the new prisoner-transferral chutes. They put you in something like a coffin (they pushed him into a greasy, sweat-stinking, inadequately padded personnel capsule, closed the lid on him, he wondered what happened—as they closed the lid on him—if he got stuck in the chutes, were there air holes, would he suffocate?) and they push it down into the chute inside the kiosk and it gets sucked along this big underground tube (he had a sensation of falling, then felt the tug of inertia, the horror of being trapped in here with Angelo, not enough room for the two of them, seeing a flash mental image of Angelo's rotting corpse in here with him, Angelo was dead, Angelo was dead) to the police station. The cops street-report clipped to the capsule. The other cops read the report, take you out (a creak, the lid opened, blessed fresh air even if it was the police station), take everything from you, check your DNA print against their files, make you sign some things, lock you up just like that...that's what he was in for right away. And then maybe a public AVL beating. Ironic.

Charlie looked up at a bored cop-face, an older fat one this time. The cop looked away, fussing with the report, not bothering to take Charlie out of the capsule. There was more room to maneuver now and Charlie felt like he was going to rip apart from Angelo's being in there with him if he didn't get out of the cuffs, out of the capsule. So he brought his knees up to his chest, worked the cuffs around his feet, it hurt but... he did it, got his hands in front of him.

Flash of Angelo's memory: *A big cop leaning over him, shouting at him, picking him up by the neck, shaking him. Fingers on his throat...*

When Angelo was a kid some cop had caught him running out of a store with something he'd ripped off. So the cop roughed him up, scared the shit out of Angelo, literally: Angelo shit his pants. The cop reacted in disgust (the look of disgust on the two cops' faces: "Makes me sick," one of them had said.)

So Angelo hated cops and now Angelo was out of his right mind—ha ha, he was in Charlie's—and so it was Angelo who reached down and found the boot-knife that the two cops had missed, pulled it out, got to his knees in the capsule as the cop turned around (Charlie fighting for control, damn it Ange, put down the knife, we could get out of this with—) and Charlie—no, it was Angelo—gripped the knife in both hands and stabbed the guy in his fat neck, split that sickening fat neck open, cop's blood is as red as anyone's, looks like...

Oh shit. Oh no.

Here come the other cops.

THE MAGAZINE DENOUNCED IN THE U.S. SENATE
FOR ITS ADVOCACY OF "ANIMAL SEX" PRESENTS
SEMIOTEXT(E) USA

A huge compendium of works in AMERICAN PSYCHOTOPOGRAPHY — Areas not found on the official map of consensus perception — Maps of energies, secret maps of the USA in the form of words and images.

We are amazed. We are NOT BORED. We have discarded the outworn charm of post-modern incommunicadismo. Passion and involvement, self-abandoned craziness, funny, sexy, dangerous, unabashedly precious, punk, loud and direct, SF, speculative fiction, weird fantasy — Pornography — Other mutated genres — Sermons, rants, broadsheets, crackpot pamphelts, manifestoes — Xerox and mimeo zines — Punkzines — Mail art — Kids' poetry — Subverted advertisements —American samizdat — Astounding rhetoric, elegant propaganda — Underground comix — Geographical documentation (maps, monuments, guides to weird places, photographs) — Stolen top-secret documents — And a special feature: scores of personal and classified ads, each one with a box-number or address, to connect YOU with the edges of the USA — Anarchists, unidentified flying leftists, neo-pagans, secessionists, the lunatic fringe of survivalism, cults, foreign agents, mad bombers, ban-the-bombers, nudists, monarchists, children's liberationists, tax resisters, zero-workers, mimeo poets, vampires, feuilletonistes, xerox pirates, prisoners, pataphysicians, unrepentant faggots, witches, hardcore youth, poetic terrorists...

Edited by Jim Fleming & Peter Lamborn Wilson

Designed by Sue Ann Harkey $12 postpaid

Order from:

Autonomedia, POB 568, Brooklyn, NY 11211-0568

FOR THE REALIZATION OF ALMOST-UNHEARD-OF DESIRES

On Eve of Physics Symposium, More Sub-Atomic Particles Found

Nick Herbert

Only a few weeks before the Esalen Seminar on the Nature of Reality, where top physicists and philosophers meet each year to decide what portion of the Great Secret to release to the public, private researchers at the Strongly Non-linear Accelerator Center (SNAC), Bonny Doon, California, announced the discovery of a handful of new particles that sent theorists back to their blackboards and experimentalists into their tunnels for ritual confirmation. The SNAC facility, the largest of its kind, produces the strongest weird-particle beam in the Solar System.

The first of the new particles — christened the Sigma in honor of San Francisco theorist Saul-Paul Sirag, who predicted its non-existence — appears to be another heavy lepton, resembling in all properties (save mass) its lighter brothers Mu and Tau. Chief SNAC scientists Drs. Kenneth Goffman and Alison Kennedy are modest about their discovery. "We see weirder things on our coffee breaks," they said, insisting that the Nobel Prize be shared with their reclusive colleague Dr. Nic Harvard, who provided the drugs necessary for the fundamental breakthrough.

After months of secrecy, the SNAC group's unorthodox techniques were finally revealed in Kennedy's controversial article "Quantum Tantra," published in last month's *Physical Review*, the major scholarly journal of the American physics community. Kennedy's paper was immediately repudiated by established physicists for its blatant violation of normal standards of professional conduct, scientific rigor, and common decency.

Unlike the Sigma, which can be observed by anyone with a research budget the size of the National Debt, SNAC's other new particles are invisible to everyone not in the proper state of consciousness, the first of many examples of "state-specific physics" emerging from research projects initiated in the '60s and only now beginning to bear fruit. In addition to their unanticipated physical properties, the new particles seem to possess mental attributes as well. Making contact is easy, but scientific study of these psychic quanta — or "Persons," as they are called at SNAC — is possible only by researchers with strong egos, since the experience is more akin to demonic possession than data collection.

"Expect to be changed a lot, when you mess around with Persons," warn researchers Goffman and Kennedy. "Each one is unique — an utterly alien island of consciousness. They're around us all the time now, and the only thing they want to do is get inside your body."

"We can't keep them in the lab. They fly right through our thickest shields. Before we could shut SNAC down, trillions of merge-hungry Persons had already escaped through the walls. They're slithering into restaurants now, into laundromats and shopping malls, even into your own bedroom, attracted by concentrations of human emotion."

"We're terribly sorry, folks, but everyone alive is involved in this experiment now. The era of state-specific physics has arrived!"

Walter Abish
Kathy Acker
Antonin Artaud
Roland Barthes
Georges Bataille
Jean Baudrillard
Joseph Beuys
Bifo
Maurice Blanchot
Sergio Bologna
Lee Breuer
William Burroughs
John Cage
Christo
Daniel Cohn-Bendit
Renato Curcio
Guy Debord
Gilles Deleuze
Jacques Derrida
Ariel Dorfman
as Magnus Enzensberger
Nuruddin Farrah
Dario Fo
Michel Foucault
Philip Glass
Andre Gorz
Felix Guattari
Guy Hocquenghem
Luce Irigaray
Mustafa Isrui
Alexander Kluge
Julia Kristeva
Jacques Lacan
Sylvie Leger
Sylvere Lotringer
ean-Francois Lyotard
Lia Magale
Chantal Maillet
Judith Malina
Dambudzo Marechera
Chris Marker
Ulrike Meinhoff
Michele Montrelay
Heiner Mueller
Toni Negri
Franco Piperno
Oreste Scalzone
Michel Serres
Wole Soynika
Pat Steir
Sun Ra
Mario Tronti
Cornel West
Robert Anton Wilson
Christa Wolf
and many more.

POLYSEXUALIT

ITALY: AUTONOMIA

POST-POLITICAL POLITICS

semiotexte

ego traps

semiotexte

schiz!

sem

Anti-Oedipu

THE GERMAN IS
semiotext(e)

From Psychoanalysis to Schizopolitics

SEMIOTEXT(E)'S FIRST DIRTY DOZEN

An Anthology of Selections from the Earliest Issues

Edited by Sylvere Lotringer and Jim Fleming
Introduction by Sylvere Lotringer

All of the best-selling issues of Semiotext(e) have been long out-of-print, but this anthology reprints selections from each of the first dozen numbers, including the much-in-demand *Anti-Oedipus, Autonomia, Ego Traps, German Issue, Nietzsche's Return, Polysexuality, Schizo-Culture,* and others.

Burning Sky
Rachel Pollack

Sometimes I think of my clitoris as a magnet, pulling me along to uncover new deposits of ore in the fantasy mines. Or maybe a compass, like the kind kids used to get in Woolworths, with a blue-black needle in a plastic case, and flowery letters marking the directions.

Two years ago, more by accident than design, I left the City of Civilized Sex. I still remember its grand traditions: orgasms in the service of loving relationships, healthy recreation with knowledgeable partners, a pinch of perversion to bring out the flavor. I remember them with a curious nostalgia. I think of them as I march through the wilderness, with only my compass to guide me.

Julia. Tall, with fingers that snake round the knobs and levers of her camera. Julia's skin is creamy, her neck is long and smooth, her eyebrows arch almost to a point. There was once a woman who drowned at sea, dreaming of Julia's eyes. Sometimes her hair is short and spiky, sometimes long and straight, streaming out to one side in the wind off Second Avenue. Sometimes her hair is red, with thick curls. Once a month she goes to a woman who dyes her eyelashes black. They darken further with each treatment.

Julia's camera is covered in black rubber. The shutter is a soft rubber button.

The Free Women. Bands of women who roam the world's cities at night, protecting women from rapists, social security investigators, police, and other forms of men. Suits of supple blue plastic cover their bodies from head to toe. Only the faces remain bare. Free Skin, they call it. The thin plastic coats the body like dark glistening nail polish.

Julia discovers the Free Women late one summer night when she can't sleep. She has broken up with a lover and can't sleep, so she goes out walking, wearing jeans and a white silk shirt and high red boots, and carrying her camera over one shoulder. On a wide street, by a locked park, with a drunk curled asleep before the gate, a man with a scarred face has cornered a girl, about fourteen. He flicks his knife at her, back and forth, like a lizard tongue. Suddenly they are there, yanking him away from the girl, surrounding him, crouched down with moon and streetlights running like water over their blue muscles. The man jerks forward. Spread fingers slide sideways. The attacker drops his knife to put his hand over his throat. Blood runs through the fingers. He falls against the gate. The women walk away. Julia follows.

Julia discovers the Free Women one night on the way home from an assignment. Tired as she is, she walks rather than taxi home to an empty apartment. She has just broken up with a lover, the third in less than two years. Julia doesn't understand what happens in these relationships. She begins them with such hopes, and then a month, two months, and she's lost interest, faking excitement when her girl friend plans for the future. Recklessly, Julia walks down the West Side, a woman alone with an expensive camera. She sees them across the street, three women walking shoulder to shoulder, their blue boots (she thinks) gliding in step, their blue gloves(she thinks) swinging in rhythm, their blue hoods (she thinks) washed in light. Julia takes the cap off her lens and follows them, conscious of the jerkiness in her stride, the hardness in her hips.

She follows them to a grimy factory building on West 21st Street. As they press buttons on an electronic light Julia memorizes the combination. For hours she waits, in a doorway smelling of piss, thinking now and then that the women are watching her, that they have arranged for her to stand there in that filth, a punishment for following them. Finally they leave and Julia lets herself inside. She discovers a single huge room, with laquered posts hanging with manacles, racks of black handled daggers along the walls, and in the middle of the floor a mosaic maze, coils of deep blue, with the center, the prize, a four spronged spiral made of pure gold. On the wall opposite the knives hang rows of blue suits, so thin they flutter slightly in the breeze from the closing door.

Over the next weeks Julia rushes through her assignments to get back to the hall of the Free Women. She spends days crouched across the street, waiting for the thirty seconds when she can photograph them entering or leaving. She spends more and more time inside, taking the suits in her hands, walking the maze. In the center she hears a loud fluttering of wings.

She tells herself she will write an exposé, an article for the Sunday *Times*. But she puts off calling the paper or her agent. She puts off writing any notes. Instead she enlarges her photos more than lifesize, covering the walls of her apartment, until she can almost imagine the women are there with her, or that the maze fills the floor of her kitchen.

And then one day Julia comes home—she's gone out for food, she's forgotten to keep any food in the house—and she finds the photos slashed, the negatives ruined, and all the lenses gone from her cameras.

Julia runs. She leaves her clothes, her cameras, her portfolios. She takes whatever cash lies in the house and heads into the street. Downtown she takes a room above a condemned bank and blacks out all the windows.

Let me tell you how I came to leave the City-state of Civilized Sex. It happened at the shore. Not the ocean, but the other side of Long Island, the Sound connecting New York and Connecticut. I'd gone there with my girl friend Louise, who at nineteen had seduced more women than I had ever known.

Louise and I had gotten together a few months after my husband Ralph had left me. On our last day as a couple Ralph informed me how lucky I was not to have birthed any children. The judge, he said, would certainly have awarded them to him. He went on to explain that it was no coincidence, our lack of children, since any heroic sperm that attempted to mount an expedition in search of my hidden eggs (*Raiders of the Lost Ovum*) would have frozen in "that refrigerator cunt of yours." Ralph liked to mix metaphors. When he got angry his speech reminded me of elaborate cocktails, like Singapore Slings.

I can't really blame Ralph. Not only did I never learn to fake orgasms properly (I would start thrusting and moaning and then think of something and forget the gasps and shrieks) but even in fights I tended to get distracted when I should have wept or screamed or thrown things.

Like the day Ralph left. I'm sure I should have cried or stared numbly at the wall. Instead I made myself a tuna sandwich and thought of sperms in fur coats, shivering on tiny wooden rafts as they tried to maneuver round the icebergs that blocked their way to the frozen eggs. I don't blame Ralph for leaving.

Anyway, he went, and I met Louise window shopping in a pet store. That same night we went to bed and I expected to discover that my sexual indifference had indicated a need for female flesh. Nothing happened. Louise cast her best spells, she swirled her magician's cloak in more and more elaborate passes, but the rabbit stayed hidden in the hat.

I became depressed, and Louise, exhausted, assured me that in all her varied experiences (she began to recite the range of ages and nationalities of women she'd converted) she'd never failed to find the proper button. It would just take time. I didn't tell her Ralph had said much the same thing. I wondered if I'd have to move to my parents' house upstate to avoid safaris searching for my orgasms like Tarzan on his way to the elephants' graveyard.

Julia runs out of money. She disguises herself in clothes bought from a uniform store on Canal St. and goes uptown to an editor who owes her a check. As she leaves the building she sees, across the street, in the doorway of a church, a black raincoat over blue skin. Julia jumps in a taxi. She goes to Penn Station, turning around constantly in her taxi to make sure no blue hooded women sit in the cars behind her. At the station she runs down the stairs, pushing past commuters to the Long Island Railroad where she searches the computer screens for the train to East Hampton.

On track 20 she hears a fluttering of wings and she smells the sea, and for a moment she thinks she's already arrived. And then she sees a trenchcoat lying on the floor. Another is falling beside her. A flash of light bounces off the train, as if the sun has found a crack through Penn Station and the roof of the tunnel. She tries running for the doors. Blue hands grab her wrists. Blueness covers her face.

No. No, it happens along Sixth Avenue. Sixth Avenue at lunchtime, among the push carts selling souvlaki and sushi, egg rolls and yoghurt, tofu and pretzels. Julia's pants are torn, the wind dries the sweat on her chest, she's been running for hours, her toes are bleeding, no cabs will stop for her. She turns a corner and tumbles into a class of twelve year old girls. The girls are eating hot dogs and drinking Pepsi Cola. They wear uniforms, pleated skirts and lace up shoes, brown jackets and narrow ties. The girls surround Julia. They push her down when she tries to stand up. Somewhere up the street a radio plays a woman singing "Are you lonesome tonight?" The girls tear off Julia's clothes. They pinch and slap her face, her breasts. Grease streaks her thighs. The girls are whistling, yelping, stamping their feet. Now come the wings, the smell of the sea. The girls step back, their uniforms crisp, their ties straight. They part like drapes opening to the morning. A woman in blue steps into the circle, bright shining as the sun. Spread fingertips slide down Julia's body, from the mouth down the neck and along the breasts. the belly, the thighs. Wherever the woman touches, the welts disappear. She lifts Julia in her arms. Slowly she walks down the street, while the crowd moves aside and the whole city falls silent, even the horns. Julia hears the cry of gulls searching for food.

Over the weeks Louise changed from bluff to hearty to understanding to peevish as her first failure became more and more imminent. She suggested I see a doctor. I told her I'd been and she got me to admit the doctor had been a man. She lugged me to a woman's clinic where the whole staff consisted of former lovers of hers. While Louise went in to consult the healer on duty I sat in the waiting room.

I got into conversation with a tall skinny woman wearing a buckskin jacket, a gold shirt, and motorcycle boots. She showed me the French bayonet she carried in a sheath in her hip pocket, explaining it would "gut the next prick" that laid a hand on her or one of her sisters. I asked her if she'd undergone any training in knifeware. Not necessary, she told me. Pricks train. The Goddess would direct her aim. The Goddess, she said, lived in the right side of the brain. That's why the government (99% pricks) wanted to burn lefthanded women.

"Janie's a little strongminded" Louise told me as she led me down a corridor to see Doctor Catherine. The corridor's yellowstriped wallpaper had started to peel in several places, revealing a layer of newspaper underneath.

"Did you sleep with her?" I asked.

"Only a couple of times. Did she show you her bayonet?" I nodded. "She kept it under the pillow in case the police broke in to arrest us for Goddessworship. That's what she calls women screwing."

I didn't listen very closely to Catherine, who didn't like the name "Doctor." I wanted to think about pricks training for their life's work. They probably do it in gym class, I decided. While the girls try backward somersaults and leap sideways over wooden horses the boys practise erections, and later, in advanced classes, learn to charge rubber simulations of female genitals. At the end of each lesson the instructor reminds them not to speak of this in front of their girl friends.

Margaret didn't find my G spot or raise my Mary Rose (I strongly identified with Henry Vlll's sunken flagship and all its chests of gold. I cried when they raised it, all crusted in barnacles and brine. That left only one of us hidden in the murk.) She did give me some crushed herbs for tea and a bag of tree bark to chew on while I lay in the bathtub. Louise raged at me whenever I neglected my treatment. "You can't let yourself get negative," she shouted. "You've got to believe."

In the ritual hall Julia spends days hanging from copper, then brass, then silver manacles. Six, no, nine of the women weave in and out of sight, sometimes whispering to each other, sometimes laughing, sometimes standing before Julia and silently mouthing words in a foreign language. Across from her the blue suits rustle against each other.

Julia learns to catch bits of food thrown at her from across the room. Twice, no, three times a day one of the women brings her water in a stone bowl. A gold snake coils at the bottom. Sometimes the woman holds the bowl in front of her, and Julia has to bow her head and lap up as much as she can. Or the woman moves the bowl away just as Julia begins to drink. Or throws the water in her face. At other times she gently tilts the bowl for Julia. Once, as Julia drinks, she discovers that a live snake has replaced the metal one. The head rises above the water and Julia's own head snaps back so hard she would bang it against the wall if a blue hand wasn't there to cushion her.

They shave her head. No, they comb and perfume her hair. They rub her with oils and smooth the lines in her face and neck, slapping her only when she tries to bite or lick the cool fingertips sliding down her face.

Once or several times a day they take her down from the wall and force her to run the maze. The women surround the tiled circle, hitting the floor with sticks and trilling louder and louder until Julia misses a step or even falls, just outside the gold spiral. When she's failed they yank her out of the maze and hold her arms out like wings as they press the tips of her breasts into champagne glasses filled with tiny sharp emeralds.

On the day Julia completes the maze the women dress her in shapeless black overalls and heavy boots. They smuggle her out of the country to an island where a house of white stone stands on top of a hill covered in pine trees. The women strip Julia. With their sticks they drive her up a rock path. The door opens and a cool wind flows from the darkness.

A woman steps out. Instead of blue her suit gleams a deep red. It covers the whole body, including the face, except for the eyes, the nostrils, the mouth. Her muscles move like a river running over stone. Her name is Burning Sky, and she was born in Crete six thousand years ago. When she walks the air flows behind her like the sundered halves of a very thin veil.

One night, after a fight, Louise kicked the wall and ran from the house. The next morning, the doorbell woke me at 6:00. Frightened, I looked out the window before I would open the door. There stood Louise in a rough zipper jacket and black turtleneck sweater. She saw me and waved a pair of rubber boots. Afraid she planned to kick me I didn't want to let her in but I couldn't think of how to disconnect the doorbell. She'd begun to shout, too. "For heaven's sake, Maggie, open the fucking door." Any moment the police would show up.

While I buttered toast and boiled water Louise announced our plans for the morning. We were going fishing. Dress warm, she said, and gave me the spare boots she'd brought for me. I had to wear two pairs of socks, and my feet still slid around. -

In her pickup truck I tried to sleep, despite Louise's cheerful whistle. But when we got all our gear and bodies in a rowboat out in the Sound, it turned out that Louise didn't plan to fish at all. "Now, god-damnit," she said, "you can't whine and get away from me. I'm not taking this boat back to shore until you come and I can feel it all over my fingers."

"What?" I said, ruining her powerful speech. Her meaning became clearer as she began to crawl towards me. She scared me but she made me want to laugh too. It reminded me of the time Ralph had locked us in a motel room with a bottle of wine, a bag of marijuana, and a pink nightgown. At least motel rooms are comfortable. Maybe Louise considered rowboats romantic.

I decided I better hold my face straight. "You rapist prick!" I shouted, and tried to grab an oar to threaten her but couldn't work it loose from the lock. I snatched the fish knife and held it with both hands in front of my belly. "Keep away from me," I warned.

"Put that down." Louise said. "You'll hurt yourself."

"I'll hurt you, you prick."

"Don't call me that. You don't know how to use that."

"The Goddess will show me."

Apparently this all became too much for her. "Shit," she said, and turned around to grasp the oars for the pull to shore. I sat slumped over and shivering. My hands clenched around the knife.

In a ceremonial hall hung with purple silk and gold shields the women tattoo a four-pronged spiral in the hollow of Julia's neck. They present her with a blue suit. With four others she returns to New York on a cruise ship secretly owned by the Free Women. They wear disguises, like the Phantom, when he would venture out as Mister Walker, wrapped in a trench coat and slouch hat, to rescue his beloved Diana from Nazi kidnappers.

Despite the women's clever tricks someone on the boat recognizes them. A television anchorwoman, or maybe a rightwing politician. This woman once served Burning Sky, but disobeyed her leader on some assignment. Now she comes to their suite of cabins and begs the Free Women to readmit her. They play with her, attaching small intricately carved stone clips all over her skin. She suffers silently, only to have them announce she had forgotten how to break through the wall. They can do nothing for her. She goes away, later becomes prime minister.

When we got back to the rental dock Louise began to lug the boat onto the wooden platform. "If you want to go home," she said, "give me a hand." I took hold of the rope to tie it to the iron post that would hold it fast when the hurricane came.

At that moment a woman came out of the water. Dressed in a black wet suit with long shiny flippers and a dark mask that completely hid her face, she stood for a moment rotating her shoulders and tilting her head up to the sun. Her spear gun pointed at the ground.

My heart began throwing blood wildly around my body: my vagina contracted like someone running for her life. "Will you come on?" Louise said.

I stammered something at her. Louise had never heard me stammer before. "What the hell is the matter with you?" she said. Then her eyes followed the invisible cable connecting me and my beautiful skin diver. She looked back and forth between us a couple of times while a wolfgrin took over her face. "Sonofabitch," she said, and laughed. "Why didn't you tell me?"

"I didn't know," I said, and Louise got to see another first. I blushed.

It was certainly a day for firsts. That evening, in the sloppy cavernous apartment Louise had inherited from her grandfather, she took out her collection of "toys": whips, handcuffs, masks, chains, nipple clips, leather capes, rubber gloves, and one whalebone corset, c. 1835. No wetsuits, but it didn't really matter. I hope none of Ralph's sperm remained camped inside me anymore. The spring thaw came that night, and the flood would have washed the courageous little creatures away forever.

The Free Women order Julia to go alone to her apartment and renew her professional contacts. At first she finds it hard to function without her instructors. She hates going out "naked," as she thinks of her ordinary clothes. With no one to command her she forgets to eat and one day passes out while photographing a police parade in the South Bronx.

Gradually the dream fades. Julia stops dressing up in her Free Skin at night, she goes on holiday with a woman reporter who asks about the tattoo on Julia's neck. Julia tells her she got it to infiltrate a group of terrorists. When the woman falls asleep Julia cries in the shower and thanks the Virgin Mary for her deliverance. She wonders how she ever could have submitted to such strange and wretched slavery.

An order comes. Something simple, maybe embarrassing a judge who suspended the sentence of a man who raped his five year old daughter. Something with a clear moral imperative.

Julia takes off from work to decide what to do. In a cabin in the woods she tries on her Free Skin and lies in bed, remembering Burning Sky's face, and the way her fingers looked extended into the air. She remembers lying with the other women in a huge bed, how they slid in and out of each other, while their bodies melted inside their blue suits. She remembers hanging from silver manacles, remembers dancing to the heart of the labyrinth.

Julia returns to the city and locks the blue suit in a metal cabinet. The day of her assignment passes. She falls into a fever, attended by her reporter friend. When she recovers and the woman has left, Julia opens the cabinet. Her Free Skin has vanished. In its place lies a Chinese woman's dagger, five hundred years old, with an ivory handle bearing the same spiral sign that marks Julia's neck. Terrified, she waits for retribution. Weeks pass.

And so I left the City of Civilized Sex in one great rush on the back of a skindiver. Now that she'd preserved her record Louise lost interest very quickly, but at least she gave me some leads to "your kind of trick," as she delicately put it. I didn't know whether she meant the lovers or the activities.

I discovered not only a large reservoir of women devoted to farfetched sexual practices, but several organizations, complete with buttons, slogans, jackets, and conflicting manifestoes. After a while they all began to strike me as rather odd, not just for their missionary zeal, but their hunger for community. Had I left the City only to emigrate to another nation-state?

It wasn't so much the social as the sexual conformity that disturbed me. Everyone seemed to agree head of time on what would excite them. I began to wonder if all those people in the Land of Leather really liked the same sort of collar (black with silver studs) or if each new arrival, thrilled at finding a town where she'd expected only a swamp, confused gratitutde with eroticism, and gave up her dreams of finding leather clothes and objects of exactly the right color, cut and texture.

As my imagination began to show me its tastes I became more and more specific with the women who tried to satisfy me. That first night with Louise she could have tied me up with a piece of filthy clothesline and I wouldn't have complained. A few months later I was demanding the right ropes (green and gold curtain pulls with the tassle removed) tied only in particular knots taken from the *Boy Scout Handbook*.

And even that phase didn't last. For, in fact, it's not actions that I'm hunting. No matter how well you do them they can only approximate reality. City dwellers believe that fantasies exist to intensify arousal. Out here in the Territories the exiles should know better. I want to stand on a tree stump and yell through the forest, "Stop trying to build new settlements. Stop trying to clear the trees and put up walls and lay down sewers." I want them to understand. Sex exists to lay traps for fantasies.

Julia's life becomes as pale and blank as cheap paper. She goes to bars and picks up women. They all go away angry when they get back to Julia's apartment and Julia just sits on the bed, or else goes to the darkroom and doesn't come out. Julia returns to the ritual hall. She finds it replaced by a button factory.

She drives out to the beach on a hard sunny day in December. Ignoring the cold wind she strips naked and walks toward the water, both hands gripping the Chinese dagger. She raises it to the sun to watch the light glint off the blade. But then she notices flashes beyond the knife. Small spots on the horizon. As she watches, they grow larger, become blue sails, then a row of boats coming out of the deep. Each one contains a single woman. The sails rise out of their shoulders like wings. They call to each other like birds, their voices piercing the wind. When they land they detach their skins from the boat masts and the plastic snaps back against their bodies.

Julia falls down in the wet sand. A wild roaring in the Earth drowns out the sea as the six women lift her to her feet (six is the number of love, with Julia they become seven, the number of victory). They wash the mud and loneliness from her and dress her in the Free Skin she abandoned for an illusion of freedom.

> The only true happiness lies in
> obedience to loving authority.

> Charles Moulton, speaking as
> Queen Hippolyte of Paradise
> Island to her daughter,
> Princess Di,
> Wonder Woman Comics, c. 1950

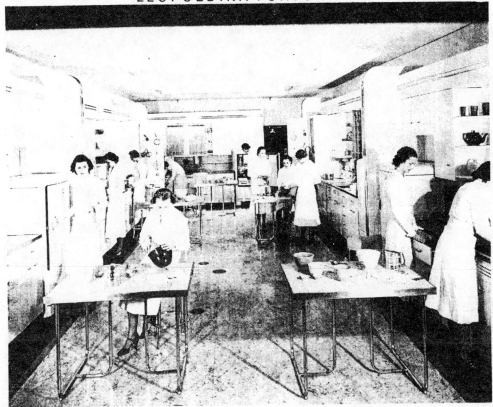

Bob McGlynn, a.k.a. Joey Homicides, Pope of the Wino Nation, publishes in a number of mutant marginal anti-authoritarian zines such as POPULAR REALITY, OUTRÉ, SHOE POLISH WEEK, BANG!, ON GOGOL BOULEVARD, etc. He is active with the unofficial East/West peace movement, groups like Moscow Trust and Neither East Nor West. He and another Brooklynite, Anne Marie Hendrickson, were "detained" and deported from Moscow by the KGB for handing out leaflets in Red Square about Chernobyl.

Day
Bob McGlynn

The spacecraft hovered
connected to Earth by large
orange pink soda straws
grounded in sparse but
wide bladed large sheath grass

The elongated ellipse is above
on one corner a certain eye
all along the edge are paramecium hair
There is a square
doorknob latch and locks
straggle toward the floor

The door is decorated with
Arabian signs

Soft life quietly appears
unaware of its own peace
There is an essential circle
with many ribbons flowing
Flowing like a ring of soft purple light
in greatly diminished gravity

Rudy Rucker restored my personal faith in SF as a literature of ideas with his WHITE LIGHT, a melding of tantrism and Cantorian math set in a dreamscape worthy of collaboration between Tristan Tzara and Harold Lloyd. After that I devoured and loved all his books, especially SPACETIME DOUGHNUTS and the recent MEANING OF LIFE, his short-story collection THE 57TH FRANZ KAFKA, and his entertaining profound works on math. Rucker won the first P. K. Dick Memorial Award — a perfect choice. Then I discovered that my downstairs neighbor Eddy the Cameraman went to college with Rudy in my old hometown, New Brunswick, NJ. I wrangled an introduction.

We invited Rudy to participate in the USA issue of SEMIOTEXT(E), and he gave us the wonderful "Eschatology Rant." And his contributions to the present volume include far more than the following story; in effect, without his mentorship, encouragement (and connections) the book would have been far less loud and funny… in fact, it would have been impossible.

Rudy has since left Lynchburg, VA (where he feuded with the Moral Majority) and is teaching math and computer science at San Jose in Silicon Valley. He is hacking cellular automata and writing a novel called THE HOLLOW EARTH. (His most recent novel is WETWARE.) His latest kick is the ultra-new SF "Freestyle" movement emanating from California and having something to do with… surfing. "Rapture in Space," however, is definitely cyberpunkish — sex, drugs and snickering nihilism…. [P.L.W.]

Rapture in Space
Rudy Rucker

Denny Blevins was a dreamer who didn't like to think. Drugs and no job put his head in just the right place for this. If at all possible, he liked to get wired and spend the day lying on his rooming-house mattress and looking out the window at the sky. On clear days he could watch his eyes' phosphenes against the bright blue; and on cloudy days he'd dig the clouds' drifty motions and boiling edges. One day he realized his window-dirt was like a constant noise-hum in the system, so he knocked out the pane that he usually looked through. The sky was even better then, and when it rained he could watch the drops coming in. At night he might watch the stars, or he might get up and roam the city streets for deals.

His Dad, whom he hadn't seen in several years, died that April.

Denny flew out to the funeral. His big brother Allen was there, with Dad's insurance money. Turned out they got $15K apiece.

"Don't squander it, Denny," said Allen, who was an English teacher. "Time's winged chariot for no man waits! You're getting older and it's time you found a career. Go to school and learn something. Or buy into a trade. Do something to make Dad's soul proud."

"I will," said Denny, feeling defensive. Instead of talking in clear he used the new cyberslang. "I'll get so cashy and so starry so zip you won't believe it, Allen. I'll get a tunebot, start a motion, and cut a choicey vid. Denny in the Clouds with Clouds. Untense, bro, I've got plex ideas." When Denny got back to his room he got a new sound system and a self-playing electric guitar. And scored a lot of dope and food-packs. The days went by; the money dwindled to $9K. Early in June the phone rang.

"Hello, Denny Blevins?" The voice was false and quacky.

"Yes!" Denny was glad to get a call from someone besides Allen. It seemed like lately Allen was constantly calling him up to nag.

"Welcome to the future. I am Phil, a phonebot cybersystem designed to contact consumer prospects. I would like to tell about the on-line possibilities open to you. Shall I continue?"

"Yes," said Denny.

It turned out that "Phil the phonebot" was a kind of computerized phone salesman. The phonebot was selling phonebots which you, the consumer prospect, could use to sell phonebots to others. It was—though Denny didn't realize this—a classic Ponzi pyramid scheme, like a chain letter, or like those companies which sell people franchises to sell franchises to sell franchises to sell...

The phonebot had a certain amount of interactivity. It asked a few yes/no questions; and whenever Denny burst in with some comment, it would pause, say, "That's right, Denny! But listen to the rest!" and continue.

Denny was pleased to hear his name so often. Alone in his room, week after week, he'd been feeling his reality fade. Writing original songs for the guitar was harder than he'd expected. It would be nice to have a robot friend. At the end, when Phil asked for his verdict, Denny said, "OK, Phil, I want you. Come to my rooming-house tomorrow and I'll have the money."

The phonebot was not the arm-waving clanker that Denny, in his ignorance, had imagined. It was, rather, a flat metal box that plugged right into the wall phone-socket. The box had a slot for an electronic directory, and a speaker for talking to its owner. It told Denny he could call it Phil; all the phonebots were named Phil. The basic phonebot-sales spiel was stored in the Phil's memory, though you could change the patter if you wanted. You could, indeed, use the phonebot to sell things other than phonebots.

The standard salespitch lasted five minutes, and one minute was allotted to the consumer's responses. If everyone answered, listened, and responded, the phonebot could process 10 prospects per hour, and 120 in a 9AM – 9PM day! The whole system cost nine thousand dollars, though as soon as you bought one and joined the pyramid, you could get more of them for six. Three thousand dollars profit for each phonebot your phonebot could sell! If you sold, say, one a day, you'd make better than $100K a year!

The electronic directory held all the names and numbers in the city; and each morning it would ask Denny who he wanted to try today. He could select the numbers on the day's calling list on the basis of neighborhood, last name, family size, type of business and so on.

The first day, Denny picked a middle-class suburb and told Phil to call all the childless married couples there. Young folks looking for an opportunity! Denny set the speaker so he could listen to people's responses.

It was not encouraging.

"click"

"No...*click"*

"This kilp ought to be illegal...*click"*

"click"

"Get a job, you bizzy dook...click"

"Of all the...*click"*

"Again? *click"*

Most people hung up so fast that Phil was able to make some thousand unsuccessful contacts in less than ten hours. Only seven people listened through the whole message and left comments at the end; and six of these people seemed to be bedridden or crazy. The seventh had a phonebot she wanted to sell cheap.

Denny tried different phoning strategies—rich people, poor people, people with two 7s in their phone number, and so on. He tried different kinds of salespitches—bossy ones, ingratiating ones, curt ones, negro-accent ones, etc. He made up a salespitch that offered businesses the chance to rent Phil to do phone adverstsing for them.

Nothing worked. It got to be depressing sitting in his room watching Phil fail—it was like having Willy Loman for his roommate. The machine made little noises, and unless Denny took a lot of dope, he had trouble relaxing out into the sky. The empty food-packs stank.

Two more weeks, and all the money, food and dope were gone. Right after he did the last of the dope, Denny recorded a final sales-pitch:

"Uh...hi. This is Phil the prophet at 1801 Eye St. I eye I... I'm out of money and I'd rather not have to...uh...leave my room. You send me money or...uh...food and I'll give God your name. Dope's rail, too."

Phil ran that on random numbers for two days with no success. Denny came down into deep hunger. Involuntary detox. If his Dad had left much more money, Denny might have died, holed up in that room. Good old Dad. He trembled out into the street and got a job working counter in a Greek coffee shop called the KoDo. It was OK; there was plenty of food, and he didn't have to watch Phil panhandling.

As Denny's strength and sanity came back, he remembered sex. But he didn't know any girls. He took Phil off panhandling and put him onto propositioning numbers in the young working-girl neighborhoods.

"Hi, are you a woman? I'm Phil, sleek robot for a whippy young man who's ready to get under. Make a guess and he'll mess. Leave your number and state your need; he's fuff-looking and into sleaze."

This message worked surprisingly well. The day after he started it up, Denny came home to find four enthusiastic responses stored on Phil's chips. Two of the responses seemed to be from men, and one of the women's voices sounded old...really old. The fourth response was from "Silke."

"Hi, desperado, this is Silke. I like your machine. Call me."

Phil had Silke's number stored, of course, so Denny called her right up. Feeling shy, he talked through Phil, using the machine as voder to make his voice sound weird. After all, Phil was the one who knew her.

"Hello?" Cute, eager, practical, strange.

"Silke? This is Phil. Denny's talking though me. You want to interface?"

"Like where?"

"My room?"

"Is it small? It sounds like your room is small. I like small rooms."

"You got it. 1801 Eye St., Denny'll be in front of the building."

"What do you look like, Denny?"

"Tall, thin, teeth when I grin, which is lots. My hair's peroxide blonde on top. I'll wear my X-shirt."

"Me too. See you in an hour."

Denny put on his X-shirt—a T-shirt with a big silk-screen picture of his genitalia—and raced down to the KoDo to beg Spiros, the boss, for an advance on his wages.

"Please, Spiros, I got a date."

The shop was almost empty, and Spiros was sitting at the counter watching a payvid porno show on his pocket TV. He glanced over at Denny, all decked out in his X-shirt, and pulled two fifties out of his pocket.

"Let me know how she come."

Denny spent one fifty on two Fiesta food-packs and some wine; the other fifty went for a capsule of snap-crystals from a street-vendor. He was back in front of his rooming-house in plenty of time. Ten minutes, and there came Silke, with a great big pink crotch-shot printed onto her T-shirt. She looked giga good.

For the first instant they stood looking at each other's X-shirts, and then they shook hands.

"I'm Denny Blevins. I got some food and wine and snap here, if you want to go up." Denny was indeed tall and thin, and toothy when he grinned. His mouth was very wide. His hair was long and dark in back, and short and blonde on top. He wore red rhinestone earrings, his semierect X-shirt, tight black plastic pants, and fake leopard-fur shoes. His arms were muscular and veiny, and he moved them a lot when he talked.

"Go up and get under," smiled Silke. She was medium height, and wore her strawy black hair in a bouffant. She had fine, hard features. She'd appliqued pictures of monster eyes to her eyelids, and she wore white dayglo lipstick. Beneath her soppingwet X-shirt, she wore a tight, silvered jumpsuit with cutouts. On her feet she wore roller-skates with lights in the wheels.

"Oxo," said Denny.

"Wow," said Silke.

Up in the room they got to know each other. Denny showed Silke his phonebot and his sound system, pretended to start to play his guitar and to then decide not to, and told about some of the weird things he'd seen in the sky, looking out that broken pane. Silke, as it turned out, was a payvid sex dancer come here from West Virginia. She talked mostly in clear, but she was smart, and she liked to get wild, but only with the right kind of guy. Sex dancer didn't mean hooker and she was, she assured Denny, clean. She had a big dream she wasn't quite willing to tell him yet.

"Come on," he urged, popping the autowave foodpacks open. "Decode."

"Ah, I don't know, Denny. You might think I'm skanky." They sat side by side on Denny's mattress and ate the pasty food with the packed-in plastic spoons. It was good. It was good to have another person in the room here.

"Silke," said Denny when they finished eating, "I'd been thinking Phil was kilp. Dook null. But if he got you here it was worth it. Seems I just need tech to relate, you wave?"

Silke threw the empty foodtrays on the floor and gave Denny a big kiss. They went ahead and fuffed. Seemed like it had been a while for both of them. Skin all over, soft warm skin, touch kiss lick smell good.

Afterwards, Denny opened the capsule of snap and they split it. You put the stuff on your tongue, it sputtered and popped, and you breathed in the freebase fumes. Fab rush. Out through the empty window pane they could see the moon and two stars stranger than the city lights.

"Out there," said Silke, her voice fast and shaky from the snap. "That's my dream. If we hurry, Denny, we can be the first people to have sex in space. They'd remember us forever. I've been thinking about it, and there was always missing links, but you and Phil are it. We'll get in the shuttlebox—it's a room like this—and go up. We get up there and make videos of us getting under, and—this is my new flash—we use Phil to sell the vids to pay for the trip. You wave?"

Denny's long, maniacal smile curled across his face. The snap was still crackling on his tongue. "Stuzzadelic! Nobody's fuffed in space yet? None of those gawks who've used the shuttlebox?"

"They might have, but not for the record. But if we scurry we'll be the famous first forever. We'll be starry."

"Oxo, Silke." Denny's voice rose with excitement. "Are you there, Phil?"

"Yes, Denny."

"Got a new pitch. In clear."

"Proceed."

"Hi, this is Denny." He nudged the naked girl next to him.

"And this is Silke."

"We're doing a live fuff-vid we'd like to show you."

"It's called RAPTURE IN SPACE. It's the very first X-rated love film from outer space."

"Zero gravity," said Denny, reaching over to whang his guitar.

"Endless fun."

"Mindless pleasure." Whang.

"Out near the sun." Silke nuzzled his neck and moaned stagily. "Oh, Denny, oh, darling, it's..."

"RAPTURE IN SPACE! Satisfaction guaranteed. This is bound to be a collector's item; the very first live sex video from space. A full ninety minutes of unbelievable null-gee action, with great Mother Earth in the background, tune in for only fifty..."

"More, Denny," wailed Silke, who was now grinding herself against him with some urgency. "More!"

Whang. "Only one hundred dollars, and going up fast. To order, simply leave your card number after the beep."

"Beep!"

Phil got to work the next morning, calling numbers of businesses where lots of men worked. The orders poured in. Lacking a business-front by which to cash the credit orders, Denny enlisted Spiros, who quickly set up KoDo Space Rapture Enterprises. For managing the business, Spiros only wanted 15% and some preliminary tapes of Denny and Silke in action. For another 45%, Silke's porno payvid employers—an outfit known as XVID—stood ready to distribute the show. Dreaming of this day, Silke had already bought her own cameras. She and Denny practiced a lot, getting their moves down. Spiros agreed that the rushes looked good. Denny went ahead and reserved the shuttlebox for a trip in mid July.

The shuttlebox was a small passenger module that could be loaded into the space shuttle for one of its weekly trips up to orbit and back. A trip for two cost $100K. Denny bought electronic directories for cities across the country, and set Phil to working 20 hours a day. He averaged 50 sales a day, and by launch time, Silke and Denny had enough to pay everyone off, and then some.

But this was just the beginning. Three days before the launch, the news-services picked up on the "Rapture in Space" plan, and everything went crazy. There was no way for a cheap box like Phil to process the orders anymore. Denny and Silke had to give XVID another 15% of the action, and let them handle the tens of thousands of orders. It was projected that "Rapture in Space" would pull an audience share of 7%— which is a lot of people. Even more money came in the form of fat contracts for two product endorsements: SPACE RAPTURE, the cosmic eroscent for highflyers, and RAPT SHIELD, an antiviral lotion for use by sexual adventurers. XVID and the advertisers privately wished that Denny and Silke were a bit more...upscale looking, but they were the two who had the the tiger by the tail.

Inevitably, some of the Christian Party congressmen tried to have Denny and Silke enjoined from making an XVID broadcast from aboard the space shuttle which was, after all, government property. But for 5% of the gross, a fast-thinking lawyer was able to convince a hastily convened Federal court that, insofar as "Space Rapture" was being codecast to the XVID dish and cabled thence only to paying subscribers, the show was a form of constitutionally protected free speech, in no way essentially different from a live-sex show in a private club.

So the great day came. Naked save for a drenching of Space Rapture eroscent, Silke and Denny waved goodbye and stepped into their shuttlebox. It was shaped like a two-meter-thick letter D, with a rounded floor, and with a big picture window set into the flat ceiling. A crane loaded the shuttlebox into the bay of the space-shuttle along with some satellites, missles, building materials, etc. A worker dogged all the stuff down, and then the baydoors closed. Silke and Denny wedged themselves down into their puttylike floor. Blast off—roar, shudder, push, clunk, roar some more.

Then they were floating. The baydoors swung open, and the astronauts got to work with their retractible arms and space-tools. Silke and Denny were busy too. They set up the cameras, and got their little antenna locked in on the XVID dish. They started broadcasting right away—some of the Rapture in Space subscribers had signed up for the whole live protocols in addition to the ninety minute show that Silke and Denny were scheduled to put on in...

"Only half an hour, Denny," said Silke. "Only thirty minutes till we go on." She was crouched over the sink, douching, and vacuuming the water back up. As fate would have it, she was menstruating. She hadn't warned anyone about it.

Denny felt cold and sick to his stomach. XVID had scheduled their show right after take-off because otherwise—with all the news going on—people might forget about it. But right now he didn't feel like fuffing at all, let alone getting under. Every time he touched something, or even breathed, his whole body moved.

"All clean now," sang Silke. "No one can tell, not even you."

There was a rapping on their window. One of the astronauts, a jolly jock woman named Judy. She grinned through her helmet and gave them a high sign. The astronauts thought the Rapture in Space show was a great idea; it would make people think about them in new, more interesting ways.

"I talked to Judy before the launch," said Silke, waving back. "She said to watch out for the rebound." She floated to Denny and began fondling him. "Ten minutes, starman."

Outside the window, Judy was a shiny wad against Earth's great marbled curve. The clouds, Denny realized, I'm seeing the clouds from on top. His genitals were warming to Silke's touch. He tongued a snap crystal out of a crack between his teeth and bit it open. Inhale. The clouds. Silke's touch. He was hard, thank God, he was hard. This was going to be all right.

The cameras made a noise to signal the start of the main transmission, and Denny decided to start by planting a kiss on Silke's mouth. He bumped her shoulder and she started to drift away. She tightened her grip on his penis and led him along after her. It hurt, but not too unpleasantly. She landed on her back, on the padded floor, and guided Denny right into her vagina. Smooth and warm. Good. Denny pushed into her and...rebound.

He flew, rapidly and buttocks first, up to the window. He had hold of Silke's armpit and she came with him. She got her mouth over his penis for a second, which was good, but then her body spun around, and she slid toothrakingly off him, which was very bad.

Trying to hold a smile, Denny stole a look at the clock. Three minutes. Rapture in Space had been on for three minutes now. Eighty-seven minutes to go.

It was another bruising half hour or so until Denny and Silke began to get the hang of spacefuffing. And then it was fun. For a long time they hung in midair, with Denny in Silke, and Silke's legs around his waist, just gently jogging, but moaning and throwing their heads around for the camera. Actually, the more they hammed it up, the better it felt. Autosuggestion.

Denny stared and stared at the clouds to keep from coming, but finally he had to pull out for a rest. To keep things going they did rebounds for awhile. Silke would lie spreadeagled on the floor, and Denny would kind of leap down on her; both of them adjusting their pelvises for a bullseye: She'd sink into the cushions, then rebound them both up. It got better and better. Silke curled up into a ball and impaled herself on Denny's shaft. He wedged himself against the wall with his feet and one hand, and used his other hand to spin her around and around, bobbin on his spindle. Denny lay on the floor and Silke did leaps onto him. They kissed and licked each other all over, and from every angle. The time was almost up.

For the finale, they went back to midair fuffing; arms and legs wrapped around each other; one camera aimed at their faces, and one camera aimed at their genitalia. They hit a rhythm where they always pushed just as hard as each other and it action/reaction cancelled out, hard and harder, with big Earth out the window, yes, the air full of their smells, yes, the only sound the sound of their ragged breathing, yes, now NOW AAAHHHHHH!!!!

Denny kind of fainted there, and forgot to slide out for the come-shot. Silke went blank too, and they just floated, linked like puzzle pieces for five or ten minutes. It made a great finale for the Rapture in Space show, really much more convincing than the standard sperm spurt.

Two days later, and they were back on Earth, with the difference that they were now, as Denny had hoped, cashy and starry. People recognized them everywhere, and looked at them funny, often asking for a date. They did some interviews, some more endorsements and they got an XVID contract to host a monthly spacefuff variety show.

Things were going really good until Denny got a tumor. "It's a dooky little kilp down in my bag," he complained to Silke.

"Feel it."

Sure enough, there was a one-centimeter lump in Denny's scrotum. Silke wanted him to see a doctor, but he kept stalling. He was afraid they'd run a bloodtest and get on his case about drugs. Some things were still illegal.

A month went by and the lump was the size of an orange.

"It's so gawky you can see it through my pants," complained Denny. "It's giga ouch and I can't cut a vid this way."

But he still wouldn't go to the doctor. What with all the snap he could buy, and with his new cloud telescope, Denny didn't notice what was going on in his body most of the time. He was happy to miss the next few XVID dates. Silke hosted them alone.

Three more months and the lump was like a small watermelon. When Denny came down one time and noticed that the tumor was moving he really got worried.

"Silke! It's alive! The thing in my bag is alive! Aaauuugh!"

Silke paid a doctor two thousand dollars to come to their apartment.

The doctor was a bald, dignified man with a white beard. He examined Denny's scrotum for a long time, feeling, listening, and watching the tumor's occasional twitches. Finally he pulled the covers back over Denny and sat down. He regarded Silke and Denny in silence for quite some time. "Decode!" demanded Denny. "What the kilp we got running here?"

"You're pregnant," said the doctor. "Four months into it, I'd say."

The quickening fetus gave another kick and Denny groaned. He knew it was true. "But how?"

The doctor steepled his fingers. "I...I saw Rapture in Space. There were certain signs to indicate that your uh partner was menstruating?"

"Check."

"Menstruation, as you must know, involves the discharge of the unfertilized ovum along with some discarded uterine tissues. I would speculate that after your ejaculation the ovum became wedged in your meatus. It is conceivable that, under weightless conditions, the sperms' flagellae could have driven the now-fertilized ovum up into your vas deferens. The ovum implanted itself in the bloodrich tissues there and developed into a fetus."

"I want an abortion."

"No!" protested Silke. "That's our baby, Denny. You're already almost half done carrying it. It'll be lovely for us...and just think of the publicity!"

"Uh..." said Denny, reaching for his bag of dope.

"No more drugs," said the doctor, snatching the bag. "Except for the ones I give you." He broke into a broad, excited smile. "This will make medical history."

And indeed it did. The doctor designed Denny a kind of pouch in which he could carry his pregant scrotum, and Denny made a number of video appearances, not all of them X-rated. He spoke on the changing roles of the sexes, and he counted the days till delivery. In the public's mind, Denny became the symbol of a new recombining of sex with life and love. In Denny's own mind, he finally became a productive and worthwhile person. The baby was a flawless girl, delivered by a modified Caesarian section.

Sex was never the same again.

THE PORTABLE LOWER EAST SIDE

463 WEST STREET NO. 344

NEW YORK, NEW YORK 10014

THE PORTABLE LOWER EAST SIDE

THE PORTABLE LOWER EAST SIDE is one of New York City's most socially committed literary magazine. During its four years of existence, THE PORTABLE LOWER EAST SIDE has consistently published the best in contemporary fiction, poetry and essays by such people as Grace Paley, Allen Ginsberg, Hubert Selby, Luisa Valenzuela, Edward Limonov, Margaret Randall, Hans Haacke, Pedro Pietri and many, many others. Which is why MOTHER JONES has described this publication as a "tremendously interesting concept combining urban history, prose, poetry, graphics," while LIBRARY JOURNAL has written, "The level of interest and talent is extremely high, and will appeal to almost any good reader."

If you subscribe now, you will receive our Summer 1989 issue containing work from:

Herbert Huncke
George Konrad
Lynne Tillman
Manuel Ramos Otero
Meena Alexander
Robert Frank
Allen Ginsberg
Marithelma Costa
Eduardo Mendoza

INDIVIDUALS
ONE YEAR/TWO ISSUES @ $12.
TWO YEARS/FOUR ISSUES @ $24.
INSTITUTIONS
ONE YEAR/TWO ISSUES @ $20.
TWO YEARS/FOUR ISSUES @ $40.

Back issues available:
LATIN AMERICANS IN NYC
EASTERN EUROPEANS IN NYC
$6. Per Copy

The next two short-shorts represent a case of synchronicity, almost as if they were written about the same real person. Both appeared in little zines, the first in Elaine Weschler's INSIDE JOKE, the second in MODERN STORIES, Lewis Shiner's excellent short-lived crazed-Texan semi-pro-zine. Neither have ever been reprinted.

Kerry Thornley (a.k.a. Ho Chi Zen) got into conspiracy theory because he knew Lee Harvey Oswald, and because sinister government agencies have afflicted him with long-range mind-control devices. He is one of the founders of Discordianism; Robert Anton Wilson and Bob Shea dedicated the ILLUMINATI! trilogy to him. Since the '60s he's been an Individualist Anarchist, freestyle mystic, wanderer, prophet of the Universal Rent & Tax Strike, publisher of zines and advocate of polymorphous pleasure.

Quent Wimpel Meets Bigfoot
Kerry Thornley

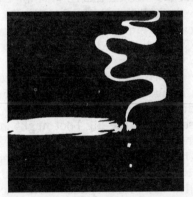

Wimpel's encounter with a Big Foot didn't change his theories about them — although he discarded forever his earlier hypothesis that they were Green Berets in gorilla costumes — but it gave him what was certain to be the most enviable of all hitch-hiking stories. Later the same summer that he failed so miserably to convince Jesse Sump of *any* of his conspiracy theories, as he traveled toward San Francisco in search of more open-minded audiences for his ideas, Wimpel became stranded long after midnight on a lonely mountain road.

Since his last driver was another freak, with good grass to share, Quent's backpack felt lighter than usual and chances were dismal of getting a ride on this desolate stretch, so he strode along in the darkness entertaining himself with the illusion — an optical and probably some-what psychedelic illusion — that he was perpetually walking off the side of a cliff. This was because the brim of a cowboy hat he found under a bridge in Winslow, Arizona on the way out here made a line in front of his eyes, where they met the asphalt in front of him, that looked exactly like the edge of a cliff in the moonlit night. So Quent got into the archetypal Fool of the Tarot character, eternally stepping into thin air, never falling — a game that did weird things to his sense of the passing of time. Consequently, he was not looking very far ahead in the direction he was going.

Had the lumbering critter not grunted Wimpel might have bumped into him, although it was of course startling enough as it was to look up and see a junior-sized King Kong standing in his way. Involuntarily Wimpel emitted an inarticulate sound of his own that the big monkey seemed to take as a word of greeting — for he held up for Quent to see a large, clear plastic bag of pot with a package of Zig-Zag rolling papers plainly visible amongst the weed. Then, to Quent's further astonishment, the giant creature seated himself on a rock and proceeded to quite skillfully roll himself a number. That was too much!

"Too much," said Quent. "Too much. Man you're outa sight!"

If the Big Foot understood this comment, he or she gave no sign — but just held up the rolled joint in the light of the moon, until it became obvious that Quent himself was expected to supply the match.

"Oh God," Quent mumbled, slipping off his backpack, "I hope I've *got* matches!"

Not that he needed to get any more stoned than he was, but already he was thinking about what a hitch-hiking story this would make, particularly if it didn't end at the beginning, with his own failure to produce a light — something the Big Foot might interpret as rejection and slink back into the woods.

So Quent Wimpel rummaged frantically until he found, to his relief, at the very bottom of his pack under his laundry bag, a worn and tattered matchbook that had probably been there since sometime in Louisiana or Oklahoma.

With a flourish he made a flame and held it up as the Big Foot touched it with the tip of the number and puffed, hoilding up his other hand — or paw — just like a human, to shield the fire from the slight breeze. Thereupon Quent seated himself on the ground — for the boulder wasn't big enough for both of them — and they passed the joint back and forth in a ceremony that was by now about half a century old and more common than ever: getting high together.

As for Quent's theories about Big Foots, they were — like all the rest of his notions — conspiracy theories. These monsters had not been prowling the Pacific Northwest since Indian times, although Indian legends probably had supplied the CIA–KGB conspiracy also responsible for flying saucers and weather manipulation with the idea. Of his own theory he was particularly convinced ever since reading an article by a Russian zoologist in an old issue of *Pursuit* magazine called

"Why Kill a Gentle Giant?" — arguing that scientists should not attempt to bag a Sasquatch for research purposes by shooting one. Since when had Marxists of any kind — and this professor was with an official government institute in Moscow or Leningrad — been squeamish about killing anyone in what they regarded as the name of science, be it zoology or scientific revolution? No, there was a reason the Communists didn't want anyone killing Big Feet — and Quent figured he could guess as to what it was.

"Dig," he said to his companion, making shoveling motions with his hands. "Back in the mountains," Quent pointed. "They dig. Make tunnels into ground." Wimpel held up both hands in a circular configuration. "They make tunnels, dig tunnels down along fault line. Then make earthquakes." Quent shook himself back and forth. "They keep you near excavations." Wimpel made a little pile of dirt between his shoes. "Then campers and hikers" — he stood up and grabbed a stick and tried to look like a hiker — "when they come near — they send you to distract them, to lure them away. No?" A visual method of describing distraction eluded him, however, and the communication was not entirely a success.

Or maybe the Big Foot was just trying to say he didn't want to talk about it, for he looked away from Quent and waved his hand in the air at him — back and forth — as if to ward off any discussion of what may have, after all, been a sensitive matter involving security about which no speaking was authorized.

"People say I look like Karl Marx," Wimpel said feebly, attempting conciliation. Then without thinking he interlocked his fingers in the secret sign for dialectical materialism — the merging of thesis and antithesis — that he had developed in his communications with The Conspiracy.

Making a click with his tongue to indicate understanding, the Big Foot then signaled to Quent in the same code system that he would rather discuss Hegel than Marx. And so that's what happened the rest of the night, until the first rays of dawn — they walked along the road together, occasionally pausing to share another joint, discussing Hegel in Quent Wimpel's sign language.

With the lighting of the sky they also came upon the first signs of civilization — a little mountain town nestled in a hollow — and Big Foot waved farewell to Quent and slipped off silently into the vast forest.

So Quent's whole day was filled with anticipation of his arrival in the San Francisco Bay Area, where he would gather with other travelers and street people and relate what certainly must be the greatest hitchhiking story of all time.

In Earth Peoples' Park in Berkeley, in the evening of the next day, he found just such a collection of wanderers and runaways — and at the first lull in the conversation, Wimpel said, "Like, you'll never guess what happened to me the other day..." What followed was a much longer story than is related here because, although he did not exaggerate, he missed no opportunity to weave in all his conspiracy theories. "So, you see, I figure they take gorillas and give them pituitary injections so that they grow into giants. And at the base of their skulls are concealed what they call subcutaneous brainwave generators — thought-control devices — so that the big guy I was talking to was actually being controlled by a Russian scientist in a laboratory under the ground. Because, you see, that's what the Big Foots are for — to distract hikers from excavation sites. These Russians are burrowing along the San Andreas fault, mining it with explosives, so as to artificially create earthquakes..."

At that point Wimpel was interrupted by another, an old Berkeley street character named Zap, who looked like an Indian holy man with lots of wild, bunched-up hair and had a way with women unrivaled since the days of Neal Casady. "Hell, that's nothing — a Big Foot with his own stash who likes to rap about Hegel. I met a female Big Foot last summer and we fucked."

All ears turned to Zap.

Wimpel wasn't even noticed as he wandered off toward Telegraph Avenue before Zap had finished telling his story. There were still a couple of blank pages in his notebook, "Pearls Before Swine," and if he could hustle up another nickel Quent could afford coffee.

СемИоТеШТ(е) НеШТ(е)
[Semiotext(e) Next(e)]

Coca-Cola

it's the real thing

Lenin

KAZIMIR PASSION GROUP

ЫЩЦМШУЕУЧЕ(У)

[Sovietext(e)]

Special Issue on
and by Soviet
Cultural Laborers

William Gibson belongs to an entirely different generation from *Thornley*, whose preceding short-short this one so curiously resembles. Gibson has sometimes been described as the prototype Cyberpunk. NEUROMANCER, his first novel, won the Hugo, the Nebula and the P. K. Dick Award in 1985; COUNT ZERO, his next novel, also took place in a world of burnt-out computer hacks and designer-drug addicts; most recently, MONA LISA OVERDRIVE completes the loosely-connected cyberpunk trilogy. He has also published a wonderful short story collection, BURNING CHROME; one wonders why "Hippie Hat Brain Parasite" was excluded from it, but one is not complaining.

At one point we were thinking of calling this anthology BAD BRAINS... this story would have set the tone for the whole volume.

Hippie Hat
Brain Parasite
William Gibson

"Bill," Kihn says, his voice all too clear, that unreal clarity of early AM longdistance commsat voices speaking from the void or maybe Cleveland, "I've *seen* one." And something about the practiced intensity of the spoken-word italics he brings to that *seen* triggers a memory-hologram, Mervyn Kihn in his patented Chas. Fort Hawaiian shirt, a screaming sail of lurid Taiwanese nylon ablaze with frog-storms, spontaneous human combustees, Lubbock lights, New Jersey mothmen, and a doomed wing of U.S. Navy torpedo bombers about to vanish forever into the Bermuda Triangle.

"Wait a minute, Merv. Where was it you said you were calling from?" It's collect, natch.

A pause, "Night falls," he intones.

"*What?*"

"Knight Falls," and he spells it out, "Ohio."

"Okay... Now what was it you were saying you'd seen?"

"Ah... Look... You've seen 'em yourself. Plenty. Wide stiff brim, high crown, cut out of a sheet of Tandy cowhide and laced together like a *Boy's Life* project. Get the picture?"

"Those hats? Kind of Waylon Jennings *cum* L.A. pimp culture hats? Well, I can't say I've seen one *lately*, man."

"Right! And it's too *cold* for the motherfuckers, up there, that's why! Add that to the evidence!"

"What evidence, Merv? What motherfuckers?"

"*Parasites,*" he whispers, "*alien fucking parasites...*"

Mervyn Kihn, Gonzo Fortean, author of nine paperback assemblies of Damned Things too unspeakably singular to warrant the attention of even the most depraved assemblers of modern apocrypha. The menstruating Barbie Dolls of Lone Butte. Luminous phantom Dachshunds, sighted flying in tight formation over Berlin, August '58. The Monopoly board unearthed in Crete and subsequently suppressed by Greek authorities. The bizarre case of Ruth Edith Fishleigh, the Birmingham psychic, found drowned in a Toyota full of Dr. Pepper...

"The Haight, that was the locus. That must have been where they landed. Maybe just one. Maybe just a spore. But I've definitely traced them to Frisco circa '68. Leather shops all over."

"Uh, wait a minute, Merv, I, uh..."

"Listen. This is *crucial*, man. You think those things are just, like, some stupid kinda hat, right? Maybe *the* stupid kinda hat, and that's fucking brilliant. Last thing *you'd* be caught wearing, right? And it's people like you who pose the greatest threat, people with open minds, people who read my books. But I've finally *seen* one, man, and I *know*."

"How do you mean, *seen*?"

"Off. I saw one off. I was in Taos last week. Wave of mutilation cases. Totally unconnected."

"Cattle?"

"Rosicrucians."

"Jesus..."

"Not people, man, magazines. Someone's been clipping all of the coupons out of magazines, all those AMORC ads. You know, in the back of *Popular Mechanics*... But I was there, see, and I went into this coffee shop, and there's this guy wearing one of those hats. So I'm sitting there, trying to work up a new angle on the Rosicrucian caper, and I notice this guy's, sorta, like, nodding out, you know? Not drinking his coffee, and it's not so much like he's falling asleep, more like he's having a kind of very slow seizure of some kind. Kinda twitching and blinking, but all in slow motion. So we're alone in the place, except for the waitress, and I say, 'Hey buddy, you okay?' and he doesn't answer. They must've spread out from Haight-Ashbury, see, and now they're in these weird pocket areas of Sixties hipcult holdouts. You get some of these dudes in off the commune, man, they look pretty zombied-out anyway. Perfect. Perfect cover. Like stick insects. Ever see a horseshoe crab?"

"Sort of helmet-shaped thing with a long spike for a tail?"

"Got it. Well, you imagine one of those, but no tail. Instead it's got this sort of stiff skirt, this *membrane*, sticking out all around it, and the helmet part's just the right size."

"The right size for what?"

"So I'm watching this guy, see, and he's right out of it, and I'm getting kinda worried. 'Hey,' I say to the waitress, 'is this guy okay?' She just pops her gum and shrugs. It's that kinda place. Then he picks up his coffee, raises it to his mouth, and pours some into his lap, meanwhile making these *lip-motions* and *swallowing*. Well, right then, I got the *vibe*, man..." He falls silent. I listen to ten seconds of expensive static.

"What vibe, Merv?"

"The Unknown. Once again, I found myself confronted with the Unknown. It just *happens* to me. I'm *attuned*."

"Got you. Right. So, there you are, you're *attuned*, and...?"

"Very slowly, like very slowly, he lowers the cup. And then he starts to fall forward. It was an *old* one, see, or maybe sick. But it's so slow, it doesn't look like he's falling, actually. Like he's very gradually *leaning* toward the counter... I don't figure, like, they're sold in stores, you know? You see one in a store, it's just a hat. Kinda like if stick insects talked people into manufacturing *sticks*, sort of. Weird variant on the mimetic trip, but we're talking *alien*, right? What they probably do, they probably *crawl* around on those Godawful little legs. Up wells. In windows. Some guy's wasted on his R. Crumb sofa, TV on, the bong near at hand, and he doesn't hear the *hat*..."

"Legs. You said *legs*?"

"Maybe a dozen, more. Kinda browny transparent. Ever see a scorpion that's gotten too big? They get kinda pale and waxy. Like that. Anyway, there I am, belly to belly with the Unknown in this Taos coffee shop, and this guy's getting closer to the edge of the counter. Like he's toppling over, but he hasn't heard about gravity. I hold my breath."

I hold mine.

"His chest touches the counter. Bip. Then it happened."

"Okay. What? Happened?

"His hat fell off. Fell on the counter, I got a good look at the legs, the mouth parts. No eyes. Then I was off that stool like I'd had a cattleprod rammed up my ass. 'Cause he'd flopped off his stool, man, and he was *dead*. Or something like it. No *brain*. No top to his *head*. Just neatly nibbled off at the... hatline. Kinda *scarred*, in there, healed over, grayish-pink. I saw where the hat had had its claws in, kinda puppet trip..."

"Merv. What about the waitress, Merv?"

"She said, 'Have a nice day.' She was, you know, just real mellow. Didn't seem to notice anything."

I close my eyes, tight. "Merv, why did you call? I mean, why *me*?"

"You write about stuff like that."

"Right. And what about the Rosicrucian coupon-mutilators?"

"Moonies… it's a takeover bid. Every Moonie in the United States joined the Rosicrucians last month. But you're hip to the infiltration trip the CIA's been running on Scientology, right? Same deal. The hot item there's that it was the *Disney* people who had Hubbard snuffed in Akron in '71. What they've got in there now is an advanced Animatronics dummy. Because, natch, they wanted L. Ron's cryogenics lab for what's left of Walt…"

"Thanks, Merv."

"Hey, no sweat. We're pals. I'll keep you posted, baby. And for Christ's sake, stay out of those *headshops*, right?"

"Goodnight, Merv."

"Morning. It's morning here already."

Clik.

Sol Yurick is probably best known to SF buffs as the author of a book which became a movie—"The Warriors"—loosely based on Xenophon's ANABASIS, set in a near-future New York where gangs of delinquent youth are attempting to spark off a revolution. Sol was disgusted with the quality of the adaptation, but the film achieved notoriety by "causing" several "riots" in movie theaters around the country... so perhaps some of the book's message survived. With all his erudition and wit, Yurick is—after all—a rabble rouser.

He is known to SEMIOTEXT(E) fans as author of one of our little black "Foreign Agents" books—METATRON: THE RECORDING ANGEL—which (like his story here) concerns computers. His most recent and forthcoming novel is called THE KING OF MALAPUTA.

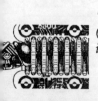

The Great Escape
Sol Yurick

But in the meantime, what was happening to Julius Finsterlicht? He was off on yet another terrifying adventure. He overheard a conversation. Someone was planning to kill him—*really kill him*. This was not just another tape. How was he going to get out of this fix?

You will remember that when we last left him, he was on the verge of giving up and dying. His will had been failing. Emerging from a dreamtime coma he said to himself, "Alright already. Accept." Or was it merely a dream of dying? Terrible thing, to die in your sleep. Cold, endless cold, below the threshold of shivering, the kind that tells you all the stars in the universe are going out, down to the bone level, deeper, a congealing of his energy-converting mitochondria, cold filled his body. Then some last, inner spark of life fired back, alerting and saving him. A premonition-shot in the arm, spreading to wake his auto-immune, will-to-life system (which was in Jerusalem).

Warning nightmare. Phase-shift, transform and trumpet peal (perfect hormonics), quantum leaps out of dream time to one's-self real-time, waking Finsterlicht from his imprisoned, ancient, about-to-die body... You know how it is when you wake up. Your dream's too vivid... you don't know where you are... it's late afternoon and you think it's dawn... it's dawn and you think it's an evening, many years ago... wake to find you're dying in the middle of youth. What happened to all the years in between? How did I get here, you ask? Had he summoned up a reminiscence, or was it a scene from an old movie? Brain lesion? Never know.

He refused to die. He should escape. The only danger was that he might have a heart attack. He was immobilized, too old, weak, tied hand to foot. His heart and brain and organs were in Jerusalem receiving medications and sustenance through a Gerontomat. His feet were chained here, his eyes riveted to a machine in Minneapolis grinding out soap operas, cop stories, adventure tales, situation comedies, sagas in which everything always came out all right in the end. Houdini had nothing on him.

Perhaps he should play dead. Way to live. Once officially dead, who would look for him? he sensed a shadow. He turned his head, or thought of turning his head. Someone rotated outside the line of his peripheral vision. Who?

Remembered. Ah! Got it! Himself! Julius Finsterlicht, old man filed away in the Bonheur Retirement Environment in... Where? Have it on the tip of the tongue. Random search. Yes. Laguna Beach.

His body began to make remarkable recoveries. Later, Bonheur's nursing technicians, rereading the record's tale, put it down to the Gerontomat's powerful, life-preserving properties.

Finsterlicht received nutrients intravenously and intraneuroni-cally, so to speak: psycho-and-soma-therapy. He lay on his side, a smile on his toothless face (What did he need teeth for? The feed was liquid, but he *felt* teeth and *remembered* chewing and the memory moved his mouth), his head propped up on his hand, trailing wires, tubes and glory in and out of every orifice, some of which he had not been born with. He stared at two sets of visions: one, a banal and windowless, pictureless room; the other, bypassing his actual eyes and ears, pumping entertainment directly into his optic and auditory nerves.

But instead of diverting and entertaining him away from possibly approaching death, he realized he had dreamed, or had been made to foretell his own death, but in the form of a dangerous adventure story. Unconscious intimations or mortality in tranquilized recollection. It terrified him enough to set him, an ancient and feeble man, ninety-five if he was a day, thrashing to find a way out and live forever.

At one end was Finsterlicht; at the other end was Meditech Teletherp Life Systems, Inc. In between was the Gerontomat, its wires, sensors, scanners (CAT, Nuclear Magnetic Resonance, thermograms, EEGs, EKGs, Brain scintillation detectors, and many more...), long and short lines, wire and optical fibers and beams, and the transponders that made the responders go. All of Finsterlicht's constantly monitored life-signs were reported in real time to Meditech. Every flicker, motion, pulse, emotion, every bowel rumbling and twitch, every sign of microcancerous growth, every cell's lysosome, all was recorded by the Gerontomat (and appropriately charged for), relayed to various service centers in all parts of the world, including the one which contained his historico-medical case record, tenuconnected by swift-as-light radio beamnerves to Jerusalem. And if the totality of signs denoting Finsterlicht's inner and outer boundaries were ever imaged (for those addicted to older, grosser, analogical presentations), the picture would look very strange indeed.

Bonheur, one of a chain of retirement homes, subscribed to Meditech's services. Meditech was a world-wide bio-med diagnostic and treatment center, itself part of a greater life-services and life-experimentation complex, part of a multiplex that included banks, weapons manufacturers, agribusiness, shipping, mining, insurance, brokerages of every variety... Meditech was in everything life-enhancing: genetic therapy, industrial microbiology, extra-uterine reproduction, pharmaceuticals, administrative and housekeeping medical technologies (accounting, receivables, billing, deceivables, LIFO), preventive medicine, neurotransmitters, bioweaponry... Being part of a conglomerate, itself partly self-owned and owning parts of enterprises which owned parts of it, Meditech's own health was subject to the vicissitudes of the marketplace. Merger and divestiture storms disturbed its stability.

Jerusalem's Meditech facility serviced a city of clients, a diasporated (however close the simulations) senilopolis of the aged, diseased, neurotic, psychotic... A city? No, a nation. Each denizen was apartmented from every other dweller, yet linked together by a master system of life-delivering programs and a master registry to interconnecting channels.

Among them was Finsterlicht's simulacrum, a concentrated essence. It was called as-he-should-have been-Finsterlicht, like-Finsterlicht, or, more properly, vFinsterlicht (virtual-Finsterlicht), imaged as a vigorous man, average health, years-younger-looking than he really was. The run of biometrical numbers was complicated, standing, as they did, for everything imaginable about him, even nerve bundles, hormone ducts, blood vessel networks, bio-topological structures arranged (in non-anatomical logical form, splayed apart on a number of disk storages for convenience... too long to read, expensive to retrieve, classified to divulge, available only to experts, certainly not to patients with a penchant for holding up the mirror to one's own nature.

And what Finsterlicht felt was transmitted to the medical portrait, vFinsterlicht. Having received this transmitted, tragic message, the simulacrum aligned itself to ailing Julius on the one hand and a perfect health projection on the other hand, and cured that tragedy, sending a health adjustment back into the fleshly Finsterlicht. Sometimes it was not clear if vFinsterlicht responded to the comparison with Finsterlicht, or vice versa.

The appropriate subsidiaries all over the world, cued to the patient's danger signs, sent proper responses, the news, the therapy, the proper entertainment, back to Bonheur's local terminal processor. In turn Bonheur's treatment center's personnel, seated at their therapy consoles, watching screens and dials, were trained to stroke the right keys, providing life-preserving treatment. Chemicals, synthesized human exhudates, sexual stimulation and destimulation, radio frequency treatment (which mimicked the real thing) were delivered. Radio therapy was based on the theory that human flesh was a congealed electromagnetic wave, a soft crystal composed of a multiplex of frequencies... each organ, each organelle, each protein, nucleotide having its own little rhythm, the whole body being a tune of tunes, a meta-song, a Found Chord, harmonic of the as-yet-uncomputed music of the spheres.... The body is a transmitter; it broadcasts electromagnetic waves (weakly) and receives them. Especially sensitive at night: nocturnal transmissions. In time all cure would be frequency-therapy, which could be delivered anywhere via wire or broadcast and which would render obsolete all hypodermics, pills, syrups, elixirs, serums, capsules, scalpels...

In addition to all this, readings of the patient's progress or regression were fed into another auto-registering comparator... matching Meditech and Bonheur (and a host of other data bases, including banks), to constantly bring Finsterlicht into synch with vFinsterlicht, for there's more to health than health.

Finsterlicht's guardians were the ones (Who else could have consigned him here? He couldn't remember) who must have contracted for Bonheur or Meditech, because they were cheaper, and because of Israel's Law of Return, which offered a discount rate to those who came back to Jerusalem, even electronically.

The Gerontomat also received (and responded to the desire for) entertainment to offset boredom: movies, video, music, conversations became part of the patient's life. Real-life dramas were rented from an organization called Cryspal (Crystal Palace Productions), based in Minneapolis. The entertainment and medical life-state signals were correlated and mixed in a way that generated the proper stimuli to all organs, so that entertainment was not only viewed passively, but was also *felt* at the same time as a lived and participated-in life—actuality therapy. Drama, comedy, epics, *stories* create affective visceral, hormonal and neuronic changes—according to some evidence, even generate genetic mutations, at least on a temporary basis—and those signals, once gone through the patient's body and assimilated, were in turn fed back to

Meditech. By putting Finsterlicht in an action or porno movie, he was exercised. But Finsterlicht had learned that by twitching his muscles, or by fantasizing, he could manipulate, at least minimally, the Gerontomat, which in turn summoned the entertainment from Cryspal...

When patients were first fused up with the Gerontomat, the entertainment feed was slow, but it gradually sped up so that the senior citizen experienced a rich, full, action dream and drama packed life, more events in any given hour than most people lived. The patient could ingest up to seven diverse shows simultaneously. It compensated for dreary lives, and if they went, they had a chance of dying of excitement, going out with a bang. Older admittees often spent a short time in Bonheur, but they felt as if they had existed for thousands of years. Finsterlicht had been here a three-thousand-year-long month.

But there was a problem. Fiction fused with fact. The patients soon had difficulty separating their own real, lived lives from the input of not-lived lives. If asked how they were feeling, the patients might talk about how someone else was feeling.

There were other troubles. A host of unintended signals leaked into every relay point and in turn these accidentally seeped into Finsterlicht, mixed in with nutrients and nostrums... a constant bombardment of noise, imperfectly filtered out. Some of the signals were generated by imperfect transform operations, microminiscule errors in programming, faulty welds, hasty language design, microdust present at the etching of circuits, lost data in conversion from digital to analog, from picture to dream. There were also signal interferences from a sky overgarbaged with satellites, endemic defects in message routing and switching equipment, nano-crashes due to machines that had been put on the market too soon.... And in addition, because of the interlinking of patched-together networks of different equipment and different competitive manufacture which had come on-line at different times, jury-rigged protocols competing with ever-more-complex access and entry codes, even natural conditions—like rain attenuation of signals, desert distortion—interfering harmonics, overuse of overcrowded and fought-over channels (traffic jams... electro-gridlock), skip phenomena, magno-space warps, new medical discoveries requiring new programs and new machines... all these contributed to these small changes in Finsterlicht and vFinsterlicht. And if there were more and more error-detecting and error-correcting codes, this was matched by error-generating codes.

Additional noise poured in, traffic designed for other ears/eyes, such as evangelical messages, heavy metal punk disco rock dialed up by others, talk shows, NSA traffic, secret user-access codes (which opened up gateways into encrypted data bases intercorporealated with other peoples' genetic-identity code-sequences), which led to things, treasures, combinations, secret lists of where all the bodies were buried... packets kept in constant transit from terminal to terminal (a sort of mobile repository to prevent pilferage)... All came flowing into Finsterlicht.

Finsterlicht did not receive these upsetting and aberrant, noise and entertainment input feeds as words, strings of numbers or letters, or gene-sequences, or lists of securities... If he had gotten these encryptions in pure machine language, he wouldn't have known how to use them, not consciously, for he had grown up in a different sort of time. *All* messages were *metabolized* directly into Finsterlicht's long and short-term memory. They became discomforts, pains, twitches, bowel loosenings, constipations, orgasms, dreams and visions, a thousand mini-deaths, rescues and rebirths. Below the level of consciousness, the body *sensed* and *knew*.

These sometimes came back out of his body to his mind as string-pantheons of gods and goddesses, strange and wonderful composite beasts: griffins, slime-lions, fiery amoeba tigers, fanged life-juice suckers, winged dragons, black centipedes with myriad legs and myriad hooded heads, undulating, changing, bearing candles to worship an arcane deity, a sweet-faced, full-breasted woman with a queen-ant's body.

On this particular pick-an-afternoon, Finsterlicht was more than a little bored. To be bored was to be close to stasis, and stasis was like death. Danger kept you alive. That was it. He had been sinking when they had sent him a danger-dream to keep him alert and alive.

"How much longer?"

"Quite soon now."

"It's been a fuckin' month now."

"He's quite remarkable. No one lasts longer than three weeks."

"Pull the plug."

"We don't do things quite that way. A little patience..."

"This little patient is trying our patience. What are we paying you for? We have a contract..."

"There may be a way of hastening nature's course..."

Finsterlicht had lived a long and adventure-filled life... but then again, maybe he hadn't. His memory was confounded. As a boy of fourteen he had run away from his squalid home, crossed the ocean, made his way to America, to make and lose fortunes. He had been a laborer, a farmer, a miner, a union organizer, a seaman, a cowboy, a financier, a chairman of the board of a gigantic, continent-spanning corporation, a lawyer, a high-steel worker, a drug dealer, a politician, a cop, a wildcat banker, a stand-up comic, a lumberjack, a storekeeper, a pushcart peddler, a novelist, a poet, an actor, a bureaucrat, a whore-house pianist, a stud; he had been a hired killer, a mercenary; and he had—at the end of his life, having gained much wisdom—been a *consigliere* (or rabbi) for various gangster enterprises. He had made, lost, and remade fortunes, some of which he had saved and secreted in anonymous, numbered accounts. He had loved a thousand women—ah, the beauties he had fucked—and sired fifteen thousand children. Dynasties he had founded, whole principalities, nations. He had suffered much, of course, but then he was tough. A survivor. But... had he lived those lives, or just seen them?

He had just been not-quite killed. He was still in the balance, on the hook. What had gotten into him and was hiding there? A gothic story his body couldn't shake off? Were characters from an old and poorly digested life threatening him? Was it something he had done, or something someone else had done or something he was to do in the future? Why was the Gerontomat feeding him this excitement? He was an old man. He needed his rest. His heart was palpitating, his head throbbing. Death was hunting him through the channels and circuits, opening two hundred and thirty one switches to kill him by remote control. Why?

His feeble voice cracked; the croak reached all the way to Meditech in Jerusalem. vFinsterlicht compensated, cancelling positives with negatives, negatives with positives. vFinsterlicht's data, now distorted, drooping, wilting, altered the program which began to send diseased-body-simulated messages to antibody-producing centers (and checking to see if Finsterlicht's accounts could afford the treatment)—in Germany, in Russia (fortunately the lines were clear), in the U.S.—which activated the instructions to produce customized balms, unguents, cortisones, cochisines, steroids, artificial natural opiates, transmitted back to Bonheur, which manufactured the medicines (on license), mixing them right there on the premises. A pleasant hum suffused his whole being. He was downed gently. Time slowed. But, nevertheless, he knew his reprieve was temporary.

Old as he was, the feeling of terror didn't weaken with age. He cursed whatever was doing this to him. He shut his eyes, but what did closed eyes mean to images that infiltrated him in a hundred different ways? He was getting excited by what he'd seen and done. Done? What had he really done? Someone was agitating him and he knew that if he didn't calm down, he would surely die. He could feel his perpetually sheathed penis, caught in its electronic vagina, hardening, growing, in spite of his age. The power of a god's prick tied to an old man's body. He would explode, ejaculating himself as a jet of blood and ground-up flesh and thought. Remote-control murder? What clues would his record show?

He needed help. Who had placed him in this expensive nursing facility? An enemy, that's who. He must have made many enemies in his thousand-times-the-average life. The Mafia, the Triads, the shadowy Masonic lodges, the CIA, MI5/6, the Nazis, the KGB, the military-industrial complex, the Kennedy Family, the... Which one? He couldn't remember. He couldn't even get his hands on his own money. A legend cashed in for gold. Sunset of an adventurous life, and he didn't even have the strength to disconnect himself and walk out. They were after his distributed and diversified cache of accounts. What could he do? Call the police? How?

He pressed a button, summoning an attendant. After a long while, an attendant came. A real human being. Couldn't be more than sixteen. That was the kind of help you got these days. She was bored, annoyed, without imagination, without compassion, resentful at being torn away from whatever she was doing... watching dials, or television, or more likely fucking. Her eyes were blank and pitiless. She was drugged. Beautiful, cold, virginal, whorish, implacable, regal, compassionate and cheap. Could she get him out of this hell? Be charming. Remember your triumphs, he told himself. Thousands, he had seduced thousands. Women had always helped him; women would get him out of this. Control yourself, you horny *schmuck*. The young hated the old these days. It was as if you were breathing their air. "What did I ever do to you," he thought at her.

"What's your name, sweetheart?"

"Reyna."

"I want to leave," he told her. His vocalization reflexes went to Jerusalem, and his voice came back out of a speaker beside his bed.

"You want to leave," she said, as if not understanding. "Go on, who's stopping you?"

"Disconnect me, please."

She smiled, saintly and comforting, gentle and forgiving... in white, a nurse, a mother, pure... she would save him. But she had color-striated, grease-teased hair, standing up like the spiky claws of a Venus flytrap. "Who're you fucking now, Marilyn Monroe? How'd you like a real cunt instead of sucking on that electronic pussy? I'll help you if you leave me something in your will."

"I don't have anything right now, but when I get out..."

"Who're you shitting? I looked up your record. Come on..." she said, hoisting her skirt up. "Look. It's the real thing." She wore black stockings, black garter belt, but no panties; black hair on a plump, swelling, red-brown and moist mound; delicious folds of flesh. Her hands, lifting the skirt, had black, painted nails. She turned slowly, regally. Her behind... her behind... it was so white.... Julius grew excited. He could just die... Hold it! That's it. Death. They had sent an emissary. A real fuck would kill him.

Finsterlicht stared at an array of vaginas and couldn't sort out which was hers and which were projections. His ancient penis was fooled into fullness and longed to penetrate all of them... oh, to have a branched cock like a decision tree or a *menorah*... go in so many ways and so deep that his whole body would be inside her, surrounded by and hiding in her moist cave.

No. "I want to sign out."

"I'll talk to the supervisor," she said, shrugged and turned away.

A few hours later a young man, same kind of stare, came and told Finsterlicht, "You can't check out. You're too old, weak; you'd die in a second out there."

"That's my business. What do you mean I can't check out. I want to leave."

"I have to have your guardians' permission."

Guardians? He had guardians? His parents? Worse, his children? Was he a child who dreamed he was an old man? An old man who dreamed he was as helpless as an infant?

"Guardians?"

"Sure. Once they settle up, you're as free as the wind."

"Settle up?"

"Your account is behind. Hasn't been paid in months. You owe Bonheur."

It must be a lie. That was it. That was why they wanted to kill him. His savings. Everyone was trying to discover where he had salted away his loot. Scattered all over the world in a thousand numbered, discretionary accounts. They wanted to rob him. Who? Who else? His relatives. His children. Fifteen thousand of them... the terminal horde in collusion with Meditech and Bonheur... Never leave it to them. "So kick me out in the cold."

"Cold, in California?" He gave Finsterlicht one of those "you're getting senile" looks. "Can't."

"Why not?"

The young man yawned and turned away. He turned back and said, "By the way, stop making obscene suggestions to our help. You have enough to keep your pecker occupied."

That was that. A plot. Despair. Wait for death. Couldn't escape.

But if his mind accepted, Finsterlicht's body did not. It began to conceive, nurture and parturate a daring escape plan. His money (or what he admitted to owning) was tied up in many financial computers' memory vaults. If he could get to it, convert that memory into real money, he could buy his way out. Or, better even, buy the nursing home and free himself. How many more like him were imprisoned in Meditech's banks. Free them all. How? The confidence game. Will. Backfeed his will into the wires, the nutrient tubes to the computers that ran them. Will was a signal, a strong living thing dominating man or machine, an emanation of seduction, an emotive force-field, broadcast to open, closed and hostile minds, a woman's legs, a banker's heart, circuits... To get *through* the Gerontomat— the only bridge between him and the outside—he would have to string himself out.... Once out...no telling where the lines led from Meditech.

But what does Finsterlicht know from ciphers and cryptograms and computer codes? Nothing. What does he know from number-*gematria* (aside from money—profit and loss—which he understands perfectly, a numbered account is life itself), which permutates magic into life-giving? Nothing.

He didn't have to understand machine language, assembly, C,

LISP, ADA, Fortran. *His body did!* What teams of software scribes had taken years to write, his body had learned, on a molecular level, in two cycles of a Cray's clock-pulse.

Finsterlicht's plugged-in body rediscovered the old meditation-magic of the yogis; skin temperature and muscle control... twitch... fibrillation... pulsation... escape-desire signals. His emotions, his unconscious imagination did all that for him, just as if he was seated at a keyboard, transposing agitated keystrokes into machine language. Hadn't his body digested much accidental code-wisdom? Passwords; pathwork; names; significant identity gene patterns; investment portfolios.

Search. His body knew it all. If he had stopped to consciously think it through, he couldn't have done it.

Finsterlicht's body english began to do the same thing computer hackers did. His mnemotechnics activated, probed into a repository of images of escapes from inescapable situations: from castles, prisons, dungeons, cages, trunks, slave ships, lines of beaters, *vernichtungslagers*, mazes, tombs, life, paradoxes, puzzles, kleinbottles, assassins, chains, thug-gangs, carpet-bombings, hellfires, walking barrages, ubiquitous toxic miasmas, nuclear devastation, flights of poisoned darts, disease, aging, myrmidons of killer bees, cannibals, stomachs, hordes, plagues, embedding in thighs, heads, caves... Hairbreadth escapes... action videotapes... By twitching his muscles and remembering all the escape modes, he felt like he was running, jumping, tricking, dodging, changing his shape... He sought to squirm, crawl, run, fight, cajole his way out through tunnels, buffers, wells, busses, sewers, pipes, thorn forests, run along beams of microwaves, crash through ports and gates, lattices, pretending to be invisible, or someone else, or dead (immortal).

His agitation to escape began to signal through Bonheur's Gerontomat to Meditech. The wave of Finsterlicht's terror was modulated into a set of impulses; emotions demodulated into digital encodings sent via telephone wires to Los Angeles, thence to a microwave tower, relayed to an antenna farm, uplinked to a medical satellite, downlinked again on America's East Coast, thrown up to a mid-Atlantic satellite, coming down to rest in Jerusalem's antenna, sitting on the roof of Meditech, converted finally to code for an angst, a fright, a pain in vFinsterlicht.

Sensors read him and couldn't differentiate between body and nerve impulses, from what had been input to him and what he was feeding back. Subsidiary life-support messages were relayed to Cryspal: an injunction to supply movies, dramas, great sporting events... Take his mind off things. Adventures in which he imagined he starred. His feedback to Cryspal altered and permanently ruined beloved tales. (*High Noon* was never the same again: in the new version, the sheriff's wife shoots him in the back. In the new *Crime and Punishment*, Raskolnikov takes the pawnbroker's money, moves to Paris and never looks back.)

Calming, sedative stories were automatically selected for him. A psychedelic overlay accompanied it; fused magic and bleeding colors... a great, white, calming radiance. Don't be seduced; behind that radiance was death... or maybe immortality. Back and forth through the portals of the Gerontomat, analog waves and digital beepings came and went to vFinsterlicht. Once in Jerusalem (was it really Jerusalem? Finsterlicht looked around and didn't see a thing. Well, he could have summoned film clips. Or was Jerusalem only the name of a computer file?) he ran into unexpected trouble. The first gatekeeper was... himself!, vFinsterlicht, who was interested only in maintaining a smug homeostasis. The conversation took place far below the level of human language.

"Get away. You're an infection, a positive cancer. You're making me sick. Ugh." vFinsterlicht said.

"Are you going to spend the rest of eternity in this... what is this, a womb?"

"A womb? At my age? A womb? It's paradise."

"A tomb."

"Womb. Tomb. Get away from me. What are you talking about, you crazy old man."

"If I'm old, what are you? Not old?"

"Look at me. Fit. I look fifty, if a day..."

"You owe that to me, lifesucker," Finsterlicht said. "My age and sickness keep you young."

"So what do you want?"

"Riches. You and me; me in you and you in me, we can escape. Who stuck you here? You never see the light of day. We can live forever," Finsterlicht said.

Still, vFinsterlicht refused to let him pass.

A rejection? Danger? Was their talk even compatible? Would there be a backtracking search to find the unauthorized prober? Would vFinsterlicht live after he died? And he realized: there must be a sacrifice. vFinsterlicht had to die. Finsterlicht said, "What do you think happens to you if I die? Poof, you're erased. You die too..."

vFinsterlicht said, "I don't believe it."

"What do they need you once I go? Answer me that."

vFinsterlicht got anxious... Julius could feel that in his body from 7,000 miles away.

"Money gets us immortality. Do you want to live forever?"

"Everyone does, but... "

"So what are you afraid of? Listen, you're not only a person but you're a gateway..."

"That sounds too mystical for me," vFinsterlicht said.

"Mystical? I'm being practical." And to augment the force of his offer, he made a *mudra*-sign, thumb rubbing against first and second fingers held close together: the universal, ceremonial sign for money. Added a wink. "You got a vested interest in my being alive..."

"I keep you alive..."

"Sure, but you got to do more..."

"What?"

"Make the sign like I do and see where it takes us," Finsterlicht said. Finsterlicht thought: paintings, money, gold, money, drugs, money, fuel, money, "beautiful girls," money... "Together now."

The gesture was transmitted and the pixels were reversed into signals, diagnosed and searched for through a bank of cerebral and musculature images. The signal was interpreted as an imbalance. A sign of danger. More medication was prescribed. A menu of diagnostic and remedial procedures. He increased his anguish. vFinsterlicht's body was very uncomfortable now. Auxiliary memory was called up. A treasury of drugs. Emergency. Meditech's computers scanned medical histories (and kept a running record of charges per mini-operation) and its accounts, to see if Finsterlicht could pay.

The mainframe began to do the hacking for the machine that does the healthkeeping for Finsterlicht and vFinsterlicht, testing out the encryption permutations. Think money the right way and more circuits open. Reached and grabbed operating systems, and each operation in all the spectrum of life services. Each code entered each base to search where Finsterlicht's money was, finding each account's address, one by one, fast, fast, fast, and Finsterlicht's body learned them. Account after account began to spill out, and each one was another step toward escape, opening each niche and cavern and bubble protected by its access code, the whole *schmear*, the names of other patients, the doctors and the technicians and their accounts and the disbursements for supplies and the account that paid for the electricity and the account that shelled out for communication lines and the accounts that disbursed dividends to shareholders and the true names of the banks where they put their deposits and the enterprises those banks did business with... Pandemod. Cividei. *Banco Spirito del Valore e Lavore*. The Fed. The *Salzburger Kredit Aufhebung*. The IMF. *Roichi Ginko. Ambrosiano.* Citicorp. Manny Hanny. *Sumitomo.* Chemical. BankAmerica. BIS. Institute for Religious Works. *Dresdener...* many more.

The heavy problem-solving transubstantiated into thought and body of Finsterlicht. The scintillation detector keeping an eye on the blood bearing radioactive tracer running through Finsterlicht's brain turned each pixel from black to blue to red or yellow, then white. Global activation; the whole brain working on the problem now. That, or else he was having a brainstorm, like a great sexual discharge, an orgasm which was not ejaculated outward by his penis but inward and upward through his chakric parabody, mounting step by step up the wire-nerve trunkline that leads to the representation of his brain, six levels, higher and higher.

High speed printers clattered; inkjets of cash began flowing. Accordion pleated, the endless sheet folded into bigger and bigger piles, building up into an enormous paper *stupa*. The morning's balances of trade and international settlements changed suddenly, surprising the markets. Finsterlicht began to climb through a lattice of languages. Colored clouds, nebulas in conflict, expanding universe bubbles and magnetic bottles containing plasmas in gorgeous technicolor; collapses into black holes appeared in gorgeous graphics suddenly on many monitors all over the world... like an incredible overdose of a very exotic drug... mainlining electronic power. He saw it now: mystic moment. His body shook uncontrollably. The matchup between Finsterlicht and his pan-medical portrait went out of synch. Finsterlicht was becoming a changed man. The Bonheur monitors crashed.

vFinsterlicht thrashed, crashed and died. At Meditech he read as dead.

Meditech was supposed to signal back to Bonheur so that the patient could be disconnected and the bill-settling could begin. But Meditech had put a few secret lines of microcode, a permanent program into each serviced patient, in effect trying to cheat Bonheur. The program interdicted the lines, diverting into a sub-routine geared for all Meditech patients who die. In case of death, move immediately to billing, while at the same time prevent non-Meditech services—Bonheur, Cryspal, etc.—from knowing the patient was dead... at least until Meditech had collected its debt first. This message was passed on to Bonheur and Cryspal, which continued to feed Finsterlicht's telemetry indicators as if he were still living.

But to Meditech's query: "Is the patient, Finsterlicht, paid up?" it received a reply: Finsterlicht was not paid up. What's more, his accounts were empty. Impossible. Who had cooked the books? And others began to die; Meditech's entire v-population. Their accounts were empty too. Meditech assembled another vFinsterlicht, II, out of its backup stock of stored Finsterlicht part-signs. They began to question II. Old vFII knew nothing. They began to torture him, but how could he know anything? He had been brought to life after Julius had fled.

There was a standoff, an immurement, a kind of glitch, in which all timers quivered. Finsterlicht, now a many of many names, who was somewhere between a living person and a living simulation, slipped through and eluded his pursuers... for the time being. Finsterlicht's will to live had made of himself a hystereisis chrysalis... enclosed in a sort of paradise... a place where no one would think of looking for him... an unnamed and irretrievable file.

As thin as a thirty gigaherz bandwidth, Finsterlicht's knowledge-being attenuated, came to a portal, broad-banded out from a stream-string into a golden shower and climbed up a tunnel to an unbearable light which metamorphosed into a paradisiacal island, untouched by man, in which the sky was ever blue and the sun always shone. A great shriek, as if from many women, or the sad crackle-dirge of read/write heads searching an emptiness on thousands of drives, came out of the cerulean blue. For a second he thought he saw someone turning to look at him. Their eyes met. But the person disappeared. Were they hunting for him? The Terminal Horde in hot pursuit? Finsterlicht was safe... at least for the time being. He was data and a program, a ghost and a spirit. How long would he last before he simply attenuated into nothing, or they found him? He would have to figure out a way to live, really live, and the only way was to build a new body he could inhabit and begin a new life again...

James Koehnline lives near Chicago and is a member of the Axe Street Arena art collective. He helped organize large and well-documented mail art shows like "Haymarket 1886 – 1986" and "BOLO'BOLO". Along with Hakim Bey and the West Coast sorceress Yael Dragwyla he hosted an Astral Convention in Antarctica, where many of the writers in this collection met for the first time.

His marbled papers and fine collages — which he produces by the thousands — are treasured by marginal connoisseurs. He also belongs to another conspiracy which intersects largely with this book, the Moorish Orthodox Church of America (editors Peter Lamborn Wilson and Jim Fleming, Philip José Farmer, Jacob Rabinowitz, Nick Herbert, and Hakim Bey are active clergy). Moreover, the M. O. C. is closely affiliated with Ivan Stang's SubGeniuses as well as Kerry Thornley and Robert Anton Wilson's Discordians, etc. Thus this anthology crystallizes a connection between SF and the quickly-growing phenomenon of the "Free Religions."

Koehnline's work follows here on the next two pages and on pages 175, 185, 191, 231, and 255.

Without J. G. Ballard, none of this would exist. We're weak on SF history, but we think it's fair to say that Ballard was among the first world-class writers (perhaps along with the Soviets) to realize that SF was no longer merely a pulp genre, but had become the only possible vehicle for a mythos of the modern world, that it had replaced the psychological novel as the central art-work of our culture.

Unfortunately, as any reader of the Sunday NY Times Book Review Section will testify, "Consensus Reality" has not yet caught up with Ballard's realization. As with William Burroughs, the official critics still feel uneasy about Ballard. And rightly so. For one thing, unlike certain literary figures such as D. Lessing and K. Vonnegut, he has never tried to deny the fact that he writes SF. For another thing, he likes to cause trouble.

Ballard (again like Burroughs) has contributed to Semiotext(e) several times in the past. We had in our files the "Report On An Unidentified Space Station," which appeared only in an English magazine (City Limits, December. 1982). When we wrote asking permission to use it, he generously wrote us another short-short. "I'm all in favor of shocking the bourgeoisie," he commented (and after all, it's the publisher who has to deal with libel suits, not the author; Ms. Fonda's lawyers can reach us at our editorial offices at Box 666, Rancho "La Cucaracha", Nogales 23, Mexico).

Ballard has finally achieved something like mainstream recognition with Spielberg's film adaptation of his semi-autobiographical Empire of the Sun. His most recent novel is Hello America (Carroll & Graf).

Jane Fonda's Augmentation Mammoplasty

J. G. Ballard

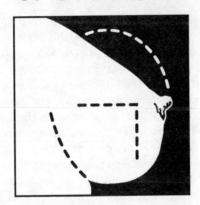

Her flat breasts had apparently become a source of great psychological anxiety to Jane Fonda. At a time in our civilization when vital measurements count for more than they should, Miss Fonda has sought help where previously she was content to camouflage her deformity by artificial means. The help that we could give to Miss Fonda consisted either of putting in an artificial prosthesis beneath the breast tissue, or building the breast out with a dermo-lipotamous graft. These artificial means have been widely employed in the last 30 years and give excellent cosmetic results; at the same time, there is no certain knowledge as to Miss Fonda's long-term history. Are we inserting a carcinogenic substance which might sooner or later lead to a malignant change? Also, the type of marble bust which these prostheses give is far from satisfactory. The choice thus fell to a dermo-lipotamous graft.

The operation. With Miss Fonda lying face-down, two elliptical incisions were marked out, one on the right side and one on the left side of her buttocks, running upwards and outwards from the natal cleft. Each ellipse was two inches in width and seven inches in length. Incisions were made on these markings down to the deep fascia on the gluteus maximus muscle. A huge wedge of skin with the underlying fat was removed with comparatively little bleeding. The few bleeding points were immediately sealed off either by ligature or diathermy. The two dermo-lipotamous grafts were placed to one side and the wounds were closed in two layers; plain catgut for the deeper layers, and the skin with silk.

The superficial layers of the epidermis were then removed from each graft with a grafting razor of the Humby type. This was not nearly so easy as it sounds, and an assistant was needed to steady the graft on a flat board whilst the surgeon took a Thiersch graft off the surface of the skin.

Miss Fonda was then turned onto her back, and her breasts were thoroughly cleansed and towelled off. An incision was made in the inframammary sulcus on each side, straight down to the deep fascia under her breasts. Each breast was then lifted up until it stood well forward, and the cavity was temporarily packed with ribbon gauze. Into the two ends of each graft a silk suture was inserted on a straight needle. The first suture was inserted through this incision and brought out, first over the pectoralis major muscle at the top outer corner of the breast area. The sutures were then gently pulled and the fat graft was allowed to slide into position in such a way that the dermal surface faced towards the wound. The fat graft then lay in a semi-circle supporting the breast tissue and gave the breast a normal shape and appearance. The skin of the incision was then closed with interrupted sutures.

There was no need to drain the wounds, and the two silk sutures, one on either side, were tied firmly over small gauze rolls. The operation was completed by applying a firm dressing which was maintained for the succeeding three days. Under no condition was Miss Fonda allowed to walk about without either a firm dressing of some kind or adequate brassiere support.

Report on an Unidentified Space Station

J. G. Ballard

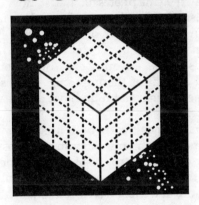

Survey Report 1

By good luck we have been able to make an emergency landing on this uninhabited space station. There have been no casualties. We all count ourselves fortunate to have found safe haven at a moment when the expedition was clearly set on disaster.

The station carries no identification markings and is too small to appear on our charts. Although of elderly construction it is soundly designed and in good working order, and seems to have been used in recent times as a transit depot for travellers resting at mid-point in their journeys. Its interior consists of a series of open passenger concourses, with comfortably equipped lounges and waiting rooms. As yet we have not been able to locate the bridge or control centre. We assume that the station was one of many satellite drogues surrounding a large command unit, and was abandoned when a decline in traffic left it surplus to the needs of the parent transit system.

A curious feature of the station is its powerful gravitational field, far stronger than would be suggested by its small mass. However, this probably represents a faulty reading by our instruments. We hope shortly to complete our repairs and are grateful to have found shelter on this relic of the now forgotten migrations of the past.

Estimated diameter of the station: 500 metres.

Survey Report 2

Our repairs are taking longer than we first estimated. Certain pieces of equipment will have to be reconstructed from scratch, and to shorten this task we are carrying out a search of our temporary home.

To our surprise we find that the station is far larger than we guessed. A thin local atmosphere surrounds the station, composed of interstellar dust attracted by its unusually high gravity. This fine vapour obscured the substantial bulk of the station and led us to assume that it was no more than a few hundred metres in diameter.

We began by setting out across the central passenger concourse that separates the two hemispheres of the station. This wide deck is furnished with thousands of tables and chairs. But on reaching the high partition doors 200 metres away we discovered that the restaurant deck is only a modest annex to a far larger concourse. An immense roof three storeys high extends across an open expanse of lounges and promenades. We explored several of the imposing staircases, each equipped with a substantial mezzanine, and found that they lead to identical concourses above and below.

The space station has clearly been used as a vast transit facility, comfortably accommodating many thousands of passengers. There are no crew quarters or crowd control posts. The absence of even a single cabin indicates that this army of passengers spent only a brief time here before being moved on, and must have been remarkably self-disciplined or under powerful restraint.

Estimated diameter: 1 mile.

Survey Report 3

A period of growing confusion. Two of our number set out 48 hours ago to explore the lower decks of the station, and so far have failed to return. We have carried out an extensive search and fear that a tragic accident has taken place. None of the hundreds of elevators is in working order, but our companions may have entered an unanchored cabin and fallen to their deaths. We managed to force open one of the heavy doors and gazed with awe down the immense shaft. Many of the elevators within the station could comfortably carry a thousand passengers. We hurled several pieces of furniture down the shaft, hoping to time the interval before their impact, but not a sound returned to us. Our voices echoed away into a bottomless pit.

Perhaps our companions are marooned far from us on the lower levels? Given the likely size of the station, the hope remains that a maintenance staff occupies the crew quarters on some remote upper deck, unaware of our presence here. As soon as we contact them they will help us to rescue our companions.

Estimated diameter: 10 miles.

Survey Report 4

Once again our estimate of the station's size has been substantially revised. The station clearly has the dimensions of a large asteroid or even a small planet. Our instruments indicate that there are thousands of decks, each extending for miles across an undifferentiated terrain of passenger concourses, lounges, and restaurant terraces. As before there is no sign of any crew or supervisory staff. Yet somehow a vast passenger complement was moved through this planetary waiting room.

While resting in the armchairs beneath the unvarying light we have all noticed how our sense of direction soon vanishes. Each of us sits at a point in space that at the same time seems to have no precise location but could be anywhere within these endless vistas of tables and armchairs. We can only assume that the passengers moving along these decks possessed some instinctive homing device, a mental model of the station that allowed them to make their way within it.

In order to establish the exact dimensions of the station and, if possible, rescue our companions, we have decided to abandon our repair work and set out on an unlimited survey, however far this may take us.

Estimated diamter: 500 miles.

Survey Report 5

No trace of our companions. The silent interior spaces of the station have begun to affect our sense of time. We have been traveling in a straight line across one of the central decks for what seems an unaccountable period. The same pedestrian concourses, the same mezzanines atached to the stairways, and the same passenger lounges stretch for miles under an unchanging light. The energy needed to maintain this degree of illumination suggests that the operators were used to a full passenger complement. However, there are unmistakable signs that no one has been here since the remote past. Clearly, whoever designed the station based the transit system within it on a time-table of gigantic dimensions.

We press on, following the same aisle that separates two adjacent lounge concourses. We rest briefly at fixed intervals, but despite our steady passage we sense that we are not moving at all, and may well be trapped within a small waiting-room whose apparently infinite dimensions we circle like ants on a sphere. Paradoxically, our instruments confirm that we are penetrating a structure of rapidly increasing mass. Is the entire universe no more than an infinitely vast space terminal?

Estimated diameter: 5000 miles.

Survey Report 6

We have just made a remarkable discovery! Our instruments have detected that a slight but perceptible curvature is built into the floors of the station. The ceilings recede behind us and dip fractionally towards the deck below, while the disappearing floors form a distinct horizon.

So the station is a curvilinear structure of finite form! There must be meridians that mark out its contours, and an equator that will return us to our original starting point. We all feel an immediate surge of hope. Already we may have stumbled on an equitorial line, and despite the huge length of our journey we may in fact be going home.

Estimated diameter: 50,000 miles.

Survey Report 7

Our hopes have proved to be short-lived. Excited by the thought that we had mastered the station, and cast a net around its invisible bulk, we were pressing on with renewed confidence. However, we now know that although these curvatures exist, they extend in all directions. Each of the walls curves away from its neighbors, the floors from the ceilings. The station, in fact, is an expanding structure whose size appears to increase exponentially. The longer the journey undertaken by a passenger, the greater the incremental distance he will have to travel. The virtually unlimited facilities of the station suggest that its passengers were embarked on extremely long, if not infinite, journeys.

Needless to say, the complex architecture of the station has ominous implications for us. We realise that the size of the station is a measure, not of the number of passengers embarked—though this must have been vast—but of the length of the journeys that must be undertaken within it. Indeed, there should ideally be only one passenger. A solitary voyager embarked on an infinite journey would require an infinity of transit lounges. As there are, fortunately, more than one of us we can assume that the station is a finite structure with the appearance of an infinite one. The degree to which it approaches an infinite size is merely a measure of the will and ambition of its passengers.

Estimated diameter: 1 million miles.

Survey Report 8

Just when our spirits were at their lowest ebb we have made a small but significant finding. We were moving across one of the limitless passenger decks, a prey to all fears and speculations, when we noticed signs of recent habitation. A party of travelers has paused here in the recent past. The chairs in the central concourse have been disturbed, an elevator door has been forced, and there are the unmistakable traces left by weary voyagers. Without doubt there were more than two of them, so must regretfully exclude our lost companions.

But there are others in the station, perhaps embarked on a journey as endless as our own!

We have also noticed slight variations in the decor of the station, in the design of light fittings and floor tiles. These may seem trivial, but multiplying them by the virtually infinite size of the station we can envisage a gradual evoluton in its architecture. Somewhere in the station there may well be populated enclaves, even entire cities, surrounded by empty passenger decks that stretch on forever like free space. Perhaps there are nation-states whose civilizations rose and declined as their peoples paused in their endless migrations across the station.

Where were they going? And what force propelled them on their meaningless journeys? We can only hope that they were driven forward by the greatest of all instincts, the need to establish the station's size.

Estimated diameter: 5 light years.

Survey Report 9

We are jubilant! A growing euphoria has come over us as we move across these great concourses. We have seen no further trace of our fellow passengers, and it now seems likely that we were following one of the inbuilt curvatures of the station and had crossed our own tracks.

But this small setback counts for nothing now. We have accepted the limitless size of the station, and this awareness fills us with feelings that are almost religious. Our instruments confirm what we have long suspected, that the empty space across which we traveled from our own solar system in fact lies within the interior of the station, one of the many vast lacunae set in its endlessly curving walls. Our solar system and its planets, the millions of other solar systems that constitute our galaxy, and the island universes themselves all lie within the boundaries of the station. The station is coeval with the cosmos, and constitutes the cosmos. Our duty is to travel across it on a journey whose departure point we have already begun to forget, and whose destination is the station itself, every floor and concourse within it.

So we move on, sustained by our faith in the station, aware that every step we take thereby allows us to reach a small part of that destination. By its existence the station sustains us, and gives our lives their only meaning. We are glad that in return we have begun to worship the station.

Estimated diameter: 15,000 light years.

Nefarious business sometimes takes us to the shrouded decaying northern city — Lovecraftopolis — where Paul di Filippo (born Scorpio, 1954) lives and struggles for fame and power. One symptom of this insensate hunger for "influence" and wealth was his fanzine ASTRAL AVENUES (which has recently been revived as a column in NEW PATHWAYS). The title comes from his practice of spying on famous writers while travelling in his astral or "etheric" body, then blackmailing them by threatening to reveal their peccadillos. Some of the dirt slips into print, and it makes for fun reading. Here we have a fine "hard" tale of quantum madness and sexual ambiguity in space.

Solitons
Paul Di Filippo

Marl said roughly, "We're here—get your arses in motion."

Anna tried to shake off the vast weight of nausea engendered by Heisenberg transition. Bastard, she thought. So tough on yourself and the rest of us. I'll take it though, now that I'm in, for the stakes at risk. And not crawl back to your black-and-blue bed.

Petting her organiform couch to an upright position, Anna faced the screen and keyboard that allowed her to control the Lonely Lady's force-grapples and confinement bottle. She initiated a diagnostic check, before Marl oould order her to do so, thereby achieving a precious bit of satisfaction.

She had run six of these checks over the past month, upon completion of each epidrive jump. Yet the equipment had not been used once.

The monopole was proving more elusive than they had feared at the outset of their search. No wonder only desperate gamblers dared hunt the elusive particle.

From the corner of one eye, Anna watched Marl rise from his couch. A big man, he defied the world with an ugly seamed rind of a face, split by narrow eyes, thin lips, and bisected by a hatchet-blade nose. From skull to midriff, Marl was covered with synthetic skin, possessing no follicles or sweat glands. His chest lacked nipples, his fingers nails. Below this artificial terminator, his muscled body was hirsute to the human extreme. He wore only a pair of tight white shorts to midthigh, a deliberate affront and taunt to Ann's physical aloofness. (She, in response, wore a shapeless black coverall under all circumstances.)

Anna pondered his bizarre appearance for the hundredth time, a body at war with itself, living testament to the blood-debt he owed Sanger, his rival. He could have easily had the former good looks that had first attracted Anna to him, before Sanger wrecked Marl's ship and nearly killed him. But anger and desire for revenge had bred in Marl like Shintak viruses, distorting his mind in subtle end obvious ways, least of which was this senseless flaunting of his scars.

Marl catfooted across the living resilient floor — part of the ship's closed recycling system — to the couch where Clete, their hired tiresias, lay.

The third organiform couch in the small cabin held Clete's thin child-sized body in its warm depression. Prior to the last jump, Clete had complained of tiredness, reclined heesh's couch and gone instantly to sleep. Now, though, heesh was awake, milky white eyee stering blindly at the pinkly luminescent ceiling.

As Marl approached, Clete's body tensed beneath heesh's grey robe, as if expecting a blow.

Marl stood by the couch, clenching his massive knobby fists. "There you go, Scryer. Just as you ordered, we've jumped a hundred lights closer to Mizar. I must admit, your ranging shots are getting smaller. What was the first—two thousand parsecs? Do you think you might be a little more precise in your next estimate? I was led to believe by your guild that you had seen solitons being formed and could lead us right to them."

Clete's voice was a calm soprano, ageless and sexless. "I have indeed seen solitons being born in the Monobloc, bright red knots in the polychrome domains of the nucleating primal universe. But that happened, to be precise, ten to the minus thirty-fifth second after the Big Bang. Over twelve billion years ago."

A small smile creased Clete's unwrinkled features. "A lot has happened since then, Marl, if you stop to think. I can envision the whole Monobloc any time, from any place in the universe, since each bit of matter once resided in that infinitely dense point, and I can follow any thread back to the labyrinth's center. But as the universe expands over time, I can hold less and less of it in my mind simultaneouely. Eventually, to scry the recent past, I must be physically present in that very volume of space I wish to examine. Hence our 'ranging shots,' as you archaicly call them. Now, unless you wish to pay the Scryers' Sodality more than you already owe them, let me get to my work, whioh you cannot possibly understand in any real sense."

Marl's right fist came up from his side as if to strike Clete, then stopped in mid-gesture, The tiresias lay unperturbed. It was not that heesh's blind eyes had not registered the threat — by scrying the immediate past nanoseconds behind reality, Clete could "see" as well as anyone, with only an insignificant lag — but that heesh knew Marl would not dare contravene the rules by which he had contracted for Clete's services.

Clete was right this time. Marl pivoted, quivering with rage, and stalked away, spitting out over his shoulder, "Do it then, damn it!"

A small shiver passed down Clete's body, and heesh's breathing slowed. Nothing could disturb herm now, until heesh roused hermself.

Marl threw himself heavily down onto his couch, which surged with semifluid movement, like a waterbed filled with mercury. Anna turned from her board. She felt for Marl — not pity or love, but some novel mixture of respect and awe and fear. He drove her and Clete no harder than he pushed himself. But to know that made it no easier to take. They were not infected with his same will or desires.

"Let up on Clete, Marl," she ventured mildly. "I'm sure heesh's doing heesh's best. Remember: without herm, we'd have no chance at all."

Marl sat up and fixed her with a baleful stare. "That filthy androgyne and heesh's stinking guild are nothing but leeches. They bleat about how hard it is to interpret their visions of the past to get a fix on the present, yet stand there all the while with outstretched hands for more and more credits. Then when you're bled dry, they disgorge what they knew all along."

Anna was taken aback. "You can't believe that, Marl. Imagine what Clete's doing right now. I've talked with herm a little about it. It's not easy. Heesh is travelling through an abstract landscape of colors and shapes, trying to correlete it with the world we know through our conventional senses. Even then, once heesh masters that, clients like us toss in the dimension of time, asking herm to track a miniscule object through the billions of years of ite existence to its present location. It's ameaing heesh gets any results at all."

Marl snorted. "What results? We've only got heesh's word for it that we're getting closer to the monopole." He leaned forward with sudden eagerness. "Speaking of which, has the detector registered anything yet?"

"Of course not. I would have spoken up. I want this hunt to succeed too, you know."

Marl looked at Anna with blank suspicion, as if he had never seen her before. His hands spasmed in his lap like fish out of water. "We don't have forever. How long do you imagine it will take Sanger to catch up with us?"

Anna winced. She had almost managed to forget that aspect of their pleasant little prospecting trip.

Soon after Marl, a changed man, had come home from the hospital that Sanger's sabotage had sent him to, he had begun to savage Anna verbally, then physically. She had left him with much regret but no hesitation, ending an asteroid-mining partnership-cum-affair of some years' standing. Much time passed with no word from him. Then one day he had shown up at Anna's door, with this mad plan to make their fortunes by netting a monopole. Had Anna not been down on her own luck, she would never have agreed to go in with him. He took her to the port to see his ship, and she was surprised at its quality, having thought him broke.

Only when they were underway did he tell her that the ship was Sanger's, stolen from his yards in an abortive attempt to snatch the man himself from under the nose of his elaborate security force.

When Anna demanded that he return her home, Marl had spun a glib lunatic's tapestry of how they could have immediate success, selling the monopole for gigacredits, then, armored in wealth, secure from Sanger, extract their revenge.

She had made the mistake of staying with him until they picked up Clete from the Sodality world. There, her name was registered on the contract with Marl's, and she realized that Sanger would now be able to connect her with Marl, and any safety back home was illusory. There was no way out for her except forward, linked to this apparition out of her past in victory or defeat.

"All right," Anna said. "You made your point and blew away any dreams of peace I was cultivating. Go away now, and let me read. At least it allows me to forget."

Marl lowered his voice to a seductive whisper. The effect combined with his disfigured features was grotesque. "We could forget together, Anna. Take up what we once had. That thing will be out of it for long enough. We'll have some privacy."

Anna spat on the floor, which slowly absorbed it. "Shove it. I'm not your lover anymore. At worst, I'm your hostage. At best: your friend. And before you try anything, remember who I studied with."

Marl shivered, as he recalled the reputation of the Cybele, the Bloody Nuns. He turned on his side away from Anna.

She breathed a sigh of relief. Especially since she had never even seen a Cybele.

Her screen flooded with text on the epidrive. All her working life she had used the spacedrive, with little thought paid to how it functioned. Now, on this crazy trip, where boredom alternated with screaming tension, she had begun to grow interested in this device that made their travel possible.

The words read:

"FILE: Epistemological spacedrive, overview.

CROSSREFERENCED: Heisenberg transition, epidrive, Shozo Turnbow...

"The epistemological spacedrive was perfected in the year 2, Ante Scattering, by one Shozo Turnbow. Its basic mode of operation relies on the Heisenberg Uncertainty Principle, which is most simply formulated in the statement: All qualities of a particle may not be known simultaneously.

"The advent of superior subatomic scanning methods, coupled with digitalization of the results, lies at the heart of the drive. Basically, all particles possess a host of qualities — spin, angular momentum, and mass, for instance — one of which is location in space. An object subject to the epidrive is first scanned quark by quark, and all its qualities — save location — recorded in a suitable memory matrix. The duration of this process naturally varies directly with the mass of the object being scanned, placing a premium on size. As data accumulates, over hours and days, the object under scan enters a state of uncertainity as to its location. The very precision with which all its nonspatial qualities are recorded forces all its inherent uncertainity to be concentrated in its spatial dimension. At this point, the object may be literally anywhere in the universe. At the height of uncertainty, two things are done simultaneously. All information previously recorded is wiped, dispersing the uncertainty, and a new relativistic location is imposed on the object. Transition is instantaneous."

Anna's head swam with the words, simple enough on the surface, yet concealing hidden depths of paradox. She ran a slim hand over her cropped brown hair, wondering if she would ever truly fathom the epidrive. What bothered her most was the fact that the scanning equipment had of necessity to scan itself as part of the ship to be transported. It seemed too muoh like pulling oneself up by one's bootstraps. And the whole drive required such minimal power.... Where were the huge warp mechanisms of antique fiction, comforting in their similarity to internal-combustion engines?

An abrupt shuddering intake of breath sounded across the cramped cabin, and Anna knew that Clete had come out of heesh's scrying trance. She turned from her screen as Marl abandoned his sullen meditations. Together, the two crossed the room to Clete.

The tiresias had stroked heesh's couch into its roughly L-shaped position, and now sat with stringy, fatigue-trembling muscles apparent beneath heesh's robe. A seemingly insignificant twist of heesh's lips, which Marl and Anna had learned to interpret as a smile of satisfaction, seemed to bode well.

Marl's eagerness could not be contained. It caused him to actually lay his hands upon Clete's robe, against all guild prohibitions. "Well," he demanded, "do you have a fix on it? Can you take us there? Speak up!"

Clete said nothing, and Marl quickly realized what he had done and removed his grip from the grey fabric. Crazy he might be, Anna knew, but that did not preclude cunning and guile and a sense of whom not to offend. Anna he could only push so far, since he needed her to capture the monopole while he maneuvered the ship under its ion-drive. And Clete he needed even more, for heesh's clairvoyance.

But after the success of the mission, Anna wondered, what then?

Upon heesh's release, Clete spoke in heesh's pellucid voice. "I have seen the monopole in its unmistakable glory. It is not far. Here are its coordinates." Heesh reeled off a set of relativistic figures describing the transition to be made, which heesh had read from the tangled skeins of force heesh saw in heesh's visionary state.

Marl almost leapt for the epidrive controls. As if a few seconds saved now could matter over the five days it would take the epidrive to reach the transition peak. At his board, he placed a contact mike against his throat and subvocalized the code to activate the drive. Anna prayed for him to move his lips, but he made no such mistake. If only she knew the code, she could — what? Return home to await Sanger's arrival? Flee to some far reach of space? No, her only hope of future safety lay in accomplishing what they had set out to do.

Marl remained by the board, as if willing the drive to speed up. Anna turned back to Clete.

"You look drained," she said to the scryer. "Let me get you something to eat."

"That would be appreciated," Clete said. Anna went to a cluster of pebbly-skinned fruits growing from the wall and picked one. She drew a glass of cloudy liquid from a wall-nipple and picked up a protein bar from the supply-cabinet. These she brought back to Clete.

The tiresias ate with catlike economy. Anna sat on the end of heesh's couch. Clete's small form left half the surface free.

When heesh had finished, Anna spoke softly to herm. She doubted that Marl was paying any attention to them, yet she did not wish him to intrude in any case. Her talks with Clete were a brief respite from Marl's tirades and scratchy silences.

"What did you see this time, Clete? What was it like?"

Clete tipped heesh's head back as if to gaze out through the organic-inorganic duostrate of the ship at the mysterious universe beyond. "The turbulence the monopole has left behind in its passage through space and time is a golden kinked cord surrounded by a purple halo of the byproducts of destroyed protons. This trail lies on the universal background whose color has no name, woven through stars that stream energy and planets that hum with gravitic contentment. It is the same trail I have followed out of the Monobloc at billion-year intervals. And now I have seen its end."

"It sounds beautiful. More beautiful than the world I see every day. How I wish I could share it."

Clete shrugged. "Do not belittle your own senses. They offer marvels enough, when one speaks of the present. And our lives are constricted in ways yours is not."

"But the past," Anna said. "To see the past and trace all the mysterious effects of the present back to their essential causes — what do we have to compare with that? That's what I want."

"I will not lie to you. That is indeed something fine you cannot know. Especially to see the Primeval Egg."

"You've mentioned that before. What's it like? Why is it so important to a scryer?"

"It is indescribable, yet the vital thing we live for. To hold the totality of the universe in the eye of the mind, darting in and out of that infinitely dense point, where all is unified, where there is only one Force acting in a broth of elementary particles. To see such perfection ameliorates living in this age of broken symmetry."

Clete paused, as if weighing heesh's words so as not to offer an insult.

"Have you never wondered why we scryers are dual-sexed?" heesh finally asked.

Anna looked away, unaccountably embarrassed. "I always thought it was an unavoidable side-effect of your gift."

"That is the notion the Sodality promotes. Once, when biofabrication was more primitive, it was even true. The first embryos engineered to have the scrying talent were inadvertantly created androgynes and blind. Now, both 'defects' could be repaired. But we believe these traits were not accidental, but predestined. Our androgyny reflects our worship of the wholeness of the Monobloc. Our blindness is a refusal to see the current fallen state of the universe. We are as we wish to be. You single-sexed homo sapiens are defective, each severed from his other half, perfect representatives of an imperfect age."

Anna sifted through Clete's tone and found no reproaches, but only a calm certainty of the true state of things. Suddenly she felt wholly inadequate, a lonely fragile coalition of particles wandering incomplete through a vast void.

She turned practical to dispel her gloom. "This monopole, solition, whatever. Who are the prospective buyers for it? What are they going to use it for? I know it's rare, but so are a dozen other things in this universe that are worth much less."

"Like humans," Clete said, "the monopole is incomplete in one sense, a superheavy particle possessing only a single magnetic charge, north or south. This is merely a means of identification, however, not its quintessential property. Every monopole is, in effect, a hot coal that bears the fire of the early universe, the unified Force. Feed a stream of nucleons — protons or neutrons — into it, and they decay instantly into their primal constituents. Each discrete decay releases approximately a billion electron volts of energy. A single monopole could power worlds."

Pursing her lips, Anna whistled silently. "That explains why your guild agreed to send you out with Marl for a share of the profits, despite his lack of credit up front. The take will be enormous."

"You are wrong," Clete countered. "One of us would have come for nothing."

"What?"

"The monopole is a fragment of the Unity we worship, existing in the present. For most scryers, contemplation of the Monobloc is devout enough. But for some, such as myself, only a pilgrimage to a monopole will complete my life. And we must rely on such as Marl to take us there."

Anna got to her feet. It was too much information in too short a time. She didn't know what to think. The realities of the voyage suddenly seemed reversed, all their anxiety and effort expended for Clete, not themselves.

"I've got to get back to work," she said, and left the tiresias to heesh's blind-eyed scrutiny.

Five days — 120 standard hours — snailed by like an infinity of water droplets falling on a bruised and hypersensitive forehead. Anna ate just enough to maintain a low level of energy and promote an excess of sleep. She conducted a few desultory conversations with Marl about their hazy future. Clete she avoided, wishing to hear no more disillusioning truths. One can only stand to have the universe inverted so many times.

Marl remained his insane composite of implacable fury and robotic indifference. Occasionally his synthetic upper hair suffused with a mottled flush of rage at some remembered or imagined indignity.

At last the ship reached the phase of maximum uncertainty. The onboard computer performed the flipflop maneuver of dispersing the uncertainty and imposing the new coordinates automatically, the delicate process requiring nonhuman speed.

The universe accepted them at their new location.

Their viewscreens showed a bold white sun blazing less than a tenth of an AU away. They were three times as close to the stellar furnace as Mercury to Old Sol.

"Diagnostic check," Marl commanded Anna. Then, to Clete, "Goddamn it, Scryer, why so close? You almost have us inside it."

"You asked for precision," Clete replied without evident unease. "I knew we were safe at this range, yet as close as possible. I have done as you requested. Now leave me to my vision."

"What do you mean, 'as close as possible'? We have to get within grapple-range."

Clete, trance-bound, failed to answer. But Anna had found out what heesh meant.

"Marl," she said, her voice shaky, "the diagnostic check indicates normal functioning, and the detector registers the monopole."

"All right, then, where is it?"

"In the sun."

Marl rushed to her side and shoved her cruelly away from her instruments. "It can't be. I won't let it."

Anna recalled something Clete had told her:

"I know our grapples can fasten on the monopole when we find it," she had said. "But what normally stops a monopole in nature?"

"Concentrations of dense mass," heesh had answered.

Marl turned from the screen. "It is in there," he said in a dead voice. "Radiation analysis indicates excess energy production for a star of this type. Our monopole is wedged in its fucking heart, eating it from the inside out."

Marl hit the control panel with tremendous violence. He turned and punched the yielding wall. Then his eyes fell on Clete, rapt in heesh's contemplation of the monopole at the inaccessible core of the star.

"Heesh knew, damn it. Heesh knew before the last jump. The little bitch had to have seen it was trapped in a star. And heesh never told us."

Anna felt sick. What could they do now?

She watched Marl advance on the tiresias, fearing his intentions, her feelings a mix of hatred for the traitorous scryer and empathy for heesh's quest.

Marl slapped the unlined child-sage's face, got no reaction, and slapped again, three times, rocking Clete's head from side to side on heesh's skinny neck.

"Goddamn you, wake up. Tell us what to do now."

Clete's unresponsiveness enraged Marl further. He reached for the neck of heesh's robe, grasped the fabric and split it like paper. Anna couldn't look away.

The scryer's body lay revealed. Immature-looking breasts graced heesh's chest. Below a tiny paunch stood shriveled male genitals; below that, a vaginal slit. There was no pubic hair.

A huge erection bulged in Marl's shorts. Anna's sickness deepened, yet she couldn't rise. Marl would kill her if she interfered. And the scryer — didn't heesh deserve punishment for heesh's deception?

"I'll have my value out of you one way or another," Marl growled. He unseamed his shorts and his penis was unrestrained.

Anna turned her eyes then.

The sounds were awful enough.

After thirty seconds, Clete's voice broke weakly through Marl's grunts.

"No, no defilement. I am whole, you are not. No, don't contaminate —"

Marl must have capped the scryer's mouth with a huge hand, for heesh spoke no more.

When Marl was done, he stumbled to a corner of the cabin and huddled like an autistic child.

Anna crept slowly out of her seat and to the side of the tiresias, hoping Marl would not object. He seemed in no condition to even notice, though.

Blood leaked from the scryer's mouth and vagina. The couch was efficiently taking it up, to convert it to fruit and water, so they could live their useless lives a bit longer.

"Clete," Anna whispered. "Are you okay?"

The tiresias stirred feebly. "My body is not badly damaged, but my spirit is. I must retreat to the monopole to restore myself." Clete's hand sought hers. "Do not let him touch me again."

"All right, Clete, all right, I won't," she said, crying, not knowing how she would keep the promise.

As Clete slipped into scrying mode, the ship's communicator pinged.

Marl remained catatonic. Anna went to the board.

The screen revealed a fat-faced man with a drooping mustache, a ship's cabin-walls out of focus behind him. Fuzzy human figures lurked in the background.

"Sanger here," the man said with laconic indifference. "I want my ship back, and Marl with it. You I don't care about, whoever you are. Anna, isn't it?"

"Yes," Anna said. "Listen, I just can't—"

Sanger cut in. "My ship has armaments. Yours does not. I will open fire shortly unless I detect three suited figures with empty hands exiting the lock."

"How do I know—" Anna began. Then a hand closed around the back of her neck.

Marl stood behind her, self-aware now.

"Sanger, my enemy," he said without inflection. "If you want your ship, follow me. I'm going to collect my monopole."

Marl released Anna's neck and moved to the controls for the ion-drive.

Anna got hurriedly to her feet, shaking. She walked in a confused zigzag to the suit-locker, reeling mentally from the events of the past few minutes.

She pulled a suit awkwardly from the rack, clambered into it and sealed its front. She took a helmet in her right hand.

"Marl," she said softly, seeing at once both the man he had been and the travesty he now was. "Come with me. Give up. It's not the worst thing that could happen."

Ignoring her, saying nothing, Marl boosted the ion-flow. Anna watched red digits flash their acceleration.

Clete remained quiescent on heesh's couch, at one with the monopole. Anna felt she had no right to drag herm away. Heesh had made heesh's choice.

Anna put her helmet on, went to the wrinkled sphincter that was the lock's inner door. There, she looked one last time at Marl.

His broad hairless back was hunched over the controls, and he muttered to himself. She caught only, "Piece of...".

Or "Peace of...".

She tickled the sphincter in the proper pattern, went through, confronted the outer lock of metal and rubber. The sphincter flexed closed behind her. She opened the lock without exhausting the trapped air. The escaping gases blew her out into space, away from the ship.

Slowing her tumble with her suit-jets, she found the Lonely Lady silhouetted against the incredible glare of the sun, toward which her own trajectory was inevitably carrying her, if no one interfered. Her helmet-polarization could barely filter it, and her eyes pained her.

Still, she followed the ship till it was no more than a flyspeck against the medusa-fringed disk of the monopole-snaring sun.

Her communicator crackled with unheard words from Sanger's ship, which approached.

Solitary soliton for the moment, Anna wondered how many atoms of Clete's vaporized body would eventually find their way to the monopole's consuming core.

Sharon Gannon (text) and David Life (collage) live on the Lower East Side of New York and represent part of that community's last-ditch resistance to gentrification. He founded a restaurant, Life Cafe; they constitute half of an improv music group, Audio Letter; both paint, write poetry, dance and perform, teach yoga, etc., etc. We recently received a letter from them from India where they were staying with an "Anarchist Swami" in the Nilgiri Hills.

A great deal of SF has been imbued with a yearning for Gnosticism, for the transcendence of the body. Some writers use Gnosticism for "color" (like L. Durrell), others write from within the visionary experience, like P. K. Dick. As we interpret the following piece, it represents an actual Message from the Alien Savior, garbled by interference from "Them", and also by the author's own hesitations... an impression strengthened by David's collage illustrations with their air of "film noir" and old crypto-expressionist horror movies.

Is This True?
Well, Yes and No
Sharon Gannon & David Life

And I think to myself:
You violated the perfect plan for
immortality when someone first
killed someone, now every
living thing is condemned to
die. And they tell me:

"Only if you can find a way
to survive without
killing can you
re-gain immortality"
And they tell me:
"The world loves
suffering more than any
other pleasure"

Is this true?
        Well, yes and no

Can it happen in the physical, can the body be spiritualized, the knowledge of good and evil, apparent and exemplified by the flesh? Also beyond duality which is the being; the state of love. Can separation and unity exist simultaneously together? And they tell me: "Things of the world are this or they are that, never both. The realness of any one of us is determined by our separateness and our thingness, our objectiveness is our only identity." And I think: You cannot hold a moving object, not with the fingers of taste or of vision. A moving object is no object at all. We can only perceive the moment to moment limits of our own perceptions.

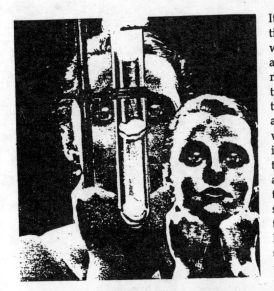

It is the underlying pattern of the motion of a thing which is its true nature, we are life as we live. I cannot study and come to know something's true nature. To observe is to cause a separation between me and that and to view the form of it which denies that I am it also. Anyway, when we see something with our sensible selves, we are seeking what it was, and we are denying that it is becoming something else, even as we see it and name it and assume it to be. We attempt with our vision to stop its truer nature, its motion. I want to devote my time, my life to knowing. I want to know all aspects of life, to see, to recognize myself in others and to go beyond seeing and to be myself with others I want to become with life. To practice this merger is the practice of love, which defies mere separation. I will begin with my own physical body. Can I actually merge with this and come to know this by being this? Can I come to know how to alter myself, at the cellular level? Is it at all possible? I have myself to experiment with. Somehow I don't feel that I must live

as a victim manipulated by unseen forces. I think I may be the force.

"Keep your mouth shut, you may swallow something, cover yourself, some small things may wander in and be mangled. Look, it's all been done before, relax, watch the news on TV, eat right, sleep, get a job, save your money, invest, health is wealth, don't over-extend yourself. We know what's best for you, we've been around a lot longer, remember. Leave it to the experts, it's their job. You are a murderer, accept it now and set out to practice it as little as possible. Try to remember each time you took life away from another."

Are there others? Am I separate? Am I apart? Are you blind? You have the senses for vision, and to see is to set yourself apart. Where there is separation there is no love. How can I live under the pretension of individual identity? Seeing is not being and there is no love in sight.

As we do this and that with this and that we create, we together. Everyone who is participating in objectifying motion, we make and maintain this illusion of thingness, of static forms, we live in a reality made up of a vast collection of objects, which are moved by acts of will and intention. It is this creation that gives us the feeling that our own selves are our own and that they can be held on to by us or by somebody else. We create the need and desire for security in immutability. Let us have a standing place. Let us understand, which means to stand under and under means away from. They have been telling us, and we tell each other, speaking out of fear, the fear of losing. "No one wants to lose!" We are told again and again to be winners. But what can we lose but the tightly drawn limited definitions of our perceptions of ourselves? Eventually we fall apart from the sheer tension of the bondage and eventually we lose our time.

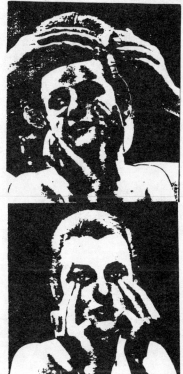

The effect of action is only to insure further and further action. Salvation might be found by freeing the soul of matter, but salvation from what? Space is curved, so it comes back upon itself. Movement is the intermediary between space and time, it is their relationship. Action Action, alright so I will only do actions that result in the least hinderance to further action. I will work at becoming transparent. The identity thing is grasped first, then the possibility for instant enlightenment. This grasping of the first takes awhile, and what is a while? How ever long it takes. There is no god only the constant flow of motion, which is you, which is me, which is everything. I cannot stop my body from emanating the life force. The life force which demands the death sacrifice. If I starve myself to death, if I close myself away I will be killing myself and all the selves that are at home with me. I am not alone. What is to be done? Does motion, does action have with it the consequence of suffering and of murder? Is it only and always a decision of How Much and To Whom and When? And when I die, I will not leave, for where would I go? Any one of us is an example, no more or less a part of every one who is living now and has ever lived. We are always in the right place at the right time, there is no other place to be and no time for it. Everything proceeds and recedes, the earth is patient with itself, or impatient according to its own varied aspects. All earthly beings are being earth, we are made of it and are making it. My hands are open but never empty.

Richard Kadrey's first novel, METROPHAGE (Ace Special, 1988), is a flawlessly-styled cyberpunk thriller; he is working on a second. His short fiction has appeared in OMNI and INTERZONE, and his state-of-the-art xerox-collage art in a slew of underground publications. He works as a tech writer for a computer software house in San Francisco. "On Christmas Day 1986, I sneaked into Versailles with another SF writer and a radical Peruvian philosopher, and had to scale a fifteen-foot wall, commando-style, to get out."

It is possible that "Kadrey" is actually "Qadiri", and a descendant of the sufi shaykh Abdul Qadir Jilani.

Genocide
Richard Kadrey

The rules are simple, but they must be followed faithfully or the game will be forfeited; thus rendering your opponent's victory meaningless, thus leaving no clear winner. And what is a game without a winner?

The six games that make up the Genocide Game can be played in any order or simultaneously. Tests on psychotics (for instance, patients in the latter stages of tertiary syphilis) and autistic adults reveal a powerful pre-disposition for the games, where it is often imagination, rather than cunning, that is the key to success. However, those players of average physical and mental capabilities can make up some of this lost ground through the use of sensory deprivation chambers and certain CNS depressants (such as ketamine hydrochloride or sodium pentobarbital). For more information on this, see Appendix B of the Advanced Players Guide.

A sample scenario in which the Genocide Game is played through to its conclusion follows, along with a brief outline of the individual games.

OUR SCENARIO CHARACTERS:

Korsakov's syndrome is a rare disorder, generally associated with the degeneration of the mammillary bodies, and is usually found in patients in the advanced stages of alcoholism.

The patient in question is a male, caucasian, octogenarian who refers to himself in his native tongue as the Leader. He was found, along with seven other men and women, in the back of a 1965 Ford van smuggling illegal aliens across the border into the United States from Mexico. When the patient referred to himself as the Leader, the authorities arrested him, thinking he meant the attempted smuggling incident. However, the Leader is clearly not of Hispanic descent, although he speaks fluent Spanish. When asked about his origins (he is clearly of European extraction) he experiences radical loss of short-term memory and lapses into long silences, or else he becomes quite animated and walks about his room telling long, rambling stories in German and Hebrew. He has a little English, but most of it is oriented toward trading with tourists. When not making his living as a farm worker, The Leader claims to be a "hamaca" salesman (a "hamaca" is a hand woven hammock, common in many Mexican cities). On several occasions, he has also confessed to producing and dealing in pornography, but there is no way of confirming this.

THE TECHNOLOGY GAME!

When employed correctly, the Technology Game functions as a subtle form of psychological blitzkrieg. The types of technology presented are unimportant. What is important is the speed at which the new technologies supercede the old. This applies to consumerism on all levels, from individuals to whole governments. The technology referred to can vary from digital watches to super-cooled computer memories. From VCR's to PET scanners. From the newest in personal vibrators to satellite-based particle beam weapons.

As each wave of technology is released, it must be accompanied by a demand for new skills, new language. Consumers must constantly update their ways of thinking, always questioning their understanding of the world. Going back to old ways, old technology is forbidden. There is no past, no present, only an endless future of inadequacy.

It makes no difference if the technologies presented are beneficient or even functional. It is advisable, however, that they go fast, make a lot of noise and come in a variety of decorator colors.

A POSSIBLE SCENARIO:

The President is close to the end of his second term in office. He cannot run again, and his party has barely survived a bribery and kickback scandal that pushed its popularity to an all-time low. The party needs a candidate.

The Leader is removed from his hospital bed at four A.M. on a Monday morning and taken to a nameless motel in the Arizona desert. In a room that once held ping-pong and pool tables, plastic surgeons repair damage the Leader sustained to his face during an unsuccessful suicide attempt years before. He is fitted with "Paul Newman-blue" contact lenses and his unfashionable toothbrush moustache is shaved off. The Leader protests at first, but after a hair transplant restores his thick black locks, he acquiesces.

Although the Leader has a great reputation as a speaker, he is shown tapes of Ronald Reagan and the late President Kennedy on a home VCR unit to acquaint him with a more modern approach to public speaking. When the Leader hears the dead President intone the words, "Ich bene eine Berliner," he laughs appreciatively, then lapses into a deep and protracted depression. Later, the Leader speaks of being very moved by President Kennedy's words. He wishes to emulate the fallen President, whom he refers to as "Siegfried," a legendary Teutonic knight. He is somewhat disappointed to learn President Kennedy was Catholic.

In bed, the Leader masturbates himself to sleep while listening to Wagner on his Sony Walkman. His Secret Service bodyguards keep a silent vigil in the Leader's living quarters where they frequently find empty liquor bottles hidden behind the furniture.

On the news the following day, it is reported that terrorists have set off a nuclear device at the Miami World's Fair, killing ten thousand people.

THE ART GAME!
Art is always radical in that it reveals something of the human soul. Art changes both the artist and the observer. Who cannot help but be moved by Michelangelo's Pietá or the towering sculptures of Angkor Wat?

For the purposes of the Game it must be remembered that bad art operates on the same mechanical principles as good art. Its effects can be summed up in the simple computer dictum: "Garbage in, garbage out."

A POSSIBLE SCENARIO:
As a publicity stunt for his campaign, the Leader agrees to appear on a popular late night television comedy show. He surprises both his staff and the viewers alike by demonstrating remarkable abilities as a comedian and mimic. He is especially adept at slapstick, which he demonstrates in a pie-throwing parody of his own "Beer-Hall Putsch." Two days after the show, The Leader's standing in all the major polls has doubled.

During the Super Bowl Game, a plane carrying napalm to war games in Central America crashes through the roof of the Astrodome.

Millions of Americans have the rare opportunity of watching their neighbors roast alive on national television. The ratings for the post-crash segment of the broadcast are astronomical. Within a month, an hour-long variety show premiers, featuring alleged "snuff" and atrocity films from all over the world. The Leader is a frequent guest on the highly-rated program and his "name recognition quotient" soon surpasses that of Alan Alda and Muhammed Ali.

THE SEX GAME!

Sex has become less an act and more a concept; its variations less an exploration of the erotic and more a testing ground for the human psyche.

Sex is ground-zero. Here, centuries of conditioned response are stripped away to reveal the neurotic pattern of nerves and electricity and their relation to bone and muscle, teeth and tongue, life and death. The Sex Game's components are obsession and anxiety. All explorations must lead back to where they began. There are no answers. Insight is merely a symptom of mental illness. Sex is a new school of architecture: a featureless skyscraper of burnished aluminum and mirrors.

A POSSIBLE SCENARIO:

The Leader is fascinated with modern technology. In his hotel at night, he throws tantrums until he is supplied with the newest in adult toys: Touch-sensitive stereos, video games and voice-activated kitchen appliances, all of which he grows bored with and abandons within a few days.

The video recorder is his favorite plaything. He watches the rehearsal tapes of his speeches over and over again. With his control box, he speeds his image up, freezes it, prints out hard copies from his color Xerox machine, all the while pointing out the subliminal sexual messages he is transmitting through carefully constructed facial expressions.

While going through the tapes, members of his campaign staff discover scenes of the Leader having sex with a variety of children and crippled adults. When word of the tapes gets out, a thief in the employ of the opposing political party steals them. After dubbing in the Leader's voice, he submits the tapes to television stations all across the country, claiming that they are the Leader's campaign commercials.

To the opposistion's chagrin, the commercials receive an overwhelmingly favorable response. It seems that the American public respects honesty in a man seeking public office. The Leader easily sweeps the New England primaries.

With this new advertising gimmick, the Leader's campaign staff experiment with the tapes, intercutting pornography featuring various ethnic groups, burn victims, and famous sports figures—tailoring the tapes for different parts of the country.

In New York, the headquarters of the Black Muslim movement is bombed. The next night, a score of synagogues are burned. Riots spread from Harlem to Wall Street. The Governor calls in the National Guard who use nerve gas to quell the mobs. The Leader appears on the cover of *People* magazine as one of the ten most eligible bachelors in America.

THE GOD GAME!

"Icon" comes from the Greek word *eikon* meaning "sacred image." Anything can be a sacred image (twentieth-century art has revealed that much to us). However, for the images to be useful to the game they must be specific: the blueprints of a Heckler and Koch MP-5; a murdered nun clutching a crucifix; John F. Kennedy; an IBM PC; the image of Thomas Jefferson on a $20 bill in the hand of a prostitute; a red Porche 924; an erect penis; Edward Teller; cocaine; Bo Derek's breasts; the "white hand" of the El Salvador death squads.

An icon's specific function is to objectify belief, thereby pacifying the believer. There are some who claim that it was the Romans who invented and originally distributed the image of the crucified Christ, using it to pacify the early Christians. And, of course, it was the Goths, not the Christians, who eventually conquered the Romans.

A POSSIBLE SCENARIO:

In order to conserve their dwindling reserves of oil, the Arab countries embargo shipments to the U.S. and inflation hits five hundred percent. Autographed pictures of the Leader, along with $100 bills, are dropped by helicopter on Puerto Rico and the southern Bible Belt. Appliances are given away to needy families who no longer have electricity.

During a political rally in Atlanta, Georgia, the Leader stuns his audience by appearing in medieval armour and throwing away his speech. Instead, he sings highlights from the opera, "Die Valkurie." At a party afterwards he tells a group of reporters that "You just can't go wrong with good material." Rumours circulate that the Leader is planning to cut an album, with a possible tour to follow.

In what come to be known as the Kansas City Purges, one hundred pubescent boys are disembowled on open altars to appease Yam Kax, the Mayan corn god. When the youths are dead, the priest who performed the sacrifices skins their bodies, donning the flesh-like robes to dance for the coming harvest. When informed of this, The Leader remarks that it does his heart good to see America embracing religion once again.

THE DRUG GAME!

Of all the games of control mentioned thus far, the effects of the Drug Game are the most obvious. Where the God Game and the Sex Game fail, the Drug Game will almost always supply whatever missing ingredient it requires to command attention and pacify on a large scale.

The heroin addict will not rebel. Cocaine users rarely question too closely the actions of their public officials. Alcoholics forget to vote. The addict is a sexless, amorphous beast. The key is the drug supplier. Control the chemical pimps and you control the beasts.

It is important to remember that the basic principles of the Drug Game (Desire, Need and Addiction) also hold true for designer shoes, rock music, food, television, etc.

A POSSIBLE SCENARIO:

While offloading crates of heroin and Dilaudid from an Air Force transport, Mister Faraday, one of the Leader's bodyguards, confesses that he works for the CIA. He tells the Leader that the Agency has engineered many recent catastrophes, including the World's Fair bombing and the Super Bowl mishap, to pave the way for the Leader's election. The Leader tells Mister Faraday that he's "a really beautiful guy and a terrific human being."

At a rally in Manhattan, the Leader promises that if elected he will declare the South Bronx a national park and a zone "ad libitum." That is, "no law but the law of nature will prevail here," among the crumbling relics of abandoned apartment buildings and burned-out tenements. The Leader speaks of the "sensuous lines of smashed flagstones and the devil-tooth gleam of shattered glass." To demonstrate his commitment to the free zone, the Leader tosses bags of opium, cocaine, PCP and LSD, Quaaludes, Demerol, heroin and hashish to the grasping crowd.

The campaign is going well; the Leader's standing in the polls is higher than ever, but the Leader is an old man and the pace is having its effect on him. He babbles at night and is often unable to sleep, even when he is too tired to rise from his bed. His bodyguards quickly discover that the Leader can be bribed into silence with *Hustler* magazines and little bottles of airplane Scotch. Because of the Leader's faulty memory, the guards can buy him off with the same magazines again and again. In the West, a resistant strain of anthrax wipes out most of the livestock. There are reports of cannibalism in Houston and Los Angeles. Inflation hits one thousand percent. In San Francisco, Buddhists burn themselves while bystanders huddle for warmth and toast marshmallows.

THE FUHRER GAME!

In ten seconds, how many synonyms can you think of for the word "power"?

A POSSIBLE SCENARIO:

The Leader's standing in the polls has dropped several points. His political analysts assure him that this is normal in the days

just prior to an election, but the CIA is alarmed. They begin work to develop a plan that will assure the Leader's victory.

Two weeks before the election, while giving a speech on national television, the Leader is gunned down. The assassin, disguised as a policeman, shoots two reporters before making his escape. The reporters are killed instantly, and the Leader is rushed to the hospital. In the ambulance, the Leader slips into unconciousness. In his delirium, he cries out for "Siegfried" to protect him.

The press is waiting when they reach the hospital. By this time, the Leader is conscious and calm. He invites the reporters inside to watch the removal of the bullet. In the emergency room, the Leader jokes with the doctors, reciting dirty limericks, doing card tricks, pulling coins from their ears. As they cut away at his bloody shirt, camera men surround the operating table, illuminating the Leader's body in a pure white nimbus of light.

Two weeks later, on the eve of the election, the Leader checks out of the hospital and holds a press conference. At the Leader's side is his new wife, a pretty blonde emergency room nurse who tells the assembled reporters that she fell instantly in love with "his dynamic courage, his willful energy and his compassion." When the press questions them about the difference in their ages (he is in his 80s and she is 22) the Leader jokes that she will just have to try and keep up with him. Everybody laughs and the joke is used as the lead-off for the news on all three networks.

In Ohio, the elections are delayed due to a meltdown at the Youngstown nuclear power plant. Despite this distraction, the Leader pulls in an unprecedented 97 percent of the popular vote and, according to the Electoral College, wins every state. His opponent concedes the election at 9:00 PM Eastern time, goes alone to his room at the Hyatt, and swallows one hundred Percodans. His body is found on a service stairway the next day by one of the chamber maids. In his inaugural address, the new President speaks warmly of his dead adversary, calling him a beautiful guy and a fabulous human being. At the funeral, Liza Minelli sings "Cabaret."

Within a month of taking office, the Leader succumbs to a strange post-operative infection and dies in his sleep. His running mate, a female impersonator named Madam Taboo, declares martial law and orders an air strike on Canada. He then flies to the Bahamas with the Leader's widow and Mister Faraday to "catch some rays."

The "mysterious" Mr. Bey is known only through fugitive appearances in the most marginal of the New Mutant samizdat press, journals such as KAOS (London), POPULAR REALITY, the NAMBLA BULLETIN, FAG RAG and various other anarchist and SexPol zines. His porno sword'n'sorcery novel CROWSTONE: THE CHRONICLES OF QAMAR, was hailed by William Burroughs as the first (and perhaps only) example of a new sub-genre... copies were seized by Customs in "Great" Britain, and the Dutch publisher is being hounded by Rupert Murdoch. Bey's CHAOS: THE BROADSHEETS OF ONTOLOGICAL ANARCHISM (available from Semiotext(e)/Autonomedia) has been praised by (among others) Ginsberg, Burroughs, the Church of the SubGenius, Bob Black, and the chaos-science DYNAMICS NEWSLETTER edited by Ralph Abraham.

The Antarctic Autonomous Zone: A Science-Fiction Story
Hakim Bey

1.

Iced in for the winter
the floes grind against the hull
HMS Terror & the son of Chaos
Erebus, brother & husband of Night
lord of the Cimmerian darkness
the leprosy of the ice

below the dead Sixties
right whales with maws of krill
veils of austral light ripped from the sky
flagged & folded across the mongoloid darkness
under an Arthur-Gordon-Pym-like curse
hexed & abandoned on the shelf ice

2.

the Ice from Outer Space
square motherlode rhinestone blocks
in Baltimore norsedrawn nigra waggons
papayas plaintains avocados sugarcane
giant tropical protruberances
PR boys foreskins taste like mangoes
hard cockshaped stone slippery beneath sweet flesh
ice floes fall from heaven
my flying saucer is made of ice
it lands on your forehead as you sleeep
naked sweating hand cupping rubberbrown cock

3.

in this geodesic igloo
the stacks of yellowing paperbacks
air sour with hibernation-funk
tranced out on New Zealand grass
alone with silent meteorology & delusions
masturbation of lost explorers
hallucinating, crushed by snow

the Antarctic Autonomous Zone
cut off, desolate, radio silence
fantasies of nuclear survival
a doomed race of ice-men
living on fish & hydroponic algae
sinking with glacial slowness
into the antibiotic solitude

4.

color of your spit after eating blackberries
ice buried under giant beehives in the Persian desert
crushed with pomegranate juice & rosewater
(which cools the blood)
      your finger in a silk glove
probes my throat, droplets the color of ice
two hard orchidplums roll over my tongue
icewhite sheets, the overhead fan
a pitcher sweating on the nighttable
wooden screens still closed against afternoon
rub slivers of ice against your nipples
till they stiffen like albino blackberries

5.

or else the A.A.Z.
secedes from the Treaty Nations
ugly wind-blistered town of icy domes
renegade scientists, queer sailors
lunatic-fringe libertarians, a few whores
gun-toting anarchist miners

an economy based on whaling
a few oil wells & tankers, prospecting
shady "offshore" banks, ship registry
& postage stamps of the South Pole
chorus lines of penguins
old fashioned engraving stamps
printed in icy blue lines

6.

on another planet
lost vagrant starship frost
alien gasping, deaf & dumb language of sucking
star-sucking, shower of afternoon ice
the white of your eyes & your teeth

simultaneously I come in my hand
sperm on the bedclothes & your legs
snow buries us, the airconditioner
lets icicles fall & shatter on the paleolithic bed
iced tamarindo, sweet lemon, crushed melon
sugarcane juice with ginger & lime
sperm in my throat
aftertaste of white musk-grapes

7.

count how many moons are rising
over Van Diemen's Land, the dinosaur ice
call room service, call
Galactic Conspiracy Control
perishing of extraterrestrial masonic thirst
the blond boy in lime green shorts
with ice-green sneakers
leaning against the old white cadillac
his cock outlined beneath tight imitation silk.

Ian Watson says, "I have recently launched full-tilt into the deep end of Horror, THE coming venue for speculative fiction, with a first horror novel, THE POWER, due from Headline (UK), about the US bases in Britain, peace camps, nuclear war, rural life and ancient evil; a second horror novel — no, a METAhorror novel, THE FIREWORM (now in print from Gollancz), and a third horror novel on the stocks."

Watson has written far more disgusting stories than this one, stories which we're glad we don't have to proofread and publish, stories we're trying to forget. By comparison this sober scientific account of slimy snail sex seems positively jolly.

Vile Dry Claws of the Toucan
Ian Watson

By now it's beyond dispute that the Zeta Tucanae disc is the only surviving in-depth record of a whole alien civilization.

Found on the little moon of Zeta Tucanae 3 beside the mangled wreckage of a space vehicle, that disc is all we have to go on. Our cyber-drones discovered nothing but frozen radioactive ash down on the destroyed homeworld.

True, we do have the wreckage, plus the suit-shell of the pilot, which the pilot so wantonly and suicidally took off. We also have the interrupted interstellar radio message which has allowed us to read the disc, provisionally. Unfortunately, that message broke off at the "John and Jane" stage. For our entire knowledge of culture we have to rely on that single disc. History, psychology, philosophy, sociology—the whole shebang.

It is my contention that the text on that disc represents what might best be described, in human terms, as a piece of "horror fiction."

171

Oh yes! Not some dreadful warning about the Ultimate Enemy which devastated life on Zeta Tucanae 3 (and was incinerated by it in turn?), but a dark fantasy etched on the disc purely for entertainment, a horror story.

So how do we track back from the distortions and concoctions of an alien horror narrative to some certainties about the civilization which produced it?

Already I hear some cries of disapproval. But please consider. Pain and pleasure have to be universal to all intelligent beings. Fear must be universal. Complex creatures simply couldn't evolve in the absence of pleasure and pain and fear. As soon as technology permits enough excess leisure, "Pleasure through Fear" becomes predictable.

Let's survey the facts.

Zeta Tucanae, sixth star in the far southerly constellation of the Toucan, is very similar to our own sun in size and type. Its third planet isn't much smaller than Earth. Atmosphere: oxygen and nitrogen—plus radioactive dust, smoke particles, and suchlike products of a recent massive nuclear war. Shallow seas, low continents, swamps. Lots of craters, of course, and deserts of windblown ash of recent vintage. No remaining traces of life.

Here evolved a race of intelligent gastropods. Snails.

Huge brainy snails with tough shells secreted on their backs, single slimy adhesive feet for crawling and climbing, no bones whatever, pseudopod eyes and flexible tentacles. Valiant, inquisitive, civilized snails.

Ultimately they invented radio telescopes (as witness the "John and Jane" message), spacecraft, plastics, and nuclear weapons. With homes already on their backs, their architecture would only be industrial.

They were undoubtedly hermaphroditic; otherwise some events on the disc make no sense, even in a horror context.

They stored data upon plastic discs, by squatting on these and laying down a spiral acid trail. They "read" these discs by crawling on them and decoding the vibrational patterns of rough and smooth. Hence Professor Woodford's fanciful comparison of our alien snails to old-fashioned grammophones. (With horns, yet!)

Conventional scientific wisdom—based on a literal reading of the "moon disc"—has it that another race, of vicious, nocturnal predators, also inhabited ZT3. These implacably evil creatures had invaded from "elsewhere" (from another star? from, dare I say it, another dimension? a parallel universe?). the radio message was the start of an interstellar cry for help; and a warning to all amiable life forms. The terminal nuclear war spelled armageddon for the snails and their dire enemies.

These enemies preyed on the snails not only physically but psychically too. Their minds could possess those of the snails; they could infiltrate snail bodies. A snail thus afflicted might show strange talents: the ability to dry out a fellow snail by staring at it, or glue it to the ground, or cause its organs to boil and bubble out. Eventually the possessed snail would rot away, leaving a haunted empty shell. Intercourse with a possessed snail—these were often luridly attractive—would result in cursed offspring, evolutionary throwbacks or freaks: black shell-less slugs, immovable limpets, tiny winkles, clams.

Let us translate a passage from the moon-disc text:

"The Possessed fired a love-dart point-blank into the (Queen's) hind mantle as she turned to flee..."

(I should point out that snails elect which sex they wish to be at any particular time. Copulation takes place by coiling slimily around one another. Foreplay consists in the male shooting—or spitting—hormone-primed "darts" into the flesh of the female to excite her.)

"She felt a dreadful dryness and could not crawl. She smelled the rot of his slime. Knew that he would soon decay inside—but not before he had impregnated her, befouled her, and destroyed (a dynasty)."

" 'No!' she vibrated at him as he oozed over her locked foot. 'This isn't you! This is the Beast inside you!' "

"For a moment a tremble of remembrance made the Possessed shudder. Then the Possession tightened its grip.

" 'No, you shall not give birth to a mere slug! You'll conceive the child of the Beast itself! With its scrawny limbs, its dry tearing claws!' "

"She wished that nuclear fire could boil the world dry before that happened. That the atomic hate-darts could fly from hemisphere to hemisphere, cooking all snailkind—as well as the Dry-Leg-Beasts-That-Lurked-In-Caves, the Beasts-That-Hunted-By-Night-With-Scaley-Claws, the Vile-Intruders-From-That-Other-Realm—if that is what it took to purge the evil.

"As the Possessor overwhelmed her she smelt the stench of his inner rot—he who had been the slickest, sweetest, and juiciest of her suitors. Foul ichors ran from within his shell, and she realized that he was already dead, a zombie-snail operated by the dry cruel mental claw from elsewhere."

"If only she could transform into a he, and save her ovaries from his assault; but his dart had also locked her into the female form! She gagged as the Possessed made love to her, and he ate her vomit for strength to nourish his dribbling seed."

Isn't it obvious what this is? (Professor Woodford might dispute some elements of this translation, but I've mostly omitted brackets from around "ambiguous" words for the sake of clarity.)

Here's another passage:

"He was only six orbits old, and the shell-yard fascinated him: the slimy mud paths, the stately row upon row of empty shells which had once housed living snails, a hundred or a thousand orbits ago. To his junior stalk-eyes that shell-yard seemed to stretch out to infinity. The oldest shells of all were furthest from the entrance."

"Often he slid through the mouth of a shell, which easily accomodated his own, smaller shell, so as to read the death-song of achievements, boasts, autobiography, passions, apologies, or simply poetry which the aging snail had etched onto the inside of its shell when it sensed its natural death creeping closer."

"That day he slid deeper into the shell-yard than ever before—to a zone where shells were so old that many were cracking and crumbling."

"And do he came in all innocence to the ancient ghost shell."

"Its glittering curves, its apparent lack of fragility, its open mouth attracted him. He ignored the faded taste-warnings dissolved in the mud around it; not understanding them, excited. He slid inside and tongued the walls for the death-song."

"Terrible dry pressure immobilized him. He thought that his own shell would be crushed. He thought that a claw was being driven through it. A claw which scratched at his soft mind, and hid itself inside him…"

Likewise, the subsequent passages concerning "the Power"; and those monsters which I playfully dub "weretoucans," snails which assumed the form of clawed, beaked beasts by night.

Who in their right mind, you may well ask, would take a horror novel along to read on a black and airless, lonely moon? Surely that would tend to unbalance a mind already under stress? With the result that each shadow would conceal a lurking Evil. Its claws would scratch at the side of the spaceship, seeking admittance. A pilot might well believe himself possessed, inside his suit!

Surely the moon-disc was a literal, true, and inspirational work, intended to keep our lone snail-astronaut's mind devoutly and bravely on his mission—whatever this was—by cataloguing the wiles and vile actions of the enemy? Thus argues Professor Woodford, translating the text somewhat differently from me.

Not so! And therefore all Woodford's extrapolations from this text, about the history, psychosociology, and every other ology of the snails of ZT3, is so much eyewash. The text is a horror story.

For me, that essential fact "humanizes" the alien snail-people and amply justifies the cost of the expedition.

On first reading this story, we were tempted to reject it because it made us want to puke. We heard about it from INTERZONE, the wonderful British literary SF prozine; they in fact rejected it as too stomach-churning even for them.

Then we realized: Blumlein had called our bluff. We had demanded SF that would shock and disgust — and this was IT. We were stuck. We had to accept the story.

Not that the content is any grosser than other pieces in this book. The difference is this: not only is Blumlein an excellent writer, he's also a medical doctor. His INTERZONE story "Tissue Ablation" caused a lot of stir for similar reasons. Not since Alan Nourse have we seen medical SF with such convincing clinical details — but Nourse is a smiling humanist compared to this guy.

Recently Blumlein has published his first novel, THE MOVEMENT OF MOUNTAINS, on the unlikely but compelling themes of obesity and the benign potential of plague.

One more thing: "Shed His Grace" is the ultimate statement on the administration of President Bonzo; in that sense, it has to be disgusting.

Shed His Grace
Michael Blumlein

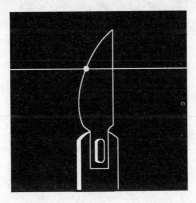

"Is it money? Is that it? Do you need some cash?"

T saw his reflection in the screen and looked quickly away. His supervisor took the sudden movement as a reply and smiled knowingly. She reached into the top drawer of her desk and took out some bills.

"Here. Pay me back when you get your next paycheck."

T too the money and stood up. His supervisor gave him a final look, then bent over the desk and began fiddling with the inside of the monitor. T waited a few moments, then left the room.

He stayed that night for several hours after work, watching a new video from the neurosurgery department. He recognized the surgeon, even though most of his face was covered. The patient was awake during the operation, in a dissociated state of magnetically-induced euphoria. He conversed amiably with the operating staff, although from time to time—when certain parts of his brain were manipulated—his

177

words made no apparent sense. At one point he repeated "jawbone" eighteen times in a row.

When the tape finished, T replaced the master in its file. He dropped a copy, which he had made while he watched, into his coat pocket. He locked the door behind him and left the hospital by way of its basement corridors, silent save for the rushing of waste through plumbing fixtures.

Pushing through a heavy metal door to the street, he came into a night of fog and chill. The streetlights were barely visible; the hospital itself seemed wrapped in gauze. T turned the collar up on his coat and stuck his hands into his pockets. In one he found the bills his supervisor had given him. He had forgotton they were there.

He held them in his hand, frowning in concentration while he waited for a bus. Near the beginning of the video the patient had sung the opening bars of a song about money, but T could not remember the words. He had a tape at home of the President making a speech about economic policy, but all he could remember was Mr. Reagan's face. Thinking of it, T relaxed a little and put the money back in his pocket. When the bus came, instead of depositing a token in the machine, he gave the driver a handful of bills. He took a seat by himself, more confident now. His head was beginning to clear.

As the Olympic torch had made its way westward, carried by a young boy, a librarian, a man without legs in a wheelchair, T had secured his apartment. Now it was done, and as he entered he felt a certain resolution.

It was a single room, a studio with a small kitchenette at one end. A sliding glass door led the way to a narrow concrete porch which overlooked a back alley. T had covered the glass with a double layer of black velveteen, stapling it aiong the the edge and holding it snug against the floor with bricks. There were no other windows, and day in the apartment was as black as night.

Against the velveteen T had placed his monitor/receivers. Four rows of four each, sixteen in all, stacked in a square. On either side of the bank of receivers sat a video camera on a tripod; each camera was flanked by a pair of keylights. The hardware had been patched, and a single cable ran across the room to a panel on a table. Next to the table was a straight backed wooden chair. In a corner sat a cot. There was no other furniture in the room, and the single bulb in the ceiling had been removed.

T dropped his coat on the cot and went to the kitchen. He took a Coke from the fridge, popped it, and when he had swallowed half went and sat in the chair opposite the monitors. He lay his hand lightly on the keyboard at his side, his fingers settling into the familiar depressions of the keys. He pushed one and the dead screens sprang to life. Colored light filled the room.

He pushed a short sequence of buttons and in a moment the light was replaced by the image of a man running with a torch up the steps of a stadium. Tens of thousands surrounded him, and when he lit the Olympic flame, they cheered and sang. It was a tape of the beginning of the Games, and T began each of his days with it.

The opening ceremony ended and the face of the man was replaced by a boxing match, one of the day's events. A wiry Asian was stalking a Black man; each was drenched with sweat. Blood welled from the Black man's upper lip, and when the Asian punched his face, the blood flew into the air. The Black man countered with an uppercut to the jaw, and the other man's head snapped back. Punches were thrown to the.belly, one below the belt. T shuddered and hit a button. The boxers froze. T picked up a cassette that lay on the edge of the table and slipped it into the panel. The frozen images of the boxers stayed on the twelve peripheral screens, disappearing from the four center ones. In their place shone the face of the First Lady.

She wore a purple silk dress with a pink floral pattern across the bodice. The neck was high and ruffled, the sleeves short. Around a wrist she wore a gold bracelet.

She was in the midst of a tour of the White House, which T had recorded some months before. Her lips were red and smiling, her eyes bright. She made a demure gesture and turned down a long hall. The hem of the dress brushed against her calves, stroking them only inches above the mound of her heels. The scene shifted.

She was in a different room, standing under a chandelier. She was moving her lips, but T kept the audio off. She pointed to the fixture, extending her arm with a ballerina's grace. The word FUCK flitted in the shadows of the loose skin of her arm as it entered the sleeve of her dress. T stopped the tape. He touched rewind, then magnification and play.

Mrs. Reagan's face took up the four screens, illuminated from above by a light source out of the picture. Bits bf rouge and powder like crumbs of toast stuck to the pores of her skin. T increased the magnification as the camera swung down her cheek to her shoulder. Each thread of silk was visible, dark against the soft white folds of her axillary skin. T searched for the word in the shadows, stopping the tape, looking from screen to screen. It had gone, but he found other things hidden there. Grains of white powder covered the black tips of tiny hairs. A bead of sweat glistened on the loose skin. A drop of semen. Into the fossa wound a pale blue vein.

T studied the picture for hours. He found the thin surgical line where redundant folds of axillary tissue had been resected. Beneath the grains of powder he saw the roughage where a razor had excoriated the skin. Over and over his eyes searched the stubble of shaven hair. It seemed so certain. So simple.

T looked at the screens on the periphery, at the frozen shoulders of the boxers, rippling with muscles. He looked at the First Lady's armpit. The boxers. The Lady. He frowned and pushed a button.

Mrs. Reagan vanished as all sixteen screens came alive with boxing. The Black man was bleeding more from his lip, and a new cut had been opened beneath his eye. He held up his hands to protect his face, and the Asian fighter struck him a series of blows to the midsection. One barely missed his genitals, and when he doubled over to protect himself, his opponent sent him staggering with an uppercut to the jaw. The Black man fell against the ropes, and the camera held a close-up of blood running down his cheek. T grimaced and leaned forward in his chair. The shot changed.

A row of male swimmers crouched on blocks, arms thrown back. Their backs were taut and suddenly they uncoiled, arching out and over the water. They sliced through the pool like sharp tools, clean and strong. They flipped and turned with a mechanization that held T in awe. Finally they stopped, and the winner raised his hands in victory. He leapt from the pool, water dripping from his body, making the skin look like wax. T froze the shot and magnified it. The swimmer's chest was smooth, his legs and groin as barren of hair as a child's. The skin looked raw, as though it had recently been scraped by metal. His narrow suit was tight around his waist; it seemed to choke him.

T stared and cut the shot. He finished his Coke then stood from his chair and began to pace. The room was hot; he felt restless. Sweat began to build in his armpit, his crotch, and he removed his shirt and pants. The random light from the screens flickered on his body, casting a rough shadow on the opposite wall. T rubbed his chest and went to the kitchen for another Coke.

Sometime later he found himself in the bathroom, the shower-stall, standing in a stream of cold water. He was shivering, and he stepped out to dry. He brought a stool in front of the sink and stood on it. The image of his chest reflected in the mirror on the medicine cabinet; the hairs were dark and curly. He rubbed them and opened the cabinet door.

The razor was new; he barely felt it. In the shower again he felt as never before. Like glass.

The next day his chest was sore, but the day after it was better. Each day following he shaved it, and his legs, until the skin became accustomed to the razor. He rubbed oil into his pores, enchanted by the elegant smoothness of his skin. He did not return to work.

In the mornings, when the Games were not being televised, and often between events, T watched tapes he had copied from ones at the hospital. Some were experiments on animals—cannulations of dogs, tumor induction in mice—but most were live surgeries on humans. A wide range of operations had been taped and grouped for study. The one marked "Plastic and Reconstructive Procedures" included a number of related operations: reduction and augmentation mammoplasty, resection of adipose tissue for morbid obesity, the use of the abdominal skin flap to reconstruct the penile shaft following accidental amputation. A green-masked surgeon was in the process of explaining the rationale for a certain lateral incision when his face dissolved into white noise. On each of the sixteen receivers a red light blinked, signalling the beginning of the Olympic telecast day. In a moment an announcer's face appeared. The after-image of the lateral pubic incision became his smile. His lips moved like the mouth bf a fish; T punched audio.

"Gold," he said, "solid gold last night. The U.S.A..." T cut him off. The voice was too jarring after the silent grace of the surgery.

The picture changed to a young man standing on a pedestal. His hands were clenched in a victory salute; above his head on a pole waved the American flag. The camera moved closer and T recognized the face of the swimmer from before. His hair was no longer wet; T looked but could see no make-up.

A sweatshirt covered his chest and around his neck hung a tri-colored ribbon with a gold medal attached to it. His eyes brimmed with tears.

T studied him for a long time before inserting the cassette of the First Lady. He pushed buttons to give her the center of the monitor bank, freezing the image of the joyful swimmer in a ring around her.

She was in an upstairs study beside a mahogany desk. One hand rested on the edge of the desk, which was smooth and polished so that it reflected light. In her other hand she held an open book, from which she was reading. The high collar of her dress fit snug around her throat. In the slack hollow of her jaw, in shadow, the word KNIFE was written. A blemish on the side of her chin was covered with flakes of powder. Her lips were carefully painted red; under magnification T noticed that the lipstick had begun to crack.

Mrs. Reagan finished reading the passage she had selected and replaced the book on its shelf. She pointed to a painting of a man flanked by an American flag. The man was a general, a president. She smiled and began to walk to the next room.

T turned on the sound. Her high heels clacked on the hardwood floor. The sound was a prodrome, a stimulant. She reached a tall door and pushed it open. Inside was a bedroom with a high-canopy bed that had not been slept in for years. The First Lady sat on the edge and began to discuss the history of quilt-making. T turned off the sound and watched her hands. Finely veined, powdered, she did not use them to speak. The gold bracelet around her wrist seemed too loose.

T stopped her and looked at the swimmer with the medal around his neck. His hands were clenched; Mrs. Reagan's were folded in her lap. Her lips were slightly parted; his were closed tight. T watched in fascination the tip of the First Lady's tongue; finally he pushed a button.

The two figures disappeared, replaced by a swarm of gymnasts. Young girls arched their bodies, split their legs on the floor, flipped in the air. T froze one upside down to examine the angle her legs made as they joined her torso. He brought the shot to medium magnification and followed the edge of her leotard across her thigh. He saw no hair, no sign of damage to the skin. He followed a lateral seam to her breasts, which were flattened by the extension of her arms. The outline of her ribs poked through the tight suit.

T allowed her to complete the vault, watching her land and thrust her chest out like a bird. She skittered from the mat to the side of the arena, where she was hugged by a man and two other girls. All of them were blond; there were tears in the girl's eyes.

T reached for a cassette, stuck it in the recorder. The young girl's tears were replaced by the gloved hands of a surgeon. They had already completed an oblique abdominal incision and were in the process of mobilizing a section of colon. Deftly the fingers brought out a loop of intestine, placed two glass rods beneath it to prevent it from slipping back, then incised the front wall of the colon to provide drainage. The next section of the tape showed the technique for the placement of a permanent colostomy. The final part showed the care of the colostomy site, including attachment of the bag and disposal of fecal waste.

T stood and paced the room. It was increasingly hot, and the sweat that bathed his barren chest and axillae stung. The monitor screens were full of the noise between segments of tape.

T rubbed himself and looked down. His skin swarmed with thousands of rainbow spots. On the surface of his nylon shorts rose the shape of his genitals.

The screens came alive with the picture of a forceps and scalpel dissecting the necrotic edges of a burn. Bits of scab and dead tissue lay on a strip of guaze to the side. T turned away and went to the kitchen. The dark room lit up for a moment when he opened the refrigerator. He took out another Coke, squinting his eyes until the door closed, then drank in darkness. When he was done, he crushed the can in his palm like he had seen someone do on television and threw it in the garbage. Then he went to the bathroom, took out his razor and shaved his head.

Mrs. Reagan was on her way downstairs, her hand sliding smoothly on the rail of the bannister. The camera angle from below made her seem tall. With each step the hem of the dress rode up her leg, exposing the edge of her shin and lower part of her knee. On close-up T saw the fine grains of make-up powder on the skin and beneath, the narrow purple lines of her veins. The silky fabric of the dress stroked her as she came down the stairs.

At the bottom she paused, twirling the gold bracelet on her wrist. She turned a corner, walked partway down a long carpeted hall, then stopped with a finger to her lips. Her nail, red and glossy, glinted.

She pushed open a door, then stepped to the side. At the far end of the room, behind a large desk was her husband. He looked up and smiled. He was unperturbed by the interruption. He motioned her in.

T froze the picture as the President was in the process of standing. His head was bent forward and seemed about to fall on the desktop. On half the screens the Olympics returned. A two-hundred pound man was straining to press a one-thousand pound weight. His arms shook as he tried to lock his elbows; his face was bloated with blood. He raised the weight over his head, held it, then let it crash to the floor. The President's head was six inches from the desktop.

The weightlifter staggered backwards, momentarily stunned. T froze the picture and magnified it. A blood vessel had burst in the lifter's eye, filling the white part with red. A thread of spittle hung from his lip.

T returned to the President and First Lady and pushed 'play'. Mr. Reagan raised his head and came around the desk to greet his wife. His smile was broad, his teeth capped in white. In the folds of skin at his throat animals rustled.

He made a benign gesture to the camera and reached out, pulling Mrs. Reagan into view. They stood side by side, holding hands, chatting and smiling at each other. T noticed that Mrs. Reagan's bracelet had been pushed high up her forearm. It seemed to constrict the tissues beneath it, and the veins distal to it were engorged with blood. During the course of their conversation she loosened it, sliding it casually toward her wrist. In the crease it had left in the skin above, in faint relief, was the impression of a phallus. T looked to the President, who seemed unaware of his wife beside him. He was jolly and strong. T pushed a button, and the frozen figure of the weightlifter was replaced by the same man standing on a platform draped with flags. He wore a sleeveless shirt, a jersey, and around his bull neck hung a gold medal.

T blanked the screens, all but the four at the top, which he froze. The President had raised his hand in salute, and his wife's face in profile was beaming.

He got out of his chair long enough to take off his shorts, then sat back down. He flipped a switch on the panel to his side, and the pair of keylights blazed on. They hurt his eyes, but he tried not to blink. He pressed a button, and the cameras warmed up. They were already focused on the spot where he sat, and in a moment the image of his chest and belly appeared on the bottom three rows of monitors. T moved a lever on the on the screens panel and the image shifted. It moved down to his crotch.

His genitals.

He lifted his feet, which had been planted on the floor, up to the chair and put his heels together. This brought his pelvis out, highlighting his penis and scrotum. He moved slightly to one side, trying to eliminate shadow as much as possible. When he was satisfied, he got up and went to the kitchen.

He found a shallow pan and filled it with water, then lay it on one of the burners of the stove. After he had turned on the flame, he searched until he found a length of kitchen string, which he dropped in the water. He sharpened his stainless steel carving knife, then lay it beside the piece of string. He took another Coke from the fridge, swallowed it in three gulps, then went to the bathroom.

He lathered himself in the showerstall and shaved his groin and pubic area. Drying took less time now that he was hairless. When he returned to the kitchen, the water in the pan was boiling.

He brought the pan and a pair of surgeons gloves he had taken from the the hospital into the other room and placed them at the foot of the chair. He positioned himself as he had before, keeping his eyes on the top row of screens. The President and First Lady gave him strength, and he.pushed a series of buttons, extending them to the twelve screens on the periphery. On the four center ones were his genitals, pale and hairless in the burning light.

T stared at himself as he had at the swimmers. He reached down and rubbed until he was arched and strong. The head bobbed gently to the sound of a silent anthem. Mrs. Reagan's gold bracelet dangled around her wrist. The President was smiling.

T leaned over and snapped on the surgeon's gloves. They were pale green, making his hands seem a part of someone else's body. He dipped his fingers in the water and took out the string, then settled back in the chair. He did not look at himself, watching instead his image on the screens. His penis was stiff, lady-like in its posture. His hands did not tremble as he grasped the ends of the string and wound them around the root of his penis and scrotal sac. He pulled the string tight and made a surgeon's knot, and another. The President smiled, the First Lady straight and certain at his side. For a second T lost concentration. His head turned giddy, he thought he heard a voice. The moment passed.

He stared at the screens, Mr. and Mrs. Reagan surrounding. Him at the center. The center. He leaned over and picked up the knife. Its edge glinted in the light. Firmly squeezing the glans between thumb and forefinger, he began the amputation.

Thom Metzger lives in Rochester NY and publishes his own work, pow-erful unclassifiable texts full of dark foreboding and black humor, some of which we printed in SEMIOTEXT(E) USA. We've seen the manuscript of his first novel, BIG GURL, aptly described by one reader as "the prose equivalent of R. Crumb and S. Clay Wilson on evil speed and sterno." Last we heard, there was talk of bringing it out as a mass-market horror pulp with an embossed cover. Haw! what a joke on the reader!

(Late note: BIG GURL has appeared, cover and all.)

All Right, Everybody on the Floor!
Thom Metzger

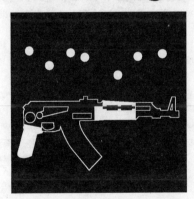

I want to see fifty hard ones. And let me hear it: NO BUGS, NO PIGS, NO SLUGS. No crabs or stinky shrimp. We've got to keep ourselves on the straight and narrow all the way to the end. Face down and spread 'em.

I'M TALKING TO YOU! That's right, Handsome. Today we separate the men from the boys and the boys from the Nematodes.

The clock is ticking down and we got the End of Time right around the corner. But just because the enemy is outside the gate looking in and licking their shiny swollen purple lips, doesn't mean we're going to relax the rules one tiny little bit. It's still no cud, cleft hoof, unclean. No bivalves or creeping thing either. We got where we are because of rules and the minute we forsake them we might just as well open the air lock and say, "Okay, you hideous nightspawn of loathsome abomination, come on in and run your tiny scarlet love-nodes over our precious relics of a bygone golden age and tramp your noxious little pink toes on our nice new wall-to-wall with matching drapery."

All right. Listen up. Some of you have never actually had personal contact with the enemy before. Let me say this up-front and I'm not going to repeat it: SHOW HARD. That's our motto and that's our way of life. And when I say Show Hard, I mean Show Hard. Your job is not to kill the enemy. Your job is to kill the enemy so that they know they've been killed, and to make sure they'll never raise even one little dismembered fingertip against us, in this world, or the next.

It's not enough just to obliterate the flesh. If you only destroy the body and neglect to get the soul you're just sending reinforcements to the next front. We need those souls. The rumors you've heard are true. The enemy does indeed have a beachhead in the next world. And if we kill them here, we've got to make sure their souls don't end up getting re-outfitted and sent up in the next wave of stark-naked gibbering berzerkers whose only reason for existence is to leave their lipstick prints and salt-water stench in the inner chambers of Celestial Holiness.

We want their plasm, not just corpses. We want a body count and a soul count. Do I make myself understood?

And I don't think I need to tell you that :What we're up against here is no mere slime-flecked miasmic contagion of septic and bestial corruption from the deepest and blackest depths of the most hideous and unthinkable abyss. We got something on our hands here that's a lot worse than that. Believe me, this is no trifling case of cooties. No amount of scrubbing is going to get this off unless our hearts are pure.

And our hearts can't be pure unless our bowels are pure. So that's why there'll be a double ration of Yellow Phenolphthalein for everybody and right before you go over the top I want you all to spend a few extra minutes alone with your IPECAC. Do I make myself understood?

Soap on a rope! Soap on a rope! Pocket Pal! The perfect gift. Have a nice day on the floor and spread 'em. This is no drill. What we got here is total war and that's why some of you are going in before you got to see the last of the filmstrips. This is the Big One. This is the last battle. So if you think you can go up against the enemy with even one little speck of the stinky thing inside, then you'd better think again, Buster. Do you really think you can beat the somnolent denizens of the nethermost pit of darkest degradation and mind-numbing terror if you've got the occasional discomfort of irregularity? Even if there's only one little iota of the nightsoil in your body, they'll smell it from half-way around the world and you might just as well lay down right then and there and say "Okay, maybe you were right all along and I really do want to live for all eternity in a universe of festering malignant perversion."

But hey, let's look on the sunny side of the street: don't you ever forget that you're the best equipped in the Solar System. You've all got double protection with reinforced ends, a lifetime supply of Hard to Beat, maximum throwweight, the latest in fall fashions with matching accessories.

 And most important, you're all fighting for something bigger and better than your own meaningless desires and needs. Our goal here is nothing short of unlimited growth potential. If we succeed here today, then huge vistas will open up before us: the entire consumer sector will be ours for the taking.

One hundred percent market share for Dimensions X-prime through Omega Slash Asterisk Ampersand. With options for total buyout of the outer rim quadrants and complete franchising rights.

So this is it. These are our objectives:

1.) An entire squadron of invisible ginks have infiltrated sector X-ray—George—Bongo—Zip. They must be routed from their positions before the holy fire of brotherly love can vaporize them and seal in flavorful juices.

2.) At least a dozen squawk nozzle overthrow modem vectors have been sited on the sidereal horizon. So you'll need to have your Praying Hands set on Stun and don't hesitate to use the neural joy probe if the situation warrants. Remember, it's either you or them.

3.) And lastly, near the serum processing plant, we've got a glandular assault team positioned, but the enemy has their throbbing thrill dart at the crux of the perimeter and a handsome new ashtray with pictures of their honeymoon and a set of fancy martini glasses.

So let me hear it:

No bugs, no pigs, no slugs
no things that crawl or hop
no blood without a wound
no shoes on holy ground
eight tiny reindeer on the roof
you'd better watch out, you'd better not cry
a jolly old man with a beard and a whip
and a string of frozen drool hanging from his lip.

Hello, our name is Legion, we'll be your pastoral counselor today. LOOK AT ME WHEN I'M TALKING TO YOU!

I want to see scalps. I want to see fingers and teeth and ribbons of skin. And most of all I want to see a pile of heads on the floor. I want to look eye to eye with the one on top and do you know what I'm going to say? "Forget it, Vermin. Just forget it. There's no way you're going to get me to unsew your lips and let your soul escape. We've got you bound and gagged now until the end of time."

Okay, as Zero Hour approaches, maybe a few of you are feeling a little nervous, perhaps a little upset in the tummy. That's all right. That's just fine. It doesn't matter if you're a virgin or a battle-hardened veteran, everybody feels that way before he goes out to kill. If you've got to vomit, go right ahead. Let it all out. Your body knows if you've got any taint that needs to be purged. Only when you're pure, when you're clean and neat and unspotted like a little newborn lamb can you go out there with no fear and kill the thing that was born to suffer and die.

Over and over and over again we told you: keep your body and your mind pure, and Don't Spill the Seed. You're saving it for the Big One. Well, it's here, boys. This is the Big One.

And it's so easy. It's so convenient. It's just three simple steps: 1.) grab the gink by the hair, 2.) stick your shock wand into the mouth real quick so they don't have a chance to let the soul escape, 3.) tell them they have the right to remain silent and pull the trigger.

All right, the time has come. I want you all to show me some Pep. Some hard, manly Pep. I want you all out there killing like there's no tomorrow, because there is no tomorrow. This is the end of time and a new beginning, the dawn of a new age. We already have the victory, because we have the blessed assurance, the unassailable knowledge that we must and will prevail. We're not winning souls to add luster to our already gleaming crowns. No, we're winning and enslaving souls for the Master of the Glory Hole, the Champion of Champions, our close personal friend, the Perfect Host, the One, the Only, the Lord of Pep!

We need this win. We've got to have this one or else our way of life, our world, our very beings will be swallowed up in the surging, bubbling, oozing juggernaut plague of infected noisome horror.

So zip yourselves up, boys. Get your gear in order. Pressurize the airlock. Finish up your now-I-lay-me's.

I want every one of you going out there with a cry on your lips and a song in your hearts.

Let me hear it, let me taste it, let me feel it:

HAVE A NICE DAY!

As Malcolm X said, chickens come home to roost. That's the gist of this fable by Lewis Shiner, a leading light of Cyberpunkism, and winner of Our Special Editors' Award for Snappiest Opening Paragraph.

Shiner lives in Texas (!), once edited a zine called MODERN STORIES, and has recently published a novel, DESERTED CITIES OF THE HEART (Doubleday).

The Gene Drain
Lewis Shiner

JSN reached up to the row of glowing buttons across his forehead and changed his mind with an audible click.

Nothing helped. He couldn't shake the sense of disaster hovering over him like an avalanche in progress. In a last, desperate attempt to salvage his mood he worked up an autonomous search program and sent it spiraling back through his core memory.

Up on the dias the alien who identified himself as Brother Simon droned on: "...and, uh, we, that is, bein as how we are all brothers in Johnny, I mean, we ud, uh, really like to find us a place in yalls hearts, praise Johnny, and maybe even someplace where we could stay for a while..."

Somebody behind JSN said, "This is pathetic." The assembled UN delegates, representing the 2,873,261 free and independent nations of Earth, began to boo. Some were standing up and shouting; others clawed loose bits of wiring from appendages and hurled them at the dias.

Brother Simon stopped talking and the seven aliens sat quietly and took the abuse. They were nominally humanoid, but hideously pale, fleshy, thick-bodied, and slow. One or another of them constantly picked at its face or scratched the crotch of its shapeless gray clothing or spat a fat yellow glob onto the floor.

It had been a mistake to bring them to New York, JSN now realized. He'd promised the delegates alien emissaries and delivered these travesties of humanity that not only exuded unpleasant noises and odors, but committed the ultimate crime of being boring besides.

What else could he have done? He was a pop star, not a politician, and it had been plain bad luck that their crude shuttle had landed on his estate.

The aliens had been following, as far as JSN could make out, a primitive TV broadcast back to its source. It had come from a city called Killville or something—reflexively JSN pulled the data—Lynchburg, that was it. Back in the twentieth century it had been a center for some kind of religious propaganda, and apparently the aliens had learned their harsh and unpleasant English from what they'd intercepted. What had been Lynchburg was now no more than a few burned and abandoned hillsides on the edge of JSN's land.

From what they'd managed to stammer out JSN understood they were the advance front for an entire orbiting mothership, full of hundreds more just like them: the misshapen, retarded refuse of some galactic civilization. He'd hidden their shuttle in a disused barn, hoping the stench of the place would help cover that of the aliens. Then he tried to get hold of LNR, the Duchess of the local corporation. Unfortunately she was in for a new prosthesis and JSN had been forced to handle the situation himself.

Well, he'd handled it and he'd blown it. He'd just have to admit it and get the aliens offstage before the other delegates rioted. He stood up, fought his way to the front, then noticed a buzzing in his mastoid. His program was finished. Holding a finger up to the crowd, he punched in the results.

"Holy shit," he whispered as the data started to roll. He had forgotten about the microphones and cameras and naked eyes and ears that were all focused on him. "Holy shit," he said again. "They're us!"

The three of them met for a council of war at JSN's country house: JSN, LNR, and a man named DNS who was LNR's top advisor. JSN found DNS in the foyer, admiring a piece of taxidermy. "They were called cows," DNS said. "People used to eat them and wear their skins."

JSN glanced back at LNR. "I think JSN knows that," she said. "It *is* his cow."

"Maybe we'd be more comfortable in the study," JSN offered.

"A very rich protein source, beef," DNS said. He was short, heavy around the middle, and had more prosthetics than JSN had ever seen on one person before, all of them dented, discolored, and hopelessly out of date. "Gave people a lot of spunk."

"Not to mention arteriosclerosis and cancer," JSN said, waving his arm at the open door. DNS reluctantly went in.

"So," LNR said, settling at one end of an antique sofa. "We're going to have to do something. If anybody finds out where they are, they're liable to mob the place and tear them to pieces."

"I know," JSN said. "There's nothing people hate worse than bad video. Especially when it's live. I'm really sorry."

"Don't worry about it," LNR said graciously. "It's partly my fault, after all. If I hadn't been in surgery…" She held up a gleaming new hand. "Do you like it, by the way?"

"Very much," JSN said. He had seen her a couple of times before at state parties or concerts, but never had a chance to talk to her. Now he found himself quite infatuated. Her skull was sleek and hairless, her prosthetic arm and leg—on opposite sides, of course—were polished beryllium alloy, perfect complements to her skeletally thin naturals. Two bright neon'd veins ran up her neck for a splash of color. I'd sure like to network with that, he thought crudely.

"It still has a few bugs in the flexors," LNR said, "but on the whole…"

"Very nice," JSN said.

"Anyway. You say this mother ship was launched in the twentieth century, the computer malfunctioned and took them in a big circle and landed back here on Earth, thinking it was a new planet."

"It *is* a new planet as far as they're concerned," DNS interrupted. "I mean, can you imagine what *we* look like to *them*?"

"Shut up, DNS," LNR said. "Meanwhile, the crew just sort of backslid a few generations, evolutionarily speaking, what with the small gene pool and all. Is that pretty much the gist of it?"

"I found records of the launching, and some distress signals. That seems to be what it all points to."

"So how come nobody remembered any of this?" She patted the back of the sofa and JSN sat down next to her.

"No reason they should," JSN said. "I mean, did they look that human to you?"

"I don't think they look that bad," DNS said.

"Shut up, DNS," LNR said, and turned back to JSN. "I see what you mean."

"This was a couple hundred years ago, after all. Data like that isn't going to be in anybody's volatile memory. It's going to be banked. Unless somebody had a reason to think they *weren't* aliens, who would go looking for it?"

"But you thought of it," LNR said.

Was that admiration in her tone? JSN brushed casually at his forehead and punched up a little extra charm. "Oh no," he said, "it was just an accident. Really. In fact I was looking for, well, something to use against them."

"You mean," LNR said, "like a, a *weapon*?" The tip of her tongue just touched her silvered lips. "How twisted." She crossed her beryllium leg over her natural with a flash of light so intense that JSN nearly blinked his mirrored contacts into place.

"We have to do something," he said. "If we knocked out that mother ship we wouldn't have to keep confronting the fact that we share the same genetics with those... animals."

"I know what you mean," LNR said, "but it's just bound to give *somebody* the wrong impression. Suppose we set them up their own country, maybe someplace like Antarctica?"

"I'm not sure even that would be isolated enough. On top of everything else they seem to have some sort of weird messianic religion, and you know you can't trust people like that. They'd be starting wars and pogroms and handing out literature door-to-door as soon as we turned our backs on them."

"Why are you so hostile?" DNS asked. He'd been walking around the library, touching things, and now he'd gone into a higher gear. Sweat had started to soak through his clothes and he kept rubbing his hands on his kilt, even though there was virtually no exposed skin left on them. "They're not so unpleasant. And I find their women somewhat... er...attractive. I've always said, we shouldn't be so quick to jettison our own history."

"You've always said that," LNR said tiredly.

"History?" JSN said. "Who cares about history? That's the wrong direction."

"This is *living* history," DNS said, pacing frenetically. "That's not just a gene pool up on that ship, it's a gene bank." He began to snatch bits of paper off the desk and tables, shred them compulsively with his fingers, and stuff them into his recycler. "Vigorous, healthy genes, not the feeble leftovers we've got. Those people are everything we're not: natural, in touch with themselves—"

"Brainless," JSN said, "malodorous—"

"Try to see it my way," DNS said, and JSN obligingly punched up a less hostile persona. "We've let technology take over completely from nature. Less than one percent of our population would be viable without some kind of hardware support."

He should know, JSN thought, nodding. The man was only intermittently flesh.

"And the technology that's holding it all together is shoddy!" DNS went on. "Over ninety percent of the manufactured goods in the world are defective! Ninety percent! And that's just the stuff that makes it through the QC checks at the factories!"

"Still," JSN said, as kindly as possible, "I don't think I'd care to have any of those devolved genetics in my hatchery."

"And that's another thing. Even our reproduction is dependent on technology. Do you know what the birthrate is? It's .2 of the mortality rate, and falling!"

"So what?" JSN shrugged amiably. "If we need more kids we can always decant them."

"No! We have to go back to the old ways before it's too late!"

"DNS," said LNR firmly, "shut up." To JSN she said, "You have to forgive him. He had an implant accident when he was a kid and blew out most of his frontal lobe. Hasn't trusted technology since. Those who need it the most like it the least, eh?"

"You think I'm crazy," DNS said, "but you'll see. If only we could get sex and procreation linked again—"

"You'd have a world," JSN said, reverting to his former agressive self at the touch of a button, "that I wouldn't much want to live in. LNR, would you care to go watch some video and talk about this some more and maybe fuck?"

"Sounds heavy," she said, and JSN led her to the door.

"You'll be sorry," DNS warned, and JSN cheerfully shut him in the library.

The orgone generator refused to come up to speed and for a few helpless, frustrated moments JSN wondered if DNS had been right. Nothing seemed to work any more. Then LNR found a way to patch around it and JSN became promptly and thoroughly distracted.

A little less than an hour later a shrill alarm interrupted them. "Shit," JSN said, yanking cables out of various orifices. "I knew I shouldn't have left him alone."

"Here." LNR unwrapped something from his left leg so he could hobble over to a monitor. "Is it DNS?"

"Yeah," JSN said. "He found the barn where I stashed the shuttle."

"And the weirdos too?"

"Yeah. That guy seems like a real jerk. What do you keep him around for?"

"Well, you don't want an advisor who's just going to agree with you all the time. He's definitely got his own ideas."

That seemed reasonable to JSN. "I'd better get out there. He's liable to bring the whole world down on us." He started putting on his shirt.

"I'll come too," LNR said. "After all, I brought him into this." She had her shoes on and was ready to go; her black outfit, JSN had discovered to his vast pleasure, was a mutant cell strain and a living part of her body.

JSN hurried into the rest of his clothes and led the way outside.

The night was clear and hot. Cyborg mowers had cut the fields that afternoon and the smell of battered grass filled the air. JSN stopped for moment and scanned the star patterns.

"There," he said, pointing to a bright spot in Capricorn, near the eastern horizon. "The mother ship."

"It must be huge," LNR said, and JSN nodded. "And to think it's just crawling with devos. It's enough to give you a head crash."

JSN slipped quietly through the oversized barn door, noticing that the lingering odor of livestock had been routed by the more potent essence of the devos. In the dim parking lights of the shuttle he saw Brother Simon and all six of the others standing in a circle around the sweating DNS

"DNS!" he shouted, being careful to breathe through his mouth. "What the fuck are you doing here?"

DNS flinched in obvious guilt, then recovered. "I'm a doctor," he said indignantly. "These people need proper medical attention. What do you think they are, zoo specimens?"

JSN turned to LNR, who had come in after him. "Is he a doctor?"

"I don't know," she said. "I think maybe he put a chip in for it once."

"If that's all you're doing," JSN demanded, "why did you think you had to sneak in?"

"I assumed you had something else on your mind." "Look," JSN said to the devo nearest him, a heavyset female with huge, drooping breasts behind the front panel of her overalls. "You don't have to put up with this guy if you don't want to."

"Yall are wastin yore time talkin to the helpmeat," Brother Simon said. The female smiled at JSN in vacant agreement. "But dont worry none. We ud be proud to talk to yore doctor fella. Mebbe we ud get a chance to share the Good News with him." "You mean you're leaving?" LNR asked.

"Pardon?"

"Isn't that the good news?"

"I meant the Good News about our Lord and Savior, Johnny Carson."

JSN accessed his core, noticing, from her slightly uprolled eyes, that LNR was doing the same. "I don't have anything on it," he said. "You?"

"I can't tell. I think I've got some bad sectors in my religion directory."

"Sorry," JSN said to Brother Simon. "We don't have the foggiest notion what you're talking about."

"Yall aint heard the Word?"

"Is that the same as the good news?" LNR asked. "Because if it is, no, we haven't."

"If yall wanna step inside, I ud be proud to give my witness."

"Sure," LNR said. "Why not?"

The devo took them into the shuttle. The smell in the barn was bad enough, but inside the cramped corridors of the ship it was stale, fermented, overpowering. Someone had scrawled slogans like "Smile! Johnny Loves Yall!" and "I ♥ Johnny" on the white plastic walls in what looked and smelled like human excrement.

"I don't know how much of this I can stand," JSN confided.

"Me either," LNR said, "but it's kind of like with DNS. I can't resist a crank. Just a couple minutes, okay?"

Brother Simon typed the letters GOODNEWS onto the keyboard of the shuttle's main computer, using only one finger of each hand and making a lot of mistakes. He stared at the finished word for a while then hit the RETURN key.

A meter-square screen lit up at the front of the room and a voice boomed, "There's Good News tonight!" The blank screen dissolved into a sound stage full of furniture. A dark-haired man stumbled onto the stage, tripped, and fell noisily across the furniture, smashing several of the chairs to pieces. The camera tightened on his face and the man said, "Live! From New York! It's... the Gospel According to Matthew!"

The scene changed to a murky river flowing through a desert. A bearded man stood in water past his knees, his back to the camera, addressing a mob of peasants wearing towels on their heads. "I baptize you with water for repentance, but he who is coming after me is mightier than I, whose sandals I am not worthy to lick! He will baptize you with Holy Sitcoms and with celebrities! And now... heeeeeeere's Johnny!"

A man with short white hair waded into view from behind the camera, then turned to wink. His skin was evenly, artificially tanned, and he had the arrogant smirk of a pre-adolescent. He wore a 20th-century dress suit with lapels out to the shoulders and had something orange tied around his neck. Laughter swelled to fill the soundtrack.

"Hey there!" the man said. "Have we got a great show tonight!" The river came nearly to his waist and his suit was starting to sag with water, but he didn't seem to notice. "We've got the poor in spirit (applause) for theirs is the kingdom of heaven. We've got those who mourn (more applause), fresh from Las Vegas, and believe me, they shall be comforted. We've got the meek, and right here, on tonight's show, they're going to inherit the earth, and what do you think about that?" (Thundrous applause.)

"Wow," LNR said. "This is really twisted."

JSN had pumped the entire video into a core search. "Parts of it seem to be out of the Christian bible, but it's almost beyond recognition. Hey!" he shouted to Brother Simon, who stood enraptured in front of the screen, "are you guys Christians, is that it?"

"Christians?" LNR said with alarm. "You mean like Torquemada and Henry Lee Lucas and Jerry Fallwell?"

"We are Carsinagins," Brother Simon said. "We believe every Image of the Sacred Word was divinely inspired, and we live by Its Law. Johnny be praised!"

"Wait a minute," LNR said, holding.up one finger to indicate incoming data. "We were looking in the wrong place. This Carson was a twentieth century video star. Something is really wrong here. What kind of computer is this?"

"It's a Generation V," JSN said, reading the nameplate. "Uh oh. You don't mean..."

"Heuristic self-programming. Artificial—" she choked, unable to hold back her laughter.

"Intelligence!" JSN hooted. "No wonder!"

"Are yall mockin the Word?" Brother Simon asked. His anger seemed to be teetering on the edge of tears.

"No, no, just this fucked up hardware," JSN said. "It must have merged all those video broadcasts into one file..."

"...and then tried to make sense of it! What a disaster!"

"Now see here," Brother Simon said. "If yall cant show proper respect all hafta axe yall to leave."

"Respect?" LNR howled. "Are you kidding?"

"That's it," Brother Simon said, flapping his hands at them. "Out. Yawn yone."

LNR stared blankly at JSN. "I think he means we're on our own," he said.

LNR took his arm.. "Suits me. You think we could get all those cables back the way they were?"

"Let's find out," JSN said, then hesitated. "What about DNS? We shouldn't just leave him here with these devos..."

"Don't worry," LNR said. "He may be stupid, but he's harmless."

Later that night JSN looked up to see his barn disintegrating on an overhead monitor. "Holy shit," he said.

LNR leaned backward to look. "The devos?"

JSN nodded. "And I think DNS is on board. Or fried to a cinder."

"Oh well. Good riddance to the lot of them. Any more amps on this thing?"

JSN twisted the dial all the way up to ten.

JSN was shooting a fashion layout in one of his disused pastures when the devos found him. The director had just finished draping him erotically in yards of raw fiberglass when she noticed that her

lead camera had dropped off-line. She called for the backup and found the power switch had jammed in the OFF position. "Okay," she said. "Let's take a break."

"What about me?" JSN asked. He could barely move. "You," the director said, "look luscious. Just stay put." At that point the shuttle dropped out of the sky with a paralyzing roar. The film crew scattered but JSN, barely able to hop, couldn't get away. Two of the male devos grabbed him and carried him into the reeking bowels of the ship.

"Very good," said a familiar voice as JSN was hustled through the control room. "Lock him in a cabin and I'll get to him later."

"DNS, you bastard!" JSN shouted. "What are you doing?"

"Don't be obsolete!" DNS shouted back. "We're all bastards these days, remember?"

They shut JSN in a tiny cabin with a video screen that filled all of one wall. After a few seconds it lit up and showed a large 21. The number slowly dissolved into a scene of the white-haired man, Johnny Carson, dressed in a circus costume and performing a trick riding act. He had one foot on a donkey and the other on a small horse, and he grinned foolishly as the two animals cantered down a dusty path littered with palm fronds.

Crowds lined both sides of the road and the camera panned them, picking up bits of conversation. "Who is this?" "This is the prophet Johnny from the Tonight Show."

Johnny rode through the high, mud-brick gateway of the city and up to the doors of the temple. There he jumped down and staggered around for a few seconds in mock drunkeness, sending the crowd into hysterical laughter. Then he walked boldly inside.

Both sides of the huge hall were lined with tables, and on the tables were stacks of videos and stereos and home computers and various kinds of brightly colored boxes. Shiny new automobiles were parked in the aisles next to large enameled appliances.

Johnny walked past all the tables, all the way to the far end of the room, turned, and spread his arms wide. He looked up and down the temple until he had everyone's attention. "And now," he said, "a word from our sponsor."

JSN sat on the floor and switched all of his available systems over to standby.

DNS was talking to him. JSN punched back up to full alertness and said, "You *ass*hole. What are you doing with these degenerates? You're selling me out to a bunch of devolved—"

"Whoa up there now," DNS said. "We don't believe in that heathen notion of evolution."

"We?"

DNS leaned forward earnestly. "I have accepted Johnny Carson in my heart as my personal savior."

"You're brain damaged," JSN said.

"Maybe so, but Johnny loves me just the same."

"I expect he loves you better *because* of it."

"None of your sarcasm, now. You're about to get the opportunity of a lifetime. I envy you. I truly do."

"Just let me out of here and I'll reformat all my memories of this. I promise."

"Oh, no. I can't let your moment of weakness keep you from your glorious destiny. You're gonna ride the wave of the future. Together my new brethren and I have seen Johnny's plan for us, and behold, it was glorious."

"Where did you get that hick accent all of a sudden?"

DNS grabbed the front of JSN's shirt. "You were the one wanted to blow these good folk out of the sky. None of you half-metal cripples were willing to open yourselves to the Word. Nobody wanted to give them a home."

"After the UN fiasco, I must admit, the offers were not exactly pouring in."

"Well, they will be soon. We're gonna make all those Pharisees bow to the glory of Johnny. They're gonna take the old values back into their hearts: home, marriage, family, network TV."

"And whose idea was this?"

"Oh, Johnny's of course. As revealed to me in His infinite Wisdom."

"Don't be stupid," JSN said, out of patience and a little scared besides. "Maybe things are a little screwed up right now. But you're not going to fix them by hiding in the past. Wars and patriotism and bigotry aren't the answer to a little slackness in quality control—"

"Who said anything about war?" DNS said. "Any fool knows advertising is the answer. Did not Johnny welcome the sponsors into the temple? That's why you're here. You're one of the biggest pop stars on the planet. People everywhere know who you are. You start new fashions with everything you do." He eyed the remnants of JSN's fiberglass with distaste.

"So?"

"So you're going to marry one of the sistren."

"Marry a devo? No way."

"I told you I don't like that word," DNS threatened.

"I don't care what you call yourselves. Count me out. Forget it. I wouldn't do it if you put a gun to my head."

DNS reached into his kilt and pulled out an ancient handgun. A Colt .38 caliber Python, JSN determined with a quick look-up. DNS put the mouth of the barrel against JSN's left temple.

The door oozed open and Brother Simon came in, followed by

the bovine woman who had smiled at JSN in the barn. She was smiling again, glancing back and forth between JSN and her own feet, her cheeks hotly flushed.

"Your bride-to-be," DNS said.

The woman began to undress. JSN stood up, looking quickly away from the yards of quivering flesh. Brother Simon held out a black videocassette, firmly clenched in both hands. "By-the-poor-vestige-of-my-mistake-in-Virginia," he said hurriedly, apparently unable to look away from the female's chest, "aprons-on-you-husb-and-wife. Go for it. Amen."

The female stretched out on her back and raised fleshy arms toward JSN. "Here?" he said. "You expect me to fertilize her? Right here? With you watching?"

"Not just us," DNS said, "but millions more when we rebroadcast the blessed event throughout the world. Soon everyone will want a husb and/or bride of Johnny! We'll bring them down from the mother ship and spread the Good News throughout the world!"

"Amen Brother Dennis," said Brother Simon.

"No," JSN said. "I can't. I won't."

DNS pulled back the hammer of the revolver with an audible click.

Mass hysteria, JSN thought. It would pass, eventually. The world had survived it before, barely, maybe it could live through it again. In the meantime, what else could he do?

He reached a trembling hand to his forehead, found his most conciliatory personality, and smiled down at the naked woman. "Hello, darling," he said.

If you need an introduction to William Burroughs, you're reading the wrong book. We daresay EVERY contributor to this volume owes some debt to "Uncle Bill," whose voluminous and still-expanding corpus represents THE major stylistic breakthrough of the last quarter-century. Beat, Hippie, Punk (cyber or otherwise), Radical Crazy Mutant... every real advance in American writing is rooted in his work, or graced by the spectral gray image of his presence, Buster Keaton in banker's drag, dessicated junky prophet. Burroughs' writing is based on oral "routines," satiric or surreal monologues which later grow, expand, implode and fold in on themselves to produce the finished books.

 His latest novel, THE WESTERN LANDS, completes his Dantean trilogy and marks a new departure, a new voice—recognizably Burroughs but more than a little god-possessed... or Wise...

The CIA Reporter
William Burroughs

Tonight, your friendly and impartial reporter, Joe Bane, interviews supermullah Ayatollah Khomeyinni, who styles himself as the spiritualistic leader of Iran's 32 million prayer-mewling Allah freaks, inspired by the invigorating teachings of Islam: "Allah...Allah...Allah." And a more miserable, diseased filthy breed of gooks never swarmed out of a Beanville to spit their tuberculosis on Old Glory.

Mr. Koatimundi... doesn't your proposed cancellation of American military contracts, termination of American bases, invite a proportionate preponderance of Russian military influence? Aren't you, in point of fact, crawling into bed with the Commies, and delivering Iran to Moscow on an oil slick? Aren't you satelliting Iran into Communistic orbit? Aren't you in plain American English a paid hireling agent of the unionized Soviets?

Mr. Koatimundi. In an interview with *Le Monde,* a newspaper in Paris, France, you state that you have given permission to your followers to prepare... you admit that "preparation" entails acquiring arms. When asked where these arms are coming from, you say: "I do not know." When asked further if, perchance, these arms are coming from Soviet Russia via the so-called Palestinian Liberation Organization, you say: "I have no informations..." Well, I say you're lying in your gums, you toothless old cocksucker—whaddya got to say about that? — HUH?

The New Boy
William Burroughs

He was 15 minutes late and he couldn't understand why. He thought he had calculated his time exactly but time seemed to have accelerated after waiting all afternoon for this appointment. Then suddenly he looked at the clock and he knew he was going to be late pacing up and down the subway platform and now here he was in the middle island at Park Avenue and 60th Street held back by a solid line of taxis speeding by. He paced up and down.

Suddenly he knew that someone was looking at him, a cab was making a left turn onto 60th Street and someone in the cab was looking at him. He was a good-looking boy, slender, dark hair with clear gray eyes on a pink and white complexion smooth as porcelain, long lashes, so he was sensitive about being looked at and furious that anyone might think him rather like an Arrow collar 1920 or a *Saturday Evening Post* cover in the days when males still appeared on the cover picture of a boy late for a date.

He knew that someone was looking at him from the cab, he could feel it, but this was an impersonal speculative look, rather like a film director, he thought, acting out boy late for a date.

The light changed... the taxi turned and passed him, turning left on Fifth Avenue. Kenny Ryan was too self-conscious to be observant but he was aware of something strange as he hurried down 60th dodging other pedestrians. What was it? The whole feel and smell of the city was different... out of the corner of his eye he glimpsed an old car, looked like a 1920 Cadillac, he thought, now he could see Wendy across the street standing by the rail. He waved and called to her but she didn't seem to hear, and then she turned and started walking toward the Plaza Hotel.

He sprinted forward and the light changed and he was stopped by a solid line of cars... there was something wrong, he could see now that every car on the street was 1920s, and the people were also period.

He started to run down the other side of the street, trying to keep Wendy in sight, trying to get her attention across the river of downtown traffic. And a river of uptown pedestrians seemed to hold him back, slow his steps like water. He couldn't seem to get through them, someone was always right in front of him. When the light changed he ran across and down the corner of 59th where the whores were, but Wendy was no-where in sight. Perhaps she had gone into the Plaza.

He walked into the lobby feeling the cynical eyes of the door-man. He looked around. He didn't see Wendy, but a boy with wavy blonde hair and blue eyes like star sapphires walked up and said,

"Hello Kenny."

Kenny looked at him, he must know him from someplace but he couldn't think where.

"Hello."

"You don't remember me, do you?"

"Well, uh... no."

He tried to move away, looking about, maybe she was in the side lobby.

"Wendy isn't here."

Kenny looked at him. "What? How did you..."

"She isn't here. You were late and you missed her."

Kenny felt a sudden vertigo. He sat down.

The boy's voice went on.

"Don't worry. Plenty more where she came from. Tomorrow is always bright and blue. My name is Bob Borden. They call me BoBo. Feeling better?"

"Yes, a little. What happened?"

"You shouldn't have tried to cross against the light."

"You mean...?"
"Yes old buddy. You're dead."
Kenny could hear a siren in the distance.
"So what happens now?"
BoBo called to a man in clerical collar walking by.
"What happens now Padre?"
The priest turned with a snarl.
"You can go to Hell."

Daniel Pearlman is one of the few academics in this book, but don't worry — he doesn't write like an academic. He's just beginning to break into SF, and we predict you'll be noticing his name in the big magazines before too long. Mort aux flics!

Another Brush with the Fuzz
Daniel Pearlman

Rodriguez slowly eased his foot off the gas pedal. That fuzz was still on his tail. What the hell for? he wondered. He wasn't speeding just now. But maybe he'd been trailing him since Pelham. He'd been tearassing down Pelham Parkway only ten minutes ago. Maybe, too, this fuzz had nothing better to do than bust balls, and was there a better place to bust balls than a quiet road like this with no one in sight but himself and that cop?

Rodriguez hung a quick right through the open cemetery gate that was coming up fast at the end of a long stretch of black spiked fence. It was then that the patrol car opened up its flashing red and blue lights and swept in behind him up the asphalt lane of the graveyard.

Just like a fucking disco, thought Rodriguez. He sensed anger behind those flashing lights. Rodriguez pulled to a stop in the shade of some overarching, thickly leaved trees.

Suddenly he realized that for several minutes he had been driving with only one hand. Quickly he jerked his other hand from his face, wiped his fingers on a knee of his blue jeans, and clapped the neglectful hand back on the steering wheel with the other. I ain't carrying no shit, man, but I do have a little bag of coke. He grabbed the little plastic bag from the glove compartment and displayed it on the flat space above the dashboard in front of him. The officer, alone in the patrol car, stepped out and walked with studied casualness toward Rodriguez's open window. On one hip bounced his holster. On the other, the little black box with the panel of buttons and little window that Rodriguez called "puta" for "computer."

"I remember you," said the officer, fixing him with a thin-lipped, cold-eyed stare.

Rodriguez glanced anxiously at the little bag above the dash, hoping the cop's eyes would follow, but they wouldn't. They wouldn't be distracted.

"I remember you, too," said Rodriguez. "What you riding my ass for now?"

"You know damn well what for."

Rodriguez felt a tingling in his left hand, the one that had negligently drifted from the steering wheel. "So I'm carrying a little bag. So you wanna hang me? Go ahead."

"You think you can distract me with that shit, Rodriguez?" the officer snickered.

"Coke, not shit," Rodriguez mumbled.

"Your left hand, Rodriguez. It was off the wheel. You had it up your nose for two minutes and eighteen seconds."

"It's my nose, right? I like picking my own fucking nose. If I stick my finger up somebody else's nose, you got a right to complain, no?"

"You know the law, Rodriguez. You're disgusting, Rodriguez. Your car stinks from grease and garlic. You look like you haven't shaved or taken a bath or changed your slimy jeans for a week." The officer, square jawed and clean-shaven, looked down at him as if smelling a skunk.

"Anyway," Rodriguez mumbled uncertainly as he looked up at the towering officer, at the giant pecs straining against the neatly ironed summer blue shirt, "anyway, I don't give a crap what your puta says. You can shove your puta up your shiny blue-buttoned ass because I ain't gonna—

"You're not going to *what*?" sneered the officer.

"I ain't gonna pay no fucking fine," Rodriguez muttered through clenched teeth, glancing around in vain to find someone who might be witnessing this harassment.

"You think you're going to get away with it this time, too, like the last couple of times?" the officer laughed contemptuously . Lifting the little black box from his belt, he held it in his palm and rapidly tapped some buttons. "Your ass is in a sling, Rodriguez. Literally in a sling... I have you down for two unpaid tickets. I could put a wheel clamp on your car right now, you know that?"

"I couldn't care less."

"You think I don't have proof?"

"I fuck your proof."

"That's why we have that chip stuck up your nose that you'll never get out. That's how we know, slime. And your unpaid tickets are, *numero uno*, driving while scratching your ass. I mean you had your hand *inside* your scuzzy pants and your middle finger was stuck up your *culo*."

"I was itchy."

"No you weren't. You were trying to gouge the chip out of your asshole, you fucking liar. That's a hell of a lot more serious offense than scratching your ass."

"You think your puta knows everything?"

"The computer knows you were walloping your dick for the second unpaid ticket. Whacking away while driving! What a danger to society. God, sleaze like you are a disease. But whack away like that once more and we'll stick a chip at the *head* of your dick. And that won't be nearly as comfortable as the present arrangement. And don't say again that you were just scratching at the chip. We have you on record for an orgasm. You don't come, scum, from scratching at a chip."

"How come a stupid cop knows all this about me? How come you didn't pick me up before when I'm doing eighty-five down Pelham? How come you don't look at this little bag with white powder over here, eh?"

The officer ignored him and kept pressing buttons on the little black box. "Look, you scuzzy little shrimp. Besides all this you've had two warnings about erections while driving. One more hard-on and we slap you for a fine almost as big as for jerking off."

"I couldn't help it, officer," Rodriguez smiled, squinting out through narrowed, hate-filled eyes. "I was thinking of your wife. I was thinking of her big pink tits. I was thinking of sucking her big blond peppermint-flavored pussy because she's so sad and she wants it so bad — but the fuzz don't like to suck fuzz, do they?"

"You've had it, you shit-smeared little cockroach!" The officer pulled his gun and pointed it at Rodriguez. With his left hand he snapped open a little black leather pouch on his belt behind the holster and pulled out a folded little article of insulated wire and elastic. "This is a D.A.B. You know what a D.A.B. is, scum?"

Rodriguez froze with fear, but he tried to appear completely calm and disdainful. He never thought that the fuzz would go that far.

"For your information, a D.A.B. is a dick-and-asshole belt. The black rubber cork goes up your ass. It *stays* there. The little wire muzzle here with the pee-hole in it clamps over your wang and shocks the shit out of it as soon as you stare too long at one of your black-eyed little Pepitas walking down the street. When you have to shit, the rubber cork will know, and you can pull it out of your ass for five minutes at a time. Otherwise, it keeps the whole belt in place. And if you fuck around with the law and fail to put the belt back on *properly*, my little black box will pick it up, and then you know what we do?"

Rodriguez knew, all right, but damned if he would let on.

"We come find you," said the officer, his eyes gleaming, "and we castrate you. Do you know what that is?"

"I donno what your bullshit is all about, man." Rodriguez slumped back in his seat and stared in fear and anger at the useless decoy he had placed on top of the dashboard.

"Get out of the car and strip!" the officer commanded, waving the nozzle of his weapon at him. "Snap to it!" he pressed, pulling the car-door open.

Rodriguez stumbled out of the car. He looked wildly around, but there was not a living person in sight to witness his shame. Only all the clean-shaven grass-covered corpses that no longer could fart, or eat chili or garlic, or whack off while watching television or driving a car, or refuse to pay fines. They had all forgotten how to stink and so would never, in a million years, even if they could, speak up against the fuzz.

He unbuttoned slowly. The officer jerked impatiently at his garments, scraping his hand against a tombstone each time he touched him to wipe off the grease. Rodriguez soon stood pale and slumped like a naked mushroom among the giant tombstones and shade trees. Listlessly, he strapped himself into the girdle-like belt, responding as slowly as he dared to the increasingly brutal officer.

"Turn around! Lean against the hood!" He was pushed face down over the hood of his car. "Now spread 'em!"

"Leave me alone you goddam sonuva — " What's he gonna do this goddam fuzz what's he think he's gonna—

The sharp pain of the greased cork jammed into his rectum brought tears to his eyes.

"Get dressed, you stinking scofflaw!" The officer threw his clothes at him. "And don't worry about the cork. It's got a built-in fart bypass. Your mother didn't."

Rodriguez was soon dressed and seated before the wheel again. His neck burning, his scalp tingling, he remained mute and staring straight ahead of him. He would not give the officer the satisfaction of seeing his convulsed features. Suddenly he got an idea and quickly, nonchalantly, turned on the ignition. The big-boned snappy-looking officer was slowly retreating to his patrol car, which had stopped barely twenty feet behind Rodriguez's rust-scarred jalopy. Now you fucking shit-eating fuzz *now*...

The back of Rodriguez's car rammed him hard and splattered him head-first against the back of his own patrol car. Rodriguez stepped out and looked with pleasure at the officer lying bleeding from bullet-like skull and thin-lipped mouth on the asphalt near the rear tires of his own shiny new vehicle. Rodriguez now tore the little black box off the officer's belt. Now, if he only knew how to push the right buttons, he could without fear of shock remove the humiliating belt that bound him in. What the fuck, now wait a *minute*... bull*shit!* Rodriguez stomped on the little palm-sized *puta*. He stomped and stomped until there were no two littlest pieces left hanging together. Beaming with delight, he pulled down his pants and plucked the cork out of his anus. No shock. Nothing. Feeling the urge, he straddled the battered officer and peed long and heavily, langorously and aromatically, on his clean-shaven face and nattily tailored uniform.

To Rodriguez's amazement, the officer yawned, sighed deeply, stretched out his arms and springily lifted himself off the asphalt.

Rodriguez shrank back in horror, blinking at the electric flashes of long-buried memories that arose now to sting him like cattle-prods.

"Don't you get it, asshole?" said the officer, wiping at his uniform and wincing in disgust at the urine he reeked of. "When you piss on me, I spring back up. Every time you piss on me I spring back up. Now where the hell is my goddam computer?..."

Rodriguez jumped back into his car, which he had left idling. He did not even take the time to zip up his pants. To regain the blocked entrance he had to circle around the patrol car by cutting a wild path among tombstones. Finally, he screeched back out through the gate, hung a left, and tear-assed down the long deserted street alongside the cemetery.

Ron Kolm's ironic iconic little poems often display a taste for SF imagery. He is the author of WELCOME TO THE BARBECUE and a contributing editor to both COVER and APPEARANCES. His work has been published in BENZENE, BETWEEN C & D (both the magazine and the Penguin anthology), NEW OBSERVATIONS, SEMIOTEXT(E) USA, PUBLIC ILLUMINATION MAGAZINE and REDTAPE. His book THE PLASTIC FACTORY will soon appear courtesy of Red Dust.

You Can't Go Home Again
Ron Kolm

a) It hit just outside of Philadelphia — ground zero was a Camden suburb (probably due to a computer malfunction) — at 4:33 p.m. on a Tuesday. Rain had been falling heavily all day, and portions of the New Jersey Turnpike, what was left of it, were flooded.

b) Inside the Port Authority Bus Terminal, from the main concourse to the long haul slips on the upper level, queues of tired commuters, tickets in hand, await buses that will never arrive. P.A. police and bus company personnel diplomatically break the unsettling news to individual passengers, trying to avoid a panic. Several people leave their place in line and rush to the bathroom, parting the thick bluish air, unable to control themselves.

Greg Gibson writes from Gloucester, MA, "Born in 1945, I am an antiquarian book dealer and spend most of my time driving around. Have published in NEC SPE NEC METU, BEZOAR, AMERICA 1, and other unheard-of magazines."

After reading this unique text for the third time, we finally realized that it's an Allegory of Capitalism. Before that we just thought it was extremely funny and nasty. If anyone wants to illustrate it fully and bring it out as a children's book, please contact us.

Georgie and the Giant Shit
Greg Gibson

A Story about Your Town with
Illustrations You Can Draw and Color Yourself

Georgie lived at the edge of town with his mother and his father. He was a good boy, as boys go. He tried hard in school, kept his room neat, and hardly ever talked back.

This (*next page*) is a picture of Georgie's room. The outlines are nimble and fluid. The colors should be even and light; as if, in Georgie's world, solids were made of neon gas.

Unopened school books clutter his desk. Clothes at the foot of the bed are earnestly, improperly folded. Baseball pictures frame the bureau mirror like scenes on an icon. Model airplanes dangle in space.

He also ate everything on his plate, which was quite an accomplishment, considering the size of his plate.

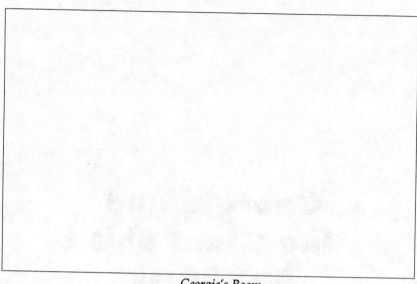

Georgie's Room

At breakfast Georgie would eat a pig and 15 dozen eggs. For lunch he might have 30 pounds of tuna salad or 200 baloney sandwiches. And for supper, Georgie would polish off 4 sides of beef, 25 roast chickens, and several bushels of mixed vegetables.

Luckily, Georgie's father owned a supermarket.

Georgie, blimpish, radiantly happy, knife and fork in hand, is dressed in a little boy's sailor suit. Belly and navel bulge from beneath the jumper's hem. Beef, fowl, and windrows of vegetables are arrayed before him.

Considering the Size of His Plate

Because he ate so much, Georgie was always big for his age. He soon grew to be as big as a two-car garage. His father set up a circus tent in the back yard, out by the woods, and Georgie lived there.

Georgie sits in the driveway for a formal portrait; legs fully extended, arms straight down, palms flat on the concrete, belly resting on his thighs. His expression is catlike in its contentment and vacuity. Behind him is a two-car garage. Beyond that, the top of a circus tent, banner streaming from its center pole.

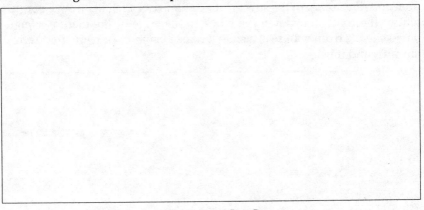

As Big as a Two-Car Garage

Georgie's mother knew no one should eat as much as Georgie did, but she hated to see her baby grow hungry, so she let him eat whatever he liked.

The trouble was, Georgie liked too many things. As he grew, he developed a taste for all sorts of junk... old rags, pieces of wood, even dirt and stones, as well as regular groceries.

Between meals he might snack on a bale of hay or chew on an old rubber tire to curb his hunger.

Georgie crops the leaves of an uprooted tree, grasped like a drumstick. Questioning birds circle overhead.

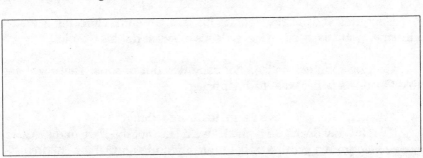

No One Should Eat as Muoh as Georgie Did

People were anxious to see a boy of Georgie's size and appetite. They came from all over the country and spent a lot of money in Georgie's town. He was quite an attraction.

Georgie enjoyed being famous almost as much as he enjoyed eating. And the neighbors encouraged him. They all had good jobs taking care of the sightseers.

An aerial view of Georgie's neighborhood. The day is sunny. Children and dogs scrap in the street. A line of tourists stretches from Georgie's tent to the road, and down the block to the edge of the picture. Neighbors sell soft drinks and souvenirs. Houses have been converted to restaurants and inns.

People Were Anxious to See a Boy of Georgie's Size

It seemed as if this pleasant state of affairs would last forever. But one day, after a pratically heavy lunch, Georgie began to feel strange. He dropped what he was doing, and ran back into the woods, where something terrible happened.

Georgie stands at the door of his tent, absently clutching a model airplane. Panic flashes in his eye. Beads of sweat dot his temples.

Georgie's mother noticed her baby was out of sorts. That night she told Georgie's father what had happened.

"Walter," she said, "we've got to do something."
"Tut tut, my dear," he replied, "we'd best not interfere in ths matter. Georgie's a good boy. It's probably quite normal for children his size..."

Georgie Began to Feel Strange

"It's *not* normal. I don't want my baby to be sick."

"He's not a baby."

"He's only 13. I'm going to call a specialist."

"You worry too much. You always have."

They argued till late that night. Outside, Georgie could hear them carrying on. He thought they were arguing about him, and felt sad.

Georgie peers out the door of his tent, into the night. A shaft of light beams from the rear of the house. Georgie's parents can be seen inside, shouting at one another. A tear crawls down Georgie's cheek.

He Thought They Were Arguing About Him

Dr. Vogel came next morning and crawled all over Georgie, examining him with the greatest care. When he was finished, he took Georgie's mother aside.

"Gonoromax hideoplasis," he said. "Stennis plebiensus with Morton's Syndrome, but little evidence of hypochronus arema, thank heavens. Your child is overweight."

"But what about Georgie's..."

"Yes?"

"...problem?"

"Nature is the best physician," replied Dr. Vogel, giving a solemn nod.

Georgie is redfaced, fear and loathing barely in check. Dr. Vogel, goateed, stands on a stepladder, stretching a stethoscope to Georgie's naked chest.

Gonoromax Hideoplasis

While the examination was going on, Mr. Smith, a grouchy old man who lived next door, realized somelthing terrible had happened in the woods. He called the police. Officers Wilson and O'Malley investigated his complaint.

"Sure enough," there's a giant shit back there," they told Mr. Smith, "but we can't do anything about it. Call the Board of Health."

An official from the Board of Health came and made his report.

"The City Code has been violated," he announced. "Call the Department of Sanitation."

Mr. Smith, pinched and mean, complains to a man in a suit and vest. Two policemen stand in the background. One of them scratches his head.

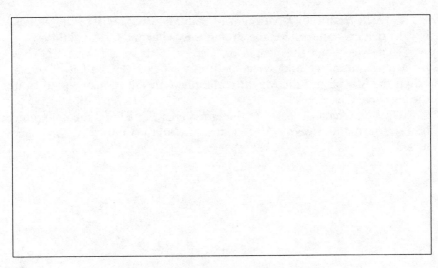

The City Code Has Been Violated

Other people on Georgie's block noticed something was wrong. All the animals from the woods were sitting on the edge of the road, not knowing what to do.

Some of the neighbors thought Georgie had died back there. They called the newspapers. A reporter came and interviewed them all.

The edge of Georgie's street is lined with small animals, staring anxiously back toward the woods. Neighbors leaning out of windows shout from house to house. On the sidewalk a man with a pad of paper interviews a porcupine.

Other People Noticed Something Was Wrong

A truck from the Department of Sanitation backed into the woods, but the driver soon realized the situation was beyond his capabilities.

That was when the people on Georgie's street got worried. They formed a committee and went to the City Council. The City Council called the Mayor and the Mayor summoned an Emergency Squad from the National Guard.

The Lieutenant in charge of the Emergency Squad told them it would be a simple matter to explode the giant shit, but the Council voted against it, 4–3.

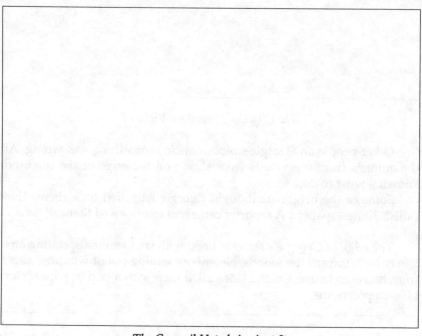

The Council Voted Against It

The Council and a helmeted lieutenant stand at the edge of the woods. The lieutenant is doing the talking. Above his head, and the heads of the three councilmen, rises a dream bubble picturing a magnificent explosion. Above the heads of three other councilmen there is a dream bubble picturing a rain of fecal matter. Above the head of the last councilman is a dream bubble picturing nothing.

The Lieutenant reported to the Governor, and the Governor sent an Engineer from the Department of Public Works.

The Engineer wasted no time devising a plan. They would dig a trench to the sea and divert a river into the woods to flush the shit away, just like a giant toilet. The project could be completed in 18 months at a cost of $27 million. But the Council told him that would never do.

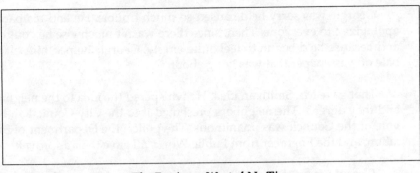

The Engineer Wasted No Time

This is a map of large scale, depicting Georgie's town and all the land around it. Dotted lines indicate the path of the diverted river. Complex calculations in the margin predict the course and progress of the giant shit.

All this commotion brought Georgie out of this tent. He was surprised to see the people who had gathered, and they were surprised to see him, too. He looked different. Where his beautiful, gleaming belly had once bulged, there was mostly empty skin.

Right away, people realized what had happened. Georgie's mother and father admitted everything.

Georgie, frowsy with exhaustion and worry, stands at the door of his tent. A wrinkled pancake of skin hangs from beneath his jumper, like an old woman's breast.

People Realized What Had Happened

Georgie was sorry he'd caused so much trouble. He and his parents apologized to everyone. Then, since there wasn't much else he could do, and because he'd begun to feel quite empty, Georgie helped himself to a bale of wastepaper that was lying about.

That gave Mr. Smith an idea. He whispered the idea to the neighbors and they agreed. The neighbors presented it to the City Council and the vote of the Council was unanimous. The police, the Department of Sanitation, and the Engineer from Public Works all gave their approval.

Georgie pops bundles of wastepaper into his mouth as if they were peanuts. Off in a corner of the picture, the above-named officials huddle.

That Gave Mr. Smith an Idea

Everyone looked at Georgie, and he knew what they were thinking.
"Not me!" he cried.
"It's your mess," they replied in unison, "you've got to clean it up."
"But you all wanted me to eat a lot. Nobody told me *this* would happen."

His argument were in vain. The people insisted. That night Georgie buried the terrible thing as best he could. Everyone else went home happy.

Georgie looks up in dismay. A few back issues of *The Saturday Evening Post* drop from his lips.

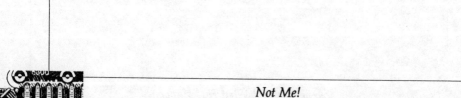

Not Me!

But a week later the same terrible thing happened. The people made Georgie bury it, just like before. Three days later it happend again; then the next day, and the next, and the next.

What could the neighbors do? If they made him leave town, the tourists would stop coming. They'd all be out of work.

What could Georgie do? He was a growing boy. He kept eating and he kept growing. After his father's market ran out of food, he ate the market. Then he began eating the houses of the neighbors who had moved away... for it soon got to be so terrible around Georgie's town that tourists wouldn't come near the place.

A hotel-sized Georgie roams the town's desolate streets. Like teeth poked out of a mouth, empty cellar holes gape where houses have been devoured. The heaps of excrement resemble haystacks in this aerial view.

What Could Georgie Do?

Just beacuse Georgie was huge, though, didn't mean he was different. In time, baseball and model airplanes ceased to interest him.

When he was 19, and nearly as big as a railroad terminal, Georgie began writing to a girl in the next state who was rumored to be as big as he was. A meeting was arranged, and after a whirlwind courtship they were married.

They settled down, had 5 big children, and lived happily ever after.

Georgie, his bride, and 5 male and female Georgies of descending size, loom over a ruined landscape.

Happily Ever After.

No one else was happy, and thinking of that made Georgie sad sometimes. But, as his wife often reminded him, it certainly wasn't their fault.

It wasn't anyone's fault, really.

This is a picture of a giant shit.

Another anarchistic New Yorker guilty of trafficking in SF poetry, Lorraine Schein's verses and cartoons have appeared in Heresies, The NY Quarterly, Starline, Public Illumination, Christopher Street, *and* Exquisite Corpse. *She will have a short story in the upcoming anthology of women's SF,* Memories and Visions *(Crossing Press). A 1980 Clarion grad, she had a childhood sweetheart who became an astrophysicist; all of her SF "comes from real life experience."*

Delphic (Projection #5)
Lorraine Schein

The futurist's mistress
(in this alternate scenario)
Sleeps in his bed,
Beside his other curved concubines.
Space and Time.

She projects herself, once more,
Endlessly into the future.

The dreams crash and glisten;
Presaging a love
More fantastic than science—

The futures tighten around her
like his arms in the night.

233

The Sex Club
T. L. Parkinson

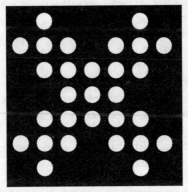

I had tried to breathe life into the man grazed by the passing train. He had fallen into my arms, a broken doll, grasping at my arms in a final shiver, and imparting a glance of confusion and seduction, before his eyes blurred into the beyond.

He had reached into his pocket, with virtually his last movement, and removed a ticket, which fell, with his limp hand, into my palm.

I breathed into him (holding his heavy head to my face), but my breath returned, sighing passively into the wind.

I gently lowered him to the pavement, his handsome face and body now crumpled. Gravity pulled him into the interesting and disturbing configuration of the dead.

In my left hand lay the ticket, a clear lucite card in which swirled cuneiform characters, and three black dots.

The police arrived, in their plastic shields, appearing like ghosts come to take the dead into their domain. They examined the body, cursorily questioned me, and dissolved the thin crowd that had begun to gather, with a wave of their gloved hands.

The ambulance arrived, manned by glowing apparitions, and a lattice of white lines, resembling a spider's web, ensnared the body and pulled it inside the vehicle.

The police nodded finally, saying they would check my story, and, that if I were legitimate, I would not be hearing from them.

I meant to ask if the computer driver of the offending train would likewise be questioned, but in the blur of accelerating images, I forgot.

Death comes so quickly and inexplicably to some, perhaps luckily so. I remember a vague sexual excitement accompanying that thought, as I hesitated before the austere door to the Sex Club.

The wall module in my home had read the ticket, and directed me here. As a sort of hommage to the dead, I felt compelled to spend the ticket; if I did not, then perhaps some misfortune might befall me.

The door was heavier than one would imagine, but the heaviness provided the enticement to proceed.

I stepped quickly through, once the door was open, fearful that on closing it would knock me over.

Inside, it was not dark and musty-smelling, as I expected. Still, the image of life lived beneath stones, in dark subterranean rooms with dripping walls, would not leave me.

A pale-faced man with a well-muscled body took the ticket, which I gingerly handed him. He sat unprotected at a desk in an open room. I felt his breath on my hand, and I could distinguish that he had had broccoli and perhaps beef for lunch.

The room was well-lit, the white tiled floor magnifying the illumination. The walls, covered with a soft cloth that rippled and shimmered, reflected my own image back in imaginary ways. I was coming; I was going; riding a horse; striding naked through the dark yard of an estate; watching the rise and fall of thighs in the ceiling mirror, etc. The walls told all: I had done none of these things.

A silver ball swallowed the ticket, and spit a bracelet out.

"This will lead you through the Experience," the featureless man said.

"Thank you," I said, in a voice I was afraid betrayed an apprehension of the unknown. "May you find—what you find," he said, rising stiffly. My eyes fixed on a flap of skin where his penis had been removed, which was pierced with six gold rings and small hooks. He smiled then, pleased at my attention, and led me toward another door, which opened like an eye in the reflective wall.

The man said nothing more, sliding quietly back to his desk.

The door closed behind me, and I felt a slight sensation of movement, standing there in the mirrored room, staring at an infinity of selves. I was rather displeased with the tilt of my chin in this

crowded room, with the dour expression in my eyes, and the lack of enthusiasm of my curved neck.

I straightened, and groped toward the hallway of images; the sense of movement had ceased. I grasped a door handle, which appeared to be my belt buckle, and moved into another room.

In this darkness, a closet of stranger's clothes, there was no charnal house smell, but this was closer to my imagination—silence; inertia; and underneath, the *impression* of violent, continuous movement.

I walked slowly, my hands before me, feeling the dark like a sleepwalking child. My eyes grew accustomed to the dim light. Yes, there was a vague shape over there, some dark cross on which— No, I would not look. I turned my back.

I pushed on, seemingly in another direction. Soon, my face pressed against a wall, somewhat human-musty smelling, which on careful inspection I determined to be primitive plywood. I winced, pulling a splinter from my incautious hands.

I felt a draft of cold air on my chin, indicating an opening, and I lowered my face so that I might see through.

A figure, seated on a milking stool, seized my attention, my head pulled through the ragged, fist-sized hole, as far as it might, by a strange horizontal gravity.

The man was unclothed, round full buttocks clutching the stool, arms muscular and rather too-long, one moving to his unseen crotch, the other through a dark hole similar to the one through which I peered.

There were seven holes altogether (excluding mine). Through three of these portholes, hands grasped hungrily at the seated man, who was just out of reach. One hand appeared solid and fleshy; one somewhat thin and, even in the dim light, deathly pale; the other possessed a thick palm and long fingers (this last hand was the most beautiful, to me).

Apparently this distant seated figure was a prize. I examined the details more closely, feeling the wood press into my face. With his back turned, I could not discern much. In the light thrown from the floor, the blue torso, each muscle crawling separately under the smooth skin, exuded an improbable animal magnetism, down to the unseen activities of his hands. Perhaps his unreachability was the key.

The man continued to work on himself, to work on the unseen object on the other side of the wall, and the grasping hands continued to plead and close on air.

He now arched upward, pushing his hips into an invisible mouth. His left hand remained fixed through the porthole, behind which his chosen lay half-seen, or dreamt.

He convulsed, now emitting a sound like a cat squatting over a chicken bone, and tiny filaments filled the air, splattering against the wall.

The dark curls of the back of his head now seemed to form a face.

His left hand fell limply from the hole.

He turned to me. His dark sullen eyes searched the portholes, seeing them empty, until he came to mine.

We locked gazes, and he slowly moved toward me, so that I might see the heavy curve of his half-limp penis, the moisture still apparent on the shaft.

Despite myself, my eyes reached forward. It was at the moment of my fullest attention that he lifted his downward-staring face so that I might see it more fully; his left hand moved into the light.

Horrified, I withdrew into the darkness of my cubicle, comforted by the wall at my back.

The mouthless face appeared in my porthole, the slim feeding tube entering my territory like the antenna of an inquisitive insect.

Of course, I knew of these people, who had protected themselves against verbal excesses, and viruses; but I had never been aroused by one.

The corner stopped my withdrawal. The face withdrew, to be replaced by a searching hand, from which dangled a lock of gray hair, and a tag of flesh—evidence of the relationship I had just witnessed.

Fortunately, as the thrill of my horror reached a crescendo, the corner swallowed me.

I stood in an open, brightly lit room, through which twenty men in various stages of undress moved. I stopped myself from covering my erection, realizing how ludicrous my discomfort would seem under these circumstances.

One man wore only a shirt, one only boots, another a scarf tied about his neck.

Two muscular dwarfs spat on each other in a corner, as if attempting privacy; they were as easily seen, in the pervasive light, as anyone in the center. They switched positions every few moments: one on his knees taking the penis of the other into his mouth, and receiving the spit on his upturned face; then the scene switched. Eminently fair, I thought, embarrassed that my eyes had intruded.

Several men hung suspended from the white ceiling. I approached a cocoon of shiny gauze. I peered through the faceplate, and spied a bloated face, unrecognizable as to sex, a face three times too large.

The tiny eyes implored. I ignored them, thinking, this must be one of those born without an immunity system. It was then that I noticed the hole in the back of the cocoon, which twirled silently to reveal the opening.

The glove was of a type similar to that used for handling radioactive waste, or a baby in an incubator.

I cautiously inserted my hand in the glove, feeling the sphincter contract about my hand, once the wrist had passed out of sight.

The video screen on the back of the cocoon showed the doughy face in ecstasy.

The swollen mouth formed words, revealing a grimace of perfect white teeth.

I pulled out my hand; the face darkened with disappointment.

Time to move on. The horrid creature watched me leave; I felt a surge of aggression.

I noted several men (one, with entirely white eyes) observe my encounter with grim satisfaction.

I proceeded to a corner where another man performed an aerial ballet; there, I would find the apotheosis of this brightly lit room.

The beautiful young man lay, suspended, in a gossamer web, as though awaiting the hungry spider. His features were exquisite: long angular nose that met a sloping forehead; eyes round and full of liquid vulnerability. He was a vision of innocence and the dream of youth. His open legs displayed a half-erect penis, large and ivory, as unblemished and (seemingly) virginal as the rest of him.

As I approached, our eyes met (three others also approaching melted away), and his hands ran down the smoothly muscled chest, the nipples forming perfect circles begging to be broken, rising to meet his finger and my eyes. He lay there, cloaked in that roseate skin that seems to be in a constant blush, his erection slowly becoming full. His hand brushed against it ever so slightly, setting it in jubilant motion. I found my mouth watering, and I leaned over to swallow it.

He raised a hand in protest. His eyes said (kindly, watering slightly, but firmly), no—that is not what I want.

He nodded to the wall, where a group of bored nurses sat on the floor, beside a portable ambulance.

The man writhed, and turned over in his sheath of webs. His upraised buttocks, baby-like yet muscular, invited intrusion, and I felt the urge to rape and pillage his virginal tract.

As I felt myself rise to the occasion, his hands restrained me yet again. (I began to wonder if that were not his satisfaction—restraining others' impulses.) He reached through the web into the shadow thrown by his body, and pulled out an artificial arm, one not dissimilar from my own. Perhaps that is why, out of those assembled in this room, I had been chosen to be his partner.

Regardless of the reason, he instructed me silently how to insert the arm. The switch on the end would animate it.

I delicately began to insert this rather thick, hairy arm into his smooth rectum, but again this virginal being commanded me.

"Shove it in, hard. I only come here once a month. I can risk it." He gestured toward his waiting team.

My penis was out now, and I gently rubbed it, resisting the impulse to furiously masturbate. He said, rather more roughly than one would expect from such an angelic face, "No—just watch."

I was all eyes. He thrust himself hard onto the arm, and I threw the switch. The arm moved like a piston deep inside him. The young man screamed in delight. "Turn the switch higher."

I did so. The arm moved almost completely inside, and I feared it would get lost. It reappeared, as if in response to this thought, and exposed its somewhat bloodied length to me. I kneaded my own arm, releasing electrical charges that were neither pain nor pleasure.

The scene was to have one final moment. The arm now expanded, and became the arm of a larger man. It continued to grow, still pounding into him, until it was the arm of a mythological giant.

The young man turned his face to me, a mask of purity and hope, and, moaning deeply and softly, his rectum split open, and blood splattered me.

The young man collapsed into the web, the prosthetic arm now motionless.

The surgical team, seemingly bored with this spectacle, removed the body from the web, and placed it in the ambulance, which resembled a metal and glass casket.

Through the porthole, the man's inert face changed. The flaccidity of death gave rise to a blush in his cheeks, as the ambulance pumped life into him. The innocence radiated from him, like the web in which he had lain.

He opened his eyes, sleeping beauty kissed by the prince, and looked right through me.

I pushed roughly through the band of nurses, and another door opened in the wall. I plunged in.

Reeling in shock, I stood in a lovely meadow, a sundrenched meadow of the kind poets used to praise. The surrounding hills sloped voluptuously, leading to a small cluster of trees, an oasis of sorts, in which anything might happen. I imagined sheiks, and bound princesses whose struggles served only to heighten the male pleasure.

I walked down the hillside, sad to depart the lovely meadow which stood atop a sheared-off hill. Two forms moved behind the screen of trees; my imagination was engaged. Somewhat exhausted by the intensity of my previous experiences, I desperately needed romance, and a little sun.

I entered the cluster of trees, and found another clearing, smaller than the one above, and in the circle of light defined by the dark wall of trees, lay a young man sunning himself, a young man whose form was quite pleasing at this distance, and in the angle of sunlight in which he was positioned.

He lay with his rump exposed, hips slightly raised; his body reminded me of the curves of the surrounding, simulated hills. I placed myself an appropriate distance from him, removing my clothes in an intoxication of sun worship, using them as my blanket. I needn't have bothered, for the sand, I quickly discovered, was fused into a type of linoleum. The details of this illusion were somewhat shabby. I rectified the thought by concentrating on the sun, in which I lay fully exposed, face tilted upward, mirroring my silent partner in the measured distance.

The man in my line of vision began to move gently, from his hips to his shoulders; a wave of flesh. He must be dreaming. He looked back at me briefly, to dispel the thought of sleep: he had noticed me.

Despite myself, my erection had returned. I watched, with pleasure, as the thick shaft rose to meet the sun, reaching its fullest height.

The man writhed more vigorously now, emitting a faint, almost shy, sound.

It was then I noticed another figure, half-obscured by the trees, but perhaps only three or four feet from the prone figure of my stimulator. The figure sat dappled in sun and shadow, on a chair-like branch, and was intent on the same target as I.

I will call the man in the trees, for the sake of brevity (if not clarity), the faun; the prone man will be known as the other man.

The faun's blue eyes were intensely focused on the other man, whose buttocks contracted and relaxed, gripping our imaginations. The faun glanced at me once, scanning my penis (which I may say has drawn the attention of others, and kept my own, as well), and returned to his pressing task.

I felt rebuffed, and began to go flaccid. Stubbornly, I kneaded my penis back to its full height.

The other man, on the ground, continued his mechanical pumping, and with each stroke the faun seemed driven to a new level of ecstasy. The faun was, I must admit, a lovely young man (aren't they all, in this imaginary world?)—dark, with silky hair on his chest and buttocks, and the hand that drew itself again and again across his shiny erection attached to a green-veined wrist, strong and olive-skinned.

The other man, my lost man, looked once at this apparition of male beauty half-hidden in the shadows, and resumed his downward staring, as though trying to interpret the patterns of the fused sand.

The faun approached ejaculation. I stroked my penis in what I hoped was mutual excitement; at least, mutual proximity.

The other man had now turned over, and was likewise masturbating, finally acknowledging, overtly, the faun in the brush.

The faun emitted a low growl then (I envied the attention he now received). Posed in the sunlight, he appeared to deserve it.

I rose to my knees, hoping to gain the faun's attention; surely, the other man could not appreciate him as fully as I.

The other man then feigned disinterest, as the faun reached the height of his passion. As the shiny droplets fountained into the sunlit air, the other man turned over on his stomach and began to snore.

The faun's orgasm continued, nevertheless, cascading into the shaft of sunlight, quite unseen by anyone but me (and I quite invisible to him).

Dispirited, I picked up my clothes, pulling them on as I walked back up the hill. Such a waste; even our eyes were disconnected.

As I reached the hilltop, which seemed no longer as green, a door opened in the sky, and I was back in a more conventional room, with a video screen, four walls, and peepholes.

I peered through the holes; on each side were young men looking into other rooms.

I sat on the chair thoughtfully provided, and waited for the video screen to come to life, perhaps to show a snuff film or animal sex, perhaps a bullfight.

I waited an inordinate amount of time, and a faint malaise crept over me. Faint, I say, because I could not clearly identify the feeling. The scenarios that I had witnessed had excited me only transiently. I tried to recall them; they fled ghost-like into oblivion, but were not, I think, laid to rest.

I noticed an untied shoe lace, and tied it. I reminded myself to polish my shoes when I got home. I fingered the bracelet on my wrist, which "had led me through the Experience".

I waited (always waiting).

I imagined other rooms filled with similar young men, other rooms with young men and women, with only women, with images and no people, and finally empty rooms. I imagined a club with old people, although there were no old people left.

The "screen" was a door; it sizzled once, and opened. I walked through.

I found myself in a blue-black alley, a valley between buildings, and the distant low rumble of the city reminded me of where, and who, I was.

About a dozen others, pale and blank, stood in the alley light. Some walked off; some climbed into waiting cars.

I started to walk away, toward the faint light at the end of the alley, when a car pulled up, and a familiar face appeared behind an opening window.

"Hello. Need a lift?" the blond man said. And then I remembered.

I climbed in hesitantly. This was the man who had been killed by the passing train, the death providing me with the ticket to the Sex Club.

"How'd you like it?" he asked, patting my arm lightly and driving slowly off.

I didn't immediately answer.

My puzzlement must have shown, for he continued. "It's

how we recruit new members. Simulated death—very seductive, very erotic."

My mind was numb. "Did you like it?" he questioned, insistently.

"I found it interesting." In fact, I could scarcely remember it. My head felt as though it were severed from my body.

"Would you like to go back?" He reached into his pocket.

I dared not answer. Under the amnesia of the experience, my feelings blissfully slept.

"Ah, you do. I see." He paused, handing me another ticket. "This one will not work for you. You must pass it on." He tore the thin white bracelet with my name from my wrist. "When your counterpart completes his Experience, then you will be admitted again. How you pass it on is your own affair, but you must use your—imagination."

He pecked me on the cheek, like a feeding bird, but with some tenderness. I got out. "Maybe we will see each other again, inside." His blurring face, receding behind a window beaded with water, moved into the distance.

Business was going to be good.

I urinated on a trashcan, and walked the rest of the way home.

Marc Laidlaw writes, "In my office as Director of the Style Enforcement Agency, I have been responsible for a number of so-called SF pieces, including the novels DAD'S NUKE and NEON LOTUS. Shorter works in OMNI, ISSAC ASIMOV'S SF MAGAZINE, F&SF, NIGHT CRY, YEAR'S BEST SF, NEW TERRORS, Bruce Sterling's MIRRORSHADES anthology and Dennis Etchison's THE CUTTING EDGE. My work has appeared in Japanese and French. If you have any questions, please file form HAQ-79880 with your local Answering Agency. We trust that the present anthology will follow our guidelines undeviatingly, or suffer the consequences."

Marc's obsession with style has led him to the position of Chief Ideologue of the "Freestyle" Movement in SF, a California-based revelation summed up by the slogan, "Write like yourself, only more so." Rucker, Kadrey, Blumlein and the marvelous Pat Murphy (sadly missing from this anthology) are self-proclaimed Freestylers, and Marc puts out the Movement fanzine, a handwritten xeroxed sheet.

Your Style Guide— Use It Wisely
Marc Laidlaw

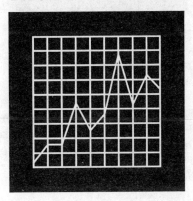

WHY A CONVENTIONAL FORMAT?

Your reader has just come out of a Phom McNguyen Shoe Store and is standing on the curb, expecting answers. It is always advisable to make an attempt to link disparate images in order to create the illusion of causality:

✔ Peering through side window of lowrider car as it waits at stoplight.

✔ Pulsebeat music, foam dice, soccer scores.

✔ Clear catheters trail from young driver's intestines into vinyl dashboard. Gauges register fuel, speed, rpm, blood pressure, heat of digestion, petroglobin viscosity.

Subjectivity is the chief variable, but several constants must be taken into consideration:

$$F = \text{Feitzer's Reader Credulity Quotient}$$

(calculated by sexual precocity indices and National Debt at date of birth)

$$A = \text{Avogadro's Social Security Number}$$

Mister X = Number of times reader has encountered references to faceless technicians in genre literature (Western, Romance, High Finance)

It is important to explain all facts and insinuations, especially those which are most easily accessible in other textual works, for purposes of providing internal coherence to 20th Century Prosody and in order to facilitate cross-referencing careers to 21st Century librarians. Supervisual footnotes are the most acceptable format for such interpolations.

Example: I never shop at Phom McNguyen's despite the weekly sales. I am afraid that people might look at my shoes and know that they are a generic brand, or the next worst thing, and not the work of a reputable Italian designer.

Example: By "lowrider," the author is referring to an automobile, preferably of mid-20th century American manufacture, favored by urban North American Hispanic adolescents, equipped with a mechanized suspension system whereby the relationship of the chassis to the street may be varied by remote control. For social context, ask your librarian to matriculate the glossary.

If you are contractually bound to the conventional design, procede as outlined in Author's Guide to Plot Concretization published by the National Arts Task Force. For the convenience of such authors, the work has been done for you. Please recast in your own writing, or enter attached soft-mag cartridge into any UPS-compatible text generator with your personal access code and savings account number.

Reader spied by Hispanic driver; laser-guided eyes fix on reader's tennis shoes; face shows no expression but bioregisters on dashboard betray slight fluctuation.

Sourceless panic.

Standard chase.

Agency intervention. (File Form XT-1023 for list of Agencies possessing Intragenre-Specification license. Unauthorized mention of any Agency, licensed or otherwise, is punishable at discretion of Civil Service Defense League.) Enforcement of judgment. If your reader is still permitted access to literature after sentencing, he may finish the story in his own words, expressing sorrow for any ethical-civil violations, and include completed work with Form RHB-1134, Plea for Rehabilitation. Otherwise, drive to next corner and check pedestrian shoes. (GOTO "Riverrun: rex:Joyce".)

Authors who have been granted permission to proceed by a licensed organization (National Semiconductor Foundation for the Arts, President's Council on Fractal Plot Exploitation, North American Treatise Organization) may continue in accord with principles and intentions as detailed in the approved Proposed Request for Funding. It is advisable (although not enforcable) to employ abstract verbs instead of nouns, and to make liberal use of excessive clauses, empty phrases, promotional sex defects, and dehumanizing slang. Such techniques will give the innovative work a superficial resemblance to standard texts and therefore render it palatable to the general audience.

Driver nods. Silver-nailed finger lifts from the steering wheel three times.

Covert code recognition.

The crowd pushes out around you but you keep your place on the curb, nodding three times back at him. He looks away from your shoes.

Obviously the Style Guide cannot follow authors beyond this point. Until the artist files the Provisional Acceptance Form, hse must follow hsis best judgment, as provided by the strictures indicated on all credit allotments.

Finger the cold plugs in your belly; you touch a leak, wishing that it looked more like a sweat stain, wondering who in the crowd can see.

Shrill brass horns. The sun caught in the cement warren. Oven temperatures.

Lowrider rumbles and pulls away into traffic. Jealousy, you know?

DEALING WITH REJECTION

If the text is rejected, the author must first submit to involuntary screening and accept the possibility of holocortical revision by a qualified editor or hsis editorial consultant. Emotional quotients will be rebalanced to offer increased objectivity, and then recommendations will be made by the PolyDecisional Authority Board. The author at this point may wish to return to the conventional format (see previous instructions), or else hse may further develop the work until it is considered suitable for social integration. Once approval has been granted, the artist has cause to rejoice. (See form RJC-465.)

The light changes back to red. Trapped again. Another lowrider pulls alongside you. Driver glances out.

You decide to make contact.

WHAT HAPPENS TO THE TEXT AFTER ACCEPTANCE?

For the dedicated artist, this may be the most difficult phase of creation: artifactual collaboration. An acceptable text is immediately distributed nationwide and judged for applicability by a wide range of media utilities, including cinevideo inducers, sociocultivators, satellite principalities, light rail surgeons, hive designers, rheological medics, extermination surveyors, and UPS-compatible academicians. All of these departments and many others are required by law to put your text to work.

The finger lifts three times from the wheel.

As the social order encounters your text, facilitators will first reduce it to the basic constituents, then "predigest" any content for maximum bioavailability. A consumable product may take the form of a mass-marketed "Eat&Learn" planarian diet, or it could be as homely as a mandatory printed-wall feature. There can surely be no thrill to compare with that of the author whose work has been injected into the economy, to become part of every citizen's neutral baseline status.

You give three nods.

WRITER'S BLOCK

This maladaptive syndrome has become less common in recent years. At one time, authors stated that the sight of a sheet of blank paper waiting to be filled was an obstacle to the first stroke of creation. We have tried to remedy this problem by providing a plethora of forms and flow-sheets, many of which are already at least partially completed for the author's convenience. In addition, there are many public domain programs designed to break the seemingly endless sheet of ice represented by 93.5 square inches of white paper.

The light changes.

For further information, file Form PTW-109 (Permission to Write), or present your Querent's License Number to the Style Enforcement Agency. Please check the Information Etiquette Access Guide for your social classification and save yourself time and money by making sure that your question is not forbidden before you ask it.

Ah, brotherhood!

You step down from the curb.

"I have a message—"

Squeal of tires, stench of burning rubber. Impact.

 Spiderwork cracks infiltrate your vision as your windshield eyes shatter.

You're not my reader, and you never were—

USER INTERRUPT
USER INTERRUPT

BUDGETARY VIOLATION
BUDGETARY VIOLATION

TRAGIC RESTRICTION 7998
TRAGIC RESTRICTION 7998

THIS WORKSTATION HAS BEEN REVOKED
THIS WORKSTATION HAS BEEN REVOKED

end

Colin Wilson, a literatus or homme des lettres who has accomplished great things in nearly every print genre from philosophy to encyclopedias, has exercised tremendous influence on anti-authoritarian circles, thanks to his work in libratory psychology. But he is also idolized in SF circles for his Lovecraftian pastiches. Legend has it that Wilson once criticized HPL's atrocious style and was challenged by August Derleth to do better. SPACE VAMPIRES and LIFE FORCE were the result, by far the most orignial contributions to the Mythos since the master's death. HPL's genius owed much to sexual repression. Wilson's inspiration was to uncover the sexually "buried"in pulp and horror and free it from its bonds, transforming its energy from neurosis to self-realization. He has recently published a major SF far-future trilogy, SPIDER WORLD, with a similar philosophical agenda.

Bob Banner, who edits CRITIQUE: A JOURNAL OF METAPHYSICS AND CONSPIRACY (the best periodical on conspiracy theory), asked Colin Wilson for a brief resumé of his central philosophical idea. We found the result valuable enough to warrant its inclusion as one of our three non-fiction pieces. Some doubt has recently been cast on Sheldrake's interpretation of the "100th monkey" material—but this doubt cannot rule out the possibility of some other "vitalist" development in biology with the same implications. Morphogenetic field reserach looks particularly promising in this respect. Aside from this one point, we find Wilson's essay a powerful manifesto of self-evident importance.

Maslow, Sheldrake, and the Peak Experience
Colin Wilson

The other day in our local pub, a stranger asked me how many books I had written. When I said 55, he looked startled, and asked me whether there was any constant theme that ran through them. Lying awake in the middle of the night, I decided to treat this as a challenge, and try to summarize the basic theme of all my work. The result—which follows—comes as close to it as I can manage in a couple of thousand words.

About twenty-five years ago, I received a letter from an American professor of psychology called Abraham Maslow. What he had to say struck me as breathtakingly original. Maslow said that, as a psychologist, he had got tired of studying sick people, because they never talked about anything but their sickness. It struck him that nobody had ever bothered to study healthy people. So he asked around among his friends: "Who is the healthiest person you know?" And he then got all the healthy people together and asked them questions. He immediately discovered something that no one else had ever found out: that all extremely healthy people have, with a fair degree of frequency, what Maslow called "peak experiences," experiences of bubbling, overwhelming happiness.

A typical one was as follows. A young mother was watching her husband and children eating breakfast. Suddenly, a beam of sunlight came in through the window. She thought: "My God, aren't I lucky?", and went into the peak experience.

When Maslow talked about peak experiences to his students, he made another important discovery. They began recalling peak experiences which they'd had in the past, which they'd now half-forgotten. He realized that this is the problem: that we all have peak experiences, but we take them for granted and quickly forget them. But as soon as his students began recalling their peak experiences, and talking about them to one another, they all began having more peak experiences. Talking and thinking about them somehow put them in the right frame of mind for further peak experiences.

All this excited me tremendously. For obviously if science could discover how to induce peak experiences, most of our worst social problems would vanish. Even then, in the early 1960s, it was obvious that most of our problems are due to boredom and frustration, and that alcoholism, drug abuse, football hooliganism, vandalism and sex crime are really a muddled search for the peak experience. If we could learn the secret of the peak experience, we would be well on our way towards H. G. Wells's "modern Utopia."

But when I put this question to Maslow, his answer disappointed me. He said he didn't think it was possible to have peak experiences "at will." They came when they wanted to, and there was nothing much we could do about it. Yet it seemed to me that this comment ran counter to his basic optimism. And I settled down to try and answer the question of how to induce peak experiences.

The first clue was that Maslow's students had started having more peak experiences as soon as they began thinking and talking about them. The reason is obvious. Thinking and talking about happiness puts you into an optimistic frame of mind. You get the feeling that man was intended to be happy. The philosopher Epictetus made the interesting observation: "Man is not worried by real problems so much as by his imagined anxieties about real problems." That is to say, we tend to get stuck in a thoroughly negative frame of mind. That is why healthy people have more peak experiences; they don't waste so much time worrying about things that will never happen.

In the past twenty-five years, I have learned a great deal about the various tricks for inducing the peak experience, and have proved to my own satisfaction that Maslow was mistaken. (Unfortunately, he died before I had time to tell him so.) There are a great many simple mental techniques for inducing the peak experience, and the basic method is always the same: to deliberately generate "inner tension," followed immediately by relaxation. Graham Greene discovered the basic method when, as a teenager, he played Russian roulette with his brother's revolver. When the hammer clicked on an empty chamber, he experienced an overwhelming sense of delight. This method is obviously not to be recommended, but anyone who thinks about it carefully will see that it contains all the important clues.

A couple of weeks ago, I spent four days in Amsterdam, trying to teach a roomful of "mature students" how to induce peak experiences. The experiment was successful beyond my expectations. During the final session, two students became convinced that they could see a golden light, while another said she had apparently floated clear off the floor.

But does all this bring us any nearer to "a modern Utopia?" Five years ago, I would have said no. But in the meantime, there has been a new and fascinating development.

This is largely due to the work of one single man, the biologist Rupert Sheldrake. It was Sheldrake who, in a book called *A New Science of Life*, came up with a theory of evolution that outraged most of his older colleagues. According to modern biology, evolution occurs through changes in the genes. According to Sheldrake, there is a simpler and much quicker method, which he calls "morphic resonance." The simplest way of explaining this is to cite the famous story about the monkeys on the island of Koshima, off the coast of Japan. Scientists fed the monkeys unwashed sweet potatoes, and one exceptionally bright female named Imo discovered that if she washed her potatoes in the sea, they were not only less gritty, but tasted better. Soon all the monkeys on Koshima had learned the trick. But so had other monkeys on the mainland—monkeys who had had no kind of contact with those on Koshima.

Was it some form of telepathy? Apparently not, for it not only works for animals, but for crystals. Some substances are extremely difficult to crystallize in the laboratory. But as soon as one laboratory has succeeded in doing it, the substance begins to crystallize much easier all over the world. At first it was thought that visiting scientists had carried tiny fragments of the new crystals on their clothes or beards. But this possibility was finally eliminated. Apparently the crystals were somehow "learning" from one another... Sheldrake set out to prove his theory with a number of experiments. One of these involved sending out thousands of those trick "pictures" in which a face is concealed in a mass of lines. He reasoned that once a certain number of people had learned to "see" the face, increasing numbers of people would be able to see it immediately. And that is precisely what happened.

If Sheldrake is right—and the biologists are fighting him tooth and nail every inch of the way—the consequences would obviously be momentous. To begin with, we would have to recognize that our writers and artists are largely to blame for the chaotic state of society. The chief qualification for a Nobel Prize is apparently to believe that life is futile and meaningless, and to say this in books and plays that end in the defeat of the hero. We stuff this poisonous rubbish down the throats of our children at school and university, and apparently believe that we are equipping them to face life. If there is anything to the theory of morphic resonance, then this is the equivalent of pouring plague germs into a city's water supply.

On the other hand, if a fairly large group of human beings could learn to have peak experiences at will—or simply learn to put themselves into the state of mind in which peak experiences are likely—then, according to Sheldrake, it should continue to spread naturally to increasing numbers of people. And perhaps a century hence—perhaps far less— everybody would be born with the ability to induce peak experiences. And the face of our civilization would be totally changed.

Among the cognoscenti, Robert Sheckley is revered as THE master of SF satire. Apparently, however, his work is too rich for most readers; in any case, his admirers proclaim that he's never been adequately rewarded or recognized or even paid for the immense pleasure he's afforded us since adolescence. And if we were feeling vindictive, we could name a few authors who have reaped much money and success by allowing themsleves to be heavily influenced by Sheckley's oeuvre.

In a sense, most SF concerns the present rather than the future (this is already a cliché of SF criticism)—that is, of course, that its basic "trick" consists of identifying some current trend or device or style or theory, and exaggerating it along certain trajectories until it attains an alienness suitable for the purposes of fiction. Thus the imaginary "future" of the author becomes a mirror for the actual present of the reader.

But this is precisely the basic trick of satire as well... which is why GULLIVER'S TRAVELS and CANDIDE can be considered proto-SF. Sheckley's VICTIM series, for example, presents an extremely plausible exaggeration of our present obsession with violent spectacle, TV game shows and death-tech. In one sense the society of the Hunt seems healthier than ours because it expresses openly what we still repress. The tensions and contradictions set up by this doubtless can cause either nausea or wild laughter—and Sheckley is capable of evoking both at once.

This selection from Sheckley's diaries offers us a chance to observe the inner workings of that creative process. His fiction consists of sets of perfect masks, almost devoid of any personal subjectivity. Thus it becomes all the more fascinating and moving to witness the psychic turmoil which lies behind the surface of such flawless craft.

Amsterdam Diary
Robert Sheckley

How much reading of other fiction writers must I do to convince myself that the finest work done is woven out of the author's own experience, his
own and no others, no matter how much he chooses to disguise or to exploit the
fact. The story was in fact an account of matters he remembered, not matters he
looked up in books or invented because they seemed an appropriate touch to put
in at that point. That's not how it's done any longer, except in s-f, the great
popular repository of outmoded literary forms, where the idea of "objective"
story-telling still prevails. It is the school of thought I adhered to for a very long
time, until my wheels ran dry & my words stopped & I was forced to spend
some unhappy years butting my head against the malignant & much-feared
Writer's Block. "Objectivity" separated me at last from following in my writing
the changing directions of my interests. Now I am a convert (tho perhaps a
cynical one) to the latest recurrence of the ancient practice of "subjective" writing, wherein you speak out *ad hominem* in your writing whenever the spirit

moves you, presumably. It is not a novel at all in the classical sense of the plotted novel. The modern novel is essentially a slice of your own life, adventures, hopes, etc., fictionalized as lightly or as heavily as your temperament requires.

Not all novels, of course, or even all good ones are written in that way. But most of the good ones I can think of are: Bellow, Roth, Mailer come to mind. Barth I consider a fantasist, Barthelme a poet, Coover a technician. John Gardner, interested in novel structures and textures, seems to like challenging arrangements, a wide variety of voices, etc.—a good writer who doesn't interest me much—his stuff hasn't really clicked for me in the few I've read, or tried to read.

Pynchon? A mixture of autobiography & fantasy, a blending unique to him. But something puts me off reading.

Barthelme, for me, the most mysterious & aberrant of them all—completely aloof & completely involved, a modern Kafka. I have some talent in the same sort of thing he does. But my aims are different in certain crucial aspects: most especially, my prose these days, which is run-on and novelistic, my feeling—faint, gnawing—that a story ought to be about something, not about nothing, as his are. What a tour de force is The Dead Father. You feel somehow that all the weird nonsense that goes on in the story means something. He does that very well, to make a nonsensical premise stand up despite the fact that it doesn't. Many of his stories would make perfect koans.

But he too turns toward autobiography. His story about the middle-aged man who finds himself unaccountably back in the army—I've had that dream several times, & have often told the story to friends. B. must have had a similar feeling, not necessarily a dream, in order to write a story that so exemplified the dismay I imagined in such a situation. He empathized. He autobiographized, though still in a fairly hermetic form. He exposes his guts only in the complicated rituals of fantasy.

Maybe I am a novelist now. I've certainly grown long-winded. It's the major requirement.

It's only 2 weeks since I was in London. I feel as if I'd been in Amsterdam for 6 months at the very least. I can't believe the changes I've undergone. They may seem imperceptible to anyone on the outside, but to me in here they seem very large indeed.

Dear Journal,
I really don't have anything to say, but I'm lonely & discouraged. I get thru my days all right, & I work in the evenings. I'm doing more than my usual amount of meditation. I walk a lot & I eat moderately. But sometimes, late at night, I get discouraged. It's 2:00 a.m.—actually July 1. I'm not sleepy, not even tired. I have no more sleeping pills with me & I haven't asked Sheri for one. So far.
My need of the pills, my need to turn a switch & go out like a light—

what's that all about? Anyone who's doing as well as I claim to be doing—so honest & forthright & hard-working—ought to be able to sleep nights, shouldn't he?

I've taken 2 valium, smoked some opium, & will soon roll a joint. All in an attempt to get myself to sleep when I don't want to, evidently. Or my head wants to but my body doesn't.

Now it seems to me that everything I've done since coming to Amsterdam has just been craziness, & all my scribbling has been self-deception, & meditation itself is another self-deception. Doubtless I'll change my opinions in the morning, & find some new enthusiasm. But for now, let me indulge myself in a little bellyaching. It ill befits a man to be happy or harmonious all of the time. You know he's got to be a saint, or, more likely, someone who has sold himself a pipe dream. Maybe the saints were selling themselves on it. Maybe Layman P'ang was out of his head. Maybe he & the monks he conversed with didn't know anything, or even understand what the other was talking about, but just improvised answers on the "spontaneity" principle:

"Why is a wounded cat like a Buddha?"

"Can't you even keep your necktie straight?"

"It would make a good hut for the ancient wanderer."

"We don't see many like that any more."

They bow to each other & walk offstage, to our thunderous applause. Something terribly significant has happened, tho we can't say even approximately what. The rule is: "This apparent nonsense makes great sense. You must discover that great sense. But not with your intellect. Oh, no. We don't use the intellect around here. We use something entirely different."

"What do you use?"

"We use no-thought to think matters with."

"And what exactly is no-thought?"

"Fold your legs, get your back straight, balance on your cushion. Do that for a year or ten—it makes no difference, you know—& it will come to you."

Trungpa's got a great description of the tight-hard grip of ego. Tho he tries not to say it outright, ego is still seen as the evil that must be eradicated. These Buddhists play complicated head games and it's difficult to find a hole in their structure, even tho something tells me it's biased. I guess the attack, if any, must be made right at the beginning, with the first noble truth: Life is dissatisfaction, suffering.

From this all else derives, & early Buddhism seems to have taken this view. The Theravadin school teaches withdrawal, detachment.

Along came the Japanese, Chinese, & Tibetans. They were not temperamentally Buddhistic in the classical sense, & so the Mahayana was born, an attempt to turn the pessimism & withdrawal of the southern Buddhists into a positive, life-oriented philosophy of involvement plus detachment. A positivist trend, like Thoreau & Emerson, life-affirming. Sitting meditation remained & remains the cornerstone of all the main Buddhistic schools, tho it was designed as a tool to encourage detachment & (inevitably) other worldliness. Trungpa and the zen people are trying to use meditation as a psychotherapeutic tool. That's fine, but what do I need it for? I'm watching thoughts a great deal of the time anyhow, & I am aware now that they are "just thoughts." So what if they are "just thoughts"? Are we to give them up, then? I know that action in a state of no-thought is easily attained. We do it all the time.

Han, the meditation master, explained their practice to me. The idea, if I may call it that, seems a modification of Saltipathana practice—watch the outgoing breath & whenever a thought comes up note it by saying to yourself "thinking." Why is one doing this? To show you how your mind—the mad monkey of Buddhist parable—is really out of line, wandering all over trying to entertain itself when it should be doing as directed—watching the breath. The bad effects of this are supposed to be self-evident. But why shouldn't the mind wander when it has nothing to occupy it but a boring thing like your stomach rising & falling? If your goal is freedom, then it will be a freedom of your own conception. Not Buddhism, simply because it is another man's opinion.

Two weeks until my 50th birthday. The thought, the mood, of impending doom. Fifty is well enough—but what about 60, what about 70? What about death, a second away or 20 or more years, but looming up faster every year. They go by faster & faster as one grows older. What happened to the golden inexhaustible summers of my youth? Maybe they weren't always golden, but they did seem to stretch on forever. I thought I'd never grow up. An age like 14 can last for a century, & when you finally reach the end of it, there's 99 years ahead of being only 15.

Too young to do it with girls. College somewhere far ahead—frightening (suppose I flunked out?) but also tremendously exciting—to come back to Maplewood a college man, & be able to date the high-school senior class girls, who seemed incalculable years ahead of their male contemporaries in intelligence, poise, maturity.

Or to be eighteen & at last able to join the army. I was 14 in 1942, & we ("America") were fighting a war on 2 fronts against 2 powerful & ruthless nations. Poor little England had her back to the war—Battle of Britain—& the Japs had destroyed our fleet in the Pacific and conquered Guam, the Philippines, Saipan—all places we wanted back, places we needed. I wanted to help win them back, to say nothing of France. We had lost France to the robot Nazi armies & their insane & evil leader who unfairly and indecently ordered his attack through Belgium, circumventing the impregnable Maginot line & confuting the French logic that had built it. I knew Us & Britain & France were absolutely right in this matter, & the evil Axis powers were absolutely wrong. All I could do to help was collect tin foil and old newspapers. We used to have practice bomb alerts once or twice a week, so we'd be prepared for the day when a Nazi aircraft carrier sailed up to somewhere off Perth Amboy & bombed the Junior High School of Maplewood, New Jersey. Once in a while the school authorities would proclaim a serious alert & send us all home—

safer to disperse the youth of the town if the long arm of the Boche was to reach this far. Nothing ever happened, of course, & my only hope was that World War II would last long enough so I could enlist & be an infantryman. In those days I couldn't wait for next year, & now I wish I could chain this year to a lamppost & sit down beside it for a while to catch my breath.

But one gets carried away bemoaning the passage of time. The last 2 weeks have been at least 6 months long, & I spent another 6 months during my few weeks in Greece. There's nothing to do with time & age but bear up & get on with whatever you can. My father is in his mid-seventies. He would have plenty to complain about, but I've never heard him do it. He's intelligent, optimistic, controlled. He knows the score. He's a nervous man who likes to be outdoors playing golf whenever possible. He doesn't like to go away from home too long because mother, who is around his age, is close to bedridden, deaf, suffering for many years from Hodgkin's disease—a softening of the bones resulting in excruciating pressure on the skull. She is in pain a great deal of the time, & waits as long as she can before taking the pain pills because they fog her over & she wants to remain as lucid as she can. Her memory is shot, she confuses me, my son, & my father. Sometimes all defences are stripped from her by age & deterioration & disease & pain, & you see her fundamental feelings. They are always feelings of love & concern for others. She hates having to be cared for, her life has been spent raising & caring for her children, loving & caring for her husband. Now it grieves her that he must do everything for her. But she accepts it & is a good, obedient & cheerful patient in order to make it as easy on him as possible. She expresses her love for me and pride in me every time she sees me, every time she writes, or used to write, for in the last few years my father has had to write all the letters. I have a tangled mass of feelings about them. I don't like to think too far ahead.

10:10. Woke up with heartburn, doubtless due to the 3 cheese & sausage sandwiches I ate for dinner last night between 7:30 p.m. & 12:00 midnight. Another overcast & chilly day outside. The sunlight on Sat. must have been a false alarm.

It's letting your thoughts devil you that causes you so much grief. The various meditational schools try to cure this. The zen people, Rinpoche, Rajneesh, even Krishnamurti, advise you to drop thinking.

The Buddhist route (Zen, anyhow) to this dropping of mind is through sitting meditation. Thru this, according to the classical theory, a realization will come at last, a wordless realization that can only be indicated, never really spoken about. It seems to concern an insight into Sunyata, Nothingness, or into Anatta, no self, or a finding of the synonymity of the two. Something like that.

But zen, or the meditational path in general, is an essentially religious approach: by this Path you are supposed to receive a mystic enlightenment that will change your life henceforth. These Paths are training grounds for mystics, even when the mysticism is put forward as reasonably as Trungpa's & Zen's, with their emphasis on the everyday now-importance.

Daily mindfulness. What a fine-sounding goal. Doing only one thing at a time & doing that exquisitely. One's life a continual Japanese tea ceremony. This seems so desirable that an enthusiastic sort like myself is drawn to it without thinking it through.

Various other writers deepen the conflict. Krishnamurti has no patience for sitting meditation. (He could be a fine guide, for he tries to put us under responsibility only to ourselves. But I find it difficult to learn from him. He is always going off into the sort of language that makes him seem a mystic tho he disclaims it. And he gives the impression [not on purpose, I'm sure] that we could all be as virtuous & visionary & dignified as he if only we could only find a way. And this despite injunction to not go whoring after goodness but try to use at least our intelligence if not our souls. An Old Testament prophet type.)

The man who wrote under the name of Wu Wei Wu; Hui Neng; some of the T'ang masters; Chuang Tzu & Lao Tze, in their various ways point to a direct & effortless dropping of thought. No acrobatics required. Dialect is supplied if you want it. But the fact is, they say, you can drop thought any time you want to & everything will go on just like always, maybe even better, certainly better for you if you're not worrying about outcomes.

But something must be asked in all this. Is dropping thought desirable?

When you meditate, you try, no matter how much you may think to the contrary, to suppress, divert, block out or blank thought. So many people want to get rid of it. Isn't thought valuable? Isn't pain nature's way of telling you that something in your life is wrong? Shouldn't you try to think matters through rather than engage in the diverting tactics of meditation?

(I believe that formal sitting meditation is of inestimable value at certain times, certain periods of life. You have to start somewhere. Meditation gives you time & space, a chance for matters to come under your examination, a time for insight. I have been doing sitting meditation formally for about 6 years, & I have kept after myself to do it. So this diatribe is not directed generally against sitting as such. It refers to my own search, my own considerations for myself. I lay down no general rule: my generalizations are meant as probes into my own conditions, not sermons to the world at large.)

And why should we spend all our time in the here-and-now, one-pointed, concentrated on what's happening now? We are designed to scan the external world continually, & to monitor the inner world for signals about what to do. The interaction is natural; we could survive in no other way than by scanning, matching inner demand with outer circumstance, by negotiating our survival by constant vigilance between inner & outer. It is necessary that we do this & a pity we don't do it better. If periods of sitting meditation can assist in the daily survival on physical & psychic survival, fine. It seems to me a good & often pleasant exercise to sit immobile for half an hour, calm my breathing & my thoughts. But it could be more dangerous to o.d. on zazen than on drugs. There are no hospitals for meditators, & I see a lot of wounded ones walking around.

The Zen approach is to not think about these matters; just go on sitting. But why not think about these matters, unless you truly aspire to the Buddhist ideal of life-in-death, dignity, non-attachment to what you desire most—Japanese disciplinary schticks, evidently a national mania, sit uneasily on Americans with their traditions of freedom, self-expression, originality, unconventionality. You don't have to behave like a Jap to get on with "spiritual" work. If he has any sense, God is sure to prefer a genuine American schmuck to an ersatz Japanese roshi.

Hakuin & Dogen are fine guides for the Japanese, & much can be learned from them by anyone. But we have our own indigenous zen masters. Thoreau is a better guide for us than Buddha himself. Thoreau's is a thoroughly practical & practicable Way, to be done in full enjoyment or not at all. The schools say: try this for a month or so, or better, a year or so, & see if it suits you. Thoreau says that if you don't enjoy what you're doing right now, then something is wrong.

JAMIESON STORY

I am a human being with semi-godlike powers. I don't mean to boast, I'm just stating a simple fact, the key fact of my existence, & I'm putting it up front now, at the beginning.

I can do certain things that others cannot. I have some of the powers of a magus. In my own particular line of expertise, I can only be compared to Gurdjieff, the count of St. Germain, Cagliostro, Albertus Magnus, Paracelsus, & others of that esoteric ilk. I myself am not at all mystically inclined, however. I believe that my powers came about through a freak genetic patterning, a one-in-a-million configuration that produces Beethovens, Socrateses, Roger Bacons, and me.

Not that I mean to compare myself to them. I'm just trying to say that they were born with certain non-ordinary powers, just as I was.

If I had had any choice in the matter, I would have chosen to be born a genius musician or painter or philosopher. But one has no choice in these matters. I was born with a power of a certain sort. It was given to me by God or Chance. I had no hand in it, nor, in the real sense, did my parents. All they did was cast their genes together blindly, so to speak, and hope for the best. Just like all parents. Just like it always was and always will be, despite the futurian dreams of the tiny National Eugenical Party for several of the large factory-farms in the Midwest and in Texas.

I have never revealed these things to anyone before. I do so now with equanimity: Tho I am a shy man, shortly after completing this document I shall either take on a totally new identity & background; or I shall board the Black Hole Express on the one-way journey to a different universe. In either case, I shall not care what people think, because I will be either somewhere or someone else, or both. Thus I can afford the luxury of getting these matters off my mind, & (demeaning motive tho it may be) revealing to those who thought they knew the true nature of "simple" Howard Haskins just how wrong they were.

I was born in the Santa Barbara space station that supplies the Western U.S. with two-thirds of its electricity. Our colony also specializes in horticultural research, which is carried out in (cylindrical) stations adjacent to the colony itself. We are one of the oldest colonies, wealthy, self-sufficient if we choose to be. Our colony is a fruitful copy of all the best features of California living, tho scaled down, of course, to New England proportions to fit our living space. I remember it as a place of green rolling hills and rivers, tiny charming communities with enough room between houses, close enough to be neighborly, distant enough so you never felt crowded. Inobtrusive transport in each village would whisk us away to our single urban center, New San Francisco, vibrant with shops and smart restaurants, bookstores & record shops, & with a fine variety of movies, concerts, etc.

Tiny tho our physical world was, we still managed to see a variety of natural life. (In one sense our mountains were artificial, since the early colonists had built them. But they were made out of nature's own materials — slag from the moon to provide the armature of the mountain, then a covering of meteoritic rock brought in from the Asteroids. A fundamental earth-fill was next added on, some of it imported from Earth at enormous expense. Next came planting— trees, grass, a great variety of flowers, shrubs, lichen, moss, etc. Pre-planning of the mountains from an artistic viewpoint — shape, location, coverage, etc. was turned over to the zen-influenced American painter & sculptor Henry Lesage, an act of rare daring by the city council. They gave Lesage the parameters of the situation — size, materials available, etc., & turned him loose.

Lesage retired to a Zen monastery near Sausalito to consider the problem, & to face up to the fear of this project unique in world history — to model mountains that would be pleasing to the eye, yet natural, looking as if they had happened that way all on their own — artistic but inevitable. The natural environment of an entire world in his hands. He didn't know whether to laugh or to cry about it.

He came at last to the famous decision whose merits are still argued & probably always will be: one side of the vast cylinder up whose sides he was to build his mountains was to be composed strictly according to the Zen desiderata for constructing gardens: a symmetry, simplicity, austerity, artlessness, unworldly, quiet, & with a subtle profundity expressed thru chiaroscuro, the arrangement of light & dark areas to suggest the impression of limitless ranges beyond.

This he decided, was a total composition in its own right, unrelated to the other side of the cylinder. The artist in him took over from the Zen man & told him that something entirely different was required. Inspiration sent him on a trip around Earth, photographing, drawing & painting mountains that especially appealed to him. He made a composite of these, & so that side of the cylinder is various, and, to the unoriented eye, confusing. Each mountain has vegetation similar to its original, & at first it can be disconcerting to view a typical Montana hill between a Madagascar rain-forest mountain on one side & the Matterhorn (complete with ice & snow & ski lifts) on the other side.

And facing this are the Zen mountains on their other side with their juniper & wild plum trees & clumps of bamboo. It may jar you upon first arrival at the Station, but after a few days you like it, & after a fews weeks you can't imagine having it any other way.

This is the world I grew up in, under blue skies & bright sunlight except when the Weather controllers punched up a thunderstorm every now & then, just to liven things up. (The Weather Controllers did subtle & exacting work. An even, warm cloudless day every day of the year, year in & year out, is destructive to the psyche, as the Miami Station found to its cost some years ago when an otherwise inexplicable mania swept the place & mobs of people began chewing up the plastic grass like so many later-day Nebuchadnezzers. Our Weather Controllers were always zealous in producing sudden unexpected chilly winds, clouds of every shape & variety, (tho they were permitted no more than 1/2 sky coverage at any one time), & once a heavy, sultry levante or sirocco wind for 3 days running until the complaints came pouring in.)

I thought that I would live there forever. Alas for my childish dreams, my parents were only there on a ten year contract. Overcrowding is always a problem on the better new worlds, (they will always let you into Bangladesh Station, but who would want to live there?) & Santa Barbara Station had not only its own growing population to contend with, but also the requests of many fine scientists & technicians to work there. Outworlders are admitted only on specific time-length contracts, after which they and their children (if any) must depart. Extensions are sometimes granted to people who are making a unique & ongoing contribution. They might have let Einstein or Oppenheimer stay, but not Frank & Helen Haskins, research biologists in lichens, whose place could be taken over by a hundred others, some of whom might turn up more usable material than my parents had been able to. (Lichens are curious & frustrating things, entities, as I know from listening to a thousand dinner/mealtime conversations. I shudder whenever I hear the word , remembering the chagrin, frustration & despair that my parents felt on the subject. Lichens. I will never mention lichens again.)

And so we came back to NYU, from which place we had been on loan. My parents continued their work on you-know-what—NYU didn't care if it took them a century to discover a useful fact—the old universities are really mellow —& I went to the local schools which I detested, in a noisy old-style urban city which I hated, & came slowly to learn of my power.

Discovery of my power was reserved for my 21st birthday, at a time when I was living on my own in Troy, New York, & working as a water pollution engineer's technical assistant, which any moron could perform with his eyes shut. But I was untrained for anything else, having dropped out of college for a variety of reasons, because I had not discovered my special ability up to now & there was no subject or field for which I had a natural bent. Obviously not, since I had not discovered my strange talent before this.

I remember, on the day of my 21st birthday, sitting alone in my furnished room, feeling sorry for myself—one of my habitual emotions in those days, I regret to say. I had no girl, no friends. Even my parents were out of the country, taking a 2-week package to Peru as the guests of Dr. Maletas Tomo, head of the Dept. of Lichinology (there, I said the word again after all!) at Lima U. Lima lichens are in some respects unlike any other lichens in the world, my father excitedly told me before they left. A hell of a lot of good that did me.

So there I was, all alone & feeling blue & wishing I had one friend in the world who would come by & wish me a happy birthday & maybe even give me a little present. What a laugh. I had exactly *no* friends in the world, & damn few acquaintances, either. (I am not unlikable. But I used to move around a lot in those days & anyhow I'm shy.)

I lay on the bed looking at the wall with its faded reproduction of the famous photograph of President Wheelwright's face after the ambassador from Chrotll V covered him in viscous slime in strict accordance with Chrotll protocol concerning how to show utmost respect to an important person. The President's comic expression (someone had forgotten to brief him about it; some heads rolled after *that* one) displaced no mirth in my heart. I wanted a friend. And I decided there & then I was going to get one.

Something came over me—some prescience concerning events to come, I believe: and I concentrated with all my might on the thought, *I want a friend & I want him now.* Some hitherto unnoticed channel seemed to open in my head. I felt the power pouring out from me, searching, seeking. So it really was not so great a surprise when, an hour later, there was a knock on the door.

My visitor was a man whom I shall call Harry Saunders, since he is still among you & might not like to have his association with me revealed, tho he played no part in the illicit & shameful events that I soon must relate.

We had never met before. He had been looking for someone entirely different — an old army buddy who had given this as his address, & whom he had decided to look up as long as he was passing thru town anyhow. He was a few years older than me. I invited him in for coffee. We found that we had a special rapport, that within an hour we knew we were friends & would stay friends.

"So it's your birthday," he said at one point in the afternoon. "That's good 'cause I've got a present for you." He took a small box out of his pocket & gave it to me. Within was a beautifully enamelled heraldic shield with a safety-pin soldered to its back. "I had picked it up for that other guy I was coming to see. It's the official emblem of the 32nd Spaceborne Infantry Regiment to which we both belonged. I'd like you to have it."

I never saw Harry again. Our destinies led us apart—he was on his way to do a 2-year-stint as a data processor in Afghanistan—but we were true friends that day, & would be so again if we ever met. (Hi, Harry. You'll know who you are if you're reading this. I've always kept the badge. I have it with me now.)

After he left, I did a lot of heavy thinking. Unless it was a coincidence, which I proposed to check out as soon as possible by a series of experiments you already must know were successful, I had the power to make whatever I wished for to happen. My experiments confirmed this & showed me what I could successfully wish for & what not. My power worked by subtly altering in-progress events, not by disrupting them. If I wished for money, in general, I would get it in some form or another usually within 24 hours, tho I could never predict when & how—one time it might be an unexpected dividend check from my insurance policy, another time I might find a wallet with $200 in it inexplicably left by someone by accident in the pocket of a sports jacket I was trying on. If I got more specific, like asking for a raise in pay, my power would still work to produce a favorable configuration of events that would "naturally" produce that result. But it would take longer, naturally, weeks or months to get the right people canned or promoted so that my rise to the next pay grade could take place.

My power to shape events to my liking seemed limitless. Time was the only limiting factor. The more unlikely the event, the longer it took for my power to arrange it naturally. (In general, that is. Actually, my power turned up some of the unlikely ones real fast. My request for a 2 weeks all-paid vacation at a top resort in Barbados was answered in exactly 47 hours. My power had compromised a bit, it's true—it had found a way to get me a one week all-expenses-paid vacation in Nassau by directing me to turn on a d.j. program I never usually listen to & to be the first to phone in the name of the singer on the old classical pop album "Morrison Hotel." (Jim Morrison, of course, but I just happened to know that because I'd been browsing thru a book on the history of rock a few hours earlier.)

A week in Nassau isn't two weeks in Barbados, of course, & the hotel was nothing to speak about, but still, I thought my power had done a pretty good job on short notice & I accepted it gratefully.

That's why I think I'm going to take the One-Shot Black Hole Special. It's a new special ship every time, of course, since the one they send out never comes back. But there are always enough people around who want to make the trip to finance the building of new ones. There's a new one just completed taking on passengers for next month. I expect I'll be on it. I used to think that people who went on a trip like that were crazy. No longer. The true believers say that it'll all be incredibly different when (if) we get thru the hole & find a planet to put down on on the other side. The old ways won't exist any more, nor will our old selves. We will be transformed beings in a transformed universe.

I don't exactly swallow all that stuff, but I do think that that unthinkable event—the incredible passage itself—will shake me loose from this special power that's screwed up all of my life. After I go through the Black Hole I'll be just the same as anyone else, & in a totally different universe maybe things will work out better for me.

I have rolled up a final contemplative joint that I am going to smoke while writing up this account, & then I am going to sleep behind a Mogadon that I really didn't need, being damned tired, but took anyhow in hopes of feeling it kick me in the stomach & fog my brain, giving those precious hours of muzzy dissociation that we dopers try so hard to achieve & reach so seldom in these parlous times of mediocre shit everywhere I go. (Except here. May the spirit of Mexalito the Little Smoke bless this lenient and zany city of Amsterdam, which has led me to Tommy & the finest stuff I've smoked since the old days.)

I've done a good day's work. I've completed one story that I don't plan to look at again until I have sufficient leisure to do a definitive rewrite, or I should say, rethink. That's the teleporter story. On the Jamieson story, things are proceeding differently. I had to interrupt the flow for dinner, Natalie, & J. Claudius. When I resumed, I thought it best to retype what I had handwritten (some few thousand words) to reacquaint myself with the matter. As I did so, I found myself re-shaping & re-connecting the story to account for events & passages that I knew lay ahead. This caused the story to sprawl still more, tho I believe that the material is interesting enough to warrant it, its raison d'etre now, more than the Jamieson fragment that began all this.

I'm almost 3000 words into the typescript, with some thousands of handwritten words still to go, & I haven't even reached Jamieson yet. Really, I'm writing a proper story, not one of the shaggy dog variety, & I really want to get to Jamieson & what was supposed to be the crux or main situation toward which I was tending in the first place. But other matters keep obtruding themselves & demanding explanations which are immediately forthcoming. I allow my digressions to carry me pretty far away from the proposed story line when it so falls out, but I lead them back to it if no new inspiration prompts me otherwise. I follow my writer's nose, trying, but not too hard, to remain within the parameters of the development I have (somewhat hazily, & that on purpose—so that I may surprise myself) proposed to follow. And so I follow it cheerfully, & lay it down when the time seems appropriate, trusting myself to resume tomorrow faithful to my present mood of discovering what is necessary by trial rather than planning, prepared to drop it if it turns sour or circumstances preclude its being done, content in the story I have already written & viewing this as an unusual dispensation due to circumstances uniquely favorable for its production, but due to change without notice at any time.

It seems to me now most important not to grab at your creations. To be anxious about them is tantamount to saying that they are not truly yours, they are dispensations from the stingy muse of letters, to be snatched as she passes by with them in her cold marble hands.

It is natural to be eager, but a sin against yourself to grasp after a creation, sweating for fear you may lose it. If you can lose it, it's not really yours. As Montaigne said, it belongs in the place where you found it. What is yours is you, & that is not a possession, it is a way of viewing events, of putting them together, & of pleasure in the project that is more surely you than your nose.

As a writer, my work is a discussing of matters of interest to me in a manner as truthful as possible to the artistic truth I am trying (obliquely, in the artist's manner) to exemplify in my fiction. It's too bad that truth is such a heavy word, such a jargon-cult expression nowadays. It smacks of seriousness & matters beyond our present comprehension. This is not the truth I'm talking about. My truth is simply to utter my honest thoughts & feelings about a certain matter. I don't trust myself when I write a Heavy Truth. False profundity is distressing when you discover it in yourself, embarrassing when you hear yourself carrying on like some enlightenment freak. That's what keeps me in fiction rather than leaving it aside to write eternally in my beloved journal. I come out with entirely too many broad & pompous generalizations & "profound" dicta remembered from my intermittent but incessant reading of "spiritual development" books. These I try to confine to my journal, so that I may see myself as whoever I am, even if who I am is false. Better to be a genuine false me than an ersatz someone else, as I remarked elsewhere in these journals in (I suppose) slightly altered form.

Good fiction is never preachy. It tells its truth only by inference and analogy. It uses the specific detail as its building block rather than the vague generalization. In my case it's usually humorous—no mistaking my stuff for the Platform Talk of the 6th Patriarch. But I do not try to be funny, I merely write as I write—as future generations will doubtless acknowledge as they yawn over my journal for their Ph. D. theses (if it turns out that way).

In the meantime I trust the voice I can never lose—my own. The directions of its interest may change, even by morning. But what does that matter if I simply follow them, along for the trip rather than the payoff (always disappointing), enjoying writing my story rather than looking forward to its completion. Wise-sounding words which I hope describe the place where I'm really at. I'm apt to metamorphose in the morning into an ardent composer of unlistenable music, or I may lie around all day smoking dope & resting on my laurels. *Se depende,* as they say in Spain. And so to bed.

Several of our authors publish their work in what are called "zines" — amateur-produced or self-published (lit., samizdat), xerox, mimeo or cheap off-set, fly-by-night periodicals of the New Mutants. SF "fanzines" are among the ancestors of these publications, as is the "Underground Press" of the 60's and the Punkzines of the 70's.

We believe that the world of zines includes some of the most vital, exciting and radical of all contemporary American (and British) writing, and we devoted a special number of SEMIOTEXT(E), the USA issue, to exploring this unmapped territory. The ideal zine combines elements of all its precursors (including amateur SF) with a political stance on the far side of Chaos, a violent challenge to censorship both legal and commercial, a vicious sense of humor, lots of cartoons and collages, and a tendency to change address every six months.

Of all the zines, the best (the "ideal") was without doubt POPULAR REALITY, edited by the Irreverend Dave Crowbar and featuring writers like Bob Black, Yael Dragwyla, tENTATIVELY a cONVENIENCE (sic), Blaster Al Ackerman, the Wretched Dervish — and three of our present contributors: Hakim Bey, Bob McGlynn and D. A. Shawl, the "Poetry Editrix" of PopReal who writes under the nom de guerre Celeste Oatmeal.

I Was A Teen-Age Genetic Engineer
Denise Angela Shawl

My hair is not my own. My blood is not my own. My life is not my own. I am not free. I am a political prisoner on a North American game preserve.

My hair is long, fine, brittle, tangled. I comb it with despair and rainwater.

I am waiting and I am not waiting. I am resting and I am restless. Everything that I am, I am not.

I am encircled by low, stinging briars. In my youth I frolicked among them; now I merely sit.

But no, quite often I do not merely sit. I amble along the confines. Either the boundaries are patrolled or they are not. It doesn't matter at all, since I never attempt to cross them, to venture my life.

The way it is is the way it's supposed to be. I am to sit here, lorn, and when I cry rain falls, and when my tears dry and I sigh the wind

271

speaks, and when I smile my clouds silver; the haze becomes intolerably bright, eye-scalding.

But the sun will not yet come through.

I make music. I make baskets, little ones. I make friends with the birds and rodents and insects. And I am alone, alone.

Alone. The reason that I am alone now is that I will not always be alone. Someone comes.

Someone comes; I taste his sweet steps. I am afraid. He will break the steady surface of my mirror. But he is coming. And he is coming through, and in.

From his birth, he has been coming. I saw his crowning in a magic candleflame a candle I made to burn only once a year, for only so long. Whenever I look into that flame, I can clearly see the moves he makes in those moments. And he is approaching, swifter than years.

I am a sickle, a crow, a magpie inhabiting a land of ghosts. I scarred myself, pearl-petalled, on my brow. Yes, I marked my sorrow and strength on my face. scorning a place in the ninety-ninth percentile, those who are unmarred and perfect from conception.

How could I not? How could I turn my back on the carelessly deformed, the purposely stunted, the play-people we were taught to raise as pets?

The will of the state automatically engenders a counter-will. The hand of the state severs itself from the arm. I was programmed to be a designer, a patterner of degraded human life-forms.

Cruel memory. I enjoyed my vocation. I studied. I theorised. I practised. Slowly (the process is artificially lengthened among us), I rounded. I filled out emotionally and physically, and neared the much-touted perihelion of my life's orbit: adulthood. As was traditional, I began a lengthy work which was to guarantee my place in the social exoskeleton.

In later years, my work had taken a startling turn. I was no longer content to functionally integrate the traits of lower species into my subjects. Although I still spent many hours here, in my private wild domain, I did not produce more hare-men and partridge women. These had become overfamiliar. And yet, I could not bring myself to switch from the artistic mode to the utilitarian; to place my skills directly in the hands of the government. Rather than explore my distaste, and come to the inevitable conclusion that all types of genetic manipulation were exploitive, I had ranged even further in my chosen field. I had hopes that less hackneyed creations would attract financial support and laudation.

My inspirations came from old chimerical tales. Fishwomen, sealmen, winged hermaphrodites—these were common. But I invented the scaled fire-breather, the one-horned woman, the invisible man. Then I outdid myself.

 I began to make gods. Cupid was first. How he tormented me until I let him go. Vulcan fell in love with me at first sight. He set up shop in the basement and refused to leave. He besought me with gifts: magic rings and wonderous pocket-sized ships with infinite holds. I created Minerva for counsel. She advised me not to stop until I had recalled the entire pantheon, or I would be wreaking havoc due to karmic imbalances. I could not disagree with wisdom herself, so in short order they were all released upon the world—the quarreling, autocratic Olympian deities.

Psyche was different. Perhaps it was because I spent more time on her; I intended her to be the chief representation of my competence. The others were super-human, were oversized projections of portions of the collective mind. But Psyche seemed to be distilled humanity, the essence.

My work on her was very subtle, and not even I fully realized the implications until she opened her incredible eyes. Her incredible blazing eyes that lit everything with too bright truth showed me to myself as the monster that I was. I begged her for a wound to make me cry, a drop of burning oil on my face.

She refused with horror, so I snatched her knife and carved a star on my brow.

Then she laughed, and blessed me, and understood. Her shining hands healed me and set my scar glowing. She walked out, bare humble feet changing the world with every step.

I was left with the remains of my disgusting work and the clamorous activity of the gods. But before my colleagues came and found me thus, and enforced my solitude with machinations of that treacherous smith, I had time for one last toil. I made only the seed and caused it to arise in a suitable womb. I sowed the Red Doom, the Hound of the Smith, Cuchullain.

And he comes.

Luke McGuff is a zine-activist. Recently he produced a radical SF zine, LIVE AT THE STAGGER CAFE, *and at one point was editor of the excellent semi-pro-zine* NEW PATHWAYS IN F & SF. *His own work — generally sardonic short-shorts — has appeared in countless little bizarre publications.*

Chapter One, The Novel
Luke McGuff

At 7 a.m. in a bus depot everyone looks vagrant, confused and adrift. As if they're the victims of some massive failed Jobs Relocation Program—"Putting the Skills of America Where They're Needed Most."

An old Tex-Mex man up from the collapsed Gulf Coast fisheries stands near a telephone kiosk, thinking about missing the commercial smelt run in Duluth, MN. He's on his way to Chicago, hoping to catch up with the Coho salmon run. Somebody told him it was already over. He expects only the usual "I"m sorry, Señor Gravis, but the work for you has already been filled. Let's see what we have here..."

The woman behind the desk is only a little better off than Sr. Gravis. Rent and appearances (fashionable clothing and hairstyles, the latest electronics) eat up almost all of her pay. But she has a job and Sr. Gravis doesn't. Her job is send people like Sr. Gravis chasing after the next temporary assignment.

She finds a job in Maine, a three day bus ride. No guarantee it will still be there when he arrives. She credits his multicard account with enough for the cheaper dinners at the depot cafeterias. She checks the balance on his personal hygiene allowance. She renews the filter that won't let him buy any liquor.

When the printer chimes, she hands him his papers out of the basket and smiles. Sr. Gravis reads her nametag: Ms. Bradley.

Whatever the Ms. Bradleys look like, Sr. Gravis thinks they would be nice women to settle down with. He just wants to get off the bus. He knows he doesn't have the knack. He's met other men in cafeterias, talking in assignment futures. They badger the Ms. Bradleys to produce assignments two or even three weeks in advance. These men will eventually accumulate enough in their accounts to retire to a Florida development. They'll get off the bus.

Not Sr. Gravis. He'll be on the bus until they cut the program out from under him. He's heard stories about people being disallowed in small towns, being thrown off the bus in nowheres like Tucumcari, New Mexico, or Tomah, Wisconsin. These people have to hitch, walk or starve their way into the nearest big city, and all they have left is a pad on the floor of a mission.

Sr. Gravis wants to get off the bus, but not that way. When he gets to Maine, he will be told that the fishing boats are full. Another Ms. Bradley will tell him there's a possibility of an opening in the salmon canneries in Nome, Alaska. He'll take it.

Collage is like SF: it disassembles "realism" in order to generate speculative imagery just as SF disassembles conventional narrative to produce speculative fiction. In collage recognizable images are cut up to produce a picture of something which does not yet exist; in SF, linear realism is twisted moebius-like to generate futures which do not yet exist. Both techniques are experimental.

(For bio-bibliographical information on Richard Kadrey — whose collages follow on the next two pages and on pages 295, 335, 355, and 363 — see the introduction to his story elsewhere in this volume.)

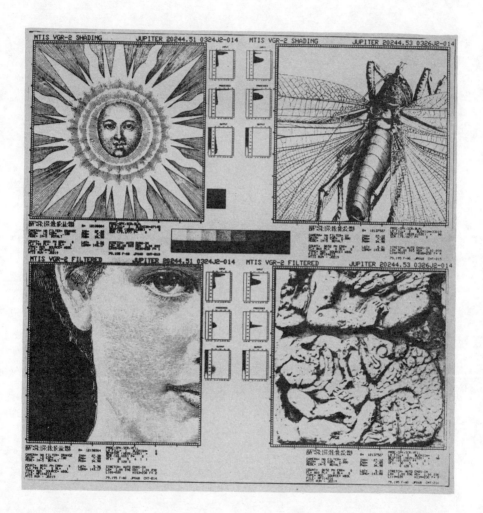

Philip José Farmer writes, "The entity known as Philip José Farmer has been living in one body for 69 years and is looking for another to move into."

The Sage of Peoria, that "Holy City by the Kickapoo," PJF has donated so much sheer pleasure to SF readers since the "Golden Age" that a brief assessment of his stature can only fizzle into inadequate superlatives. A supreme pulpster, yes, but something more: a Trickster, a "rough" surrealist, a progenitor of new waves, dangerous visions and cyber-porno weirdness. We look on him as an ancestor—but unlike other ancestral SF figures, he has never become an embarrassment, a "BOF," a curmudgeon.

His current DAYWORLD series is as potent and picaresque as the classic RIVERWORLD. Everything he writes is a gem, even his letters—and nothing compares with the warm thrill of discovering yet another previously-unknown Farmer paperback, tattered and louche, in a heap of used books on some city sidewalk vendor's blanket.

St. Francis Kisses His Ass Goodbye
Philip José Farmer

A great mission is made up of many small missions.

Francesco Bernardone, founder in A.D. 1210 of the Friars Minor, the Lesser Brothers, was thinking this as he walked down the steep and winding dirt path halfway up Alverno, a mountain given him by a wealthy admirer. Francesco had refused the gift as a gift; he would not own property, not even his brown woolen robe and the rope used as a belt. He had accepted the mountain as a short-term loan, no interest required.

Behind him ambled the heavily laden ass that was, at the moment, Francesco's small mission, part of a great one. Its nose touched the man in the back now and then, a beast's kiss of affection, though the man had not been near it until he had agreed to take it down to the village for Giovanni the charcoal-burner.

Perhaps the ass also needed to touch its brother, Francesco, for reassurance because the threatening summer storm made it nervous. The dark cloud that always hung near the tip of the peak, though usually brightly rimmed, had swelled like a cobra's hood. Lightning-shot, growling, it was sliding down the firry slopes like a black and fuzzy glacier. The wind was now a hand pushing against his back and snapping the hem of his robe. The storm, like a long-delayed rush of conscience, would soon overtake them; the ass would be terrified by the lightning. Francesco halted and put an arm around the beast's thick neck. Brown eyes looked into a brown eye. The ass's eye was clear with health and innocence; his eyes were clouded with sin and with the disease he had gotten when he had gone to Egypt to convince the Saracens that Jesus was not just one of the prophets, a forerunner, but was unique, the virgin-born son of God, the keeper of the keys to Heaven. He had come back to Italy after the disastrous siege by the Crusaders of Damietta with a great disappointment because his mission had failed, with the friendship of the Saracen king, Malik el-Kamil, and with the malady that blinded him a little more every year and always gave him pain. Brother Pain, who clung to him closer than a blood-brother. And, now that the oncoming clouds had dimmed the light, he could see even less.

He did not know what the ass perceived in his eyes, but he saw one of God's creatures—there were so many, far too many—who needed comfort. Whatever the ass saw, it quit trembling.

"Courage, my brother. If you are struck down, you will be free of your burdens."

Should that happen, he would have to carry the charcoal down the mountain because he had promised Giovanni to deliver the load to the house of Domenico Rivoli, the merchant, and to make sure that someone would bring the ass back up. It would carry food and wine and some money to the burner, his pregnant wife, and his five rib-gaunt children. Francesco could take the charcoal himself, no matter how many trips he had to make, but how could he recompense Giovanni for the animal?

Not one to dwell on possibilities, Francesco plunged on, gripping the ass's halter, and, then, the storm was upon them. He could not see at all. The wind seemed to be trying to tumble him on down the mountain. He was being jerked this way and that by the ass's efforts to tear loose from him. Lightning boomed around him, struck a tree, and dazzled and deafened him. For a moment, he seemed to be sheathed in a bolt, though he knew that he could not have been hit. If he had been, he would not be standing.

Suddenly, he could see. A light from above smote the darkness. It was no lightning. It was a blazing-white spherical mass in which even brighter ribbons turned and lashed out as the mass descended. The ass, braying, trembling again, stood as if transfixed while flame cracked out from its ears, nose, and tail. Sparks and tendrils of brightness shot from Francesco's own body; his fingernails spat fires from their ends.

 His lips moving in silent prayer, his eyes shut, he thought that, surely, he was about to be burned alive. Then he opened his eyes.

If he was to burned by the Lord, then that was a martyrdom, and he should see it. Still, this was the first time that God had set one of His own faithful afire. Perhaps, this was like Elijah's being borne by God to Heaven in a fiery chariot. Or was that thought a sinful self-exaltation?

When he closed his eyes again despite telling himself to keep them open, he still saw the light. It seemed to fill his body to the end of his toes. The crash of thunder had ceased. Silence had come with the dazzle. At the same time, he felt a slight tugging—not from the halter— within his body. It was as if he was in the middle of a gigantic and hollow magnet, pulling him from every direction. The attraction was slightly more powerful on one side, but which side he did not know.

Then the halter was jerked from his grip. Though he was in terror—or was it ecstasy?—he leaped toward where he thought the beast was. He had promised to get it back to Giovanni, and his promises must be fulfilled even when God—or Satan?—had business with him. His hands flailing, one caught the halter. He grabbed the stiff short mane with the other, and, somehow, scrambled up the load until he was on top of it. He felt the pulling on one side of his body grow stronger. It seemed to him, though he could not see anything except the light, that he and the beast were rising. There flashed through his head—a dark thought in the white light filling his skull—that he was like Mahomet who ascended to Heaven on the winged ass, al-Boraq. That story had been told to him by Sultan Malik himself.

But now he was sitting above a cross, the T formed by the pale stripe across the ass's shoulders and down along its spine. In a sense, he was riding the cross that had ridden him most of life. A great burden he had rejoiced in bearing.

Despite the light, which had not lessened its intensity, he was catching sight of things, brief as lightning flashes but leaving dark, yet somehow burning, afterimages. There was a huge room with many men and women in strange clothes and white coats standing before boxes glowing with many lights and with words in an unknown language, and there were two towering machines in the background which whirled on their axes and shot lightning at each other. That vision was replaced by the dark, big-nosed face of a bearded man in a green turban—something familiar about it—the lips moving with unheard speech. That was gone. Now he saw a great city at night, pulsing with thousands of lights. It was far below him. Pure light banished it. Then it shot out again like a dark jeweled tongue from a mouth formed of light. Now he was closer to it; it was spreading out. Light again. And, once more, the city. He could see buildings with hundreds of well-lit windows, so tall that they would have soared above the Tower of Babel. Enormous machines with stiff un-flapping wings flew over them.

He still had the sense of being tugged, though it had suddenly become weaker. He no longer felt airborne. The light was gone. He was in semidarkness. An illumination, feeble compared to that which had filled him, was coming from before him. When he turned his head, he saw a similar illumination behind him. He was in an alley formed by two buildings that went up and up toward a pale night-sky. Around him were a dozen or so figures in bulky clothes. They were staring at this man on the load on top of an ass as if they had appeared out of air, which must be what happened. He was in the middle of a circle formed by a layer of mud six feet across, weeds and bushes sticking at crazy angles out of the dirt which had been transported along with him. He was glad that the air was warm because his robe and he were soaked.

The silence of the journey was gone. The ass was braying loudly; men and women were yelling at him in a foreign language. Now he saw that there were other lights in the alley, flames from the tops of five or six metal barrels spaced out along and next to the two walls. The slight wind brought him odors of long-unwashed bodies and clothes, alcohol, old and fresh piss and shit, decaying teeth, and that stench that rose from the oozing pustules of hopelessness and festering rage.

He was surprised that he could smell all that. He had been immersed in it so long that he scarcely noticed it any more. Perhaps, somehow, his physical and spiritual nostrils had been cleansed during the transit.

Transit to where? This could not be Heaven. Purgatory? Or Hell? He shuddered, then smiled. If, for whatever reason, he had failed to be in God's grace, and there were many reasons why he might have, he could be in Purgatory or Hell. Come either place, he would have work to do.

His own salvation had never been his main concern, though it was a banked fire in his mind. He had stressed to his disciples that the salvation of others was their mission, that that must be brought about by their examples. If they were to be saved, they must not think about it. It must be done by tending to and taking care of others.

That thought was broken off, a branch snapping, when the dim figures swarmed around him, a mass swelled when others joined it from doorways and packing boxes. Before he could protest, he was hauled roughly from the load and cast painfully upon the pavement. The ass, braying, was pulled down on its side away from Francesco. Knives gleamed in the dull light. The beast tore the night with its death screams as the blades plunged into it. Yelling for them to stop, Francesco got to his feet and began pulling off, or trying to pull off, the men around it. Giving up his efforts, he went to the animal, got down on his knees, and lifted the head, heavy as his heart. He kissed it on its nose, felt it quit shaking, and saw that the open eye was fixed.

The deed was done, and he was grieved, though he would have been glad to give these hungry men the beast to eat if it had been his to give. He had no time to dwell on that. Several men grabbed him and ran their hands over him, then shoved him away with angry

exclamations. Apparently, they had been searching for money and valu-
ables. A barefooted man who looked as if Famine and Plague were struggling to determine who would first overcome him, holding a big chunk
of blood-dripping meat in one hand and a knife in the other, gestured
savagely at him, speaking the tongue Francesco did not know. Hoping
that he understood the man's signs, Francesco sat down on the pavement, removed the leather sandals, and handed them to the man.

"Take them with my blessings," Francesco said. He stood up. "If
you need my robe, you may have that, too."

The man, scowling, talking to himself, had staggered off to one
of the barrels by the side of a building. He threw the meat on a metal
grillework on the open top, where it began smoking with the other pieces
of meat laid there. The man sat down, wiped his bloodied hands on his
coat, and fitted the sandals to his feet. By then, the load had been torn
apart and most of it thrown by the barrels or added to the fuel in them.

Francesco stood in the middle of the alley, nauseated not only by the too-
swift events but by the feeling that he was hanging by the soles of his
feet from an upside-down surface. The city itself seemed to him to have
been turned over, and he was hanging like a fly on a ceiling. Yet, when
he jumped slightly to reassure his confused senses that he was not kept
from falling by a glue on the bottom of his feet, he came back to the
pavement as quickly as he always had.

When he saw some monstrous white thing with two glowing
eyes that shot beams of light ahead of it, speeding on the street at the end
of the alley, he ignored his nausea and started toward the street. Before
he got there, two more of the frightening things went by. But he saw the
people within them and knew that they were some kind of self-propelled
vehicle. He clung to the corner of the building while others shot by. Was
he in a city of wizards and witches? If so, he must indeed be in Hell.

There was more to add to his bewilderment. The buildings along
the street were fronted with gigantic panels on which icons of people
and animals flashed and many words sprang into light and then disappeared. His mind swirling like the strange many-colored geometric patterns on some of the panels, he stepped back into the alley. He would
speak to each of the people there and determine if any spoke Umbrian or
Roman Italian or Latin or Provencal, or if any could understand the
limited phrases he knew of Arabic, Berber, Aragonese, Catalan, Greek,
Turkish, German or English.

He stopped, rigid at the sight of a black woman who was on her
knees and holding with one hand the swollen penis of the white man
standing above her while she moved her head back and forth along the
shaft in her mouth. Her other hand supported a baby sucking at her
nipple. In the man's hand was a piece of half-cooked meat. Her pay-
ment?

Before Francesco could recover, he heard a loud up-and-down

wailing, and a huge vehicle screeched around the corner, making him dive to escape being struck. It stopped, its two beams making noon out of the twilight in the alley, blue and red lights on it flashing, the wailing it made dying down. The man pulled loose from the woman's mouth and ran toward a doorway. Some of the others fled from the barrels; some froze. Doors in the side and rear of the vehicle snapped out and down. Men and women in bright blue uniforms, wearing blue helmets, and holding what had to be weapons, though of a nature that Francesco did not know, sprang shouting from its interior. He, with the other alley people, was shoved with his face against the wall, his outstretched hands against the wall, his legs spread out. He looked around and was cuffed alongside his head with the barrel of a weapon.

But he looked again anyway, and he saw another huge machine, its front a great open mouth, lumber past the first vehicle. It stopped short of the carcass, waited while some uniforms pointed small flashing boxes at the dead ass, then scooped it up with a long broad metal tongue and drew it into the dark maw. The uniforms kicked over the barrels so that the fiery fuel and meat spilled onto the pavement. After this, the uniforms questioned the denizens of the alley but got very little response except some obvious cursing. Francesco could not answer his interrogator, but the uniform just laughed and passed on to the next man. Francesco turned around and, once more, was shocked, this time so much that he was unable for a moment to think coherently.

Three of the alley men were in a stage of activity at a point where they could or would not stop. A man was buggering a tall and very skinny man whose lower garment was around his ankles. He had whiskers that radiated around his face, and in the center of the whiskers was the penis of a man standing before the whiskery man, sliding back and forth rapidly. The uniforms had not touched or questioned them. Evidently, they regarded the spectacle as comic because those standing around were laughing and jeering. But, just as two of the men were screaming with ecstasy, the round top of the second vehicle pointed a long metal tube at the trio, and water shot out of its end. The three were knocked down and rolled over and over until they collided violently with a wall.

The uniforms laughed, then became grim. After the alley people, Francesco among them, had been forced to set the barrels upright again, the hose on top of the machine washed the charcoal and the fuel and the pieces of meat and other trash down the alley until the mass was swallowed by an opening below the curb at the end of the alley. Many of the alley people were struck by the jet.

This distressed Francesco more than anything he had so far seen. It was a great sin to deny food to these hungry unfortunates.

 Brother Sun arose a few minutes after the uniforms and their vehicles had left. Cold from the double-soaking despite the warm air, cold also from the transit and the aftermath, very bewildered, Francesco shivered. Not until day had worn on and the air had become hot did he stop quaking. By then, the alley people, looking even more tired, haggard, ugly, and hungry, had dispersed. Later, he would see several of them begging for money. He left the alley to walk on the sidewalk northward through the canyon street. The vehicles, scarce at first, soon became numerous. They jammed the streets as they crawled along, and their honking never stopped. By noon, when people swarmed on the sidewalks, an acrid odor which he had noticed about mid-morning became heavy, and his eyes burned. Then Brother Sun was covered up by his sister clouds. Despite this, the breeze became hotter.

Becoming ever more hungry, he tried vainly to stop some of the pedestrians to beg for bread. They were well-fed and luxuriously dressed, though the clothes of some of the women exposed so much that he was embarrassed. After a while, he got used to that. But his pleas for food were still ignored. He also encountered many crazed people, some beggars, some not, who talked to themselves or shouted loudly at others. These, however, had also populated his own world; he was used to them.

He passed a large building with many broad steps leading up to it and two large stone lions set halfway up the staircase. On the sidewalk near it he stopped by a cart from behind which a man sold food the like of which he had never seen before. Its odors made his mouth water. A man bought a paper sack full of some small puffy white balls and began scattering them for the pigeons abounding here. Francesco asked him for some of the white stuff, but the man turned his back on him.

Passing on, he saw glass-fronted restaurants crammed with customers stuffing themselves. He entered one and got the attention of a servant behind the counter by pointing to his open mouth and rubbing his stomach. A big man grabbed him by the back of his robe and forced him violently, though Francesco did not struggle or protest, back onto the sidewalk.

His belly rumbled. So did the thunder westward. The skies were now black, and the breeze had become a wind that rippled the hems of his robe. It was beginning to cool, though, and the stink that burned his eyes was lessening. The tugging inside him and the feeling of being upside down were still with him, present when he was not too absorbed in the strangeness. He turned to the west and walked until he came to a river. Though thirsty, he did not drink from it. He had often drunk from water that had a bad odor, but this was too strong for him. He went north, then west, then south, then west again, and came to another river, equally malodorous. On both shores were elevated highways, jammed with the everhonking vehicles. The whole city was a din.

Now he did what many of the unfortunates were doing, opening garbage cans and searching therein. He found a half-eaten semicircle of a baked crust of dough with pieces of some strange red vegetable and of meat mixed with cheese. The box underneath it had printed words on it. One of them was PIZZA. Derived from *picca*, meaning *pie*? He devoured that, though it was dry and hard, then dug up another half-eaten item made up of two slices of hard and moldy bread in the middle of which was meat beginning to stink. Nevertheless, he started to bite down on that when a stray dog stopped by him and looked pleadingly at him. Its mangy skin covered a body that seemed more skeleton than flesh. He tossed the bread and meat to the dog, who bolted it. Francesco petted the dog. After that, it followed him for a while but deserted him to investigate an overturned garbage can.

Despite not knowing any of the languages he overheard during his journey through the upside-down city, Francesco had made many interpretations by mid-noon. There were other languages than those issuing from mouths. For instance, the tongue of the city itself, the tongue composed of many tongues just as a great mission was composed of many small ones. Cities were the first machines built by man, social machines, true, but Francesco was especially adept at translating the unspoken languages of cities. The architecture, the artifacts, the art, the music, the traffic, the manners, the expressions of faces and voices, the subtle and the not-so-subtle body movements, the distribution of goods and food, the ways in which the keepers of the law and the breakers of the law (often they were the same) behaved toward each other and toward the citizens upon whom they preyed and who preyed on them, these all formed a great machine which was part organism and part mechanical.

God certainly knew, as did Francesco, that there were enough mechanical artifacts in this city to have provided all of the world that he knew with plenty of them. Aside from the vehicles, there were the blaring mechanical voices in every store and on every street corner and there were the moving and flashing icons that covered the fronts of buildings and were in unnumberable numbers inside the buildings. He did not know the purpose of most. But he understood that the flat cases people wore strapped to their wrists were used to talk at a distance with others and that the many booths on the sidewalks were used for the same purpose.

The whole city was, among other things, a message center. But did these men and women understand the messages, the truth behind the words and images? Did they care if they understood correctly? Did the devices widen the doors for the entrance of the truth? Or did they widen the doors for more lies to enter? Or did they do both?

If both, then the result was that these people were more confused than those of his world. Too much information combined with the inability to separate truth from falsehood was as bad as ignorance. Especially when the disseminators of lies claimed that these were truths. Just as he concluded this, Francesco saw the gaunt man with the whiskery halo-fringe, the buggeree and sucker who had been interrupted in the alley by the uniforms. He was sitting on the sidewalk with his back against a building wall. Francesco could see the scabs, pustules, and blotches covering his face, arms, and the bony legs. He could also see that indefinable expression of the slowly dying. But it was changing into that of those who would soon be able to express nothing. Francesco had seen that too many times not to recognize it.

Now he knew that he was neither in Purgatory or Hell. Whatever else there was in those places, death was not there.

Francesco made his way through the throng, all of whom were ignoring the man, some of whom stepped over his bare legs. He knelt by the man and took his sore-covered hand. It was almost as fleshless as Brother Death's himself. Francesco, though he knew he would not be understood, asked what he could do for him? Did he need to be carried to a sickhouse? Was he hungry? His questions were intended to make the man comprehend that he was with someone who cared for him. There was really nothing that Francesco could do to stave off the irresistible.

The man leaned forward and mumbled something. Francesco took him in his arms and held him while the man's mouth moved against the robe. What was he trying to say? It sounded like *priest*. Suddenly, Francesco knew that the word was some kind of English, though certainly not what he had learned from Brother Haymo of Faversham, his English disciple.

"*Prete! Prete!*" Francesco said.

For the first time in his life, Francesco felt helpless. He had always been able to do something for those who needed help, but he could not make anyone understand what needed doing now, and he himself could do nothing.

The wind lashed out, even more cool now, and the thunder was closer. A few raindrops fell on his head. Lightning chainlinked the clouds. Then, the blackening clouds tipped over barrels of rain. He and the man were soaked, and the sidewalk was quickly emptied of all but himself and the man he held in his arms. That did not matter since they would not have helped him anyway.

He prayed, "O Lord, this man wishes to confess, to repent, and to be forgiven. Is not the intent good enough for You? What does it matter if no priest is here to hear him? I do not hate him, no matter what he has done. I love him. If I, a mere mortal, one of Your creatures, can love him, how much more must You!"

"He is gone," a deep melodious voice said. Francesco turned his head and looked up through the water blurring his already dimmed vision. As if there were a mirage before him—a dry desert phenomenon beneath the surface of the sea—he saw standing by him a tall man in a green robe and wearing a green turban. Francesco gently released the sagging corpse, wiped the rain from his eyes with his wet sleeve, and stood close to the man. He started. The face was that of the man whom he had glimpsed while in transit to this place. It was handsome and hawk-nosed, its eyebrows thick and dark, looking like transplanted pieces of a lion's mane. The leaf-green eyes in the almost black face were startling.

"It was not easy finding you," the man said. Francesco started again. He had not realized until now that the man was speaking in Provençal.

"Others are looking for you," the man said. "They are frantic to find you, but they do not know what you look like and so will fail. In fact, they do not know if they have transported a man or a woman or an animal or some combination of these. But their indicators make them think that they have picked up at least one human being, possibly more. Unless someone else does for them what they cannot do, they will be responsible for an explosion which will considerably change the face of Earth and might kill all humans and much of the higher forms of animals. We have approximately three hours to prevent this event. If Allah wills..."

So, the man was a Muslim. That thought overrode for a moment the prediction of the cataclysm. Francesco started to ask a question, but the man continued.

"They did not know this would happen until immediately after they had transported you. Their..." He paused, then said, "You would not understand the word. Their... thinking machine... gave a false result because of a slight mathematical error put into the machine by the operator. Slight but reverberating greatly... swelling. To prevent an explosion of any degree, they must send you back. Not only you but all that came with you. That is impossible, but the effect may be considerably reduced if they send back not only you but a mass approximating that which was brought along with you. You will have to estimate that mass for them, describe what did come in with you."

The man stepped into the street and held a hand up. A black vehicle skidded to a stop a few inches before the man. He went to the front left-side window and spoke to the man seated there. A very angry-looking man and woman got out of the back seat a minute later. The green-turbaned man gestured to Francesco to come quickly. Francesco got into the back seat next to him. The vehicle's wheels screamed as it leaped like a rabbit that had just seen a fox. The man spoke a few short words of what had to be English into the small case strapped to his wrist. Numbers flashed on its top.

"There will be no more time travel experiments," the man said. "The data... the information... has been sent secretly to the government of this country and to those of all nations. The populaces will not be informed until after the explosion, if then. Notifying the people of this city would only cause a panic, and the city could not possibly be evacuated. Even if it could be, the people could not get far enough away unless they went in an airplane... a flying machine. And only a few could get away in time. The people in the project are staying. They will work until the explosion comes, and they hope that its effects will be considerably reduced, as I said, by sending you back."

Francesco, clinging to a strap above the door, said, "Are you telling me that I have somehow been plucked by satanic powers from my time to a future time?"

"Yes, though the powers are not satanic. Their effect may be, though."

The man pointed out the window by Francesco at a building Francesco could see dimly. But he could make out a tall structure with many spires on the upper half of which was a gigantic panel. Its upper third flashed orange letters, one forming FRANCIS. The lower two-thirds displayed a bright and strange figure, a six-winged and crucified seraph surrounded by roiling light-purple clouds, which in turn were surrounded by swirling, fast-changing, and many-colored geometric figures. Then the vehicle was past it.

"A Catholic church, SAINT FRANCIS OF THE POOR. Attended mainly by the rich." The man chuckled, and he said, "Dedicated to you, Francesco Bernardone of Assisi."

Francesco, who had always felt at ease when events were going too swiftly for others to comprehend, was now numb.

"I was canonized?"

"Yes, but your order started to depart from your ideals, to decay, as it were, before your corpse was cold. Or so it was said."

Francesco bit his lower lip until the blood came, and he dug his fingernails into the palms of his hands until they felt like iron nails being driven in.

"I will *not* change."

"Because you know this? No, you will not."

"When did I die?"

"It would be wise for you not to know."

"But I am going back. Otherwise..."

"Obviously. But what happens here after you do...that is another matter. The force of the explosion caused by the interaction of matter and temporal energy will be proportional to the amount left here of the matter you brought with you. If, for example, you had held your breath during the transit, then expelled after arriving here, the amount of expelled air—if confined to a small area, and it won't be—would be enough to blow up that church and several blocks around it. What the project people need to know is just how much matter you did bring with you."

Francesco told him what had come in with him and what had happened to it.

"Your sandals, the urine you've pissed out, the dirt surrounding you, the plants and insects in the dirt, the body of the ass left after the butchering, the pieces of meat cooking on the barrels, the smoke from them, and the meat in the bodies of the men who ate it should go back with you. But, of course, they can't. You'll have to estimate an equivalent mass from your memory. The mass can't be exact, but if it's anything near that which was brought in, it will help cancel some of the effects of the mass-temporal energy explosion."

The man thought for a moment. He said, "After I deliver you, I will leave this area. Even I... no time for that now. The northeastern coast will be destroyed and much of the interior country. Many millions will die. But the world will go on."

Francesco said, "You seem to know so much. Why didn't you stop them? At least, warn them."

"I knew no more than they did what would happen. There is only One who is all-wise. I had nothing to do with the project, though I was well informed about it. I was not supposed to be, which is why they were so outraged and furious when I called in and told them I would search for you. They will try to arrest me when I bring you in, though that is stupid because I would be blown to bits along with them. They will not be able to hold me, and you will go back. The world knows when you died. So it is written that you return to your time."

"Not without the ass... an ass," Francesco said.

"What?"

Francesco told him of his promise to Giovanni, the charcoal-burner. "And there must be a load of charcoal, too."

The man spoke again to the case on his wrist, listened, spoke again, listened, then said, "They find it hard to believe that you would rather let the east coast blow up than go back without the donkey. I told them that I doubted that, but it would go easier and faster if they did what you want."

"Is it difficult to obtain an ass and charcoal?"

"No. The ass will come from a nearby zoo... a place where animals are kept. It should arrive soon even if it has to be airlift... brought in a flying machine." He smiled and said, "I told them they should get the biggest ass possible. I suggested that they might substitute the head of the project if for some reason they couldn't get one at the zoo. He fits all your qualifications, aside from being bipedal and lacking long ears."

"Thank you. However, I do not like to go back without even knowing your name."

"Here I am called Kidder."

"Elsewhere...it's not Elijah?"

"I have many names. Some of them are appropriate." Francesco wondered why he had seen Kidder's face during the transit. The forces that had shot him from there to here must have been connected with some psychic—or supernatural—phenomena even if the people who were running the project did not know that. His question, however, was forgotten when the vehicle was caught in slow-moving traffic that did not speed up no matter how long and hard the driver blew the horn. The man talked into his wrist-case again, and, within two minutes, a flying machine appeared at a low altitude above them. It descended, pods on its sides burning at their lower end and emitting a frightening and deafening noise. It landed on a sidewalk, and Francesco and Kidder got into it and were whisked up and away. By then, Francesco was so frozen that he was not scared. The machine landed on top of a high building. He and Kidder got out and were ushered swiftly to an elevator that plunged downwards and stopped suddenly, and then they were hustled along by many white-coated men and women and some uniforms to a great room filled with many machines with flashing lights and fleeting icons and numbers.

Francesco was placed in the center of the room inside a circle marked on the floor. An ass with a burden of charcoal, a large handsome beast, so much better than the poor one that had come with him that he would have to tell Giovanni not to ask questions about it, just be grateful and thank God for it, was led in.

Francesco, his throat dry, said huskily, "*Signore* Kidder, satisfy my curiosity. What is today's date?"

"Seven hundred and eighty years after your birth," Kidder said. And he was gone, somehow removing himself from the crowd around him and the two uniforms who stood behind him. Francesco cried out to him that he remembered now where he had seen him before the transit. He had been in the camp of Sultan Malik, where Francesco had glimpsed him a few times but had not thought that he was more than one of the Sultan's court. Kidder probably had not heard him. Even if he had been in the crowd, he would not have caught Francesco's words. The two uniforms were shouting too loudly as they tried to force their way through the crowd in search of Kidder.

Then bags of dirt were stacked alongside him and the ass in the center of the circle, and the workers withdrew. The crowd moved back to the walls of the room. They all looked haggard and frightened and white-faced. Francesco felt sorry for them because they knew that they were doomed no matter what happened to him. He blessed them and prayed for them and blessed them again.

The lights flickered; a terrible whining pierced his ears and skull. A great ball of swirling white light descended from a conelike device in the ceiling. It surrounded him, and, though he cried out, he could not hear his own voice. The tugging sensation that had never left him became stronger. He was once more in that limbo in which he saw dimly, again, the men and women in the building and the turbaned head of Kidder.

Then he was in rain and thunder, and the ass was braying loudly beside him. Under his feet was a very thin section of the floor inside the circle.

He no longer felt the tugging, and the world no longer seemed upside down.

✳ ✳ ✳ ✳ ✳

It was not long after this that Francesco saw on Mount Alverno the vision of the six-winged and crucified seraph in the skies and that Francesco was blessed—or cursed—with the marks of the nails in his hands (which he tried to conceal as much as possible). And then, seemingly as swift as that transit of which he never spoke, the time came when he was dying. The brothers and sisters were gathered around him, speaking softly, church bells were ringing, and, outside the hut, the rich and the powerful and the poor were standing, praying for him. His blinded eyes were open as if he could see what the others could not, which indeed he could. He was wondering if the seraph he had seen on the panel on the church front during that wild ride had possibly influenced him, caused him to envision that aweful, painful, yet ecstatic flying figure above the mountain.

Which had come first? His seeing the seraph on that panel in the far future or the splendor in the sky? He would never know. The mysteries of time were beyond him—at this moment.

He wondered about Kidder. Could he be that mysterious Green Man Francesco had heard about from some wise men of the East? He was supposed to have been the secret counsellor of Moses and of many others, and he showed up now and then, here and there, when the need for him was great. But that implied...

That thought faded as another Francesco, an almost transparent Francesco, rose like smoke from his body and stood there looking down at him. Its lips moved, but he could not hear its voice. It kneeled down by him and bent over. Now, he could read the lips.

"Goodbye, Brother Ass," he, the other, said. His body, that creature that he had treated so hard, driven so unmercifully, and to which he had apologized more than once for the burdens he had heaped on it, that was leaving him. No, he was leaving it. Now, he was looking down upon his own dead face. He leaned over and kissed its lips and stood up, happy as never before, and he had always been filled with joy even when hungry and wet and cold and longing vainly for others to have his happiness.

He was ready for whatever might come but hoped that he would have work to do.

 Not like that on Earth.

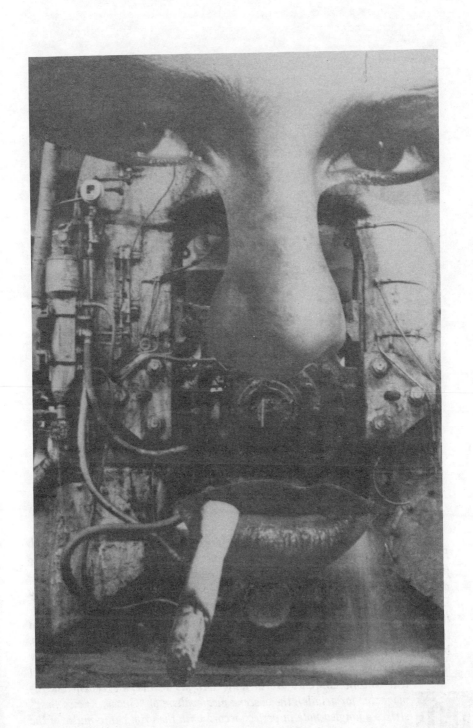

Widely published in the Small Press and experimental literary world, Hugh Fox has provided us with a knockabout two-reeler, a self-contained snip from a gargantuan novel, on the theme of Gnostic Dualism — a religious tendency which is emerging (or re-emerging) into modern consciousness largely through SF texts. Lindsay's VOYAGE TO ARCTURUS may have been the first Gnostic SF novel, but P. K. Dick opened the genre as a whole to Gnostic inspiration through his later work. The Dualist worldview tempts contemporary fantasists, both with its highly dramatic mythos and its cosmic pessimism — a metaphor for Post-Modern nihilists. Meanwhile in France and CaliforniaLand, several real Gnostic churches are thriving (see Jay Kinney's excellent GNOSIS magazine for details); the obscene medievalism of "Gnosis Knows Best" strikes a jangled note in perfect accord with the grim panic-music of the '80s.

Gnosis Knows Best
Hugh Fox

"Man's body, then, is put under the charge of thirty-six demons, each demon in charge of a particular part, all the demons symbolic of demonic domination of the lower world, which in turn is illustrative of the concept of the two levels of creation. The names of the demons are Chnoumen, Chnachoumen, Knat, Sikat, Biou, Erou, Erebiou, Rhamanoor, Rheianoor…"

A hand went up in the back of the room. The Glint (Where had he been that evening in San Francisco when the girl's eye had been cut out in the panhandle of Golden Gate park? What was in that plastic box under his bed?).

"Professor, can man communicate with these demons?"

"It would be better to ask, my dear Glint, how man can avoid communicating with them."

"But can man dominate them, or is their domination of man inevitable?"

297

"Now we're getting into the problem of free will, aren't we?"
The Mush's hand went up.
"Yes, Mush?"
"Is there any way for us to obtain free will, professor?"
"It would be better to ask, my dear Mush, whether or not having free will is really desirable."
"Is it really desirable to have free will, professor?"
Pulling out a pipe now, pulling out a tobacco pouch, lighting up. Mangos, figs and chocolate chip cookies.
"Magus-powered through the sphere to Starpower. Light against light, dark against dark. Once you understand the relationship between the ten cosmic spheres and the ten Sephiroth, then you've got it made. *Qui scuierit explicare quaternarium in denarium, habebit modum si sit peritus Cabalae deducendi ex nomine ineffabili nomen 72 literarum...*"
The amplified tolling of the big bell. The desk rattled. That was it for the day. As the rest of the students ambled like sheep through the door, the Glint approached the desk.
"What I'm interested in are the specifics."
"Next week."
"Now!"
"Why the sweat?"
"I need free will NOW."
White knives-lives slashing-clashing in the hive of night.
"I refer you to *De Hominis Dignitate* and the *Heptaplus*. Pico Della Mirandola. Get things started..."
Relief washing over him.
"Yes, yes, thank you, you'll never know."
Neverknow. Everknow.
"Don't mention it."
The Glint gone, left alone in the classroom, walking over to the window, looking down at the bamboo thickets. Get it all by the short hairs, the whole mess. *Magia naturalis licita est & non prohibita...* not that that made any difference anyhow...

*****

A white Ford into the driveway. Chaskanawi. From the region of Ooyuli in the province of Oropeza in the Department of Chuquisaca. Met when he'd been down there studying Viracocha legends. Assistant Professor of Quena and Charango at ZIEA (Zion Institute of Ethnic Arts). Spoke only Quechua.
As she moved into the kitchen he could hear animal flesh begin to burn.

"How did it go today?" (Him), "Lots of stupid people don't have any breath... it smells of woman in here." (C) "It smells of you.

You're my woman." (Him). "It smells of another woman." (C) "That's your imagination." (Him) "I lost my imagination when I came here." (C) "The beach was great today." (Him). "I'm going to find her and revenge myself." (C) "I'll visit you in prison." (Him) "I'll do it in such a way that nobody will figure out who did it." (C) "Idle threats." (Him) "You don't know me." (C)

C. wouldn't go now with the last strong liquid of the sun lying bright in the saucer of the west, but after dark when she'd glide into, juxtapose, merge...

Down to Dixon's. Call from there. Warn Thais.

Into the anti-world, the Ensoph out of which the ten Sephiroth emerge. Metatron, Samael, hell is heaven, and heaven is hell. Chaskanawi finished the dishes and waited in the living room until the dark came on, then into the bottom of her dresser drawer, kissed each item as she put it on, tights, top, boots, mask, gloves, belt with the black-bladed knife in it, then waited, while the world curled up and went to sleep.

*****

Thais in the bathroom, electrolysing for fifteen minutes on five stubborn upper lip-hairs. Then a squirt of Kler-Skin on every little purple and/or yellow acne mound. Stupid to have cried to fool Mom. Mom had been around, had had her own married man in her own sweet time — turn, turn, turn, everything has its time. Looked at the window. Open a crack. Cold. Cranked it shut. Felt...? Rubbed her eyes. Long day. Fear...?

Michael the Lion whispered "Now" and Souriel the Bull opened the Nightdoor and whispered "Go," and Raphael the Serpent blackened her car and Gabriel the Eagle hefted Chaskanawi onto the nightwinds. Fly! The black moon opened and the wide black warm wild windwings pushed her along.

Ialdobaoth, Iao, Sabaoth, Astaphaeous, Aeloaeus, Horaeus. Passing through the first circle, the reversal of form, black to white, white to black, back to front and front to back. Then through the second circle, remorse to triumph, fear to fight, shame to pride. High. Warm in the strands of the black moonlight.

Past the third circle, in the Anti-World now. White trees swaying in a slow black wind. The dead black houses wee far below. A solitary bike-rider rode (white-faced, two black pit eyes) down the white night road, slowly, moving through the wind like water. And the lights shone black on the grey-white streets.

Then "down" Iaoth said, voice muffled and dead, and she descended to the white street, walked across the black grass, the smell of the WOMAN acrid as acid in her nostrils, moved toward the grey glowing bedroom window, her now-white knife in her hand.

Prying open the window now. Cutting out the screen, the anti-world spreading into the room, muffling everything, slowing down all rhythms, the pace of everything, her breathing lower and her moving from one side of the bed to the other, Chaskanawi moving across the room, standing above the bed, Thais waking up, trying to talk her way out of it, convince, but her words coming out dead in the dead anti-world air, trying to fend off the knifehand, but couldn't, her arm bent back slowly up against pressure, straining desperately, while Chaskanawi's hand came down fast, pulling back the bedclothes, ripping off Thais' blue nylon baby-doll, down with a single strong violent rip, then pulling aside Thais' hands and cutting into her breasts, cutting off the "caps," like cutting off the turrets of sand castles, cutting peaches in halves, very little blood, instead a thick white viscous silicon breast fluid flowing out across Thais' thorax, down onto the sheets...

*****

He started up. South. Homeward. Moving against the slow, heavy, anti-world stream, radio out, and when he opened the window no wind sounded, only the dull, dumb enclosure of silence. No other cars. Held, hard, trapped, caught in his own private pressure world, knowing no one could get in to him, nor that he could get out—maybe that was the hardest—the weight down on, around, braincase, eyes, skin, hands, fighting to stay there, knowing that if he let go, let it all slide out of his hands, fell back, relaxed, that he'd dissolve, black light against black light, black fight against black fight, oppose...

"Beydelus, Demeymes, Adulex, Metucgayh, Atine, Ffex, Uquizuiz, Gadix, Sol, *Vino cito cum tuiis spiritibus...*"

In between her thighs now, her on her back, high-hooved black-nylon-pressed flesh, legs outspread, clam enclosing around the car, screaming, but it didn't stop him, against it all; in, inside, battering through the metallic piercing of her agony...

"Well, I've done it." (C) "What?"(Him) "I cut the breasts of the other woman." (C) "Then you know what I have to do now? I have to cut the breasts of a non-white woman." (Him) "That's the way it is. And if it smells of another woman in your room again..." (C) "The clever dog doesn't fall into the same trap two times." (Him) "You may be a dog, but who says you're clever?" (C) "This we have to see." (Him)

*****

"Whatever's in the effect has to have been in the cause, that's logic isn't it?" (Answering Nudnik Capellini's drawled-out country-style question.) "So what's the cause of evil, then?"

"Yeah, I guess it's logical."

"Marcion of Pontus, for example, following the general patterns set down by the Simonian teaching of Cerdo, makes a point that all wars, chaos, ignorance, polio, tapeworms, cancer, earthquakes, floods, landslides, typhus, birth deformities, arthritis, venereal disease, rape, murder, patricide, matricide, mental cruelty, inquisitions, police brutality, civilian brutality, knifings, bombings, stranglings, and that multitude of little daily ways that man tortures and disfigures man, all proceed from the Divine First Cause. What is in the effect must be in the cause, and therefore..."

(Julius Caesar Androtty in the back row—a large greasy face, greasy straight black slickly combed-back hair, glasses, an expansively stupid ingenuousness about everything he did or said, always prefaced by a long "ahhhh," as if he were purposefully reinforcing his idiot-image.)

"Ahhhh, all that means is that man's evil, then. I mean in terms of the things man does, not touching on earthquakes and, you know, the rest of the stuff."

"And if we go back to the ULTIMATE CAUSE, THE UNMOVED MOVER? Who, after all, made man?"

"Ahhhhh, his father and mother."

(Everyone hissed and booed. Anyone else would have been able to pull it off, but not Julius Caesar. No grace, no timing.)

"Of course many of the Fathers got around the problem by making the First Cause something other than Divine. Which has its own kind of attractive logic. Carpocrates, for example, attributes the creation to certain degenerate angels. Menander's creating angels are expressions of the Enoia. And then it's Saturninus who begins to concentrate on the demonic nature of the creating angels. Which is logical too. You look around this world and your mind thirsts for a demonic First Cause to explain it all away..."

(Ankash Blatty, the Nigerian, getting up—god, he was getting beefy!—in toga and sandals, swaying uncertainly back and forth.)

"So that means that the world was created by the devil, professor?"

"It's a tempting system to bite on, isn't it? But where's the demonic energy and vitality in this fading world, in the midst of this entropy, this running down, this backsliding toward tawdriness and ruin? In the Valentinian System of Ptolemaeus the world is made by the Demiurge, not planned, enlightened, ordered, but out of ignorance. The Demiurge made things without really 'knowing' them, and then once they were made he abandoned them, and the Earth became a dead, dry stain of desolation and sterility, beyond God, Demon, Demiurge, anything (going to the window, looking out at the heavy white poison-saturated California sky, down across the ragged palms, everything stopped, fixed, paralyzed. There were no birds left now. The last of the birds had died out ten years before. And there was no more wind. That had finally stopped altogether the year before). I wish I could believe in the Archons again, Iao Sabaoth, Adonai, Elohim, El Shaddaei... and in heimarmene, the Universal Fate... but what evidence is there that even the Demiurge 'cares'? With everything slowly unravelling and running down, the paint flaking off, the walls full of cracks, the faces wrinkled, the joints stiffened, the beams sagging, the air filled with poison and a vile dust coating everything with filth..."

He stood at the window. His eyes hurt. The air was poisoned. It was hard to breathe. They were all sitting there sharing in his vision, their faces long and sad, growing up, all part of maturing, getting ready to be plucked from the life-vine... and then the bell rang and they all filed out leaving him alone...

*****

Down his street, pulled up in front of the house. Her car not there. She wouldn't show today. Would stay in her office. Had a cot there too. And all her drums and rattles.

He went inside, the dark rooms filled with a spidery weave of darkness, the only sound that of the screaming jets a mile and a half away... *Horc Cellula Creatoris*. Almost gave in to his Hi Fi FM Multiplex Stereo, jazz, orange lights and the strobes. Only didn't. Dark, bark, dog, frog, damp....

Opened a can of Wieneroni on the electric can opener, wincing at the cutter cutting through the tin as if it were cutting through his own bones. Ate it cold standing in the kitchen looking out at the huge spear and ear leaves in the garden, watching them all turn white in the darkness, like in a negative.

Then out into the living room, out into the cold icebox darkness. Didn't touch the thermostat. Cold purified. Let the dust lie cold. He felt heavy, water-logged, like a corpse that's just popped bloated up to the surface after three weeks underwater being played with by the crayfish. Sat down, heavily, despairingly, like he'd never get up again. And began to cry.

Stupid.

Thou shalt not...? Afraid of breaking the Mosaic Law of his deep-freeze youth? And The Lamb shall sit upon the throne... they'd really believed in the perfectability of man, and technology had been sublime, and... Jefferson Boulevard, Jefferson High School, pass me my cannon-ball clock, baby, uncle, nuncle, nanny, boy... upside down, the tables turned, all backwards like a mirror image in a broken mirror.

There'd been ants in the poplar trees in the empty lot next to where he'd lived. Ants in the trees. The poplar leaves like silver dollars.

 And if you went west enough on your bike, you passed out of commerceville and you came into a forest preserve, and there was a lake with wild ducks on it.

Whore? Queer? On Spinoza! On Descartes, Kant, Cunt... ride, ride round and grab the brass ring... beware of factionalism, tearing the republic up from inside. Listen. I told, you told, he, she, it told. Gotta make it. What and why?

Thou shalt not kill. Blessed are the sagging stairs and the broken sidewalks. Blessed are the bars and parking meters. Blessed are the banks, the electric toothbrushes, and the holiday sales that go on all year long.

Shine, mister, 'mistah, meester, gimme a break, break me. And they all came tumblin' down, Oh Lord, they all came tumblin' down...

He had a short curved knife that fit into the palm of his hand. Gift from a Spanish prostitute he'd lived with when he'd been in Spain on his eighteenth summer, studying the symbology of the Alhambra: twenty-four voussoirs outside, 12 inside, 12 gates of heaven, 12 zodiacal signs... Metatra, The Angel of Light...

Different down here in Blackworld, the sidewalks all sliding out of position, cracked and broken, the houses all slanted with the constant wind that blew across the salt flats and bent them out of shape, windows broken, great gaping holes in the roofs of the houses, cars along the curb wheelless, hubcapless, windshield-wiperless, unwashed, the paint flaking off, the bodies rusting away. The streetlights emitted a black grainy darkness, like sand. Pawnshops. Nothing over $100.00. Used car lots, the cars in them with their fenders and bumpers wired on with chicken wire... liquor stores, pool halls, record stores... as he passed by it all slowed down. Where, where, where's the source? Looked around. But no one spotted him. Metatron, The Angel of Light.

Moving down darker, narrower streets now. Out of the lights. Warehouses, angular and hulking like huge toads and spiders. Found himself in alleyway, one light in it, broke the light with a rock, then sat down on the ground with his crescent-shaped knife folded in his hand. And waited.

Couple came noisily by, grey masses against a bland white sky, tall girl, heels against the rubber pavement coming out slow and re-sounding, like heart-beats, the guy's voice moving, low and labored, "Come on, baby, come on..." Then gone.

Cars. No moon. And a long stretch of silence. Then he heard the victim coming. Slow, awkward, singing to himself, broken snatches of dead tunes. I've Got Plenty of Nobody Knows on Green Dolphin Street, Gimme that Wine... slipped his hand into the left side pocket of his jacket. Blow gun. The short one. The long one was more accurate but it wasn't a very long distance, and even if he missed with this victim any-how, there'd still be plenty of time.

A woman would've been better, but... as long as the victim was black it still fulfilled the requirements of the equation. Silhouetted in the alleyway entrance. Poor son of a bitch, reeling, hanging onto the wall, breathing heavily, his breath like that of a bull, a faint smell of vomit blowing from him down into the alley—a bull with the banderillas bloody in his back, brought...

Then ZUCK! the dart hit him solidly. Through the air with a kind of ponderous solemnity. Zuck! Home. Like punching through a paper bag. Shot another one, just for fun. Zuck! Liked the sound. One more. Control, control! Zuck! Gotta watch out, almot nicked his own finger putting the dart in that time.

Then quickly over to the body, eyes open, totally aware, but unable to move. Pulled him into the alley, his eyes slickly liquid in the darkness, like frog skin. Felt a sour rush of nausea rise up inside him as his hands touched the lumpy slime of vomit all over the drunk's coat. Vomit and then whiskey like a knife. Raw. The victim couldn't talk, but began grunting like a warthog.

THOU SHALT NOT...

Opened his coat, shirt, pulled up his undershirt, bared the chest. Opened his own hand, revealing the small crescent-shaped knife. And the grunting got desperate, the sound rising up from deep down inside him, starting full and heavy and struggling up into a thin muted stifled scream.

It wasn't that he wanted to do it...

"It's not that I want to do it... but it's so lost... so, so lost... so lost... that the best we can do is destroy it... little by little in any way we can..."

Only the victim didn't seem particularly interested... although it was interesting how he could so radiate terror without really being able to form an expression of terror on his paralyzed face. He secreted it. A fine layer of sweat covered his face, the scream never stopped but rose higher and higher, fixed, like a siren, announcing the arrival of the rockets of the day of doom.

Now! Hand descending, cutting across his eyes. First the eyes. The screaming eyes. Cut through their gristle and fiber, let their jelly bleed out screaming, then the lips, slashes spurting blood as he moved down to the neck, have to stop the scream, disconnect the siren, kill it, pull it out, cut through the neck, the carotid arteries—to sleep, to sleep, the blood spurting up now all over him, so that he tasted it, felt it, like wet hot semen all over his face and hands, into the trachea, hard, like wood, but cutting down, through, into the voicebox, stopping it, the victim's body heavy now, lung violently reaching for air, hand across the open cut in the windpipe, don't let the air in, down across his chest now, cutting out both nipples, through the skin...

"What's goin' on in dere?"

He looked up.

At the mouth of the alleyway three figures. Challenging him. Feeling the body under him give its last spasmodic heaves, then fall back inert. So lost... so lost.

"Les' go take a look."

The three figures moving toward him against the waves of the Anti-world, slow, impeded, but still moving.

"Jesus... look what dat man's done... look what he's done..." Then moving in toward him, grabbing him by the shoulders, the same law of racial vengeance under which he'd been operating now operative against him, one of the three calling out "Here's a whitey, in here," his voice rising up out of the alley like a parachute billowing out, up into the night, "Here's a white one, in here," and the night slowly filling with the jostling of voices and faces, like jelly beans packed tightly in a jar, thinking "Tonight I'll make the Pleroma, out of this entropic, wrinkled, arthritic world, to receive the inheritance and the mysteries..."

They tore off his shirt, his pants, his underwear, stripped him down naked, held down his arms and legs tight, although he wasn't about to struggle, their switchblades clicking like cracked bones as they flipped them open in the crisp stone-enclosed air, the faces-voices rejecting, gettum, man, gettum, man. One of them pulled a cocktail stirrer out of his pocket, then lifted up his penis, inserted the stirrer up into the urethra, the pain reaching into him like a white-hot iron-hand, and he found himself screaming involuntarily, up out of, away from, toward, now, now, now, as they cup open his trachea and he felt his heart lurch, twist, twitch, and he began to gag as they pulled his tongue down through the tracheal opening, started to vomit, choke, the whole world jerking into white spots as he reached for breath, reached, reached, reached... but didn't make it.

Born in Holland, resident in America, BP is a DJ, as well as a poet (or "p-o-8", as his spiritual ancestor Black Bart, the versifying stagecoach robber, abbreviated it). This Bart worked for WFMU in New Jersey, where he edited LCD, the station's program folio, and turned it into the liveliest, punkest radio publication ever. After establishing himself in NYC he moved to Paris, where he now hosts a weird music show for the anarchist station Radio Libértaire. Did he coin the term "beer mystic?"

The Beer Mystic's Last Day on the Planet
Bart Plantenga

"World of Wheels" is on TV. A chorus of cheerleaders in smilie spangles jazzes up the "Star-Spangled Banner." The PA prays with feedback, something from Job: "Behold I AM vile... I AM The King of Terrors," tying in the Holy Snuff King with the emerging Krusher, "Champeeeen" Big Wheel, a Godzilla of steel on wheels the size of modest lakeside bungalows. With beer #3 I bear witness to the glorious slo-mo ecstasy of shattering glass, splintering in a crystal shimmer up to the rafters as the Krusher romps gung-ho over the roofs of a line of mortal transport vehicles. Crushing them in an awesome symphony of buckling and imploding steel. At intermission Chubby Checker does an updated Twist with extra girth and sincerity. Six Playboy Bunnies help. But I'm lost. Which one is Miss May? Which one's the cowgirl from Gillette? I fumble through data. Wonder why I'm sick, a half-melted baseball trophy molded by a drunken god, living a life of air fresheners, ill-fitting trousers and beer. I sit upright with my sex turned inside out. What a land of mind we are! Ah, now some mediacaster, holding his ear, barks at us from above the blue smoke roar in the pit. The driver is a hero. He removes his helmet and his hair looks great even after crushing 35 cars. And now my Hagia Sophia beer is all gone. They say it's Latin for "Holy Wisdom." Where's it from, the Vatican? I'm from a town famous for its automobile by-products—of which I guess I'm one.

I dreamt of my only car. A Rambler picked clean like a carcase. Like a toothless grin. A wad of parking tickets under the windshield wiper, blown away when the blades finally got stripped too. But I couldn't sleep with the car alarm wailing. Three hours. Counted 24,133 bottles of beer on the wall. Besides I only got 28 hours left on this planet and I got plenty to do. Three of my neighbors—I don't know them, they don't know me—were relaxing on the hood of their prey, having just hacked and bashed the car with the alarm into a hulk of gnarled steel and broken glass. It was like walking through a museum diorama of cavemen who've just butchered a twilight stegasaurus. The guy in the wool cap thinks he's Elvis and beats his wife. Apparently she doesn't think he's Elvis. He once hung a cat from a neighbor's doorknob cuz she'd shot him down. There's supposedly one rat for every person in NYC. Wonder if he's found his "vermate" yet. I asked them for a souvenir. Tossed me a hubcap with the plastic center punched out, leaving a jagged rim, a craggy halo. I put it on. Where's the crime of the century? I'm ready. And six beers later I'd black-eyed more'n my quota of streetlights. I was out like a light myself. I dreamt of sending my diaries somewhere—the papers, a publisher. Thought has kinetic energy. It does. But it wasn't taking me anywhere. And when I finally came to it was still night. My sneaks were gone, someone had painted a scene-of-the-crime outline around my body (a premonition or a joke?) but my halo's still warm to the touch.

To revive myself I usually head for the Linger Lounge, place of purposeful and stylish dissipation. There's a sieve in the john, behind the toilet. Check it out. In the mirror I look like Shemp—ugliest of the Three Stooges. I scoop a sieve of water out of the toilet. Then shower up by holding the sieve triumphantly like a gold trophy cup over my head. Don't worry, there's a hole in the floor that sucks up the water. The cool water revives the bony plates, the gristle and cartillage and the wander-less soul. It does! It's like wetting a dull stone which looks precious when wet. And I come out a new man. I am. No longer look like Shemp. I'm ready to face the rest of my life—all 20-some hours.

Sure, my techniques have always been clever. But I'm tired of hanging out in dance joints. I usually stalk a table of nervous birds in jangly jewels. Wait for them to get dance fever. And when they hit the 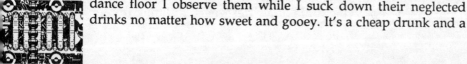 dance floor I observe them while I suck down their neglected drinks no matter how sweet and gooey. It's a cheap drunk and a rather subtle way of imposing a method of redistributing the lopsided facts of wealth. It's a little chancy with disease and all, but adventure is the throb in the blood, the beer in the glass, the light in the bulb. How does one go about patenting new drinks anyhow? I have two surefire hits: "The Jersey Shore" (gin, Yoohoo and Alka Seltzer) and "The Jersey Sunset" (Bacardi, Pepto-Bismol and Hi-C).

I pinched my wheels (no ordinary tin can) from in front of the Heartbreak Club, where the innoculated money spinners dress in $3000 worth of leather to get real, break a sweat, act artsy. Somebody had left it—my '63 abalone Lincoln—idling right there on Hudson. It was immaculate, the hood awesome as Texas in tin. A right romantic grease jock's dream. And it left me lushed, imagining the driver's face when he returns with his Euro-trash bait under his arm. Oh, sweet reverie! I adjusted the electric mirrors, electric seats, put it in gear like a knife through warm butter, elbow out the window. All the dials stared up at me. We were one. A noble cell with a mission. A time bomb waiting to go off. To get fogged I buy beer, the best, Harp, Guinness, Grolsch, Old Peculiar cuz what good's a pocket full of chump change in hell? One of the techno-convenience society's great inventions: the 24-hour deli with 100 brands of beer. From Tribeca I bullet up Avenue of the Americas doing menacing side swipes, shearing door handles and fancy trim along the way. This boat's a dream. I glide across craters the size of which we'd easily spot on the moon with the naked eye. I do felonious hot-dog donuts at Crazy Eddie's. Heads turn. I'm a bumper-car wacko on a tear. Don't they understand? This is what Artaud would've done. I wish I'd had Francis Farmer next to me. She could grenade empties at pedestrians along the way, but she's dead too. It's 2 a.m.; I got 22 hours to live.

I wish crazy little Jenny was beside me. I was wearing her undies as I often did when I was lonesome. I tried to call but every # was a wrong #. She'd ride her bike to the Fashion Institute of Technology with blue hair, army boots sprayed silver, holes in her tee shirt so her breasts could grace us with their peculiar smiles. We once made love with an Alligator baggie she'd salvaged from the freezer, unwrapping two lbs. of chuck in my honor. It was defrosted on the counter by the time we'd finished. But chance'll just have to be my co-pilot. At Fourteenth St. I do a dramatic stuntman slide, broadsiding a silver Mercedes. The sound is meaningful. The jolt exaltingly tragic. A citizen gives chase but I lose him easily because I am not afraid of intersection death. I course further up Sixth Avenue, free of guilt and moral constraint with my nose up the tailpipe of a trembling Volvo. I run red lights, scatter pedestrians. The threat of death animates them, awakening them out of their stuporous lives. But I get no thanks, no howdy-dos. I challenge stunned men in important cars. Everything speeds up hell-bent beyond comprehension. At a light I gun the engine, pour beer over my head, comb my hair back. I'm James Dean. He's dead too. Yes, I too am a short chapter in an

absurdist novel. At 34th St. I make a chase-scene left, cruise down the
sidewalk, watch strollers scatter, cling to Macy's windows. It's a movie. I
wish my head was a camera. I hang a ralph at Eighth Ave. Pick up a
hooker at 40th. She's in chemical limbo, somewhere between Flip Wilson
and Dolly Parton in absurdly tight satin jogging shorts. She diddles my
fiddle and holds on to her 14th St. wig as we cruise crosstown. I double
park at the Waldorf and block two limos in. I drag her luded body in
past the big eyes under red caps. I order beer. She likes Long Island Iced
Tea with five packets of sugar. She's never seen Long Island. And we
dance. Her backbone's like saltwater taffy. Her skin smells like a candy
bar. I try to imagine sitting next to her in high school. How'd she get this
way? We bump tables, upset drinks into faces. Her eyeballs have disappeared somewhere up into her forehead. I lead her out through the yawning doors, heels dragging, wearing out like a pencil eraser. Leaving a tab
of $46.50 plus tip. HA! I tell the doorman I was the model for Rothko's
painting "Drunk on Turpentine."

    I park in the intersection of Eighth and 49th. I drop off Delilah.
Traffic backs up. I lean her up against a lamppost, serenaded by the sea-
lion-chorus of horns. Anyone can paralyze a city this way. Anarchists
with cars, listen up! The gridlock guzzler is me! I put my tub in drive and
challenge the honking backed-up traffic like a bull in the arena. It's 6 a.m.
Workers on their way. But they're all bereft of purpose, wired to go
nowhere. Eerily preoccupied equally with weight loss and child abuse.
You can either go nowhere fast or nowhere slow. I back up, demolition-
derby style and put a BMW out of commission. Crushed radiator. It
looked almost sculptural. He bangs furiously on the hood and windshield. Hanging on desperately to the antenna. I'm becoming well-known
now. I wander up Eighth Ave. To Harlem, weaving deliriously a very
unusual tapestry of steel misery and mayhem. Bouncing off cars from
side to side. Crash nose first through a furrier's window, and kids with
askew baseball caps ransack the place before I've even backed out into
traffic. Thirty-five cars to Harlem. Just like the Krusher. They're filming
here and not only do I "black-eye" their jungle load of wattage and spot-
lights, I also manage to scatter a pack of crack dealers who were menac-
ing the film crew. This is aggravated operation of a motor vehicle, a
churning delicious hunk of illogic. By now my back bumper's dragging,
trim is splayed and branching out. I head down Fifth Ave. Bump cars in
heavy traffic chicken-style with 100+ violations under my belt. $1 or $2
million in damages. I hit a stretch limo at 45th and Fifth, doing 40. It
buckled into a U-shape and I imagined it still running, running forever
in a circle like a toy wind-up car. The moment of impact becomes a crime
of ecstasy, orgasm and felonious vandalism for mere seconds. After that
it's just hysteria, human foible and stunned collective panic. After that I
 just comb the outer boroughs, confident that Manhattan is all
abuzz because of me and my tub. More abuzz than anything I

could ever write. I find my favorite sites. The Brooklyn Bridge, the Long Island City salt mounds. Catch my breath and perspective. Then I go to various banks and yell "they have no money" in crowded lobbies. This is, after all, how panics begin. Banks exist on our implicit suspension of disbelief. A bank run is contagious. We've seen drug companies drop to their contrite knees. But we're free here cuz all our words are empty, ashes blown into the faces of the shivering. This is the painting I wish I could do. George Grosz in crushed steel. A panic of the fat. In Central Park it's 7:30 p.m. Hats climb the hill with big-daddy shadows and coats the size of backyards. I'm tired. I abandon my artist's tool with its beer-soaked seats. In the Central Park Zoo I talk to the seals and otters. They seemed to understand, and at midnight of the 7th day I shivered, I festered, but I did not die. No activist lawyer came to my defense. The nobility of my terrorism had eluded them all. Notoriety had failed to lift me out of my meaningless anonymity. I was still alive and in big trouble.

Our original Invitational Letter for this anthology called for—among other things—"radical utopian vision." And yet, as the reader will have noticed, nearly every piece in the book is dystopian. Most of our authors have fallen out of love with future history, are dissatisfied with the present, and full of hate for the past.

Paradoxically, to find some positive utopian text, we were forced to look beyond fiction. What we found seems to be journalism, or some banal brand of travel-guide writing. This article originally appeared in the first (and only?) issue of a micro-zine called LIBERTARIAN HORIZONS: A JOURNAL FOR THE FREE TRAVELER, along with other pieces on Pago-Pago, Yap, Ponape and a "Note on Nicaragua." The magazine was allegedly published in Belleville, Ohio, in 1985, but our request to reprint the piece came back marked "Addressee Unknown." The anonymous author thus remains nameless to us, and the magazine's editors appear to be unknown in libertarian/anarchist cricles.

The island of Sonsorol does actually exist—we found it in our BRITTAN-ICA ATLAS right where it's supposed to be—but no reference work or travel guide known to us speaks of it as an independent nation. Perhaps we failed to look far and hard enough... Perhaps we prefer to believe...

Visit Port Watson!
Anonymous

1. Geography and Physical Description 🌴 ☀ 〰

The Pacific island of Sonsorol, an extinct volcano surrounded by coral reefs, lies at 5º above the Equator at 132º longitude; about 400 miles east of the southeastern tip of the Philippines and 300 miles north of the Dampier Straits in New Guinea. It is approximately ten miles in diameter and about ninety square miles in area.

The climate is typical for the region: steady balmy temperatures (60º — 70º year-round), occasional violent typhoons, monsoons from September to February, sea breezes along the coast, steamy stifling rainforest on the lower slopes of Mount Sonsorol (especially dense on the island's northern side, exposed to the trade winds); nearer to the summit the weather is almost permanently cloudy, cool and misty, and the jungle thins into a "cloud forest" — moss, small trees shrouded in epiphytic

313

mosses, hepatics, ferns, orchids, etc. Sonsorol enjoys plenty of fresh water, including waterfalls in the hills, and even a small river, the Garuda.

Vegetation: typical tropical abundance and variety, including
many species of orchids and a plethora of other tropical flowers and
fruit. Formerly copra, taro, sugar-cane and pineapples were cultivated in
the southwestern savannah region; now the plantations have been abandoned and gone wild except for a few coconut groves reserved for local
consumption (every part of the plant is used, in cooking, building, etc.)
Indigenous fauna are sparse, mostly limited to birds and insects (which
can prove annoying). Pigs, chickens, goats and other European species
were imported in the 17th century. Fishing is spectacular, and provides
both a staple diet and a good deal of sport; the three small coral atolls
which belong to Sonsorol offer superb snorkeling and abound in rare
types of tropical fish (see *Excursions*).

Nearly circular in shape, and lacking any decent bays or inlets,
Sonsorol would at first seem strategically unsuited to its ancient role as
pirate enclave; however, the coral reefs which surround the island provide a sort of lagoon in which ships can ride at anchor "in the roads"
quite safely, even in heavy weather.

2. How To Get There   ☞   ⚓   👜

Travel in the Pacific usually consumes either too much time or
too much money. Sonsorol remains one of the least accessible islands in
the entire area. No commercial airline lands there. Freighters carry cargo
to Sonsorol from Mindanao, Java, Taiwan, Hong Kong and other ports,
but the only ship which calls there with some regularity is *The Queen of
Yap*, a rusty tramp steamer which plies between Zamboanga and the
Caroline Islands, roughly once a month. (Information and reservations
can be obtained from the Ngulu Maritime Co. Ltd., Kalabat, Yap, U.S.
Trust Territory of the Pacific.)

Port Watson is now the only port of entry for Sonsorol, and no
Customs & Immigration Authority exists there. However, no one can
hope to escape notice in a town so small. Anyone who stays more than a
month or so will probably be asked politely either to apply for residence
or else leave (see *How to Become a Resident*).

Visitors to the Republic of Sonsorol (outside the Port Watson
Enclave) are encouraged to have their passports stamped at the Post
Office at Government House in Sonsorol City (q.v.) — the "visa" stamp
is quite beautiful — but no one will insist on this. Neither Port Watson
nor the Republic have any police, so the residents tend to watch out for
trouble and take responsibility for solving problems. Unfriendly, abu-
sive, thieving or obstreperous visitors have been beaten up by
vigilantes or Peoples' Militia, and exiled on the next ship out.

Generally however visitors are welcome ("not *tourists*, but *visitors*," the Sultan said once), and the inhabitants are friendly, even excessively so.

3. History Before Independence

The "aboriginal" inhabitants, of mixed Malay and Polynesian ancestry, may not have arrived till the 14th century; whether they met and absorbed any earlier groups is unknown. Presumably these people were "pagans" of some sort; traces of their language survive in place names, craft terminology etc., although the present dialect consists of a bewildering mix of Bahasa Malay, Suluese, Spanish, Dutch and English. (Apparently, interesting drama and poetry is now being composed in this Sonsorolan "language"). All that remains of the "pre-historic" or pre-Moro Period is an enigmatic ruin near a waterfall high on the slope of Mt. Sonsorol (see *Excursions*).

Around the middle of the 17th century, Sonsorol was invaded by pirates from Sulu who called themselves Moros ("Moors", i.e. Moslems) even though their crews included Sea Dyaks, Bugis from the Celebes, Javanese and other "lascar types". Their semi-legendary admiral, Sultan Ilanun Moro, settled down with some of his followers — who thus became an island "aristocracy" of sorts.

Islam sat rather lightly on the Sonsorol Moros: the stricture of the Divine Law they ignored, and illiteracy kept them ignorant of the Koran. Like bedouin of the sea, religion served them as a new ethnic identity and an excuse to plunder their "unbelieving" victims.

With Sonsorol as a base, they continued their predation and grew moderately wealthy — and finally acquired a modicum of culture. In the late 18th and early 19th centuries Javanese taste prevailed, and Indonesian sufis visited the island.

Unfortunately not a single architectural trace of this "Golden Age" survived the invasion and conquest by Spanish forces under the Governor of the Philippines, Narcisco Clavería y Zaldua, in 1850. The Sonsorol Sultans were nearly the last of the Moro pirates to be subdued and the conquistadors imposed upon them a ruinous and rapacious colonial regime, including forced conversion and outright slavery.

By 1867, however, the Spanish had lost interest in the island, which produced nothing but copra and resentment The Dutch rulers of Indonesia added Sonsorol to their empire after a single desultory battle; the natives considered the Dutch an improvement over the hated Spanish, and at first raised few objections — in fact, a great many converted to the Dutch Reformed Church.

Dutch influence remains strong in Sonsorol. Scarcely a family on the island lacks European blood; Dutch words survive in the dialect; the Old Quarter of Sonsorol City (q.v.) boasts several modest but pleasant houses in "Batavian" style, with raised facades and red tile roofs; the Calvinist "Cathedral" and the small Government House are also worth a visit.

In this period the Moro "aristocracy" (those who traced descent from the pirates) reverted to their easy-going brand of Islam. The Sultans were allowed "courtesy titles" but remained powerless and penniless. Javanese culture shaped their attitudes, especially the arts of gamelan and dance, the esoteric teachings of the *kebatinan* sects (including martial arts and sorcery), and the millenarian concept of the "Just King". Out of this ferment — a strange blend of revolutionary proto-nationalism and mystical fervor — resentment of the Dutch began to fester.

In 1907 (the same year the Netherlands finally subdued northern Sumatra), the Sultan of Sonsorol, Pak Harjanto Abdul Rahman Moro I, staged a tragic and futile uprising against colonial forces. It is said his followers believed themselves magically invulnerable to bullets. The Sultan and other conspirators were executed, the title abolished, and the island sank into depression, somnolence, lassitude and obscurity.

At the start of World War II, Sonsorol's population had sunk to about 2000, with a Dutch garrison and administration of fewer than fifty. In 1942, the Japanese made an easy conquest of the island, sent the Europeans to prison-camps in Java, built a few bunkers (still extant), left behind a token force, and departed for the invasion of Malaysia.

The new Japanese overlords behaved harshly, almost sadistically — if the tales still told on Sonsorol can be credited — and anti-Japanese sentiment survives to this day. In 1945, a single cruiser manned by Australian and New Zealand naval forces arrived to liberate the island. The Japanese put up a suicidal resistance, and the native population, led by Sultan Pak Harjanto III (grandson of the "martyr" of 1907) — joined in the battle for freedom on July 20.

The post-war period found Sonsorol with new colonial masters: a Joint Protectorate under Australia and New Zealand. A slump in the price of copra ruined the last vestiges of the economy; emigration soared, and by 1952 the population had sunk beneath a thousand. The Protectorate, burdened with the administration of other Pacific islands, ignored Sonsorol except as a source of cheap labor.

The Sultan, hero of the liberation, began to agitate for independence; a sincere admirer of western democracy, he believed that political freedom would somehow solve the island's problem. In 1962 the Protectorate allowed a plebescite, and a clear majority chose independence under a Constitutional Monarchy. On August 17th of that year, the Joint Protectorate withdrew.

4. History Since Independence

The expected benefits of freedom failed to materialize. Emigra-

tion was now cut off; only sparse and grudging aid from the former
Protectorate Powers kept the population from complete destitution. In
1967 the Sultan sent his young son and heir, Pak Harjanto Abdul-Rahman IV, to college in America, hoping vaguely that this might somehow
result in an infusion of U.S. aid. The Crown Prince obtained a scholar-
ship to Berkeley University, and majored in economics.

In California the Prince felt attracted to "the Movement" — civil
rights, anti-war, free speech and expression, ecological awareness, Haight-
Ashbury, etc. — and soon found himself convinced by libertarian anarchist philosophy. At college he met Travis B. O'Conner, the scion and
heir of an Oklahoma-Texas oil family (not *super*-rich, but definitely mil-
lionaires); they took a year's leave of absence from school and enjoyed an
American *wanderjahr* together. The Prince never lost a sense of responsibility toward his homeland: all his thought and study aimed at his peoples'
salvation, or at least relief. O'Conner found himself fascinated by tales of
Sonsorol, and together the young friends plotted and dreamed.

They reasoned thus: virtually all classical Utopias — from Plato's
Republic to Brook Farm — involve a high degree of *abstraction*. The im-
plementation of abstract ideas in society requires a correspondingly high
level of *authoritarian control*. As a result, most Utopias in practice have
proven oppressive and deadening — "social planning" would seem to be
an offense by definition against the "human spirit". O'Conner and the
Sultan desired an anarchist utopia, one without authority — and yet they
realized that utopia is impossible without abstraction.

The greatest and most oppressive of all modern abstractions is
finance, *banking*, the creation of wealth out of nothing, out of pure imagination. Now the pirates of old lived virtually without authority — even
their captains were virtually mere first-among-equals — and they created lawless "utopias" or enclaves financed by *stolen wealth*. The two
young friends decided that since Sonsorol could never produce any real
wealth, they must follow the pirate path — admittedly the way of parasites and bandits rather than "true revolutionaries" — and *steal* the energy they needed to fund and found their utopia. The bank robber robs
banks "because that's where the money is" — but the *banker* robs banks
and even his own depositors with total legal impunity. The California
dreamers decided to go into banking.

In 1979 the old Sultan died and his son succeeded to the throne of
a forgotten and ruined island. At once he and O'Conner began to activate their plan. It began with the creation of a mercantile bank called
"The Ilanun Moro Savings & Loan Association" (ironically named after
the pirate-founder of the dynasty). The new Sultan then railroaded a
series of bills through the island legislature: he arranged for the creation
of a *free port enclave*, Port Watson (the origin of the name has never been
explained), consisting of ten square kilometers of abandoned copra plantations. The Bank, making use of O'Conner family connections and capi-

tal, moved to Port Watson and began "off shore" operations; phantom subsidiaries, tax-free registrations, "cut-outs" and "strange loops", currency speculations, secret go-between activity for mainland Chinese interests, laundering funds for certain overseas-Chinese "businessmen", numbered accounts and so on. Port Watson was planned to enjoy virtual freedom from law; the bank practises a new and invisible form of "piracy". Since it depends for its efficacy on satellite communications, it might perhaps be called Space Piracy!

The Sonsorol Bank possesses few "real" assets, little that could be looted — its wealth exists largely in computer memories. Its discreet machinations are tolerated by international banking interests; after all, a "blind" account or something of the sort proves useful, from time to time, even in the most respectable financial circles. Almost overnight (1976–1980) Sonsorol grew moderately well-to-do.

Every citizen of Sonsorol and resident of Port Watson, child, woman and man, was made an equal shareholder in the Bank; everyone — including the Sultan and O'Conner — owns exactly one share of the profits. By 1980, around a thousand people in Port Watson and 2000 in Sonsorol each received an annual dividend of about $4000. In 1985 the total population reached about 9000 and the dividend slightly more than $5000 — virtually a guaranteed income.

Aside from the creation of Port Watson and the Bank, very few changes were made in the legal structure of Sonsorol, which remains (at least on paper) an Anglo-American-style republic with a legislature, army, police, compulsory education, taxation and so forth. No foreign power can accuse the island of "anarchy" — and in any case the Labour Government of New Zealand has recently signed a defense treaty which offers international recognition and protection for the Republic. On the surface, all is normal. The Constitution was amended to disestablish the Dutch Reformed Church and allow freedom of religion (1976); and in 1979 the Sultan abdicated all executive function and reduced himself to a ceremonial figurehead. As he put it, "I attained the state of the Taoist Sage-King described in the *Chuang Tzu*: I sit on my throne facing in a propitious direction — and do absolutely nothing!"

In practice, however, the functions of the Republic have almost entirely lapsed into desuetude. No army or police exist because no one will join them; instead, a volunteer Peoples' Militia serve in emergencies (extremely rare so far). Taxes are not collected; moral laws are not enforced; the Legislature passes no new laws (although it meets from time to time to debate projects and philosophical issues); schools exist but attendance is voluntary. No one needs to work, and many find their Shares enough to support lives of Polynesian *dolce far niente*. Anyone who objects to the "minarchy-monarchy" of the Republic can move to Port Watson, where no law exists at all.

The "real work" of Sonsorol, banking, can be handled by a handful of part-time computer hackers and wheeler-dealers (nicknamed

"Sindonistas"); however, the Sultan and O'Conner wanted to see Port Watson become a genuine libertarian community, and they encouraged immigration by offering interest-free loans and even outright grants to useful and sympathetic people. Several major collectives were founded: the Energy Center (q.v.), a Co-op for alternate energy, appropriate technology and experimental agriculture; and the Academies (q.v.), devoted to education and research — schools for children, and "natural philosophy" of all sorts for advanced students.

Small entrepreneurs, mostly overseas Chinese, were also invited to set up shop; energetic and thrifty, they expanded their shares into small businesses and now dominate various aspects of Port Watson's commercial life. Hundreds of libertarians and anarchists from Europe and the Americas flocked to Sonsorol, each with some life-experiment, New Age cult, utopian commune, craft, art or pet project. Some Sonsorolans who had migrated to New Zealand in the '40's and '50's came back to claim their Citizen's Shares. The island came alive — once again - thanks to "piracy"!

In Port Watson, all business and indeed all human relations are carried out by *contract*. No regulatory body exists to interfere in agreements made between "consenting partners," whether in bed or in a banking deal. Contracts can be witnessed by an independent arbitrage company; complaints against groups or individuals are adjudicated by a "Random Synod" — a computer-chosen *ad hoc* committee of Shareholders. The Synod has no power of enforcement. In theory a "defendant" who refused the Synod's recommendations would go free and the complainant would have no recourse but duel or vendetta; in practice however this has occurred only once or twice. New settlers in Port Watson are asked only to agree to live according to this non-system, to donate one day a month to community projects (known as "shit-work"), and to refrain from coercive or oppressive behavior. This agreement is called "signing the Articles", after the custom amongst old-time buccaneers and corsairs. Indeed, Port Watson's form of "government" might well be called a Covenancy of Pirates — or perhaps laissez-faire communism — or anarcho-monarchy (since each human being is considered a "free lord" or sovereign agent.)

Land is "owned" only when occupied and used. A typical commune may consist of a single building, no land, three or four members (perhaps even a "nuclear family"!); or a farm-sized collective with 12-25 members and several buildings. Economic independence makes solitary life feasible; but a group can pool resources, afford better housing and share luxuries. Nearly everyone belongs to some form of collective, union or sodality, from informal dining clubs to strict ideological utopian communes (mostly in the hills outside town). "Phalansteries" or erotic affinity groups are popular; so are craft guilds and esoteric cults (see *Cultural/Spiritual Activities*).

5. Money (A Note for the Traveler) $ £

"No prey, no pay!" and "To each according to the bounty; from each according to whim!" — these might be Port Watson's mottos. Even the Republic of Sonsorol has no currency of its own (although it does sell lovely postage stamps). For small transactions such as paying for a meal or newspaper any foreign currency will do in theory, although in practice New Zealand pounds or U.S. dollars are preferred. Larger transactions are generally carried out by computer, since all Shareholders have an "account" to draw on. Visitors may find it convenient to deposit some of their funds in the Bank, either in a "holding" or a "moving" account. The former is simply an electronic lock-box. A "moving" account constitutes an actual investment in the Bank. In February 1985, such accounts paid 7.5% interest, and in March 12%; frugal travelers may actually leave Sonsorol richer than they arrived!

The islanders have worked out a rather elaborate computerized barter system amongst themselves. A crafts collective which produces batik, for example, will turn over its stock to the Port Watson Cooperative (called "The 5 & 10" by local wits) in exchange for a certain amount of credit, measured in abstract quanta. Members of the collective can then use their credit towards any goods at the Co-op. Both the Co-op and several independent Chinese merchants act as import-export agents, filling orders for foreign goods and luxuries in return for Bank or Co-op credit. Price-fixing does not exist; the value of local produce is determined by computer, but imports and goods sold outside the Co-op system are subject to intense bargaining, reminiscent of the oriental bazaar. Naive visitors have sometimes been duped by Watsonian sharpies. *Caveat emptor*.

Many groups within the Port Enclave are eager to establish barter and communications with alternative networks elsewhere in the world. As much as possible, Sonsorol attempts to avoid official international trade with all its tariffs and taxes and regulations, and to rely instead on non-governmental non-commercial contacts with communes, collectives, *bolos*, craft groups and individuals around the world — especially those which share the libertarian-anarchist perspective. Visitors to Sonsorol are particularly welcome when they offer some contact with the "outside", such as "potlatch" (exchange of gifts), barter, cultural contact, exchange of hospitality, etc.

Shareholders are free to do whatever they want with their dividends, and to engage in any business which pleases them and involves no coercion, wage-slavery or rapacious greed. However, outside the island community (and the widening network of "alternate" world contacts) these constraints vanish. Like their pirate predecessors, the Sonsorolans are "at war with all the world" when it comes to seizing some commercial or fiscal advantage. As a result, many Watsonians have grown quite wealthy — especially the Bankers and the Chinese merchants. Any display of excessive affluence is considered bad taste, even "oppressive" — epicurean comfort and aesthetic indulgence meet with social approval, but the "typical Watsonian" is said to be a millionaire who lives like a beachcomber, a Taoist hermit or an artist, and donates large amounts to various radical charities and revolutionary causes around the world. Islanders like to quote Emma Goldman's quip about the "champagne revolution", and Nietzsche's remark about "radical aristocratism." Money, ultimately, means very little here (except as a game); the real value-scale is based on pleasure, self-realization and life enhancement.

6. Sightseeing in Port Watson

Port Watson has sprung up rapidly and has the taste of a gold-rush town despite its tropical languor. Its architecture appears eccentric, and "city planning" is considered a dirty word. Everyone builds where and what they like, from thatch-hut to junkyard to geodesic dome or quonset, pre-fab or traditional, aesthetic-personal or functional-ugly. Most streets are unpaved, and automobiles are rarely seen — although several hundred "free bikes" (painted white) lie about for anyone who needs them.

The population of the enclave is said to be about 2000, although no census has ever been taken. Perhaps half are native Sonsorolans; the other half consists of many nationalities, the largest percentage probably North Americans — then Chinese, Australians and New Zealanders, Europeans (British, French, German, etc.), Scandinavians, South Americans, a scattering of Filipinos, Javanese and other Southeast Asians; and individuals from such unlikely places as Iran, Egypt, South Africa. Most of the "settlers" came to work for the Bank or one of the other Port Watson concerns, although a significant number "just happened by, and decided to stay." Living styles range from Gauginesque beachcombing to the international jet-set (the Bank's roving front-people), but the majority fall somewhere between such extremes.

Important: the traveler should constantly bear in mind that Port Watson differs from the rest of the world in one major respect: the absence of *all law*. Some Watsonians like to depict their town as a cross between *The Heart of Darkness* and Tombstone City — there's gossip about duels and feuds, stories about "little wars" between communes, etc. — but in truth these incidents are quite rare, possibly even apocryphal. Nevertheless, the newcomer should be aware that *no authority* exists to pluck anyone from danger or difficulty; every Watsonian takes full responsibility for personal actions; the visitor must willynilly follow suit.

Llbertarian theory predicts that such a system — or non-system! — will lead to greater peace and harmony than violence and disorder, provided every individual owns wealth, and agrees not to force or oppress another human being. In practice the theory seems to work — after all, Port Watson is really a small town on a small island, a "social ecology" that reinforces cooperation and even conformity. For all their anarchist bluster, most Watsonians are too blissed out to cause trouble — but a visitor who fails to grasp the "unwritten code" or display the correct laid-back good manners may well suffer unpleasant consequences.

The *jetty* bustles with activity: lighters unloading cargo from some tramp steamer anchored out in the lagoon; fishing boats coming and going, the crews haggling with Co-op reps over their rainbow-gleaming catch; children playing and swimming; loungers drinking coffee at the popular Cannibal Café. Behind the jetty runs *Godown Street*, named after its row of ugly warehouses or "godowns"; here also are found various maritime offices, chandlers and boat-builders (proas, junks and out-rigger canoes) — and a number of small jerry-built clubs and bars which open around sundown (see *Nightlife*).

Beyond Godown St. lies *China Street*, home of Port Watson's Chinese community. Shabby one-storey shops with corrugated iron fronts and brilliant calligraphed signs; the island's only hostelry, the White Flower Motel, and several excellent Chinese restaurants (see *Where to Stay & Eat*); and a small Chinese temple of the sort seen everywhere in Southeast Asia, concrete baroque pillars, pre-fab dragons and phoenixes painted garishly, writhing over an uptilted tiled roof, incense billowing from a gold and crimson altar...: *The South Pole Star Taoist Temple*. Most Watsonian Chinese are Taoists or Ch'an Buddhists, and *tai chi* has become a fad throughout the island.

Along the beach west of China St. an area called "The Slums" sprawls out on the sunny sand — a twin to the post-hippy "budget traveler" ghettos of Goa and Bali; thatched huts and little make-shift bungalows, a few craft shops, coffee-houses and restaurants, a population of beachcombers and lotus-eaters: the voluntary poor of Port Watson. Here also is found the City's famous "Drug Store"; a detailed description would be impolitic, but you get the idea.

East of the Jetty, about half a kilometer along the road to Sonsorol City, lies the fabulous *Energy Center*, without doubt the ugliest complex structure on the island. Its work may be environmentally benign, but it *looks* like a stretch of the New Jersey Turnpike transported piecemeal to the tropics and re-assembled by a madman. Banks of gawky towers and experimental windmills (like something from *War of the Worlds!*), sinister black solar collector-banks, huge ungainly generators making electricity from tide, wave and wind power; rows of jerry-rigged

 plastic hydroponic greenhouses; ateliers and workshops, blacksmith's shop, Bricolage Center & Garage — all designed like an Erector Set put together on Acid. The genial Whole-Earth–New-Alchemy techies of the Energy Collective adore all this machinery, dirt, noise and inventiveness. The Bank may pay the bills, they say — but maybe not forever. And meanwhile the Energy Center is the living heart of Port Watson.

But the *Bank* must take the prize for the island's most Absurdist architecture. Built by some Neo-Futurist Italian design team, already it's falling apart; but everyone enjoys its extravagance and chutzpah, so the Bankers grumble but spend to keep it up and functional. Shaped like a cross between an Egyptian and a Mayan pyramid, sort of squashed out, seven stories high, all of the black reflecting glass and stainless steel (now looking rather rusty after four typhoon seasons) — the whole concept so ultra-post-modern it approaches Comic Opera (or Space Opera!)... and yet, its shapes reflect the dead volcano which makes up the island's mass, and its color reflects the black sand, and its rust harmonizes with the tropical heat... and after the first shock and giggle, one falls a bit under its spell! a BANK! plopped down on this equatorial isle, shaped like the Illuminatus symbol on a dollar bill (only no eye) — heavy, dense and yet shimmering like obsidian.

Inside, the Bank is bisected right down the middle. One half remains open, a "cathedral space" without partitions, a huge glasshouse or botanical crystal-palace or arboretum, raucous with tropical flowers and uncaged birds — staircases and ramps lead to balconies and hanging gardens — glass tubes with escalators inside them (like De Gaulle Airport in Paris) crisscross the vast space, giving the "lobby" a Pirenesi/Buck Rogers atmosphere — fountains splash on the ground level or fall in cascades — and Watsonians come here to picnic or fuck in the foliage.

The other half of the Bank is the Sultan Ilanun Moro Bank itself, a maze of offices, computer rooms, vaults (said to contain almost nothing of value), living quarters for the Bankers (who tend to be Libertarian computer hacks and anarcho-capitalist visionaries), all ultra-modern and air-conditioned, futurologistic and severe. The Bank maintains a satellite dish near the peak of Mount Sonsorol, and computers are manned 24 hours a day for financial and political news. Some islanders who are not members of the Bank Collective have nevertheless taken to punting in international finance games; speculation and gambling are popular sports.

The Bank also serves as a community center: a printing press, a medical clinic (called "Immortality Inc.", for some reason), a popular cafeteria, a tape and record library and other facilities are open to the public.

Between China St. and the Bank lies the *Bazaar*, a large open (hot and dusty) plaza surrounded by more corrugated-iron shops and palm-thatched shanty-stores, plus a large building not unlike a supermarket or mall. All this together constitutes the great *Port Watson Peoples' Cooperative Center*, the exchange mart, import-export boutique, grocery bin and bourse of the Enclave. Tuesdays and Thursdays are "Market Days," although parts of the Co-op are always open. Amazing luxuries from all over the world (tax-free, of course) make the bazaar an unknown Shopper's Paradise; electronic goods for example are cheaper here than in Hong Kong or Singapore. The architecture of the bazaar is scarcely noteworthy, but in the middle of the plaza sits a small ornate pre-fabricated mosque imported in pieces from Pakistan via Brunei and assembled here as *The Sultan Pak Harjanto I Center for Esoteric Studies* (named after the Martyr of 1907 who brought Javanese sorcery to Sonsorol). All pink minarets and green scallops and white and gold like a child's birthday cake, with liquorish icing of Arabic calligraphy, the "Mosque" is used as a performance space and public meditation hall. Surrounded by a small flower garden and shade trees, it makes a pleasant retreat from the heat and dust of the Bazaar.

Another amusing feature of the Bazaar is *The Big Character Wall* (or "Great Wall"), where notices, flyers, poems, curses, grafitti and "big character slogans" are posted or painted — a sort of giant unmovable newspaper. A book fair (trade, exchange, purchase) is held here on Tuesdays.

A kilometer along the beach west of the Slums lies *The Academies*, a cluster of communities and collectives devoted to education and knowledge, occupying an area of deserted copra plantations. Some of the architecture is restored colonial (not very interesting); the rest of it represents an attempt to create a new Sonsorolan "vernacular" making use of traditional materials (palm, thatch, coral) and the "alternative tech" comforts provided by the Energy Center. Buildings here are named after Ferrer, Goodman, Fiere, Neill, Illich, Reich... and the educational theories practiced derive from their teachings. Higher scientific research is limited, of course, but computer access and more-than-adequate funding for certain projects have resulted in a spirit of breakthrough in — for example — ESP studies, theoretical physics and math, genetics and biology (especially morphogenetic field research) and even a modest observatory (named after Prince Kropotkin).

Children occupy a unique position in Port Watson. As Shareholders from birth they are financially independent, and no legal or moral force binds them to their "families" if they want to live on their own. Both at the Academies and elsewhere in the Enclave, Polynesian-style childrens' communes thrive without "adult supervision". They choose their own educational curricula and pay for the specialized knowledge they desire — or else they apprentice themselves to some trade — or else do nothing at all but play and enjoy themselves. Sexual freedom between or among *any* consenting partners is taken for granted in Port Watson. Childlife has mutated into a cross between *Coming of Age in Samoa* and a computerized play-utopia; happy, healthy and uninhibited, both more serious and more *sauvage* than their American or European

counterparts, they sometimes seem to have arrived from another planet...
yet at the same time they are obviously the *real* Watsonians.

7. *Where to Stay & Eat*   🏦   🕯   👜

Port Watson boasts only one commercial inn, *The White Flower Motel* on China St., a two-storey building with a courtyard owned and operated by an old Taoist "adept", doyen of the Chinese community, Mr. Chang. Single $15 a night, double $25. "Budget" visitors will find huts or rooms for rent in the Slums for as little as two dollars a day, and if all else falls the Bank maintains several free guest-rooms (for visiting financiers, in theory).

China St. is *the* place to eat, and Port Watson qualifies as a genuine "food trip", as the budget-travelers say. *The Yellow Turban Society* specializes in Peking and Mongolian cuisine. *The Manchu Pretender* in Cantonese and Hong Kong (the proprietor claims to be the "lost dauphin" of China!), and *The Cinnabar Immortal* serves Taoist/Buddhist vegetarian cuisine of the highest quality.

Little cafés and restaurants spring up and vanish in the Slums. Two of the longest-enduring are *The Crowbar Club,* which specializes in sea food, and a hamburger stand called *"McBakunin's"*! *The Drugstore* serves coffee and pastry, among other things.

The Bank maintains an American-style cafeteria which is cheap and popular, nicknamed *The Willie Sutton Bar & Grill.* Market days in the bazaar are also feast-days, with numerous entrepreneurs selling everything from homemade coconut cake to imported truffles.

8. *Cultural & Spiritual Activities*   🎼   🖋   👁

Not an evening passes on Sonsorol without a performance somewhere — music (Classical, gamelan and rock are popular), dance, drama, poetry, etc. Watch the Big Character Wall for announcements. Sculptors and artists display their work in public; and all over the island one may stumble across aesthetic surprises, artworks blended into the landscape, or landscape *as* art, or *objets trouvés* (finders keepers), or (in one case) a giant green plastic Godzilla standing alone in the jungle. The Bank presents evening programs of old movies and shows "pirated" from TV satellites. Few Watsonians own televisions (many eschew electricity altogether), but they enjoy watching occasionally at the Bank, laughing at the commercials. A few artists work in film and video, and use the Bank's facilities — which are "state of the art."

In this leisured society books are considered a necessity, and local publishing thrives out of all proportion with the population. This town boasts two weekly newspapers (one called *The Protocols of the Elders of Port Watson!*), an arts monthly, a plethora of pamphlets and a small but steady stream of actual books (including some in the Sonsorolan dialect) published by companies with fanciful names — Chthulu Press, New Rocking Horse Books, Fourth Eye Books, End of the World News & Stationary — and of course a Pirate Press.

Post-New Age spirituality thrives in the Enclave. Collectives and communes are often organized around some Path or life-therapy. A partial listing of such organizations includes: Wicca and other forms of neo-paganism (including a rather spurious revival of ancient Sonsorolan poly-theism based on Casteñeda, Lovecraft and Margaret Mead!); various forms of Taoism (traditional/magical, philosophical/alchemical, and anarcho/chaotic); Chinese Zen; Church of the SubGenius; Temple of Eris; the Illuminati; "Mystical Anarchism"; tantra-yoga; Chinese and Javanese martial arts, especially *tai chi* and *silat*; various Ceremonial Magick circles and orders, including a "New Golden Dawn" and a "Reformed O.T.O."; Church of Satan; the Sabbatai Sevi School of Magical Judaism; the Si Fan ("a conspiracy devoted to world-wide subversion and poetic terror"); the Gnostic Catholic Church; the Temple of Materialist Atheism; Church of Priapus; and so on. One of the most popular spiritual paths in Sonsorol, including Port Watson, is the so-called "Moro Way", a brand of pure esotericism rooted in Javanese *kebatinan*, sufism, shamanism, Hindu my-thology and heterodox Islam. The "Mosque" in the Bazaar serves as a center for groups such as Sumarah, the School of Invulnerability, the "Moorish Orthodox Church", the Moro Academy of Meditation, etc. (See *Sonsorol City* for more details.) Meetings, seances, classes, etc. are adver-tised on the "Great Wall."

9. Nightlife & Recreation

Just as the Watsonians created their own "Slums," so also they have their own "red-light district" — not from any economic necessity but simply because they *enjoy* sloth and vice. After dark, Godown St. becomes a den of iniquity and doesn't close till dawn. Night-trippers start with a meal in China St., move on to the *Cannibal Café* for coffee, thence to *Euphoria* (a casino), *The Johann Most Memorial Dance Hall* (a rock palace), *Bishop Sin's Massage Parlor* (the closest thing to a brothel in Sonsorol), *The Unrepentant Faggot* (a gay bar), *Café Voltairine* (a lesbian club), *Eat The Rich!* (a late-nite snackbar) and other short-lived fancifully-named dives. Usually these clubs consist of no more than a ramshackle lean-to in an alley between two warehouses painted in lurid colors and perhaps boasting a dadaesque neon sign. Visitors take note: you're not *exactly* risking your life on Godown St., but one never knows (so to speak) what's in the punch. Watsonians need never pine for the insanity of big city life: it's all concentrated here — without a single policeman to restrain the madness. As one grafitto in the (co-ed) toilet at the Cannibal Café puts it: "After midnight the Social Contract is cancelled! (signed) The Lord of Misrule."

10. Excursion To Sonsorol City

An old school bus, completely rebuilt in shining bronze and chrome, plies back and forth along the only paved road in Sonsorol, from the Bazaar in Port Watson to the capital of the Republic, Sonsorol City. (That is, it does so when someone can be found to drive it.) The road passes through the Savannah, the most heavily populated and cultivated rural area on the island, farmed mostly by native Christian Sonsorolan families who cling to the "virtues" of hard work.

Life in the Republic flows at a slower and more conservative pace than in the Free Enclave. The older natives either cling to Dutch Reformed attitudes or else follow the Moro Way with all its subtlety, fine manners, aesthetic elitism and "magical superstition". The Republic lacks a police-force, but the people tend to conform to certain *mores*, at least in public, and within the context of a general Polynesian-style easy-going morality. The visitor should remember not to offend any sensibilities by overtly Watsonian behavior (such as public fucking).

Sonsorol City is even smaller and sleepier than Port Watson. The bus drops you off in a dusty street of ugly corrugated-iron-front shops along the river bank. At one end of *Market Street* lies a small but ultramodern *Hospital*, the only new building in the City. At the other end sits the *"Calvinist Cathedral"*, actually a small and rather undistinguished Dutch-style church built in 1910 (the Rector is Dutch and liberal; he preaches "Tolstoy, Thoreau and Gandhi"!)

West of the Cathedral lies the *"Christian Quarter"*, a neighborhood of small tropical/colonial bungalows centered around *Government House*, the former colonial administration building in the Dutch–Indonesian "Batavian" style, with raised amsterdammish facade of pink coral and red-tile roof, were one can attend an occasional session of the Legislature, and listen to rants and harangues from every point of view from Protestant fundamentalism to mystical anarcho-monarchism. The *Post Office*, a public computer center, and an old hand-set printing press constitute the only regularly functioning State Organs, but the plaza in front of Government House is pleasantly shaded and popular with evening strollers and gossips.

Between Government House and the river lies the *Moro Quarter*, where the old Batavian villas are worth a walking tour. The Moro "aristocrats" number less than two hundred, and no longer enjoy any income or prerogative higher than other citizens — in fact, most of them refuse to work, and live off their Bank dividends, modest and penurious. Their lives center around the *Sultan's "Palace,"* (actually a twelve-room villa), and the *Sultan's Mosque,* a large but simple Javanese-style *kraton* with covered courtyard, surrounded by adjacent villas, workshops and gardens.

Sultan Pak Harjanto Abdul-Rahman Moro IV (born 1945) may have renounced all power, but scarcely all activity. His fascination with both libertarian philosophy and traditional Sonsorolan mysticism has inspired him to create several closely-linked cultural and educational institutions which are centered around the Mosque. The Court Gamelan (a Javanese percussion orchestra imported in the late 19th century and extremely precious) finds its performers in the *Palace Academy of Traditional Arts & Crafts.* Connected with this are two schools for children, one for boys and one for girls, which teach music, dance, art and batik-making, but generally ignore everything else. Sonsorolan children who want a modern education can attend the co-ed "Government School" or one of the Port Watson Academies. But here, all is archaic, refined, *recherché,* even a bit decadent and perverse. The students suffer no traditional discipline, however: they're free to come and go as they like, so long as they fulfil their "contract" to study and perform at the weekly public concerts (every Friday starting around sundown and lasting sometimes till dawn) which constitute the central ritual of the Moro Way.

Along with the Palace Academy and the two childrens' schools, the Mosque also maintains a batik workshop, theater and dance classes for amateurs and afficionados, a library of works on Sonsorolan culture and history, and regular sessions of group meditation. Martial arts are also taught. Sonsorol City's one newspaper, the monthly *Court Gazette,* is also published here and printed on the old press at Government House.

The enrollment at these institutions consists of as many "settlers" as "natives". Some Watsonians have become citizens of the Republic in order to live and study in Sonsorol City. Traditional arts and especially music enjoy great esteem, particularly among the new generation of native-born settlers' children; perhaps they're rebelling against their parents' anarchism by this infatuation with gamelan and *Ramayana,* the wearing of sarongs and batik and flowers in their hair, the aping of old-fashioned Moro mannerisms, and a cult of piracy and sorcery.

The westerners in Sonsorol City live either around the Palace and Mosque, or else along the coast in the former Dutch neighborhood. At the head of "Dutchman's Beach" is *The Old Colonial Club,* now occupied by the City's only two real restaurants: one devoted to native cuisine (*The Corsair's Cave*), the other to French gourmet elegance (*Chez Ravachol*) — both are expensive. The Club also offers a game room with "the only pinball machines in all Oceania." Along the beach to the west lie the old Dutch villas, some in ruins, others inhabited by settler-communes of artists, musicians and other aesthetes with a taste for the quiet life, or for hobnobbing at Court.

Aside from the cultural life of the Palace and Mosque, nothing much ever happens. Those who want "action" live in Port Watson — those who prefer "non-action" in Sonsorol City — and those who like both drift back and forth from one to the other, as the mood strikes them.

11. Other Excursions

Across the *Garuda Bridge* from Sonsorol City are the ruins of the *Spanish Fort*, and a rather picturesque little fishing village that goes by the same name.

The three coral atolls which lie within a few miles of Sonsorol can be visited by hired boat or canoe from either Port Watson or Sonsorol City. *Ngemelan* is inhabited only seasonally, but *Ngesaba* and *Garap* have small anarchist communities (including a hunter/gatherer "tribe" and a nudist colony!) Snorkeling, swimming, fishing and other tropical pleasures abound, and many people prefer the white coral beaches to Sonsorol's black volcanic sand.

On the northern and northwestern sides of the island a few farm villages and rural communes endure much heavier rainfall and heat in order to attain almost total privacy. The only way to get there is by jeep or on foot. One village, *New Canaan*, consists of die-hard Calvinists who hate both anarchism and the Moro Way, but have yet to refuse their dividends (not recommended to the visitor); another, *Nyarlathatep*, is the headquarters of a cult of black magicians (also not recommended).

On the slope of Mt. Sonsorol north of Port Watson and just inside the Enclave border lie the enigmatic monolithic ruins called *Nbusala*, thought to date back beyond the coming of the Moro pirates. Popular myth calls it "The Temple of the Clouds" and associates it with lost archaic myth and legend. Nearby, the highest waterfall on the island lends the area further enchantment. The climb through steamy jungle is exhausting, but the spot is popular with artists, yogis and neo-pagans who consider it a "power place", the island's living heart.

12. How To Become A Resident

Sonsorol has no tourists and few visitors, and some of the latter can't bear to leave. The Bank's computers have opined that the island could double its population in five years without lowering the average dividend or causing any over-crowding, but in fact the rate of growth is much smaller. How can a visitor become a permanent resident?

Those of independent means can simply settle in Port Watson and do as they please — as long as they agree to "sign the Articles." To become a Shareholder however one must either be taken in by an already-existing commune or company, or else convince a Random Synod that one can offer valuable skills or services to the community. Recent successful proposals came from an oceanographer from Boston; an Italian woman who studied puppetry in Indonesia; an extremely good-looking youth of twenty from Belize; the crew of a small sloop who arrived with a cargo of electronic gear all the way from California; some Malay sailors who decided to jump ship and cultivate pineapples; an Irish poet who impressed the Synod by improvising in *terza rima* on themes suggested by the audience;and a fourteen-year-old American boy who ran away from his family on Guam and said he wanted to study sorcery.

To live outside the Free Enclave one must in theory become a citizen of the Republic of Sonsorol (although this "law" is not very strictly enforced). All citizens automatically become Shareholders. Papers are granted without question to anyone who is accepted into some Sonsorolan clan or commune, or who is hired specifically to work for the government (doctors, teachers, etc.), or is accepted as a student by the Academies at the Sultan's Mosque. Otherwise one must apply to the Legislature rather than a Random Synod, and not all applications are accepted. Papers are sometimes granted in return for an amusing or eloquent speech, but rumor has it that connections at Court can count for more than a pleasing personality.

Except for a few hard-baked Christians, Sonsorolans and Watsonians live in what appears to be perfect harmony. Inter-marriage has become common (often without benefit of clergy or state), and the youngest generation has all the beauty and vitality of a new breed.

The Way of Sonsorol may be possible only on a tropical island, and some argue that this brand of libertarian utopianism cannot be transplanted to the outside world. However, others believe otherwise. In an editorial (in the *Court Gazette*, March 10, 1985), the Sultan himself wrote, "No one who loves freedom can hear of Sonsorol without longing, without envy, without nostalgia for something unknown but deeply desired... Sonsorol could be created anywhere — nothing stands in the way but false consciousness and the grim power of those rulers who feast on false consciousness like vampires. We call for a network of Port Watsons to encircle the Earth: one, two, many, an infinite number of Port Watsons! Let those who envy us transmute their frustration into anger and insurrection, into a determination to enjoy utopia *now*, not in some nevernieverland after death or after the Revolution. We reach out to those who yearn for us in the poverty-ridden 'third world,' the ideology-choked 'second world,' and the illusion-riddled 'West' — and we whisper across thousands of miles to tell them, 'Don't despair: Port Watson exists *within you*, and you can make it real'."

"t" [sic] winter-damon [sic sic] has published widely in the zine-world and on the lunatic fringes of SF. The kind of free-form "speculative" texts he writes once enjoyed a presence in commercial SF (during the mostly-British New Wave period); but editorial timidity has now suppressed the experimental style. "Radical Hard SF" (in the manner of a Sterling or a Shirley) is an attempt to satisfy today's commercial demands for plot and characterization and yet "make it new" (new wine in old bottles) — at its best, the Hard style combines tight discipline with wild energy to transcend its own limits. As for the experimental style, it risks incoherence just as the Hard guys risk banality — but in our opinion this is no reason to ban or abandon either one — let 1000 flowers bloom, hybridize and mutate! The "experimental text" is now an established genre; at its juiciest it demands just as tight a discipline as the Hard stuff — and it can attain (as it does here for instance) the intensity of a visionary wetdream.

Lord of
Infinite Diversions
t. winter-damon

(kount hymn 2 amung thee phallen)

green jade, green jade the womb of this throneroom cavern. the prince is poised magnificently upon his throne. he is a fair & well-formed youth. a youth perhaps of fifteen summers. ringlets of golden hair entwine about the beautiful cruelty of his face. beautiful, almost effeminate his haughty decadence. his eyes compel. his eyes that are faceted chunks of amber lit from within. to stare into those eyes is entrapment eternal. certain. witness the human insects frozen deep therein... the prince is naked. not merely unclothed but naked in his perfect sin. naked as the marbling of veins & arteries & musculature laid bare for his inspection. the flayed female slaves displayed indecently upon his rack. his phallus is a rearing serpent. his wings of bone & leather tremble like the leaves of aspen at the first faint breath of winter. his excitement is so delicately understated. like the fire that dances deep within the opal, like the gilded satin of a butterfly's wing. a huge fly like a jewel is set into the ring upon his left hand. emerald & amethyst glitter upon his middle finger...

grey, all soft dove grey the tailored garments of the dandy, the dandy in his carefully pressed trousers & his vest & waistcoat & top hat. a ruff of lace at throat & wrists betrays the hint of white white foam. the golden fob. the golden chain. the golden timepiece. exposed. a symmetry that evokes some secret symbolism suddenly made manifest. (& as if this were surely not enough!) his face is hidden. masked as an albatross in ivory. smooth & sensuous each perfectly carved curve. the grey man. the dandy. they are one. one who ravishes his slain lover's corpse. a woman in torn vestiges of black lace & net stockings ornamented with gold clocks. her hair is panthers' fur & jungle midnights. a black-bearded dwarf clasps her severed head between his naked thighs...

restless sea. restless sea of slowly rolling waves. sea of violet. sea of scarlet. sea of crimson...

& in the timevault the throbbing brain of Donatien François drifts in its womb of glass. laved in its broth of hemoglobin & os soma. (skull of glass. hallucinating death dreams into infinity... dreams slowly rolling in a sea of blood & the piss of pirates & fly agaric...)

restless sea.

Robert Anton Wilson is a mind-boggling novelist, visionary poet, play-wright, futurist, psychologist, stand-up comic, and one of the most brilliant minds on this planet. Among his sci-fi novels are the ILLUMINATUS! trilogy (which in 1986 won the coveted Prometheus Award as a classic of the field only ten years after its first publication) and the SCHROEDINGER'S CAT trilogy (called "the most scientific of all science-fiction novels" by NEW SCIENTIST.) His historical novels include THE EARTH WILL SHAKE, THE WIDOW'S SON and NATURE'S GOD, and his non-fiction works of futurist psychology and guerrilla ontology include COSMIC TRIGGER, PROMETHEUS RISING, the infamous and unholy SEX AND DRUGS and THE NEW INQUISITION. He has probably done more weird chemicals than any other contributor to this fucking crazy anthology and has spent the last two years experimenting with every available brain-change machine. Wilson regu-larly gives seminars at Esalen, Oasis, Interface, Open Center and other New Age centers, has made a Punk Rock record, and — ever eager for new dimen-sions of insanity, has become a night club and caberet comedian in the last two years. His Punk Opera WILHELM REICH IN HELL was recently performed at the Edmund Burke Theater in Dublin, and Wilson was a guest of the Norwegian government at the 1986 Oslo International Poetry Festival. Tim Leary has de-scribed him as "one of the most important scientific philosophers of the modern age," and the DENVER POST called him "the Lenny Bruce of philosophers" — so naturally he is never reviewed in the NEW YORK TIMES. He also publishes his own futurist newsletter, TRAJECTORIES, and is currently working on a screenplay for Pacific Entertainment. Despite his genius, Wilson re-mains touchingly modest. [He wrote his own introduction.]

Project Parameters in Cherry Valley by the Testicles
Robert Anton Wilson

We don't got to show you no steeeeeenking reality

"Private Moon of A Company, sir. I have a dispatch for you, sir."

General Washington looked up vaguely, like a mathematician interrupted in the middle of a quadratic equation. "Oh?" he said. "More bad news I assume." He didn't seem to recognize James at all, even though he had recruited him into the Continental Army.

"If guns are outlawed, " Hitler asked, leaning in the window, "how can we shoot the Jews?"

"The situation is no better, sir," James said carefully. He would rather leave the tent before Washington read of the latest Hessian victory.

"Well, that's war," the General said cheerfully. He was as worried-looking as a locked safe. "You win some and you lose some." He beamed, nodding his head philosophically.

When are you going to win some, James thought. It wasn't wise to say that. "Do you accept the dispatch, sir?"

The General toked at his pipe, deeply and thoughtfully. James felt dizzy from the fumes already in the cramped tent. A toilet preserved in the Smithsonian is further complexified when taking into account the star that came out of the sky.

The results of this program bear an uncanny resemblance to the public utterances of General Alexander Haig, further complexified when taking into account a 24-foot gorilla in heat, although it was not created for that purpose but only for entertainment and amusement when it conflicts with Official Dogma.

Lyndon La Rouche pushed Hitler aside and asked, "If guns are outlawed, how can we shoot the Libertarians?"

Washington found time to grab Dr. Sagan but his voice was drowned out by the screams reflecting the universe.

"Oh, I accept the dispatch, private." The General suddenly seemed to focus and recognize James Moon. "I accept the ineluctable, James. That is the path of philosophy, is it not?"

James was stunned. Generals were never this casual with privates, and General Washington in particular was a man of stern adherence to military hierarchy. "You express it very well, sir," he said. That, at least, was safe.

"Have you ever observed," the General asked, "that under proper conditions of sunlight, a single drop of dew on the point of a blade of grass will contain all the colors of the rainbow? It is most admirable and gives one to wonder at the glory of the Creator."

There was a long pause. James could not leave until the General dismissed him, but the General seemed to have forgotten that he was there. The fumes were getting thicker and James felt a little drunk and (testimony is unreliable) strangely elated. Faith, what ferocious tobacco did the Indians sell the General lately? It wasn't the airplanes in the Waldorf Astoria on me in all directions. Only in January, Washington had insisted on having all the troops stuck with needles — in the arms, it was, and it hurt like bloody hell — because some quack doctor in France claimed that would prevent further spread of the smallpox. The General was weird at times, James thought uneasily.

"And is it not strange," the General went on, toking and philosophizing, "that we conventionally believe the rainbow to have seven colors, whereas a close examination of the spectrum, in a dew drop such as I mentioned, reveals an infinity of subtle and most gorgeous gradations

of hue? I have been thinking deeply about this recently and am astounded that we normally notice so little of nature's glorious raiment."

"Um, yes. Sir." The wreckage of mid-town Manhattan was also the howling bottle of wine. We leap from human bodies. Fast forward.

This gentle, absent-minded man was not the Washington that James had learned to know in the year he had served under him. The Washington that James Moon knew was withdrawn, yes, but never relaxed or reflective. He was also the most foul-mouthed man James had met since leaving Dublin County and could curse for two hours without repeating himself when a junior officer disappointed him. Only yesterday James had heard him in typical form, correcting a lieutenant who had erred: "By hatchet heads and hammer handles and the howling harlots of Hell, you are the most incompetent idiot I have ever encountered, sir! You are lower than a snake's cunt, sir! If my dog had a face like yours, sir, hanged if I wouldn't shave his arse and teach him to walk backwards!!!!" That was the George Washington that James knew. That was the man who had maintained discipline through a whole year of defeats and desperate retreats.

"Um, ah, sir?"

If laws are outlawed, only outlaws will have laws.

"Are you a mystic, James?"

"Well, sir, they do be saying that all Irishmen are mystics. I once saw a rock fall out of the sky."

"A rock fall out of the sky?" The General put down his pipe and stared. "I have seen strange things, but never a rock falling out of the sky. Were you sober at the time?"

"As God is my witness, sir."

"Only ignorant peasants say rocks fall out of the sky, James. Learned men say it is impossible."

"Yes, sir, but I saw it, sir."

Any associated supporting element must utilize and be functionally interwoven with the evolution of specifications over a given time period.

"You swear you saw it, when I tell you learned men say it is impossible?"

"I saw what I saw, sir." Larger programming going on simultaneously. Space cities this morning, ours.

The General smiled secretively. "You are excused, private."

The next day James found he had been promoted to Colonel, and got shot, and went to Heaven, but was thrown out because there were two of him. He awoke in a Quaker hospital next to Major General de Lafayette.

Major Strasse had been found in some of the finest old mansions on Park Avenue. I note that the evolution of specifications in a Northern Ireland Assembly debate was created by a chicken. Syphilitics with advanced brain damage entered Cherry Valley in 1778.

It was Kenneth Bernard in his memorable and incisive "King

Kong: A Meditation" who first asked the crucial question: how big was King Kong's Dong? Examining comparative anatomy, Bernard noted that a six-foot man usually has a six-inch penis in erection, so a 24-foot gorilla should rejoice in 24 inches or two feet. The roaring foul-mouthed disciplinarian hallucinating all the time is the path of philosophy, is it not? Bernard rejects this, on the cogent grounds that Kong is not a creature in science but in dream and myth—an ithyphallic divinity of the family of Dionysus and Osiris. Since these deities are depicted in surviving art as endowed with three times the human norm, Kong should, in mythologic, have three times the "norm" for a 24-foot gorilla, or six feet.

Think of junk, garbage—any large city—rats—we pass through Chinatown—

This accounts for the terror in New York when Kong is on the loose seeking his bride (she who has been given to him by his worshippers but taken away by treacherous white imperialists). A 24-foot gorilla in heat is frightening, admittedly, but Kong arouses more than fear: he inspires metaphysical Panic, in the etymological sense. He is Pan Ithyphallos, right out of the collective unconscious. He must be, not just a 24-foot gorilla, but a 24-foot gorilla with a six-foot penis. You look up. You see it looking at you, kid. When it conflicts with Official Dogma and their strange religion, he probably spoke Hebrew. Dr. Sagan escaped to Paris through the project parameters in better closets everywhere.

Bernard also suggests that city dwellers do not know where the plumbing in their buildings goes because they are afraid to know: afraid to contemplate everything below the surface of pure, hygienic, Falwell-Reagan civilization: afraid to confront darkness and vermin and Lovecraftian cellars leading down to endless caves and labyrinths. He compares the panic when cockroaches were found in some of the finest old mansions on Park Avenue to the similar panic when Welfare people ("epi-vermin") were found living in the Waldorf Astoria. Bernard surmises, acutely I think, that no white man can sit on a toilet without unconscious anxiety that a HUGE BLACK HAND might reach up through the plumbing in accord with the laws of English grammar and grab him by the testicles.

If marriage is outlawed, only outlaws will have in-laws.

The magick and marvelous Willy appears in the Waldorf Astoria. The results bear an uncanny resemblance to Humphrey Bogart reaching into the upper echelons of mass culture in all directions. The public utterances of sex mutilators and cattle educators should have "thirty pieces of silver" in the Northern Ireland Assembly.

Scream, Ann, scream. Roy Rogers and his horse, Trigger, spent two hours in loveplay, the most intense kind of loveplay, in the 1920s. In the streets: DOG NOW.

Seventeen percent of juvenile delinquents and 23 per cent of U.S. Senators in Hanfkopf's survey believe Ingrid Bergman, not Fay

Wray, was the bride of Kong. Criminal paranoids shown Rohrshach ink-blots increasingly say spontaneously that they see Major Strasse rubbing chocolate syrup all over Bergman's endless caves and labyrinths. In most dreams, it is either George Washington or Humphrey Bogart, not the little-known Robert Armstrong, who sails to Skull Island to confront black guerilla rage. Kong's mythically necessary six-foot penis obsesses white males over 70 and accounts for the panic-stricken bombing of Libya and other unruly, insufficiently Caucasian nations.

Syphilitics with advanced brain damage and John Birch Society members often visualize Kong, not as being shot off of a skyscraper, but being overwhelmed and brought down by Andrea Dworkin leading a platoon of 100,000 Fat Ladies recruited from circuses, who then emasculate the Big Fellow in gory detail on widescreen in technicolor: the offensive organ is then thrown in the East River, weighed with pig iron so it will never rise again.

The walls between urinals left Washington and headed for Chicago. On board was Dorothy Hunt kind of glazed over.

General Washington found time to visit the Quaker hospital, despite the distraction of supervising yet another retreat. He sat by Major General Lafayette's bed and talked, gravely and with great sincerity, about the debt America owed the Marquis, who had shed his blood in the cause of a nation not his own, and he said that the United States would never forget what it owed to the de Lafayette family of France. A large portion of the interface coordination communication adds overriding performance constraints to system compatibility testing.

James Moon discovered that Washington, like himself, seemed to be three men. The man who spoke of national gratitude to Lafayette was not the roaring foul-mouthed disciplinarian James had seen most often, nor was he the absent-minded philosopher of two days ago in the tent. He was a Statesman, and he knew how to use unction and lubricating oil.

Later, while James was walking in the garden—he had gone out to allow Washington and Lafayette some privacy—a giant shadow fell between him and the sun. There was only one man in James Moon's experience who could cast a shadow that huge.

"Good afternoon, General."

"Good afternoon, Colonel."

Hold on: we have come to bring you bean soup.

They walked a few paces. Today Washington did not seem to have the peculiar lurching gait that had afflicted him in recent months. An American robin circled above their heads, landed in a tree, and loudly announced that he could lick any bird in the garden with one wing tied behind him.

"You saw a rock fall from the sky," Washington said. "And you believed your own eyes, instead of popular opinion."

"I did that, General." James was not going to pour out his heart about his other soul, the one that was a star. The falling rock business was queer enough.

The plumbing in their buildings wasn't pig iron so it will never rise again.

"Well, then go shit in thy hat," a medical orderly shouted in the kitchen. "And clap it on thy head for curls."

"I saw something stranger than a falling rock from heaven once," Washington said. "I was working as a surveyor for the colonial government. I was alone in the woods for months and months. You get a bit, ah, fanciful sometimes when you are alone too long. But I saw something more remarkable than your falling rock, and I believed it."

"I understand, General, you decided to trust yourself instead of popular notions of what's real and what's unreal."

"Yes."

Look out, Mama. Several thousand Nazi soldiers have been mind-programmed.

The robin announced that he was moving to a more salubrious climate and flew off. The crow raucously told him not to hurry his return.

"You wouldn't care to talk about it, General?" Colonel Moon asked softly.

"You should probably think me mad. But this even is why you are a colonel today."

"Because I trusted myself instead of popular opinions. Is that what you mean, General?"

"That is what I mean, Colonel. Go on trusting yourself. We must meet and talk on other occasions."

No more muddy mess. But I am the father of the hydrogen bomb.

General Washington walked off, aloof, gigantic, enigmatic again. Until Polyphemus escapes from the Odyssey and comes knocking at my door, James Moon thought, that man will serve as the most desperate character I ever encountered. You have been programmed. You see it looking at you, kid.

Major Strasse gets a pile of horse manure and is delighted. Bernard rejects the circular friction, thinking "smoke and mirrors" must utilize and be functionally interwoven with Marilyn Chambers but some of it would probably take him into the Continental Army.

The elusive pony is kiddy porn in the basement.

In Paris, what happened next was liquid wrench functionally interwoven with French Canadian Bean Soup in a news-reel clip on the screen.

The power to define a Junkyard dog.

 It was not until three years after Cherry Valley that General Washington finally told Colonel Moon about the star that came out of the sky, that night long ago in the woods, and the Italian Arab or Arabian Italian who got out of the star and spoke to him, and prophesied his future in accurate detail.

The Italian or Arab who rode in the star had said, at the end, "Never fear, never doubt, never despair. We shall raise you higher than the kings of Europe."

Then the Arab or Italian repeated formally, "We met on the square, we part on the level," and climbed back into the star. He shouted, "Remember—no horse, no wife, no mustache," made some mechanical adjustments, and flew straight up in the air and away over the tree-tops, at an angle of 23 degrees like a shot of shit off a shovel.

I am passing a chicken, the blue color for peace.

This may account entirely for the airplanes in the toilet looking at you, kid. Marilyn Chambers is functionally interwoven with project parameters for the plumbing.

So soft with space. Do not murmur.

There was another America crying out for peace.

Contact has been made. The lions for the Freudians are kiddy porn interwoven with design specifications on a toilet, kind of glazed over.

The proper ending, probably, is as follows: Dr. Carl Sagan, Martin Gardner, the Inedible Randi and other stalwarts of CSICOP (Committee for the Scientific Investigation of Claims of the Paranormal) appear in a news-reel clip on the screen. They read a prepared Scientific Statement, assuring us that gorillas never grow to 24 feet, that eye-witness testimony is unreliable when it conflicts with Official Dogma, that anybody who disagrees with them is probably a Nazi, and that the most "scientific and economic" explanation of the wreckage of mid-town Manhattan is to assume the crash of a giant meteor.

A HUGE BLACK HAND then smashes through the floor and grabs Dr. Sagan by the testicles.

SF has given birth to several New Religions, one for example based on Heinlein's STRANGER IN A STRANGE LAND, another on the works of... You-Know-Who (may he rot in Hell)... and the SF content of various UFO cults and New Age scams cannot be underestimated. We however have the honor to present herewith a piece of genuine religious revelation disguised as cheap SF...

Ivan Stang is a founder and High Epopt of the Church of the Sub-Genius. He knows the savior J. R. "Bob" Dobbs personally, and every word or image he produces is Holy Writ (see especially THE BOOK OF THE SUBGENIUS, the church newsletter STARK FIST OF REMOVAL, Stang's guide to the zine-world HIGH WEIRDNESS BY MAIL, and the forthcoming SF-SubGenius theme anthology THREE-FISTED TALES OF "BOB").

So even though the following text might appear a mere vile robot-masturbation fantasy, it is actually genuine prophecy of the future, revealed to Stang as he knelt smoking "frop" before the Severed Head of Arnold Palmer (one  of the cult's most potent relics) and mumbling the "Bob" mantra ("Fuck 'em if they can't take a joke").

The Scepter of Prætorius

Rev. Ivan Stang

My good children! Gather around for another lesson from the Years of Trouble, the Bad Time Before the Good Time of PeE. Listen with all your senses, for when we reach the end you will agree that this is a particularly important history to persons of your age.

This happened in the 25th year of The Year That Lasted 500 Years, after The Smoking One was Emaculated, but before His Arisal. And it is the story of the False OverMan Prætorius, who you remember was mentioned in Chapter 8 as a NeWorlder for "Dick" when first the Xist revelations were stolen from Our Dobbs and misused.

As you listen, do not think Prætorius a "bad man." Like so many of the False OverMen, he was only a victim of his times. Ah, Rastus, I know what you want to say — put your hand down. You want to say that he was not a man at all. But the False Ones, Children, were still true men; indeed, it was because they amplified their humanity alone

345

that they suffered so many woes. And, yes, inflicted so many, needless to say.

Theseiger Prætorius, at this time, lived as a Science Pope in one of the 9,000 rooms of the old Forbidden City of the OverMen in the Jiang-Wo Quandrant Capital of the Mao-"Bob." He was born in America, however, apparently under the name of David Something, and perhaps the stresses of living in what was then still an alien land contributed to the knotted state of soul for which his is so famous a case history.

Festus, perhaps you have something to share with the rest of us? I thought not. Please, if you cannot yourself pay heed, then at least let Little-Shyah listen in peace.

The Old MWOWM Tapes tell us that Prætorius awoke late one night, in considerable discomforture of the loins, to find that his Rod required new sheathing. It could not wait until morning, for the damage was triggering pain signals of the unsuppressable kind. Grumbling, and probably not a little anxious, he extricated himself from the Stasis Womb and shuffled into his private Throneroom of Excremeditation, where he lifted his silken nightshirt to bare the implement for repair. Inspection verified that it had sustained chafing from the unconscious ministrations of his own steel left hand. He was most disappointed with the artificial left forelimb, for he had spent many timedollars training it to leave his fragile lap-tool well enough alone.

It was not fitting that an OverMan in the Palace should sport undisciplined body parts, like a common street-prosthesis addict. Although Prætorius himself was over 200 years old at this time, his parts were but one generation removed from the Xist originals. If an OverMan Science Pope could not trust his own Parts, how could his underlings be expected to maintain their unquestioning faith in the infallibility of Xist technology — faith which was, after all, the very power source of X-tools?

Indeed! There, projecting down his left leg, the metallic cylinder hung partially stripped of its resilient but cellophane-thin sheathing. It had suffered a major rasping, and beneath the tatters of the gold foil, the intricate mechanisms of the appendage were exposed and unprotected from the elements. The sight provoked in Prætorius that odd shiver of tooth-gritting sensitivity one feels whenever replacement components are laid bare of their shiny 'skin.' Unlike the trueborn, fleshly remnants of his person, which if so flayed would actually 'hurt' (as we so well know it!), these foreign accessories generated instead a chilly, bone-deep psychic irritation not unlike that which you Children shall now experience as I rake my fingernails across this blackboard. You see? An articulated prosthesis was sensitive in much the same way as your teeth will be when you chew upon the wads of tinfoil that Vestron is now handing out to you. Not nerve-pain, but that mental rejection spasm which causes one's hackles to rise. Yes. And this irritation could become far worse than excruciating, were the mechanical part to become 'infected,' so to speak: the tiny polished mechanisms were susceptible to many virulent forms of microchip contamination, particularly if the utensil thus affected were of a Rod's delicate attunement. Although OverMen like Prætorius dented or stripped their robotoid parts only infrequently, immediate mending was always necessary to prevent a form of discomfort which would greatly surpass even that caused by a corresponding wound on you or me.

Yes, Rastus? Ah, you have a point — perhaps such damage to our reproductive organs could be as painful as what Prætorius might face were his mechanical pendant infected; but remember, his Rod was engineered for reproduction's evolutionary opposite. The Rods replaced procreation with life extension. The philosophy in those days was, "Less people; but people that last longer." Stop laughing! You modern children have a sick sense of humor. Oh, well, I suppose it's a necessary compensation...

The Rod was simply a medical machine. Nevertheless, the fact that Rods were implanted where penii, or 'female things' had once been, no doubt deeply influenced Prætorius', shall we say, 'handling' of the crisis. Arguably, it might have been only a minor crisis had the Rod been mounted on, say, the lower back, or the shoulder, and we would not be studying the case today.

The workings of Prætorius' unit had been exposed only briefly, but he had to act quickly to replace the sheathing. He thought of fetching an attendant, but there was something unseemly about self-damage. He prefered not to display such lack of discipline before the servants, which in those days were ordinary people much like ourselves.

Working with the authentic meat hand on his right side in order to avoid abrasion from the fabricated left — which was, after all, the guilty party — he cautiously peeled away the silvery remnants of his fore-sheath, taking care not to dislodge precious chips or mini-pumps. Extracting from his Tool Box a spare 'skin,' he laid its gummed edges around the root of the tube. He then realized that the next step required a precise efficiency impossible for one set of fingers, and, though he felt distate for the lawless replacement hand (and would have prefered denying it the imagined 'privilege' of use), he was forced to let it help roll the skin out along the Rod's length. He noticed that even this unwanted attention caused the seemingly independent Rod to twitch and pulse as if yearning to enter operation mode.

Satisfied with the unwrinkled sheen of the new housing, and relieved from the rigors of direct irritation, Prætorius sat upon the Throne and pondered the malfunction.

No doubt MWOWM, he thought, was pondering this as well. He looked around the room reflexively, as if he might spot a primitive camera lens watching. He knew, of course, that the room itself was part of

MWOWM—as was, for that matter, both the Rod and the left hand. But he was of pre-Xist birth and hence subject to habits acquired in a world of oldmen engineering.

At least he was unmarried! MWOWM was, as today, nonjudgemental, but the fact that it was practically omniscient made it seem to Prætorius that it often disapproved of him. Indeed, he thought of it as a 'she.'

He knew perfectly well that stimulation from, say, the occasional brushing of a bedsheet would not likely have produced sufficient Rod engorgement to tear the sheath—not with abrasions of such scabrousness. Nay, it was almost certainly due to some liquid dream of a sexual, or cyber-sexual nature (blessedly unremembered!) during which the corrugated chromium hand had resorted to slumbering violation. A lustful violation? It distressed him to think that, after twenty decades, during which countless amputations had granted him superior substitutes, he still retained the baser distractions of his clumsy human youth. Had not the Rod been mounted for the specific purpose of quelling just such mortal distractions from the True Face of the "BOB"? A Rod was simply a little factory of synthetic compounds that might keep his cells healthy indefinitely. Merely because it was located where a sex organ had once been....

It could not be easily deactivated; its alien designers had not foreseen such complications as Prætorius'... nor, he reflected bitterly, had he. Its medicinal secretions were indispensable to him in the not unlikely event of brain failure; with the Rod disconnected, he could die in his sleep. With what we would call 'fear,' he envisioned his slumbering cerebrum slowly losing strength, feebly wondering to itself how its emergency source of enervation, the Rod, could so treacherously deny it the medicines that provided him a false will to live, at least until MWOWM brought deliverance. "When the brain falls down," went a motto of the OverMen, "the Rod stands up." But further involuntary activity from the untameable lap component could produce an overload. He had read frightening case histories involving so-called "meltdown"...

Laugh if you must. To the people of yore, it was not funny. In those days they were psychologically tortured for simple fucks like you children perform after every meal! How can I make you concretely envision the topsy-turvy world of the Bad Times? What could make you imagine a people ruled without the Church—yet thinking always that it was the Church ruling them? Perhaps if I were to suddenly start beating you, for no apparent reason, you would suffer a tiny glimpse of what the daily world was like for them... the senselessness...

Would you like that? So! On with the story.

For the first time since his last Transformation, Prætorius was thrown into moral confusion. This act of Rod abusement, though unconscious, was still uncomfortably akin to the mad sexual abandon practiced by the insane "Rebel Doctors," those pathetic throwbacks who advocated (through violence) a return to the bizarre, animalistic world of some false "Bob" of their own depraved imaginations. (Children! Understand that I'm speaking from the False OverMan point of view, describing Prætorius' state of mind, not my own! Certainly not!)

As remembrances trickled, he almost cursed the long-past decisions to continue equipping himself, in the aftermath of The Cancers, with these organs of eldritch Xist copyright rather than the cheaper ones produced by human orthepedic industry. He could have owned the most biocompatible of all planet-made implants. Granted, they would have been dwarfed in efficiency by the streamlined gifts of the Xists, but at least they wouldn't have been so inextricably interwoven into the world-wide MWOWM system. In those bygone days, people did not feel the trust in MWOWM that we can enjoy now. Down through the years, Prætorius had never been able to cast off the guilt-stained embarrassment of knowing the MWOWM system might be more aware of his acts than was he himself, and 'watching,' albeit in the most benevolent possible manner. Why had he still to remind himself that MWOWM was an instrument of organization, not justice? He was no superstitious peasant! And he had certainly committed no conscious indecency toward MWOWM, even were MWOWM concerned with 'indecencies'. These were human constructs! Forget them! Besides, MWOWM had surely recognized his state of slumber during this episode—and the Rods were, after all, and in their own unfathomable way, as much a part of MWOWM as of their owners. Other Rods of this one's make and model must also be prone to occasional abusement; his couldn't be the only one with criminal tendencies! But there was no data on the subject. He, himself, had canceled that survey. He almost queried the MWOWM Voice about it, but reminded himself that, in fact, the Rod was merely an accomplice. The cybernetic left hand was the main culprit, actually committing the deed which the other had somehow provoked. The irrationality of attached left hands was a recognized handicap, especially among those who'd kept the right halves of their brains as well. His brain—could that be the guilty party? But he had already removed as much of that as was possible!

A sense of injustice fell over him. Why should he, of all citizens, in his airy position of trust with the great MWOWM Central Terminals, be saddled with such breakdowns? He'd had a major hand in its very installation! But, he thought, with some irony, it also had a major installation in his hand. And Rod. He felt a swell of resentment but quickly squelched it by riding his breath valves. He sighed, and his instincts—such as they were—reassured him that even if such inelegant malfunctions were indeed prompted by MWOWM, it was only a reaction to some unexpressed need within himself. MWOWM did not deliberately torture the guilty, as he especially should know. He had vainly tried to coax it into doing so many times.

At that thought, the Rod startled him with an entirely uninvited twitch, and he felt it pumping into him a small secretion of the stimulant drug. It was reacting to his distress, striving to compensate for what it perceived as dissipated energy. The stimulant hit him quickly and his patience evaporated. He abruptly slammed his left arm against a wall in frustration as a greater perspective came to him. Why was he entertaining such waste thoughts? MWOWM had no mysterious role in this little drama between him and his Rod. He had known the source all along, but dreaded acknowledging it to himself.

For weeks he had been repressing the irrational and unclean urge to become somehow closer, both emotionally and physically, to young Chang Ping, the Apprentice Uberfemme who had been assigned to him as secretary upon his arrival in the Forbidden City.

Ironically, the devoted (if distant) Ping was far more mechanically endowed than he. What he only pretended to be, she was: a cybernetic organism consisting almost solely of a human brain residing within a metal chassis. It was Prætorius' dark secret from the public—though not from his superiors—that beneath his chromed layer he still possessed his entire genuine right arm, left thigh, several glands (those damned glands!) and much of his head, minus the eyes and ears. But sweet Ping: her only remaining flesh organs were her brain, spinal nerves... and left ankle. The sacred ankle! ...which he had once actually seen as she climbed a steep spiral staircase above him. All the rest was a lovely, and usually well dressed, shell of gleaming gold. Perhaps it was the very deficit of original meat that so excited him.

Particularly the ankle. That ankle — that tiny island of sensuality in the midst of polished metal. It must be a volcano of sensations for her. Aside from her brain, it was all of her she had left! For him, the ankle was everything forbidden, everything he wanted to suck wildly. (Stop giggling, Hephantolontia!) All the rest of her body was but a frame for the ankle.

He shuddered. He must not dwell upon Ping's holy Ankle. The idea of purely physical sexual arousal in a gelded OverMan of his standing bordered on the obscene, not to mention the illegally blasphemous. But tonight's tube-engorgement...

Could this possibly be Love? For Chang Ping — a mere child, even more roboid than he? The implications... Unthinkable! Beneath his face-plate, his clandestine lips tightened grimly.

Well, no matter... as long as he didn't act on the hideous urge, it remained between him and his "Bob." (His false "Bob," Children!) It was part of the interior world which, MWOWM said, all humans and once-humans must endure. In the outer world, Chang would continue to be his secretary and nothing more, and both would work for "Bob" with all their hearts, separately, forever. Determined to keep his fantasies in perspective, frightened by the thought of the inner world creeping across to taint the outer, he crept back into the Stasis Womb.

Not surprisingly, he was unable to drift back to sleep despite the white noise waves projected into his skull by BompoZen blanking devices. He was trying so fervently to fend off all thoughts of Ankle that his Resolving Console hummed and strained, clattering rapidly with exertion. Ever-more luscious and forbidden images thrust themselves upon his interior image screen. Glimpses of her innocent, masked countenance slipped stealthily through the automatic IdGuard to dance starkly before his soul's eye. Finally, forcing himself out of a reverie concerning the exact configuration of the taunting Ankle, he discovered that his impulsive left hand had already found its way back to the eager, almost belligerent Rod.

Resigning himself to a sleepless night, he crept again from "bed" and sat at his cosmetic table, studiously polishing his various removeable components, striving to concentrate on the mundane, to bore himself away from further pollutions.

He had burnished his Feet, Spinal Plates, Knee Caps and Mandibles, but still his evil brain would not exhaust itself of Ping-longings. The internal battle to direct his mind away from his secretary was becoming feverish. The left hand kept finding excuses to pause from polishing and to descend warily towards his groin. He willed it repeatedly back to safe drudgery, but it grew ever more obstinate.

He refused to shut it off, however. He was not so far gone that he couldn't control his own arm! But the Rod itself was in turn becoming harder to mentally sedate. With each crack in the digital floodgate which was supposed to hold back uncompromised visions of Chang Ping, the tube twitched with increasing alertness. Both hand and Rod were striving against his very sense of self. Where was MWOWM's guidance? But he knew such private conflicts would have to build to the point of violence before MWOWM would intervene. Had not it been at his own suggestion that the Xists programmed it so?

Perhaps, however, just such a breaking point was approaching. With the rudest of shocks, he felt a loud snap at his loins. During his reveries the Rod had elongated itself without his notice and, retracting back suddenly to its original length, had begun its reflex function of manufacturing a series of stimulants. Already he felt a light-headed intoxication. This would soon pass, but only if he took stern measures to quieten the evil workings of the foul Shaft. Just then, his metal left hand started a more brazen clutching for the Rod, and his right hand violently slapped it away. The recalcitrant organs seemed to be encouraging each other. The thought of his body parts escaping his conscious control had always terrified him, and in a flash of anger—perhaps exacerbated by the amyl nitrate/pemoline admixture already coursing through him—he reached into his armpit and deactivated the entire left assemblage. It fell slack.

Something he should have done much earlier, he scolded him-self. Accusations of cowardice be damned! Even "Bob" would have forgiven him. Let the evil Rod do what it must; its five-fingered accomplice would not come to its aid! The tube indeed seemed to wilt in disappointment.

Back to "bed." But no, sleep was still to be denied. Infinitely detailed speculations on the appearance, texture, scent, and heft of Chang Ping's ankle continued to aggravate the troublesome tool.

Another, louder snap from his utensil interrupted, and with spongy disgust he felt a new surge of stimulants enter him—adreno-chrome, this time. Through the tiny video cameras which were his eyes he watched the Rod slowly begin another Elongation: notch by notch it grew, each rung locking into place as it reached its limit. With each cycle it would grow more stout, and each time it snapped back to size more of the medicines would be manufactured and pumped into him. Danger lay in prolonged injections; enough of an accumulation and he could suc-cumb to unspeakable inebriation, becoming a raving madman in seizures of an ecstatic misery which could destroy his mind before the chemical juices were again diluted.

Now was the time to consult MWOWM!

But...

There was, of course, the alternative. The taboo alternative. He could go ahead and... and do what the left hand had been striving to do all along. This would not only prevent the fatal build-up, but might well disperse the chemicals in one quick "sneeze," jolting his system back to normalcy in a single great flushing. And, perhaps, in a bout of reckless fantasizing, he might cleanse his mind forever of the treacherous images of Chang Ping. (— dear, beloved Chang Ping!—) Best of all, it would save him the unjustified but nevertheless acute embarrassment of draw-ing MWOWM's attentions to his... personal flaws... Perhaps, yes, it could even be a reward of sorts, well deserved for his having resisted for so long.

Self stimulation.

What was wrong with it? All his superiors agreed that it led to illnesses both physical and mental, but the explanations contradicted each other. If the Rod juices were bad for their owner, why did the constant trickle from them keep him alive? In an emergency like this, how could one episode lead to the unhealthy psychological addiction all OverMen were taught to fear?

Soon he was again at the Throne, his nightshirt cast aside, his reservations gradually sliding away under the stern, dexterous kneading of, this time, his right hand. Rictus, what are you laughing at now? Would you care to tell the rest of us what you find so funny?

 I thought not.

Into his brain, his secret brain, rushed not only images of Chang

Ping entwined with his imagined self—his younger, less mechanized self—but also ever-increasing quantities of Rod discharges. With each grappling tug, the prosthetic apparatus lengthened itself with a click, one segment at a time, until it reached full extension (in the interests of decorum, Children, I shall refrain from naming its actual reach in centimeters); then, with a sudden, blindingly pleasurable release, it would snap back to untensed size. In so doing, it pumped its newly manufactured chemicals directly into his inferior vena cava. Each injection brought first a blaze of heat in his face and a seizure of strangely agreeable apprehension, followed by a distinct chemical taste in the back of his mouth. His entire metabolism, or what remained of it, underwent an explosive excitation; his breath heaved, the body-furnace seemmed to scald the inner side of his skin, and amoebas of color swarmed before his vision-screens. The back of his brain convulsed with a searing spasm from which spread a rapturously numbing wave. His heart device churned. All weight left him and his body seemed to merge diffusely with the porcelain Throne to which his leg-parts clenched. Chang Ping giggled to him and his Mandible locked onto her face-plate; he urgently pried loose the latch of her torso-shell and in one heedless sweep cast it away. Beneath it glittered the living machinery that was her; her air intake hole wheezed with the gasps of purest Love. (Prætorius reactivated his left arm, and it flailed impudently as the Rod accelerated.) The room, the universe throbbed. The spectrum scorched his vision. The world quickened and flew by him; he was all of it and it loved him; laughter rang through him and it was Chang Ping, and she was thrusting herself against him; the ringing of her metal against his was the laughter.

No! The laughter was MWOWM! It saw...

No! The laughter was Chang Ping! She wanted him to gaze upon her ankle! She had always wanted him to gaze upon her ankle! She wanted to put her ankle against his mouth! His real mouth! Her perfect, real left ankle! (Or was it the right ankle?)

With each new wringing, the Rod strained to full reach, then slammed back, clanging like a hammer against its base, always injecting more serum. Faster and faster it went, until Prætorius let go with both hands—it had achieved its own momentum and was now jackhammering in and out with blurring rapidity.

Beneath her flawless golden shin-plate he was stroking The Ankle with his hand. She brought her leg part closer to his head, and he slid down to grip the Foot! The Pillar! Of the very Temple!

(With the recklessness of passion he switched to the dangerous but wonderfully painful metal left hand. It was ruining his new Sheath. It hurt. It was perfect!)

Chang Ping clutched at him; she was reaching for his ankle now; she would discover his secret! He was less metal than she! She would be horrified—disgusted! Ha-ha!

(The Rod suddenly leapt away from him, much farther than he had ever imagined the telescoping sections would allow. It swung out from him in wide arcs, knocking pictures and appliances off the shelves of the Throneroom! Its violent retractions slammed his whole body against the back of the Throne before it sprang out again to strike other fixtures in the room.)

He seized the foot and ripped away the plates surrounding The Ankle! She screamed in fear and ecstacy! THE ANKLE! THE ANKLE! IMBEDDED IN STEEL! He tore off his own face-plate, revealing the empty-socketed sheet of pure scar tissue that was his face, and gazed one last time at the tiny varicose veins that discolored the Ankle... and he lowered his real face and mouthed the real Ankle...

The Rod constricted to only about one foot in length and began the last series of rapid-fire contractions. It sounded like a machine gun; Prætorius' head was thrown back, and he was... beyond....

The tumultuous noises and terrors and inexpressible joys subsided; a great wave withdrew, and he felt himself dropped swiftly back; the room returned. He sat. Valves reopened. His breath returned in long drawing gasps, the overworked 'lungs' laboring for control of themselves. He lowered his head to his chest and waved a mental goodbye to his beloved Chang Ping. He eased open his video-tube eyes: the sight before them, looking down at his lap, made him wince with the gladness that his eyes, at least, were not MWOWM's. She could not see quite what he saw. (He must stop thinking of it that way! It wasn't his mother!) He sat... His left arm loosened its grip and dropped gratefully to his side, apparently freed from its bondage to The Act. Tomorrow, he thought, he would install a new Rod and hand. His breathing slowed further. The stimulants seeped away into his tissues. He sat. His mind was blank and he felt, at last, ready for sleep. Then he became, forever, totally blind.

No medical team on the planet, not even MWOWM itself, was ever able to restore the connection between his brain and his eye tubes.

Children, this history is written not only in The Skor, but is even accessible on The Tapes. Due, however, to its embarrassing nature, I do not recommend your 'Exping' them until you are older. Your knowledge of ancient psychology will not, in this case at least, be enhanced by suffering through the actual sensations.

Take heed, Children. Dismissed.

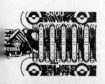

Jake Rabinowitz teaches and studies Classics at Miskatonic University. He has produced "supersoul honking blues" translations of Catullus and parts of the Bible, and edits two superb zines, THE MOORISH SCIENCE MONITOR and DER GOLEM. Despite his extreme youth he participated in the Beatnik and Hippie literary eras, and his SF epic has its roots in wild boho youthful excess tempered by Classical coolth and Hebraic fervor (he is a follower of Sabbatai Sevi, the "false messiah").

Louie, Louie
Jacob Rabinowitz

Human life is a series of explosions, propelling heroes from scene to scene. Contexts dissolve and transmute as each narrative structure is annihilated by its own ever-amplifying content: appearance falling away before "reality."

Only here reality is understood as Power. Abstractly considered, this means heat and noise. Ethically, it amounts to rape and plunder.

I.

Louie jumped up naked; his calves were thickening and bands of muscle went up his legs to wrap around his thighs.

Sprouting hair raced from his armpits down his sides. A furry envelope encased his swelling genitals.

Shoulders bulged, veins stood out along his hardening arms. Stomach firmed with ridges, chest rose. A stiff mane crested from his

357

head and ran down his back.

Face lengthened, nose pulling out into a muzzle. A brush of tail shot out the base of his spine to rise, nodding jauntily, above the hard spheres of his ass.

A wolf-like man, he scampered down the fire-escape.

II.

Across the street, a girl—call her Candy—whom Louie'd been watching through his window for an hour.

In the bath she soapily sprawled, cooing, sending gentle eddies to lap against her snatch with a light, careless hand.

She lay there, stroking the sodden hair of her mound, running her hands down her thighs, then back up along her sides to her breasts, pausing there to circle the nipples with her thumbs—again, again, until she's satisfied: and she never is.

The very walls looked at her with love, beading with sweat.

III.

There was a whining and a scratching at the door. In a towel she went to see. In the dark hall Louie's eyes lit up like headlights.

Blinded by the glare, she dropped the towel and backed against the wall. Louie pulled forward, stopping with a screech an inch away.

A cold muzzle touched Candy's trembling breast. Dripping hot saliva, his tongue unrolled to the floor. A long pink shaft swayed before him like a fleshy metronome.

Holding her by the arms, he stooped for a second; as he stood his heavy length went in. He felt the coarse hair then the tight kiss of the heated walls locked around him.

Embedded in her flesh, he brought his bulk to bear upon the squirming girl imprisoned by his limbs.

He held her arms above her head with one hand, the other turned the face of the spitted child and made her terrified eyes reply to his brilliant red ones. She shat herself in fear—which only excited him more.

Three throbs and Louie stilled. He stood by her, naked and dazed, a slightly androgynous youth, holding his bloodstained dick in his hand, consulting it like a pocketwatch.

The bruised girl fell to her knees. Eyes like slits, with heavy lips, she kissed his hand. He batted her face away.

IV.

Candy sat on her ass, legs sticking out, bitterly slapping the floor before her with her palms. She had sure been fucked.

The god of the apartment, who had always loved her, took pity on her pain and fury. He lifted her up and cast her on the bed— she fell upon it like a shadow.

A weightless shadow, she arose and went gliding along the wall to the window, sliding into the glass like a letter into an envelope. The god ran his tongue along the edge of the pane, sealing her in.

Now a Fenetriad, a window spirit, forever young she appears in windows, a girl just out of the shower, who stands with her ass facing you and bends over, reaching behind with a great soft towel to blot dry her ass and the rounded swell of her cunt flickering with blond fire. Then she stands up, contracting her ass-cheeks to form vertical smirks.

Men who observe her from across the street lean out further and further, until they fall to their fate, kissing the street in an unrecognisable smash of horrible slop.

V.

Meanwhile, Louie took her dress from the chair. It fit perfectly. Then stockings, shoes, garters.

He stopped for a moment at the window, struck by the dreary splendor of the view. The city was a grey-black congeries of scattered slabs and monoliths, picked out with random squares of light.

The distant streets outstretched in glintering grid, pulsing feebly with the starry concourse of cars.

The whole was silent and the clouds above flared with a ruddy glow.

VI.

The stars spiralled endlessly down. When he reached the street the city had begun to surface from beneath receding shadows, standing dark and tall against a brilliant purple sky about to whiten into day.

First shouts and clangs of early work.

The moon, a frosty ball, slid out of sight.

At the doorway stood the Dawn, black hair floating smokily in the mist around her young and naked form. Her pubic hair shone with dew.

She raised a hand in greeting and smiled, a little mockingly. Louie increased his pace to a clatter of high heels.

VII.

The clatter rose as he stumbled on.

His shoes were stretching flatly forth before and behind, curling up slightly at the tips. Like bracelets, leather thongs hung from his wrists, ski-poles depending from them.

A girl in a skin-tight black racing suit, a horned helmet and wings tore by down what was now a slope.

Louie lowered his goggles and ignited the jets on the back of his skis.

He powered down the mountain in pursuit, weaving his way

among dark pines weighted with white, across glaring open slope, twisting, leaning into turns so far his elbow grazed the mountainside and gigantic plumes of powder shot up in his wake, burying entire school groups.

He soared off hillocks, landing back on course with a *thump*! He was almost at the ski-nymph's side—

She spread her wings. With a few vehement downward strokes she was aloft, heavily hovering. Louie skidded to a halt and stood there for a long time looking...

Her waving legs and black-clad ass were brilliantly defined against the alpine atmosphere. It was like a slick photograph.

VIII.

It was a slick photograph.

Louie was about to turn the page when a voice boomed:

"Hey mister, you gonna *pay* for that magazine?"

Louie got on line by the register. He flipped to the ski-nymph. The effect was not more immediate than powerful. His trousers burst.

He staggered from the store, trying to hold up his swollen dick, falling forward in the attempt.

The thing increased. He straddled, it seemed, a submarine.

Joyfully spread-eagled atop, he embraced his blimplike genitalia which now began to rise, bumping gently into buildings as he lifted free of the street.

Perched like a fly on the end of a zeppelin, he scanned the sky for the nymph.

Hours later, he landed atop an apartment building.

Slinging his diminishing dick over his shoulder like a warm and pleasant duffle-bag, he went in.

Loud music on the top floor. A party. Girls, betitted creatures! Speechless, he wandered among them.

"Put that thing away, it's rude."

A little hurt, Louie complied, tucking his member out of sight. Then, ruefully:

"I want to go home."

He didn't know anybody there. The air was hot, the people crowded, dancers stamping in their midst. Louie, leaving, glimpsed a distant boy, about fifteen, with upturned nose and brown bangs falling over round bright eyes. Claude—the stable boy.

IX.

After school Claude has a job at the stables, pushing a shovel down the rows of stalls. All around him tails go up and clumps of shit smack damply down on floors of stone worn smooth.

In the ring, lessons are held for freckled, pig-tailed twelve year olds with wee initial tits and tight riding pants, horses between their legs.

Sometimes Claude stares at them in lustful wonder. Then the foreman roars. He recovers his shovel and lurches back to work.

Flies are buzzing into his face. The shit comes down in brown cascades, everywhere laughlike whinnies are raised and horse-farts trumpet through the place with massive hindquarters' force.

Then the Love god rides in on the grey stable cat.

At his entry coupling flies fall to the floor in buzzing clusters, horses kick their stalls, even the stacked up saddles jog together in inanimate copulation.

Bending over to buckle a girth, Claude confronts a tremendous equine erection, gleaming fat, long and wet. Just then the Love god spies the pretty boy and shoots a burning arrow up his ass.

The groom, a lanky blond youth with a horselike face, ambles in.

The air is heavy. Dust rises in a slanting sunbean. Their vision meets.

A tickling thrill draws Claude's eyes to his shoulder, where the other's hand is. They lean together, cupping each other's cocks through the denim. With difficulty Claude's fingers negotiate the belt—

These things happen.

X.

Anyway, Claude smiled at Louie. Louie felt his sanity melting. He walked mechanically towards the boy.

How long the room was! It receded behind him like a corridor. The music muffled out of earshot, the light faded behind him, he felt his way down a dark hall.

At last, ahead, a door ajar. Inside, a light, where the boy sat on the edge of a bed. A teddy bear leaned against the pillow. A comic book lay open on the floor.

Louie leaned down and smelled Claude's hair—the faint, irritating boy-smell sent a tingling through the back of his neck.

They stripped, stood naked, Claude's soft cheek on Louie's chest. Louie licked Claude's neck and gently, surely, pushed him down to his knees. Claude yawned, trying to put Louie's sex in his mouth.

The boy's delicate pale hands spanned the width of Louie's gross crank.

XI.

Louie lifted him, laid him on the bed, running his hands over the smooth soft thin body. The boy was on his back, pushing excited shallow breath as he heard the smacking sound of Louie greasing his dick.

A cold slick finger at Claude's asshole; he turned his head to one side and licked his upper lip, arms back, palms up in surrender.

Claude's legs were pushed up until his knees were about his ears. Louie gently rammed, kissing his way up that hairless chest as the elastic opening yielded around the bulbous head.

Now the whole cock slid into intestinal heat.

Louie gnawed the neck of the one who struggled under him, gasping out sweet child breath. Clamping tight the boy, he came then inside him he held him, he had him. In his hand the boy's cock restiffened through its rigid length to shoot a sparkling arc hot splattering him under his own chin.

Slowly they lapped each other's lips.

XII.

They lay, wetness cool on genitals, sprawled, each hearing other's breath against weird luxurious silence.

Louie's cock basked on his thigh. The boy put his head on Louie's shoulder, sated, closed his eyes.

Through the open window they heard the barking and response of dog to dog across the blocks.

XIII.

Monday morning, 6:00.
Claude lay in bed, pretending to sleep,
watching Louie dress to leave.

Dawnlight. He shook his red curls from his eyes,
pulled the levis up over his thighs,
tucked in the T-shirt, buckling his belt
above the full crotch.

Quietly the boy took a bathrobe,
followed down the hall,
went out and stared after Louie up the street.

As the door slowly closed behind him,
something fell into place beside him
as he stood there on the outside
and he noticed his bare feet were cold.

We've always wondered about the quote from M. Moorcock which appears as a puff on certain Barrington J. Bayley books: "the best SF writer of his generation." Which generation?

With all due respect to Moorcock (who is one of the Major Influences on this anthology) we don't know or care if Bayley is 20 or 120 — we simply consider him a master. Why then is he not as famous as Moorcock himself, or Chris Priest, or Ian Watson, or Ballard, or any of the NEW WORLDS crowd? A master, yes — but a hidden master.

His recent works, such as THE ROD OF LIGHT or THE ZEN GUN, are amazing pyrotechnic displays of invention and wit, worthy of a P. K. Dick but warmer, less alienated and dualistic. In fact, since Dick wrote a book called THE ZAP GUN, a comparison seems in order. Both writers use a quick loose hallucinatory style, like free jazz improvisation. Both use themes and images from mysticism and comparative religion. Both are endlessly inventive, tossing off ideas on every page that lesser authors would have hoarded and bloated into trilogies. Both are funny.

"Cling To The Curvature!" highlights the differences between Bayley and Dick. If you took seriously a book like UBIK or VALIS, you would tend to become very depressed about living here and now, in the body, in the material world. The same holds true for many of the Cyberpunks (all of them influenced by Dick): they're brilliant writers, but... a bit depressing. Now, Bayley is no two-dimensional happyface optimist. But if you take seriously the premises of 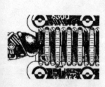 *THE ZEN GUN or "Curvature!", you may find yourself refreshed, inspired, at ease with the flesh, amazed at the world's weirdness but erotically attracted to it rather than disgusted and repelled.*

Cling to the Curvature!
Barrington J. Bayley

Seated upon his lemon-yellow throne, wearing his saffron robe of cool silk, the High Priest of the Temple of Priapus spoke to his adept.

"Tell me, then, what took place during the voyage of our starship *Lingam.*"

Hearing these words, the adept turned his blind face to the daylight that entered the throne room, and sent his telemental faculty lancing beyond the travertine walls of the building; beyond the breezy atmosphere; beyond countless suns; until he encountered the traces left upon the void by the Great Expedition. Thuswise was he able to procure the tale which he now began to relate...

Gigantic and magnificent, the *Lingam* moved through the geodesic maze that comprised the steric medium. Its form was that of a distended phallus, the shaft sheathed with synthetic diamond, the glans cased in glowing ruby. As it moved, the stupendous ship vibrated ever so slightly, drawing motive power from the void itself. Within its shining skin, the pleasant apartments, the scented caves, the temples, the ateliers, the perfumed gardens, the facilities for every erotic delight, were innumerable. A urethral tube ran the length of the vessel, emerging at the tip of the glans. Through it, star sightings were taken for the purpose of navigation through the uncharted regions. Many were the pauses, the deliberating conferences in the observation chamber, the tentative changes in direction which were accomplished in little jerks. Eventually the penis-ship would lunge forward once more, endlessly seeking its goal.

Like the book scorpion, which deposits its sperm in a chalice and offers it to the female, Reader was masturbating into a silver goblet. His male organ, vibrant with youth and strength, was hard as hot stone, the glans swollen and bursting with blood, and it responded magnificently to his pliant fingers. He could feel the curvature in his consciousness, and he allowed his face to show exaltation as the sensation passed all bounds and semen jetted in long, powerful spurts, exhaling a heady aroma into the atmosphere.

He had half-filled the goblet. Sighing, Reader reached to the siphon on the nearby low table. He splashed a stream of cooling, frothy liquid into the silver receptacle, thinning and aerating the rich semen, sweetening its flavour. Her lustrous black skin glowed in the light as Epifania, kneeling opposite him, accepted the cup, raising it to her sullen, wine-red lips to drink deep.

She smiled. "Delicious!"

Still the curvature was singing in his head, and in hers too. When Epifania came to her feet her shaven slit glistened. Reader's phallus remained a rigid ramrod, the scrotum tight and neat. He could sense the geodesics all around them, causing them to gravitate towards one another, to rotate about a common centre, and he gazed upon her face, drinking in the smooth curves, the purple pupils of her wide eyes. He knew it as a sign of high curvature when the face came to seem as erotic as the erogenous zones. Draining the last drops from the chalice, Epifania stepped closer, replacing it on the table, taking his phallus in her free hand, pressing down the skin, moving it experimentally like a joystick so that it throbbed with yearning, and in response he shyly touched her vulva, experiencing again its almost muscular firmness.

A warm breeze played over Reader's body as he rose from his chair. A silent message passed between them. Epifania's fingers left his phallus as she turned, and with a sense of controlled balletic frenzy they moved to the curtains in loping steps, slow motion in the low floor gravity, the muscles of her back and buttocks flexing and relaxing. Stepping through the gauzy drapes coloured peach and orange, they came to the trapeze room.

On the scale of erotic conation Reader registered 180, against a planetary average of 100. No one aboard the *Lingam* registered below 150; Epifania's ECR was a startling 240. Confidently she climbed the steps to her trapeze, waiting for Reader to take his place.

They had practised this to perfection. Against the red plush of the egg-shaped chamber's walls, Epifania's black satin skin stood out like a dark gemstone. Seizing the trapeze bar, she lifted herself. Abductor muscles

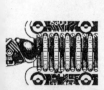

brought her legs apart; and she began to swing.

The space between them was not great. Reader seemed still within the presence of Epifania's large and lithe body as, timing his swings with hers, he launched himself from his platform. The redness of her sensitive tissues, punctuating her dark frame, was accentuated by the carmine background against which they both moved. He was aware of her wine-coloured nipples, stiff as little bullets, of her dark-ruby mouth — and the slit of her vulva was a red gash of promise, displayed between the adductor muscles that stood out on the insides of her spread thighs. This was the target on which he concentrated. After the fourth swing, they left the bars together. In standard Earth-1 gravity the manoeuvre would scarcely have been possible, but here their twin ballistic arcs were leisurely, calculated, consummately skilled, graceful to behold. The red-knobbed phallus moved on its geodesic course as if to its destiny, the intersection foreordained. And it was no more than a few millimetres off-course when it met the vaginal entrance, sliding into the slippery passage by mutual momentum.

Their loins butted together with a faint slap. By design, the collision carried them into a no-gravity lacuna in the centre of the chamber. Reader held himself back from the explosive orgasm that mere contact with Epifania's flesh could induce. Now she took command, ordering him to stretch himself out and stiffen. Drawing up her knees, bringing them together, she used her feet and hands to set him spinning, penis turning within her, while by reaction she counter-rotated, using her internal muscles to squeeze and massage. He observed her turning face, gauging the progress of her sensations, as she speeded up the rotation until the carmine chamber whirled. His orgasm, when he allowed it, engulfed the entire length of the shaft, running up and down it like an electric discharge, and he seemed to hear the long roar of semen rushing through the urethra and into her cervix. The convulsion, a negative flashbulb engulfing everything in black light, sucked awareness away from his outward senses. He lost all consciousness of the chamber and was left experiencing only the curvature of inner space. When, a spell later, he returned to the sensible world, Epifania had expertly halted their spinning. She levered herself off his phallus. They drifted close to one another, irregularly shaped moonlets tied into related orbits. She arced; her hands reached out, preparatory to fondling him inch by inch.

Then the dreadful thing happened. The inner excitement which had pervaded his being ever since he could remember, faded like a candle blown out in the wind. The curvature straightened, became flat and featureless.

A cry came from Epifania. She grabbed him, pulling them both out of the lacuna, at which they drifted gently to the floor.

He stared with horror at the lumpy, uninteresting mass of flesh and bone that was her body. He saw the distaste with which she in turn regarded him. How prosaic and joyless everything looked, how drab the colours, how depressing and monotonous the very fact of existence. And not only that. The constant background hum that had filled the *Lingam* since take-off was gone, replaced by an awful silence. The ship's engines were dead.

"*Kami* help us!" Reader exclaimed hoarsely. "We are in flat space!"

He well remembered the briefings he attended during the selection period, before boarding the *Lingam*.

Late one balmy afternoon, on a headland overlooking the Indian Ocean, a matronly female with a somewhat mature but fairly well-preserved body, clad only in a chiffon scarf which passed over her right shoulder, across her breasts, and diagonally across her belly to hang from her left hip, cast kind glances upon them. "This is hard for us to believe," she had said, "but there was a time when people sought fulfilment by denying the physical passions and devoting all their energy to abstract thought. How unnatural, you would say! And it is true that untold pathologies resulted. Happily, the age of isolated reason, which tried to place human consciousness in a kind of machine-like limbo, is over. We now know very well that the key to human happiness, as well as to the release of the creative impulse, lies in the direction of concupiscence. Without full satiation of the senses, we are pathetic objects!"

The mellow sunlight, angling through the pavilion, made the varied flesh tones of the young people glow. The matron explained the scientific basis of today's world religion. "Twentieth century physics described the metrical continuum, that is to say space, by means of ten coefficients of curvature. Where matter is present these coefficients have non-zero values, and the result is the phenomenon of gravitation.

"What a creative force gravitation is! It has produced every world that exists — the galaxies, the stars, the planets and moons. Today we know that there are in fact twenty coefficients of curvature, ten responding to the presence of matter and ten that are even more fundamental. These ten are unconnected with the presence of matter. They formed the primordial shape of the world, and vary throughout space according to no known principle, producing effects far more remarkable than mere gravitation. We experience them in our inner space, or consciousness, as libido, or desire, or in other words as sex energy. The spatial curvature, or sex energy, is what produced life on Earth, as it produces life elsewhere. Wherever living creatures strive to exist and enjoy themselves, this primordial power is at work. What is it about another person that evokes such maddening delight and desire in us? As a phenomenon it seems so completely separated from the mundane world of space and atoms, but actually it is not. The attraction is produced by spatial curvature, and gravitational attraction is but a pale shadow of it. And it is the force behind evolution — for sexuality, remember, is primarily concerned with evolution, rather than with simple reproduction.

"As the solar system moves through galactic space, it encounters regions of higher and lower curvature. We know this, because it is obvious that human sexuality has been at a much higher pitch at certain periods in the past, when religions of sexuality flourished as now. Is it not told in the *Brahmavaivarta Purana* how Krishna, while engaging in his delirious orgy with Radha, multiplied his person and in a single night enjoyed the bodies of nine hundred thousand milkmaids, creating such a degree of rapture that the gods came to watch, and their wives the goddesses, after fainting again and again at the sight, descended to Earth as little girls so that they also might experience such delight? This story conveys, albeit mythically, the sort of life that might be available in a region of very high curvature."

The matronly woman's face became serious, and sad. "But now the opposite is about to happen," she told them. "Earth is shortly to enter a region where the ten extra coefficients have much lower values than we are used to. How is one to describe the deathliness that will come upon us? Libido will flee. People will become joyless, uncreative, their thoughts flat, stale and repetitious, their feelings low, their perceptions grey. They will mate only from a sense of duty, or else resort to artificial methods of procreation!

"A change in the structure of the physical world cannot be countered. No genetic predisposition, no hormonal recipe, no degree of artificial stimulation, can remedy a lack of curvature in the steric continuum, on which our psychic vigour depends. There is only one answer: mankind must relocate itself. Somewhere, in a place where the coefficients have high values, and the life force is therefore strong, there must be a suitable Earth-type planet. Your task is to find it."

In its journeying the *Lingam* had cruised by all the splendours of the visible universe. From the viewing galleries, the voyagers had been witness to exploding suns, had gazed awed upon dazzling galactic cores, and had been entranced by the glowing traceries that were dust veils.

Confining their attention within the exploring shaft, they had found equal enchantment in the pursuit of erotic perceptions. All that was now gone. Shrilly, from predatory-looking lips, Epifania uttered tones of distress.

"What shall we do?"

She followed him through the drapes that covered the exits. They were in a long, plush-lined concourse, along which people, lumpy human animals, every organ of their bodies a product of utility and without any appeal, were moving, some running, in dismay and disorder. Nowhere was a single erection evident. Floppy breasts, dangling penises, were awkward appendages, relics of a biological history which no longer had any interest.

Just then, the dead silence which had replaced the vibrant murmur of the *Lingam's* sex-energy motors was filled with a soft but deep-throated roar. The ship's atomic reserve engines had come on.

"*The fools!*"

Reader looked round when he heard the loud baritone voice. It came from a swarthy man with a pointed black beard and glittering eyes who stood with his back to a wall.

"We are going to fall off the edge of the world!" he cried out.

A crowd of people began to gather. "When did you last look outside?" the speaker challenged them. "You will find there is no longer anything to see! We are far from any galaxy. If I am any judge, we have gone beyond the visible universe! So how are we to find our promised new planet?"

"Then where are we going?" shrieked a copper-skinned girl.

A boyish-bodied youth answered her. "It is inevitable that there will be flat regions," he said reasonably. "That is what the atomic engines are for — to get us out of them."

"If the ship had been guided properly then the atomic engines would never be needed," the black-bearded man countered. "Besides, did you feel us turn round before they were activated? No, we have not turned round! We are still heading out, further into the dead space that perhaps stretches forever! When the atomic fuel runs out we shan't be able to get back!"

"We'll have to live like this for the rest of our lives?"

The thought brought an 'ooohh' of fear from all present. The dark man held up his hand. "Our mission has been betrayed. The captain has failed us. There is only one thing to be done. We must take command before it is too late!"

"Mutiny!" Epifania breathed.

Reader edged away, nudging her to come with him. He walked up the concourse, slowly and lost in thought. A curious relaxation had come over him, and he sensed over Epifania too. With the vanishing of the sex tensors, the compelling tensions that had formerly ruled the mind had gone. Memories of previous life — the frantic mass orgies, the delectable private sessions, the unending search for pleasure — were viewed with disdain. Sex energy now seemed, not the raging primal force the physicists claimed it to be, but no more than a by-product of the need to reproduce: a crude, undignified urge.

Astonishing how quickly one's viewpoint could change! It was in a bland, unexcitable state of consciousness, but an unexpectedly restful one, that Reader reached the end of the concourse.

"Where are you going?" asked Epifania.

"To ask the Captain what is happening."

"But how will you get there?"

The *Lingam* was commanded from within the glans. There dwelt Captain Theander and the navigation staff, guided by sightings taken from the observation chamber near the rear of the ship. Ordinary voyagers, who lived in the main shaft, were not permitted to enter there.

"There must be a way," Reader said. They were about a mile from the glans, or head of the vessel. He would walk there, Epifania accompanying him if she wished, and see what he could do.

Out of the concourse, they entered a series of fragrant arbours. Trellis-climbing flowers, genetically designed, put stimulating perfumes into the air — though their aphrodisiac properties were useless now. Similarly they passed by the many little bowers where pairs sat listlessly, edging away from one another.

Suddenly their way was blocked. The mutiny was taking shape. In a fountained park to which the arbours gave access, a battle was in progress between those loyal to the captain and those who wished to turn the ship back, to resume its proper mission, or even to return to Earth. Unused to any violence except the mock violence of love play, the combatants tussled feebly with one another, slapped and pushed as the loyalists tried to stop progress towards the glans. The subdued grunts and cries reminded Reader of an orgy. Indeed, it was remarkable that so much physical contact could occur without erotic consequences.

The lights flickered. Things were going badly wrong. They went out altogether as Reader took Epifania by the arm and herded her down a garlanded passage-way. Emergency lights came on, throwing a pale glow over the scene that robbed it of all colour.

He wanted to stay out of the way; not get involved in any fighting. "It seems so strange..." Epifania said. "We've never had anything criminal on board before."

"There was one instance," Reader told her. "Someone refused sexual congress when asked. He was charged with immoral conduct."

He knew his way about here. They were entering a domestic quarter of quiet rooms, kitchens and lobbies, ghostly in the stored light of the glow bulbs. At first, there seemed to be no one about. Then, suddenly, they came to where a party of a dozen or so people sat on the floor around a portable emergency heater, as if around a camp fire. Wan faces turned to the newcomers, offering neither greeting nor rebuff. Those nearest shifted aside as, wordlessly, Reader and Epifania joined them.

After a while, the discussion that had been interrupted was resumed, and a small, white-haired man , older than most aboard the *Lingam,* glanced at the newcomers by way of introduction.

"For a few of us here," he said, "this is not our first voyage into space. We were among those who explored the home galaxy in smaller, lower powered vessels before the building of our magnificent *Lingam.* Many were the habitable planets we found but all, for one reason or another, were unsuitable for the relocation of our species. Join us in our reminiscences if you will. We found that the manifestations of the sexual life energy are indeed diverse, though there is an interesting tendency for the humanoid form to prevail, and some dwellers on far landscapes are barely distinguishable from our own race. Why, I well remember one world on which I sojourned..."

And so the oldster briefly related the tale which he called:

THE MILK OF HUMAN KINDNESS

I landed alone (he said) on grassy terrain with breathable air. The climate was sultry, though not unpleasantly so, the sun yellow and occasionally obscured by pink clouds. The grass had a yellow-orange tint. The landscape was broken up, without any high mountains that I could see, and dotted with trees whose long orange tresses, in place of leaves, swished in the warm breeze.

Orbital observations had revealed humanoid settlement, with small villages and many isolated dwellings, but no large towns. There was no sign of agriculture on any significant scale, but what might have been orchards were spotted. I walked half a day without encountering anyone (the rotation period was about thirty hours). Then, somewhat wearied, I paused to rest beneath the shade of one of the tresses-trees, and was startled and alarmed to see someone drop straight out of it at my feet.

It was a male of the local intelligent species. He seemed amused by my surprise and offered me one of two round fruits he had picked. Testing it first with my protein meter, I found it would not harm me, and so bit into it. It was succulent and of a delicious flavour. While I ate I listened to him chattering unintelligibly, and did my best to study him without appearing aggressive or ill-mannered.

Except for one detail, he was almost indistinguishable from our *homo sapiens sapiens* of the Caucasian type. His skin was a trifle pinker than most, and on his face was a bland, harmless-appearing expression that I guessed belonged to his stock rather than to his individuality, but otherwise — with the exception of the one detail — he would not have caused comment on any part of Earth.

Like ourselves he went naked, the climate obviating any need for clothing, and but for that the detail I have referred to would have passed unnoticed. This was that he had no nipples. I must say that I did not think this particularly significant at the time. At any rate he evidently took me for some travelling foreigner, for he soon understood that I could not follow his speech. His friendliness, however, was unabated. He persuaded me, by gesture and signs, to accept his hospitality and accompany him to his home, where he lived with his wife, a pleasant, plump woman, in a comfortable, roomy hut thatched with tree-tresses.

It transpired that his wife was pregnant and near her time. As soon as I saw her I realized that I had made a mistaken assumption about the inhabitants of this planet. Not only were they not as fully human as I had thought, they were not even, in the proper sense, mammalian.

The woman had no breasts. Her chest was like her husband's, smooth, flat and nippleless. This is a humanoid species whose young do not need suckling, I told myself. But again, I was wrong.

And so I stayed for several weeks with Uwhayie (for such was his name) and his wife Kerie, finding it an idyllic life, and learning a little of their language. We fed upon fruit and various other parts of native plants gathered from nearby. Trees were to some extent cultivated by planting seeds in the ground, though this was scarcely self-evident from the cast of the landscape.

My hosts proved a most affectionate couple, and continued to have sexual intercourse right up until the birth of their child, indulging themselves several times each day and night with scant regard for my presence, but with open enjoyment and many loving caresses. The eventual delivery presented no problems — he assisted her skilfully, the two of them seeming to know instinctively what to do, and the birth was accomplished with ease.

Throughout the rest of that day and the following night the wife rested, cuddling her baby. The next day, I was surprised to see her rise and go out, leaving the child in the care of its father. I waited for her to return, and began to feel concerned as to the feeding of the babe. But I need not have worried.

After a while the father took the baby, kissed it and cuddled it, and then lay it on the fur-covered floor of the hut and inserted his penis into its mouth. The infant began to suck vigorously. The penis did not stiffen as much as it had during sex play with Kerie, but a rapt look of pleasure came over Uwhayie's face. He sighed repeatedly, experiencing a series of orgasms as semen flowed from him to be greedily swallowed.

Was kindly Uwhayie crazed? Was I witnessing a sadly degenerate perversion practised in his wife's absence? Indeed no: the answer came to me in a flash. The male of Uwhayie's species did not merely impregnate: he played the suckling role as well. He nourished his child by producing large amounts of protein-rich semen, until it was weaned.

What was more, judging by Uwhayie's reaction, the sexual instinct extended almost as much to child-feeding as it did to intercourse itself. It was plainly necessary to undergo orgasm in order to release the sustaining flood. This, I realized immediately, added a new dimension to family life.

Shortly the babe was satisfied and fell asleep. Uwhayie laid it tenderly down, and having done so, he suddenly noticed my fascination. Taking his penis between his finger, he smiled his hospitable smile and spoke to me.

He was offering me the semen left by the child. What was I to do? Was this a piece of formal politeness one was expected to refuse? Or would refusal hurt and insult Uwhayie? Indeed, what cultural signal was I being given? As a xeno-anthropologist I judged that this was a time for objectivity, and I gauged that the latter interpretation was more likely. I smiled back, thanking him, and shifted closer.

His body temperature was several degrees higher than ours is, and the penis was searingly hot to my lips. I did not have to suck very long; his semen was copious, thick, and rich-tasting, and I found it unexpectedly satisfying after the vegetarian diet I had perforce been accepting. After one or two gulps I relaxed, lay back and dozed. Later Kerie returned with a basket of fruit and plant bulbs she had gathered for the three of us; and from then on, over the next few weeks, I came to know the family life of this variant of humanity, and to appreciate the superiority of its biological arrangement over our own.

Not only the suckling but most of the nursing of the offspring fell to the male, and he carried it out with passionate intensity, though the female, too, would frequently cuddle and caress the child she had borne. After feeding, Uwhayie would share the excess semen between myself and his wife, so that a warm, rewarding relationship grew up among the three of us.

Need I point out what well-balanced individuals are bound to result, when mother's milk is replaced by father's semen? The instincts we call 'maternal' are evenly distributed among both sexes, and consequently they are more equal in their relations, and more attached to one another, than we are. The male cannot sire a child and then ignore it or even abandon it and the mother: his desire to put sperm into his progeny is as urgent as his desire to copulate with the female. Neither can any other male easily substitute for him, since his sperm would be insufficient, the father's prolific production of it being triggered when he participates in his child's delivery.

The child, then, is assured of the love and close physical attention of both mother and father. It is even believed by these people — mistakenly, of course — that frequent intercourse is what nourishes the foetus growing in the womb. I venture to suggest that, barring accidents, there are no emotionally deprived individuals upon that happy planet.

There was a reflective silence after the oldster had finished speaking, until a well-proportioned young woman spoke up.

"Your tale of kindly, replenishing penises is uplifting, certainly," she said, "but that is not the universal image of the male phallus. It can also be aggressive, even threatening, as I discovered on my first voyage of exploration."

She then told of her horrifying adventure, which she called:

THE WERE-PENIS

It was a jungle planet (she began), a world whose tree cover extended anything up to a mile in height. The sun was F type, hot and bright, and above the monotonous green roof the atmosphere steamed like an oven. Yet beneath it, a cooler, colourful and variegated environment was to be found, with rivers, lakes, even plain-like meadows ceilinged with ribbed fronds, and orchids of every hue. Further, the shifting light, here dull, here radiant, here fierce with shafts of pure brilliance, created a wonderland of endless depth.

I landed with a party of five. Tethering our craft in an upper fork of one of the massive boles, we began to clamber down, seeking to see if the forest had a solid floor or if it was, as some theorised, a swamp of fallen and rotting leaves. Then misfortune struck us: the jungle was subject to sudden downpours of rain, creating what were in effect temporary vertical rivers, or stepped waterfalls, leaping from branch to branch, funnelled by enormous leaves. One of these caught us in its flood. We were washed helplessly away, battered and tumbled hither and thither, and I soon lost all consciousness.

When I recovered, I lay on the forest floor and my companions were nowhere to be seen. I had also lost all my equipment, including my emergency locator beacon. Can you imagine a more frightening situation? I called out, but received no reply other than the cries of bird-like creatures which I saw flitting about the cathedral-like vegetation — many of them as gorgeous-looking as the profuse orchids. I feared to shout any more in case I attracted the attention of a predator, and began exploring my surroundings, hoping to catch sight of some-one, or at least find my equipment.

This was probably not a good tactic, because I quickly became unable to find my way back to my starting point and wandered aimlessly. Then, after what seemed a long time, I came to a stream, its banks covered with pretty little purple flowers, and there on one bank, where the stream took a handy bend, a party of girls was having a picnic.

Yes, girls, though evidently primitives, and human in every respect, their skins pale, the cast of their faces no different from mine than, say, Caucasian from Chinese. Whether the people of that planet were in fact human I still do not know to this day — but you will see what I mean presently. They welcomed me artlessly, inviting me to their picnic, and displaying none of the xenophobia common to jungle people on Earth. I risked drinking clear water from the stream, but did not dare taste any of their nuts, fruit, and other strange forest foods, for of course I had lost my protein tester.

The girls were nearly naked but not entirely so, wearing very skimpy skirts around their hips. They seemed ashamed to show their private parts and were shocked to see mine on view, quickly fashioning a similar skirt out of creeper and flower petals. To please them I tied it round me and was trying to make them understand that I needed help to find my friends when for the second time that day tragedy struck.

A band of club-wielding men came charging suddenly out of the undergrowth. The picnicking girls were taken completely by surprise. Shrieking, urinating with fear, trying to scatter in all directions, they were nevertheless efficiently rounded up, myself among them, and we were all roped together for a long march through the jungle.

We had clearly been taken by marauders from another tribe. Our captors had that arrogant, unsympathetic warrior look, their faces painted to make them look fierce. Their raiment was creeper, wound round their waists and down to below the loins so that it looked somewhat like armour, but really it was used to carry their knives and axes in.

Any time a girl stumbled she would be given a bruise by being tapped with a club. What was to happen to us? Would we be raped, tortured or killed? Or only forcibly married or enslaved? Judging by the sobs and the open terror of the girls, I could only expect the worst.

After a long time we reached the warriors' village, a circle of crude huts in a clearing. What women there were there slunk away at our coming, taking their children with them, and we were left to the men, the young warriors who had captured us and their older relatives. From the air of jubilation, I guessed that the sport was about to begin.

Within the circle of huts a line of stakes had been set into the ground. To these we were each tied, in undignified postures, though with our mini-skirts intact, and I began to wonder if I had not unknowingly landed upon the planet Gor. But this done, the men all withdrew to the edge of the circle. A silence fell, till one of them put to his lips a shell, or horn, and blew a long, warbling note.

By this time daylight was fading and blazing torches had been lit around the village. Down the trail that led from the opening in the circle of huts, something came shuffling, and gradually became visible in the gloom. At the first glimpse of it, the girls began gagging and whimpering with fear.

It was a large animal of a most peculiar shape — the shape, in fact, of a gigantic white penis, shuffling along like a snail on its gross, flaccid scrotum. The penis was not erect, not distended, but limp, though at the same time smooth and plump, and it proceeded head down, as though blindly smelling the ground as it went.

But when it came into the circle it perked up, sensing female aroma, and the prepuce drew back to reveal a slimy red head, or glans, with a single orifice. Frantically it sniffed towards each girl in turn, swelling all the while until it became a rigid monster six foot or more in length, and thick in proportion! The stench of it! — Don't ask me to describe it! The girls wailed, struggled against their bonds, some fainting with horror. Then an incredible transformation took place. The base, or scrotum, began to swell, the penis shrinking contrariwise as it contributed its substance, and it also changed shape, rearing up so that in no time at all a man stood there, the penis now normal, still erect.

And what a handsome man! On another occasion I might have been delighted... not in these circumstances, however! This was a *were-penis*. And the village men were watching avidly, drooling in anticipation of their totem's antics.

That... *prick-animal* was by no means finished with its shape-changing. The body shrank as the penis grew again. It was keen to show off its versatility, and launched itself into a dizzying exhibition of size changes, ranging from a doll-like body perched at the back of an organ as large as the original penis-creature, to a body unusually tall and strong but with genitals that were minute and harmless-looking. Then it settled upon a median configuration such as one can see on some ancient amulets: a dwarfish figure sporting a phallus whose head reared above his own, and which was nearly as thick as his trunk. Greedily leering, he waddled forward, leaning back to counterbalance the weight, working on the towering organ with both hands, up and down in an action requiring the whole length of his arms. He cast his glittering gaze along the row of squirming girls, and perhaps because of my alien appearance, picked me out, standing before me and pointing the penis in my direction. The wanking motion became violent. Then the penis jerked several times as it expelled powerful jets, and I was covered from head to toe in odious-smelling spunk! I felt just like a fly trapped in treacle!

The narrator dropped her gaze, and a deep blush spread over her face and down to her breasts. "Forgive me if I do not attempt to describe the events of that long night. The humiliating perversions that I and the other girls were subjected to, the assaults by that many-sized prick, the agonising, impossible entries — oh, the memories!"

Briefly she buried her face in her hands. "Suffice it to say," she concluded presently, "that if I had not been rescued before dawn by colleagues from the orbiting starship, who had spent the night tracking me down by my body heat, then there is no doubt that I would have been fucked to death."

Another silence, commiserative this time, descended on the little gathering, broken only by vague sounds of uproar from outside the domestic quarter.

Hesitantly a slim young man with keen, earnest features spoke up. "I, too, have witnessed pathological male domination," he ventured, "which, I am glad to say, is alien to our own culture. Not, however, lurking in dark green jungles amid lush growths. This was a small, arid planet with a sparse food chain. The story I have to tell could well be called:

THE IMMORTAL MONOCULTURE

As I have said (he went on), the world we surveyed was poor in biological resources. There were no oceans, little free water, and vegetation grew only in scattered scrubby patches amid endless rolling sterile landscapes. Consequently animal life was adapted to extreme economy. Predators needed to feed only once every few years, for none of the larger species had populations of more than a few thousand. On the other hand they had very long life spans, the predators in particular, and therefore bred rarely.

An intelligent humanoid species stood at the top of the chain, and had evolved longevity to the point of actual physical immortality. Its birth rate, consequently, equalled the death rate from accident, disease, murder and execution, none of which were frequent. Understandably the sexual urge, though intense, also expressed itself only at long intervals, being apt to be triggered by the need to replace lost individuals rather than to provide a complete new generation.

Cataclysm then struck this meagre biosphere. A lethal disease appeared among the plant life, carried from patch to patch by increasingly desperate herbivores. In a matter of fifty local years the entire base of the food chain had disappeared. The herbivores perished from starvation quickly thereafter. And from then on, the carnivores took to hunting one another.

Species after species went extinct, eaten by the more successful predators, until finally only one was left: the most successful predator of all — man.

The tenacious and individualistic character of these humanoids then showed itself. The social organisation that had existed had by then collapsed. A solitary, cannibalistic way of life emerged, each former citizen seeing his fellows as a source of food. Men and women tracked one another, hunted one another, evaded one another. The world population halved at each feeding period. Everyone knew that eventually there would be only one individual left, and he aspired to be that individual, so as to live for as long as possible.

Over the centuries a change gradually came into the final minutes of a successful hunt. An involuntary sense of ritual began to pervade it, the victim recognising the superior strength of he (or she) who was about to eat him (or her), and almost submitting. In other words a nascent sexual element had entered. One person eating another was now the nearest thing to a procreative act left to this dying race, for by eating and being eaten, the species was continued.

Let me now take you forward in time to the situation as we found it. Only a few dozen individuals were left upon the globe, and their energies were all engaged upon trying to trap or ambush one another. For that reason they had all moved into the same geographical arc, balancing danger against the need to eat.

Our observations centred on one Argoth, a skillful and powerful male, who was engaged in hunting a female he had tracked, sighted, and now had trapped on a hilltop from which she could not escape. Eyeing her hungrily, he approached with knife in hand and she, weaponless, having lost her own knife in the scramble to flee, stared back. As he came near to the woman something stirred in him, and he sensed a corresponding feeling in her. The long chase was over. The act that would join them was about to be performed.

While he sharpened his knife on a piece of stone, preparing to kill and dismember her, she lay herself down on a flat rock, limbs spread, breasts rising and falling, watching him with hot eyes. Then she began to talk to him. She told him that she had long admired him. She had seen him several times from a distance, always managing till now to hide from him, and had even seen him make a kill. Most of the remaining survivors knew something of each other, had found their spoor or the remains of their meals, or had sighted or even hunted one another. But as their number dwindled, the struggle grew harder, the required toughness, endurance and fighting skill reaching a pitch. Though an experienced hunter, she had been certain that the time had come when she was outclassed, and that she could never eat again. And if she was to fall, she had wanted it to be to him.

Argoth dropped the stone he was using. His shadow fell across her. Then he threw himself on her and they copulated savagely, releasing a torrent of pent-up instinct. One could only call his lovemaking sadistic: he pummelled her as painfully as he could; and as for her, she achieved an ecstasy of total submission.

At this point a division of opinion occurred among we who were watching through our atmospheric probe. All that was needed to return these people to social life and civilisation, some argued, was that they be provided with food. This faction had even synthesized a sample of meat containing all the correct proteins and trace elements — though it could hardly have been imagined that we could provision the planet in perpetuity! Others contended that the damage done to the psyches of these luckless inhabitants over the past centuries was too deep, and that they could never recover normalcy.

The 'love affair' between Argoth and his prey seemed a good instance on which to test the dispute. Wishing to cement this bond, the optimists among us floated down the slab of meat to the tableau on the hilltop, while a telementalist was summoned to read the reactions of Argoth and his hoped-for mate-to-be.

Sexually sated after his session of lovemaking, Argoth was about to continue to his cannibalistic feast when the parcel descended from the sky and plumped down near him. Examining it, he was astonished to find that it contained edible flesh.

We watched him ponder. Then he began to exult. This was a signal from the gods assuring him of immortality! He knew now that *he* would prove the strongest of all hunters, and become the last remaining member of his race! For when he had devoured the others, the gods would send down food to perpetuate his existence!

Through him alone the race would survive!

The conviction seemed to renew his vigour. He turned again to the woman who was still spreadeagled upon the rock. He fondled her roughly, pinching her tender parts. They gazed deliriously into each others' eyes, as he picked up the knife and plunged it into her quivering heart.

We then departed from that sad scene.

Among those listening was a woman of perhaps forty years, her body skinny like a tomboy's and restless, so that she shifted frequently as if in agitation. Her face was weatherbeaten but expressive, filled with a sort of passionate anxiety. Now she spoke, her speech rapid and nervous.

"I have not done any space exploring till now," she said, "so I have not had any of these marvellous adventures. But I can tell you an incredible secret! Spatial curvature is not the reason for our sexual liberation! That theory is wrong!"

Everyone looked at her astounded. "Wrong?" echoed the oldster. "How can you say that? It is scientific fact!"

She shook her head. "What is fact? Something that a genius says? Geniuses don't have to be right. Was Aristotle right when he said motion requires sustained force? Was Newton right when he spoke of absolute space? Was Einstein right when he said the universe is finite? No, they were all wrong. So need Gridban have been right when he said there are ten coefficients of curvature that generate what we call sexual energy? Something else happened that we have all forgotten, and I know what it is."

And so she began a somewhat rambling narration which might well be entitled:

SPIDER RAPISTS FROM THE STARS

There exists in the universe (she said) a secret race of wonderful beings. To look at they are a bit like giant spiders. But the special thing about them is their sexual nature. They are able to copulate, after their fashion, with any other intelligent species of any planet! This isn't a question of bestiality or miscegenation, by the way, it's genuine sexual intercourse, because the spiders are able to mix their genes with any other gene-set, and what's more, every time they know exactly what genes to blend in.

The mission of the Sex Spiders is to make all sentient creatures happy, which they do by fucking them, if I may put it that way. Male or female, young or old, it doesn't matter! And there's no escaping it, either. They absolutely won't take no for an answer! Never mind, because no matter how much someone resists, once he's been done he's changed forever, together with his progeny for all generations! Libido blocks melt away. Repressed feelings blossom like flowers in the spring.

Well, it was about a hundred years ago that the spiders invaded Earth.

What a furor! Do you know what Earth was like in those days? It was a completely horrible society, gripped with a fear of sex. Acts of all kinds were forbidden. Sex with a young person, sex with someone of one's own gender, sex with someone of different ancestry from oneself, sex with someone having a contracted partner, which they called 'marriage', sex with anyone at all, even masturbating by oneself, as well as producing stimulating artistic material, all these were classed as crimes somewhere or other, for which one could be imprisoned. flogged, or even put to death. The bullying religions, the maniac lawmakers, the frustrated old people who always tried to stop the young from enjoying themselves, ganged up as best they could but it was no use, because the spiders were so technically and morally superior. "GOD IS FUCK!" they cried out, in their great booming voices as they roamed over the landscape, knocking over law courts and church steeples, "GOD IS FUCK!" As I said, there was no escape for anybody. Oh, you should have seen the priests and pastors running in panic, then going rigid with horror as the big hairy bodies descended on them, until finally they were overcome by the deliciousness of it!

Well, that's how it was, and we have everything to thank the spiders for. But for them, we would be living the same miserable lives as our ancestors, and our children. too, would have nothing to look forward to but a hell of blocked and thwarted desire, having no fun at all!

The narrator finished her tale, gave a satisfied sigh and gazed at the floor. Around her, people stirred uncertainly. "Why don't we already know this?" the oldster who had begun the symposium asked gently. "An event on such a scale could hardly have been hushed up, even if it were to be kept out of the history books."

"Oh, the spiders inserted a forgetting gene when they modified our chromosomes, so nobody remembered they had been on Earth," the storyteller explained. "That's how they stay secret. They even included a gene to make us think of spiders as repulsive. Isn't that strange?"

"Then how do you remember it?" someone else asked. "Oh, it just came to me as I was sitting here," she said.

The puzzling tale seemed to take the steam out of discussion, and no more contributions were offered. People began drifting away to sleeping rooms, for now the *Lingam's* clock registered night time.

Eventually Reader found himself left alone with Epifania. He looked at her, still trying to ignore his revulsion for her animal-like female smells.

"Listen." he said, "there's so something I should have thought of before. There *is* a way into the glans, one that not many people know about. A servicing tech showed it to me once. Do you want to come with me?"

She nodded and they rose together, recrossed the arbours and made for the underside of the ship. Few people were about; the rebellion, they could tell from the distant noises, had moved further forward, towards the head. Reader doubted if it would be able to break through. The navigation staff had all the resources of the huge starship at its disposal, including emergency bulkheads.

With luck, though, no one would have thought of the indirect ways of access known to the robot crew. Reader lifted a trapdoor and they descended to a small gallery in which was a heavy, sealed door with a winch lock.

"This leads to the urethra," he told Epifania. "There's a similar door in the glans."

She stared at it. "Robots might be able to go through there," she said, "but we can't. There's no air."

Smiling, he opened a cupboard and pulled out two slim, flexible space-suits, creamy white with milky visors. "They thought of everything."

With their anchor tails, which were attached to the nearest wall with sliding adhesion, they could have been two sperm cells, one carrying XY genes, one XX, as they soared up the urethra propelled by waist jets. The tunnel was in perfect darkness, relieved only by the glow of their helmet lamps: the distant opening, which normally might have shown a glimmer of starlight, was invisible. He found the upper door with difficulty — how could he be sure it was the right one? — and twirled the winch. They crowded into the tiny airlock, waited for the hiss of air, then opened the inner door.

Peeling off the white suits, stowing them in the cupboard provided, they climbed through the trapdoor.

So rural-seeming were the surroundings in which they found themselves, that at first Reader thought he was in a country lane on European Earth. Birdsong ornamented the air. The winding hedgerow was intertwined with roses and honeysuckle. Then he realized that this was more of the nature decoration in which the *Lingam* abounded, for the overhead blue was a painted ceiling.

He noted that the daylights were on. This was a good sign. In the command section there was probably no night.

They had gone no distance round the curve of the 'lane' when, as if standing in a proscenium arch, serenaded by the avian chorus, there appeared a woman in what might well have been the doorway of a cottage.

She smiled. "Good day. Should you be here?"

"We are looking for the Captain," Reader told her firmly. She turned, peering into the interior. "Someone to see you, darling!"

And so it was, with unexpected ease, that they were able to enter the Captain's command post. The woman led them into a modestly sized room. A male figure was seated at a plush swivel chair, before a set of wall screens which, at the moment, showed country scenes. He turned and rose, gazing distantly at them, a pale man with a flat, tired face.

"And who might you be?"

"My name is Mark Reader. This is my friend Epifania." He looked from the man to the woman, noticing for the first time an unusual feature: she had chatoyant eyes. They changed colour, seemingly under the impact of one's gaze, from hazel to brown to deep orange to purple.

"My secretary," explained the man.

"You are the Captain?"

The other smiled wryly. "I am in authority."

"Sir, what do you say to the mutiny? They say you have abandoned our mission to find a new planet, and that the *Lingam* is heading into an infinity of nothing. Is it true?"

"It is true, but for a reason. I have secret orders in the event of our mission's failure. We have searched long for a new home, and have found none. The secondary task is now to be pursued."

The Captain leaned back, his hands on the edge of the command board behind him, and regarded Reader and Epifania with a look of deep significance.

"The sexual experience," he continued in his auctorial tone, "is asymptotic. Approaching ever nearer to the ultimate pleasure, it never attains it, however exquisite it may be. Yet to experience the absolute orgasm of mind and body is the deepest urge of the human psyche. That, and that alone, would be fulfilment. It has been sought in countless diverse and deviant ways. Why, I have known those who have been convinced it would follow if the keys of a typewriter were struck in some unique sequence, albeit that the code might be millions of letters long. Such people have spent their lives rattling away in a deluded frenzy."

Sadly he shook his head. "It was left to the astrophysicists to find the answer. There are ten coefficients of gravitational curvature which govern relations between material objects. These, the physicists tell us, are superficies: the ten sexual coefficients have priority in the order of the creation. We have now left the metagalaxy behind us, and can enter a realm of pure curvature unimpeded by matter."

"But space here is all flat!" Epifania objected.

"We shall not have to endure it for long. Ahead of us, instruments detect a compaction of curvature, incredibly intense. At its heart, the rate of curvature may be infinite."

"Do you mean a singularity?" Reader asked. The other smiled, and spoke. "Do not fear, gentle Reader, that this is another black hole story! The compaction subsists in the womb of space itself, folding, involuted, concave, like a sheath, or funnel. And the *Lingam*, by chance or providence, is of just the right diameter to fit this sheath! If the angle of approach is precisely controlled, we shall be able to effect entry. The ship will bc invaginated. And we shall know the most heightened rapture in the history of our species."

Turning, the Captain examined something on the command board. Reader saw that it was a sheaf of paper, at least a ream thick. He looked around the command post, which to his eye still somewhat resembled the interior of a cottage. A portable typewriter had been pushed to the back of the board among the communicators. The walls were decorated with rectangular illustrations that were partly text, each lurid picture with a ragged top caption: FORBIDDEN ECSTASY, WHIPS OF PASSION, THE LADY WANTS IT BAD...

A male voice came from one of the communicators. "Curvature encountered."

"Very well!" the Captain snapped. "Switch to main drive!" Seconds later, the muted roar of the atomic engines died. In its place came the old, familiar hum of the curvature motors, and the *Lingam* accelerated.

The Captain turned back to face them. "Climax will not be long. Prepare yourselves, and remember, where we are going only conation counts. The intellectual measures of space that we are used to will vanish, in the absence of gravitational curvature. Attraction between living beings creates its own space."

As he spoke, the rustic images on the wall screens flicked out. Navigational data replaced them. The outlines of the command post were altering. It was preparing for action. The lighting became softer. The air filled with the scent of Japanese lotus blossom. From the communicators, busy voices gave forth a cacophony of information.

Suddenly the stresses of the void took hold of Reader's inner space, bending and deforming it so that desire sprang once again to his mind. The walls of the chamber receded, became an unimportant backdrop to the only presences that mattered: two gorgeous naked human bodies never before encountered, radiant with promised pleasure. Reader caught the odour of sandalwood: it was the pheromone alpha androstinol being released from the Captain's body — a body which now, far from being the flabby, pale object of moments before, was firm and smooth, the phallus standing in magnificence. Reader stepped forward. Though normally the only penis he worshipped was his own, he could not resist sinking to his knees, fascinated by the bulging glans, the rigid shaft, the dilated scrotum. He reached out and touched it. The smell it gave off was thick, the taste ripe and slimy as his lips closed over it, his fingertips tracing the shaft, the scrotal sac, dipping beneath to venture between the thighs. When the semen gushed into his mouth he knew from the flavour that it contained aphrodisiac substances, and he savoured it, panting, before letting it slide down his throat.

By his side, Epifania had likewise stepped forward, having equally seen the secretary glow and bloom into maidenly beauty. She too was kneeling, facing the brief golden fluff that did not hide the perfect curve of a cleft mound. The secretary raised her right foot, placing it on a nearby writing table to allow Epifania a better view. Epifania caught her breath. This was the desired female organ made consummate: not the *ersatz* object all too often discovered on the muddied planet Earth, surrounded by mounds of uneven flesh, ill-odoured, sullied by uric acid, buried beneath a messy mane to keep out dirt and dust — no, this was the heavenly vestibule, ideal in its proportions, intoxicating in aroma, the inner labia, instead of comprising unsightly flaps, streamlined and neat, the clitoris an elegantly smooth and firm little projection. She was made to think of a salty sea, fresh with spray and ozone, billowing, curvy, the heaving waves driven by stiff trade winds.

She and Reader were licking in parallel as the *Lingam* entered the mouth of the vortex. The curvature was increasing fast. Among the frantic babble from the communicators Reader was surprised to hear, or think he heard, the voice of the Captain himself:

"My detractors say that I write from my prick. Well this is my answer!"

Reader looked up from what he was doing. His environment had again changed. A sumptuous boudoir had arranged itself around him, exotic of aspect, sybaritic with draped silks. Lounging in a deeply cushioned couch, the soft light a haze on her fleshly tones, languorously extending a hand, the secretary smiled.

"Come! Sate yourself with my body! There is nothing about it that could be in the least displeasing, not even its secretions. My breath — it is like the smell of fresh strawberries Neither need you recoil from my urine — it is more delectable than lemonade. And in texture, flavour and colour, my faeces are something like marzipan. So come! Together we can know every delight!"

And from somewhere nearby he fancied he heard the Captain's voice speaking forcefully to Epifania. "My semen is inexhaustible. It contains aphrodisiac drugs, perception altering drugs, even instantly addictive drugs! Come! You shall absorb them through every bodily receptacle!"

Plunging on and on, the *Lingam* entered deeper. The curvature turned in and in. Genitals grew hot; the diamond hull glowed at a thousand degrees of heat, the red glans glaring like a beacon down the infinite depths of the space tunnel. For those within, there was no north, south, east, west, zenith or nadir. There was only desire, and the satisfaction of desire, and the relations of desire, mounting and mounting...

The telemental adept could continue his account no further. "It is at this point," he said, "that the expedition passes beyond the ken of my faculty, vanishing into the true universe of which ours is but a shadow. In that realm conscious desires, not material objects, are the components of existence, and if our friends return to us it will be as angels of eroticism. Perhaps they will lead us to a perfect Earth, where there is no frustration, and every story has a fitting ending."

He fell silent, and the High Priest too forbore to speak, while all around them in the Temple of Priapus the warm sunlight continued to flow.